Heating

Up

PARADISE

D1613519

Other Titles by Lizbeth Selvig

Seven Brides for Seven Cowboys
The Bride Wore Denim
The Bride Wore Red Boots
The Bride Wore Starlight
Betting On Paradise
Heating Up Paradise

Love From Kennison Falls
The Rancher and the Rock Star
Rescued by a Stranger
Beauty and the Brit
Good Guys Wear Black

Chandler County
Missing By a Heartbeat
Missing One Angel

Anthologies
Love in the Land of Lakes – What's Up Dock?
Festivals of Love – Bun Wars
Wild Deadwood Tales – Gotta Have Faith

Heating Up PARADISE

A Seven Brides for Seven Cowboys Novel

LIZBETH SELVIG

Webster Publishing

Heating Up Paradise

Copyright 2021 by Lizbeth Selvig

Editing: Megan Records – Megan Records Editorial

Cover Image: Royal Touch Photograph
Cover Design: Dana Lamothe—Designs by Dana

This book is a work of fiction. Names, characters, places, and incidents are the products of the author's imagination or are used fictitiously. Any resemblance to actual events, locales, or persons, living or dead, is coincidental.

To Jan

You have shown me for forty-plus years that no matter how long things take, how much I fret, worry, try to give up, and whine—you'll stick with me. And things usually turn out pretty well!

Love you forever.

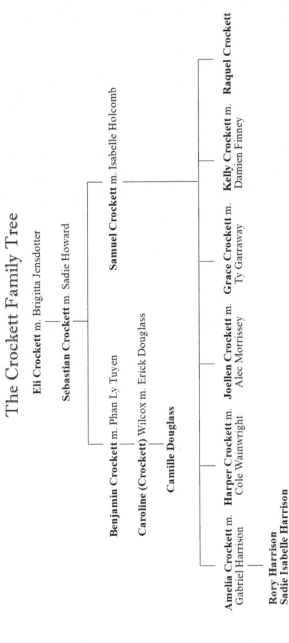

The Crockett Family Tree

Eli Crockett m. Brigitta Jensdotter

Sebastian Crockett m. Sadie Howard

Samuel Crockett m. Isabelle Holcomb

Benjamin Crockett m. Phan Ly Tuyen

Caroline (Crockett) Wilcox m. Erick Douglass

Camille Douglass

Amelia Crockett m. Gabriel Harrison

Harper Crockett m. Cole Wainwright

Joellen Crockett m. Alec Morrissey

Grace Crockett m. Ty Garraway

Kelly Crockett m. Damien Finney

Raquel Crockett

Rory Harrison
Sadie Isabelle Harrison

Prologue

"ALL YOU HAVE to do is jump into hell, get the devil's attention, kick him in the ass, and get out before he grabs your soul."

So went one saying every smokejumper rookie took to heart. Experienced jumpers loved to brag that hell was no big deal. In truth, however, jumping into a remote forest fire was one of the hardest jobs in the world, and only the bravest—probably the craziest—men and women on the planet could pull it off. It been drilled into Damien Finney's rookie head that to be a smokejumper, you had to hate the devil fire almost more than you loved your own life.

Despite all he knew, his knee jiggled fitfully and his stomach churned as he stared at the floor of the DH-6 Twin Otter plane that had started the tell-tale bouncing warning the six men and two women they were over the fire site. Hot air streamed upward from the orange dragon Damien knew was below, meeting the cool air of fifteen-hundred-feet, and the resulting turbulence started his adrenaline flowing. Less than ten minutes to fly time.

"Ready, Shark? Fifth jump's a milestone."

A hard clap on his back pulled Damien out of his mental prep, and he looked into the ebony eyes of their crew leader.

Captain Stone Rayburn was nobody's idea of a pushover, yet he was a loyal friend and compassionate leader when he wasn't being a genuine hero.

"Sure thing, Cap."

Damien was the only rookie from his Montana-based company on this crew. Three others—the captain, Forty Juarez, and Ace West—were seasoned veterans with almost seventy-five years' combined experience. The other crew members were newer firefighters but had at least two years each under their belts. Damien wiped his hands on his thighs, troubled by his leg's restless, double-time bounce.

He pressed down on his knee with both hands to stop the old tic-like sign of impending panic—a sign he hadn't experienced in nine months. It had disappeared after his acceptance into the smokejumper program and hadn't returned, even during the intense training period. With a sense of blessed relief that all the intense therapy after his time in Afghanistan had done its job, he'd allowed himself to believe the warning sign had permanently faded. Ever since this take-off, however, he hadn't been able to halt its unwelcome reappearance.

He couldn't figure out the difference in this mission. He remembered with crystal clarity the rush of his first real fire jumps—the exhilaration of abandoning gravity and expertly navigating the air currents, the utter relief upon a safe landing followed by the immediate, adrenaline-fueled charge of fighting against a power as destructive as fire. And when the fight was won, there was the exhaustion—soul-deep but so satisfying he couldn't wait to fight again.

He'd made four of those successful jumps since gaining his place on the crew, each granting him more battle hardness and pride over his hard-won spot in a profession only three-hundred people in the country held. He was taking on fire number five, and Cap was right. He should be jubilant, charged, more ready than ever. He wanted to jump. This regression was out of the blue.

"Okay, we've got the go," Cap called. "Final gear check, boys and girls. Order of exit: Ace, Forty, Snake, Texaco, Poppy, Hermione, Shark, Stone. You've all studied the terrain—heavy tree line to the west, a ravine well to the east but not out of range should you hit a bad current. We'll be a quarter-mile south of the leading edge. See you on the ground."

Through the wide-open jump door, they saw the smoke. Though they couldn't smell it yet, within fifteen minutes, every orifice and wrinkle of fabric would be clotted with it.

Anna "Hermione" Swenson, an eight-year veteran, had gotten her nickname because she'd been the "smartest witch of her age" her rookie year. Damien hadn't jumped with her before and was looking forward to it. Her reputation was stellar. She took her place in front of him and fingered a photo she held in one hand. He swallowed, shrugging his shoulders to ward off the uncomfortable hitch in his heartbeat. She'd shown him the picture on the way onto the plane.

"Adrenaline levels always jump twenty points right about now, don't they?" she asked with a grin that said she wouldn't have it any other way.

Damien's adrenaline levels always skyrocketed the moment the plane took off and didn't approach normal until after he'd jumped and landed.

"Adrenaline is a gift from the gods." He forced a cheerful response. "Numbs the bad, heightens the good. Best drug ever."

"Good one! I'm stealing that." She laughed and turned the photo for him to see again. Two kids around seven or eight. "Maybe I'll use it with these guys when they get older."

"Your boys," he said dully.

"I put them in my pocket every time I jump. Reminds me who I'm doing this for."

The picture had weirdly unnerved him the first time, and at her words, an alarming chill, unlike anything he'd ever felt before, blasted down his spine. A flash of memory he couldn't quite grasp slipped in and out of his brain, followed by ghostly words: *Don't look down.*

He blinked at the phantom voice in his mind and staggered one step back, confused by the anguish swirling in the memory. He strained to place the voice, but as eerily as they'd come, both the memory and the voice slithered away, leaving hollow sickness behind. All he held in his mind was the wavery image of Hermione's two boys.

What the actual fuck?

Swallowing again against a tightening throat, he adjusted his pack, fastened the final straps, checked his rigging, and blew out his breath to shake off the remnants of the bizarre sensation.

"Tracer's away," the jump master called. "Looks perfect. Go, go, go."

Ace West stepped into the blue-gray sky, and Damien watched as one by one his fellow crew members followed.

Hermione stepped to the door, flashed him a thumbs-up, and that's when it happened. Damien's stomach rolled as if it had been pierced by a guided missile, and his eyes blurred so badly he had to reach a gloved finger behind his goggles to wipe them. He could make no sense of the symptoms and fought to shake them off. Then Hermione was away, and Damien stood at the doorway, looking not into a clearing but into a whirling void. A pit of blackness.

Don't look down.

"Shark!"

Nothing registered except the sharpness of Captain Rayburn's voice in his ear.

"Dammit, Shark. Go." Stone nudged him, but Damien stood, frozen solid as death. He was scared, but numbly so, and he had no explanation other than the image of a swirling black hole before his eyes.

A sudden jerk on his arm yanked him away from the door so hard he stumbled and landed on one knee. Stone peered down at him, an unreadable expression in his eyes.

"I don't know what the hell is happening, Damien, but you just put our lives in danger. I'm out of here. You have ten seconds after that to get your ass out of this plane or you're going back with the flight crew, and we have a serious problem."

His captain was gone seconds later, and Damien's head spun in confusion. He stumbled to the door again and looked out. This time he could see the ground, see his crew members' 'chutes opened below him, snaking in precision toward a swirling vortex in the middle of the landing area. Only then did the full-body fear hit—as if an earthquake fissure had opened directly beneath his feet. With a groan, he staggered backward and gripped the grab bar above his head like a lifeline.

Chapter One

THE FIRE'S AFTERMATH was clear enough in Denver's orange-and-yellow August dawn. Nobody needed a professional film crew's unforgiving lights to add harshness to the sad scene, yet the cameras rolled, ten feet behind her, and Kelly Crockett hunched her shoulders to ward off the brightness. She stared at her restaurant's scorched façade, her mind numb despite the shock buzzing through the rest of her system on live-wire nerves.

Rivulets of water-logged soot lined Triple Bean's eaves-to-sidewalk picture window, and half the shingles on the blackened roof curled in on themselves like dead autumn leaves. Through the smeared plate glass, she could see Triple Bean's interior had escaped total destruction, but one wall sagged pitifully, and she didn't need the results of an investigation to tell her the smoke damage would be disastrous.

Standing on the boulevard across the street from their restaurant, Kelly wrapped an arm around her sister's waist. Raquel stood statue-straight, regal and sad as a queen in mourning. Triple Bean was as much her domain as it was Kelly's. Neither of them wept—yet. Tears would come later. When it all finally felt real. When they could be alone.

At the moment, they were anything but alone. Beside them, along with the film crew and the unwelcome lights, Marley Beckham, host of one of the most popular food shows on television, murmured directions to her production team. The team that was supposed to be *inside* Triple Bean interviewing Kelly and Raquel for *Undiscovered Gourmet*, a show that introduced locally popular chefs and their establishments to the world. Kelly should have been on camera, creating two of her signature dishes, while Marley highlighted the fact that in six short years, triplet sisters had created an award-winning bistro and coffee shop. Instead, the crew was filming the aftermath of an overnight blaze in the bookstore adjoining the Crockett sisters' restaurant.

Raquel shifted and startled them all with a first break in the somber silence.

"Say something funny," she said, her eyes fixed on the last fire crew, packing away hoses and equipment.

Kelly swiveled her head at the absurd command. "Say what?"

"Something funny. You're the funny one, and we need..." Raquel trailed off. She didn't look at Kelly, but the barest hint of a tremble in her lower lip showed the first crack in her tough exterior.

Kelly swallowed and slowly shook off her brain fog. Raquel was wrong; she wasn't funny. Funny took intellect. A good stand-up comic was funny. What humor Kelly did possess relied on the ridiculous, cheeky, and irreverent.

And the snarky—she could do snark on autopilot.

Under normal circumstances.

She almost told Raquel not to be insane, but when she took in her sister's stoic, pale profile, arrows of pain pierced her heart. The two of them had been at serious odds for the past ten days, but Raquel was clearly traumatized enough to put not only their disagreements aside but to make this ridiculous request. Normally, Raquel's most positive response to Kelly's irreverence was a censoring scowl. Kelly drew in a breath and squinted at the mess across the street. The words came without effort.

"See that smoke smudge above our name on the window? It looks like a giant weasel on a bicycle."

Marley Beckham choked.

Raquel covered a snort with both hands, and her first tears leaked free. "Oh, lord, it does."

"And the bike has a flat tire," Kelly added. "It looks...melted. Maybe from a fire or something?"

Marley—tall, black-haired, and built a little too much like Halle Berry for Kelly not to be jealous—beamed with delight. "And there it is. The famous Kelly Crockett wit everyone we interviewed mentioned."

If she considered that wit, Marley Beckham needed some serious humor therapy. A Jim Gaffigan marathon maybe, or a *Schitt'$ Creek* watch party.

"What do you think?" Marley asked, her smile a notch past brilliant. "Are you feeling up to that quick interview yet? A couple of questions and I can get out of your hair."

An interview? Now?

No.

She didn't answer out loud, although the request dragged at the curtain of privacy she wanted to draw over herself. Even though Kelly normally loved the spotlight.

Even though the host was only doing her job—one she'd literally been asked to do when they'd applied to be on *Undiscovered Gourmet* in the first place. It wasn't Marley Beckham's fault that the wiring in their neighbor's business had picked a piss-poor time to short out.

Kelly grabbed her sister's hand and tugged gently until they stood eye-to-eye. She looked deeply into the face that mirrored her own. For twenty-seven years, it had been second nature to see herself in the faces of Raquel and their third identical sister, Grace. Right now, however, the image she saw disconcerted her. Sad circles beneath Raquel's eyes had turned puffy with unshed tears, although she blinked hard keeping them at bay. If she, the one they called Rocky for a reason, looked like she'd been on an all-night bender, Kelly, the party girl with no trace of a party to bolster her, couldn't possibly look any better. Out of the corner of her eye, she spied Anya Patel, the owner of Magic Pages Bookstore, moving to stand on the curbside a few feet away.

"Sure, Marley," she said, not looking away from Raquel. "Give us a minute to check on the bookstore owner and make sure she's okay."

"That's fine. We're in no hurry. Tell me when you're ready."

"And could I ask a favor? Don't film us talking to her. Maybe turn off the lights for a moment? I'm pretty sure she won't want to be on camera."

"Of course." Marley smiled in acquiescence.

Even though Marley and company had arrived the night before, gotten a start on background footage, taste-tested some of the restaurant fare they were supposed to film the next day, and then been awoken in the middle of the night just as the girls had to the news of the fire, the gorgeous cooking show host looked fresh as the gentle morning breeze. She truly seemed like one of the nicest people—not remotely conceited or celebrity-like—and still, in this tired, disheveled moment, Kelly wanted to dislike her for her perky calm.

She blew her unkempt hair—assuming her style more-or-less matched Raquel's—out of her face and gathered the shoulder-length strands into a ponytail, holding it off her neck while she turned and took Raquel gently by the hand so she could follow.

They could put aside their quarrel for one moment.

Watching Anya Patel survey the remains of her bookstore shook Kelly to her core. At twenty-five, Anya was two years younger than Kelly and her sisters, but what she'd accomplished in two years with the bookstore she'd inherited from her grandfather matched anything the Crockett triplets had accomplished with Triple Bean. It was a source of joy to have her as a neighbor, another young entrepreneur in a once up-and-coming area of unique shops and fun eating establishments.

Now, three-quarters of the businesses had moved away from the block, and one of those remaining had been reduced to a brick shell filled with thousands of dollars' worth of precious inventory turned to ash.

"Anya?" Kelly said softly and put a hand on the girl's shoulder. "You must be exhausted."

Their friend turned, her features tired, her eyes calm but filled with uncertainty, and gave them gentle smile. "I admit it. This is draining. It's sadder in the light of day."

Raquel nodded. "I'm so sorry, Ani."

Their friend let out a wavery sigh and shrugged. Then she turned and gathered Kelly and Raquel both into a hug, bending to make up the five-inch difference in their heights. At five-foot-two, Kelly was used to being shortest among her friends, but Anya wore her height with pride — like a taller, more elegant version of Raquel. She released the embrace and straightened, forcing cheerful words through the tears clogging her throat.

"Even when things are darkest, you guys have always known how to fill my days with sunshine. Thank you. I made some decisions overnight."

"Decisions?" Kelly frowned.

"I have to move on. I'll miss you both so much, but there's no other way."

Kelly's heart fell in a turmoil of understanding, despair, and a little guilt. Raquel shook her head vehemently.

"No! You can*not* give up, Anya. All of us here will help you. We'll rebuild."

It was a kinder, gentler version of the lecture she'd been giving Kelly for nearly two weeks.

Anya smiled sadly. "You are the best business neighbors I ever could have hoped for. You've given me so much help and you've become the best friends, but you know as well as I do there aren't enough of us left on this street to help rebuild anything. Four shops out of nine? Now three? The streets will be closed for the redistricting projects another year."

And that was a version of the same argument Kelly had been giving Raquel. The dilemma in a nutshell.

"I know it feels that way," she said softly.

"I can't replace my inventory even with insurance money."

A tear traced down Anya's soft brown cheek. Kelly pulled her sweater sleeve over her hand and wiped it away. "I do hear you. I don't want you to quit. You're a phoenix, Ani, I believe that with all my heart," Kelly said, even as a wave of despair washed over her looking at her own damaged property. "I do hear you, though. In some ways, if the restaurant had gone, too, it would have made things easier."

"Hey!" Raquel pulled back, her eyes sparking. "Don't you bring all that up now. This is a convenient enough disaster."

Kelly stared, heat rising in her cheeks. "What, exactly, is that supposed to mean?"

"Nothing. I'm sorry." Raquel looked away.

Tears beaded in her own eyes. Few people knew what a perfect storm this truly was; she didn't look forward to the next big conversation she would be having with her sister.

"Come on, Rocky," she soothed and held back her sadness. "This is all so awful, everyone is on edge. I only meant if Anya goes, that leaves Triple Bean, the antique store, and Walt's tobacco shop on a street no one can access without a flipping safari guide. We've gone into the red ourselves for the past three months. I'm not sure we're in a great position either."

Raquel took a step back her eyes filled with angry despair. Kelly's heart sank. Fighting with her sister had been unheard of until recently. The entire past year had been fraught. But she loved her lookalike best friend and business partner. She might think of Triple Bean as her restaurant because she was the chef, but the business had been Raquel's brainchild. Without her, and without Grace, to be honest, there never would have been six years of success and awards.

"I'm sorry, Rocky. Really. This is a terrible time to talk about business."

"You're right." Her sister's words, sharp and brittle, drove home the depth of her hurt. "It's an even worse time for you to play the pessimist card. Or is it easy because you're leaving anyway?"

Stung, Kelly's mouth opened soundlessly. A week-long trip to San Francisco to meet with her old mentor did not constitute "leaving," but Raquel refused to look at it that way. The sad thing was, Raquel had always been the steady Crockett triplet, the smart one. Since Grace's departure, however, she'd been distant. Seeing her so lost and angry at this new disaster threw Kelly's world even more off-kilter than it already was. Her own preferred coping tools were parties and humor, but even she was resorting to doom and gloom.

"We have a lot to decide," she said simply. "I won't abandon you."

Raquel let out a wavering sigh and clutched at Kelly's hand. "Sorry. Sorry. Forget it. Nothing comes out the way any of us means it."

With a manufactured smile, Kelly wrapped Raquel's upper arm in a hug. "Except that the spot really does look like a weasel."

Raquel punched her upper arm lightly. "You're not well."

"That is my superpower."

Kelly tried to gather strength from the brief lightness—to collect her thoughts and form them into some kind of a plan. Or into words that could be used for the slightest comfort. But that was neither her forte nor Raquel's. That was their sister's.

"I wish Grace were here," Raquel spoke the exact thought in Kelly's brain.

Kelly stared, although the mind-reading

phenomenon wasn't unusual. "I was just thinking she'd have the right words."

Raquel allowed a slow, dejected half-smile. "She'd just tell us it's all in God's hands."

Kelly sighed. "Never thought I'd miss her endless Sunday School wisdom as much as I do."

Grace was the nice triplet. And a year ago, she'd been the first to leave the restaurant all three had founded and strike out on her own. Nothing had been the same since she'd moved back to Paradise, the family ranch in Wyoming.

"Once we do Marley's interview, let's all go get coffee." Kelly took Anya's hand. "Come along; we all need a break."

"Thank you," Anya said, "but I have a meeting with the fire marshal in about fifteen minutes. You two go. My parents will be here within the half-hour, and I can use is a few minutes alone to prepare for them. They'll be devastated. Magic Pages was my grandfather's pride and joy."

Anya's mother had emigrated from India at age three and was a dedicated teacher who'd grown up in her father's bookstore. Her father, a software engineer, had been born in Colorado and never left the state he loved. They'd been so proud when their entrepreneurial daughter had jumped at the chance to run Magic Pages books. This would devastate Mr. and Mrs. Patel as much as it had Anya.

"All right." Kelly offered her another huge hug. "You have our numbers. If you need anything, just call."

"I'm sorry." Anya brushed away tears.

"What on earth for?"

"This started in my shop. I feel so responsible."

"Stop it. They already say they think it started near the circuit box. This is a terrible accident." Kelly fixed her with stern eyes. "Ac-ci-dent."

Anya nodded. "Thank you."

"Are you sure you're all right?"

"I'm fine. I promise."

They hugged again, and Kelly turned reluctantly toward Marley and the crew. Closing her eyes, she groaned. "This sucks."

"I agree. It's not a good time to do an interview."

"Marley Beckham's show would have gotten publicity for us, but it is built on a lot of hype, and now I don't know what to expect from her. She could turn this into a huge sob story that will overshadow everything about the food."

"It's not just about the food, Kel."

She sighed. Raquel was all about entrepreneurship and promoting the uniqueness of three identical sisters starting a business. It could have been a clothing store, a paper clip factory, or a gas station, and Raquel would have used their triplet-ness for promoting it. Contacting Marley Beckham had been her idea.

"It's a restaurant. She focuses on food."

"Of course. But it doesn't matter now anyhow, does it? We're stuck talking about the future, and who knows what you want that to be."

"Not fair. You know I love Triple Bean and I've always wanted to grow it into a proper high-end restaurant, but you're right; the fire makes a lot of things unclear. Tell you what, you do the interview. Say whatever you want."

Raquel laughed without humor. "Now that's funny. The people-person trying to palm off an interview to the introvert?"

"I have no idea what to say to the woman. I'll just get it wrong."

Raquel straightened beside her and seemed to gather resolve. "No. You'll do fine. Off-the-cuff is your wheelhouse, big sister."

"Bigger by four minutes, and only because you probably had your nose stuck in a book you wanted to finish in utero."

"Yeah, and that joke never gets old."

Kelly gripped Raquel's arm again firmly. "I'll start, but you got us into this, so you're staying stay right here. I'll let you elbow me and take over if I say something stupid."

"Well, there's a once-in-a-lifetime opportunity. Let's go."

Kelly smiled, and for that moment, she felt in sync with her sister.

It didn't last long.

Marley showed her easy interviewing skill from moment one. They sat on tall, director-style chairs, once again in front of the unforgiving lights, and chatted like best friends—Marley filled with sympathy and concern, and Kelly, despite her protests, falling into the conversation the way she always did: enthusiastically, letting talk fill her with energy. Raquel filled in details, turning to facts for comfort. Kelly forgot to begrudge the host her cheeriness and perfect Halle Berry allure even though it was barely seven in the morning when Marley's questions turned out to be kind, her sincerity genuine.

Do you know how the fire started? *No. The inspectors are still investigating.*

Was anyone hurt? *Thankfully not.*

Any idea yet how much damage was done? *The fire started in the adjacent bookstore and the shared wall is destroyed. Since that's at the end of the restaurant where the kitchen is located, it's hard to know what might have been lost. There'll be significant smoke and water damage.*

Raquel shared stories about the history of the restaurant and answered questions about the massive rezoning and reconstruction project that was sending the old neighborhood into near-isolation and the businesses toward financial crises. Kelly's thoughts, way more scattered than usual, drifted to Anya's announcement that she was not rebuilding the book store. It made sad sense. Raquel, with her business degree, was the numbers person, but Kelly wondered if their own insurance would fully cover repair and replacements on their elderly building.

Maybe Anya did have the right idea…

"And Kelly." Marley jerked her out of her internal musings. "Raquel is optimistic. Tell me your thoughts about the future. Does adversity make you more creative as a cook? Will you and Triple Bean come back better than ever?"

She sat silent for a long moment, her brain racing with the question she'd just been asking herself. Absolutely she wanted to come back better than ever. But as Triple Bean? What could she say out loud right now about the dreams burning deep inside of her that Raquel didn't seem to understand anymore? Raquel's eyes were fixed on her, and Kelly felt waves of confusion flow from her sister. She could hear the worried question: *Why are you hesitating? Tell her. Tell her we're going to be fine.*

"We will come back," she said at last. "There's a lot to think about because of all the difficulties in this part of the city. But here's something. I'm about to go meet with Chef Landon O'Keefe in San Francisco. Your viewers will know him as the owner of the Michelin three-star restaurant Bayvio. I spent a year working at his restaurant after I graduated from culinary school, and I'm looking forward to getting some ideas from him. Especially now that we're more or less at a crossroads. Maybe we start Triple Bean 2.0 right here, or maybe we'll start all over in a new location. You'll have to watch and see what comes next."

Raquel's quiet gasp told Kelly she'd let more than she should have out of the bag. None of her statements had been definite, but she knew Raquel loved this location and loved what they'd created. To even muse on such major changes when they'd barely been discussed would seem disloyal.

Yet voicing her dreams didn't feel wrong.

"Well, that's a teaser if ever I heard one!" Marley rubbed her hands theatrically, like a child anticipating offered cookies. "I promise we'll stay in touch and follow Triple Bean's progress and resurrection. Or…will we have a big surprise?"

She left her question hanging, gave a smile to her camera, and then indicated the crew could cut. As soon as Marley relaxed back in her chair, Raquel shot out of hers, the full-fledged fury in her eyes slamming Kelly as physically as a slap.

"Want to tell me what exactly that was all about?" She might as well have been a steam train bearing down for all the hiss accompanying her words.

"That was wonderful, girls!" Marley interrupted the scene with genuine warmth and praise. "You two are great interview subjects. I think we'll generate a lot of interest and sympathy with your spot. And anticipation, of course."

Kelly's heart lifted a little. She hadn't promised or announced anything official, and Marley was right. Their unknown future would be good publicity in the long run. She didn't blame Raquel for being sensitive—this was a huge trauma for them both. But it would be all right.

"Thank you." Raquel's reply came out as tight and high-pitched as an overwound violin string. "Please excuse me, Marley. I see the fire chief across the street, and I want to talk to him before he leaves."

She walked away, shoulders nearly at her ears, arms rigid as sticks.

Then again, maybe it would take some smoothing over to convince her everything would be fine.

"Yes." Kelly looked away from Raquel's retreating form and took the hand Marley offered. "It was really good of you to stay and do this even though it wasn't what you came to do. I hope you really will stay in touch."

"I absolutely will."

"Forgive me, I should go see what the chief has to say, too."

"Of course. We're going to start packing up now anyway. If you learn anything important, let us know before we leave."

"I will."

She made her way to Raquel, who wasn't talking to the chief at all, but staring again at the ruined bookstore and the restaurant that only looked sadder as the morning grew brighter.

"Rocky, I—"

She spun, her eyes still spitting hot despite fresh tears dripping from their outside corners. "You what? You're still going to meet with Landon and actually consider leaving for some crazy new internship after this? You'd abandon me with a mess like this?"

A wave of Kelly's anger crested at the unfair charges.

"Who said I'd abandon you? Who said our dreams had to die just because of some bad luck? From the day we first opened this place, we planned on turning it into more than a coffee-and-sandwich restaurant. Yes, we were going to give it ten years and it's only been seven, but Grace leaving made a difference, and now this fire makes a difference. I have a chance to meet with one of the top chefs in the world. What can it hurt to pick his brain—*especially* now? What if this fire is a sign it's time to move on?"

"Because after something like this, it's pie in the sky, Kelly. We can't possibly move on until we're re-established. We can't sell before Triple Bean is rebuilt. Nobody will loan us expansion or start-up capital when we're in the shape we're in; you said so yourself. As for you, you've been itching to leave ever since Landon O'Keefe came by out of the blue and said you were wasting your life here. If you leave, you leave for good."

"Wait. What? Is that some kind of threat?"

"Of course not! It's a prediction. You'll want to stay in San Francisco."

"You know nothing of the sort."

"You're bored here. You've been telling me so in a hundred ways since Grace left. We live in each other's heads. Don't try to deny it."

Kelly looked around at the firemen dragging equipment, at the gawkers starting to get bored and drift away, at Marley's crew suddenly busy as rock band roadies packing up all their equipment. She didn't want to have this argument here, but nobody was paying attention to two pathetically bedraggled women.

"I'm a better cook than one who makes up one new sandwich a month to put on a menu. Yeah, I want more. I want people to know I can work with more than mayo and mango chutney. Once, you wanted more to manage, too. Or were you simply nodding and smiling to appease me when we planned to strive for a Michelin star in a bigger city? If so, when were you going to tell me?"

They stared at each other for a long, silent moment until Kelly dropped her gaze to the ground, hating the argument even more.

"How about we don't talk about this here?" she asked when Raquel didn't answer. "Let's go do what we always do when we're stressed. Check out a new restaurant. That place over by the botanical gardens has some crazy jungle theme. We can call Grace. We can make a real plan."

She willed her sister to catch a little of the optimism she herself felt peeking through the sorrow at the thought of starting fresh, but Raquel didn't soften. All their lives, the family had joked the triplets were permanently synced on the same page. Raquel was not only far from on the same page, she was reading from an entirely different book.

"Maybe this isn't a sign we should move on but that we need to re-focus on the basics and get our ducks back in a row before taking on ideas we can't possibly afford. Isn't that what my role in this business is? To know when hard financial decisions need to be made? Maybe you need to stop being so immediately focused on becoming the next Gordon Ramsay and be practical."

That arrow couldn't have been sharper or struck more deeply than it did. Never had either of her sisters said anything that hurt as much. But before she could regroup and reply, the fire chief appeared before them.

"Miss Crockett?" He looked directly at Kelly. "I'm afraid I have some bad news about your building."

"What?" Raquel spoke first.

"The wall you shared with the bookstore is unsalvageable. The wiring throughout the building was destroyed, and the plumbing into the kitchen area is badly damaged. You wanted to know if it would be possible to be cleaned up and running soon, but I'm so sorry; you'll be looking at major renovations. Of course, that's simply a place for your insurance people to start. Those are just my preliminary findings."

"But you still think it was an accident?" Raquel asked.

"We'll have an arson investigator on-site when everything's fully cooled down, but I don't believe she'll find anything suspicious. These buildings are close to a century old."

Kelly sagged, her flicker of optimism fading as Raquel asked a few more questions. The perfect storm. Everything had been wellchoreographed, like a play. Once Marley had agreed to feature the restaurant, Kelly had formulated the plan. Grab the spotlight on Marley's national stage; the exposure would bring an influx of customers to Triple Bean; lenders would be impressed with the success and happily grant them a small business loan so they could expand. She'd meet with her old mentor, which would lead to a short refresher stint as a three-star sous-chef, then Triple Bean's enhanced reputation would ensure it could be sold within the year, and two months later Kelly would have her own new, high-end restaurant with Raquel as her brilliant business partner. She'd get her name known in the world of serious restauranteurs. *They'd* get their names known.

Then had come the call in the middle of the night. Fire. Not even a fire in their own building, but next door. It shouldn't have derailed everything, but it had.

The fire had scuttled Kelly's timeline, but that could be rewritten. Far worse, the fire had cracked open Raquel's true feelings about Kelly's ambitions the way a wildfire forced open lodgepole pine cones to release the seeds. The seeds of Raquel's anger and unhappiness couldn't be gathered back together—they were in the air to spread. Seeing the damage to the restaurant wasn't a fraction as painful as Raquel's barbed accusation.

Maybe you need to stop being so immediately focused on becoming the next Gordon Ramsay...

She didn't want to be Gordon-flipping-Ramsay. She wanted to be herself. She wanted her own signature fame. Raquel knew this.

Her sister turned from the fire chief and Kelly knew they reflected each other's hard, glassy-eyed-with-shock stares.

"We need to talk," Raquel said.

"Do we? It seems you have the answers already."

"Not fair."

"This whole thing isn't fair." Kelly shook her head. "We can talk, but this is my part of the conversation in a nutshell. You figure out the financing. I'm going to San Francisco the day after tomorrow. We'll rebuild the restaurant if it makes sense. Then we'll decide what's next."

"Kelly, I—"

"Don't apologize." Kelly looked away, anger giving way to a soul-deep sadness mixed with her resolve. "I heard you, and you don't have to worry. It isn't Gordon Ramsay I'm chasing."

Chapter Two

THE INSTANT DAMIEN stepped from the car in front of Paradise Ranch's main house, he felt better than he had in nearly two weeks. With the first breath of Paradise air, a slight weight lifted from his mind, if not from his soul. He could escape here for the few days he planned to visit, even if bubbles of joy weren't part of the respite. Feeling "better" was a relative term.

After Damien's disastrous, aborted jump twelve days earlier, Captain Rayburn had been sympathetic. He knew Damien's history with PTSD and had supported him fully during the past year of training, praising him for the effort he put into getting past old traumas. Since the jump, Stone had given every bit of help he could—offering retraining, talks with the base doctor, all to no avail. Damien hadn't even been able to manage training jumps attached to zip lines. Whatever had injured his brain while serving his country was not healed. Whatever had scared the living shit out of him—and there were so many things he'd talked about over the past two years that he couldn't imagine there was anything more to be exhumed from his subconscious—wasn't going to let him go. The black abyss his mind saw from the precipice of every jump remained.

Finally, Stone had authorized four weeks of medical leave and required more counseling. Damien had a month to figure himself out—to find out what truly lived in that swirling black hole in his brain.

He'd spent the two years before joining smokejumper training around the people and the land of Paradise, and it was as close to a home to return to as he had these days. When he'd asked if he could stop for a visit, the Crocketts had welcomed his request with happiness.

"You know you can come home anytime."

"We love having you here."

"We can't wait to see you. We missed you!"

Their genuine warmth was a form of love, he knew, but in some ways, it made coming back harder. It was hard to accept their love when he'd failed so utterly.

Damien closed the door of his black CRV and eased his back into a stretch. He'd only stopped once on the eight-and-a-half-hour drive from Missoula to Jackson. With a grunt of relief, he straightened and gazed past the house to the enormity of the view behind it. The sky curved toward the horizon, a rich, robin's egg blue decorated with the kind of scallop-edged clouds a child would have drawn. Eighty-odd miles away, across a landscape of swelling hills, expansive pastureland, and sweet, clear air, stood Grand Teton, its cocked-hat silhouette greeting him like a welcome home gesture. Although he'd been born a city slicker in Pennsylvania, his small family had moved to eastern Wyoming when he'd been in junior high school, and he'd never looked back. His mother still lived in the Big Horns south of Sheridan.

Since his tours in Iraq and Afghanistan, however, Damien had fallen in love with the wilder, mid-Rockies country of western Wyoming.

He turned back to the house the Crockett family called "Rosecroft." The massive log home had always been intimidating, with its front porch big enough to host most peoples' weddings, its two stories of windows, and overflowing gardens surrounding every side. Damien never felt worthy of being in the big main house, and yet he knew it was one of the warmest places he'd ever find.

As he neared the first of the wide porch steps, a sharp burst of frenzied barking stopped his progress, and he looked left as a black-and-white bullet of energy raced around the corner of the house. A border collie. In general, he wasn't much of a dog person, but he knew this pup.

"Asta?" he called. He swore if anybody didn't believe a dog could smile, they hadn't seen this one.

"Damien!" A tall teenage girl trotted into view behind the dog.

She wore jean shorts and a purple T-shirt with white lettering that read "All I care about is my horse… and, like, maybe 3 people." Damien chuckled for the first time in a week.

"Well if it isn't the one and only Skylar Thorsen. I figured you'd be long gone and running your own business somewhere by now."

She ran at him and unabashedly threw her arms around his waist. He'd come back here for three things, and Skylar was one of them. He and Skylar, the ranch foreman's daughter, had become friends when she'd helped him learn to ride during hours on the trail—the crazy veteran and the rebellious teen.

"When Gabe told me you were coming home, I

couldn't believe it. I'm so glad you're here. Pan will be, too."

Gabe Harrison, the man who'd invested so much in Damien's healing after Afghanistan, was the second reason Damien was back. But the first was, without question or guilt, a gray-and-black mustang mare named Pan.

Panacea, the Greek Goddess of healing.

He'd named the horse himself in a fit of optimism back when he'd gotten involved in Gabe's program here at Paradise, pairing wild horses with injured vets. There was not a single doubt in his mind that, more than all the therapists and doctors in the world, he owed his sanity to the little grulla mare. All eight of the men in that inaugural program had found healing with the mustangs they'd adopted. A couple of them, like Damien, still owned their horses. He had no idea, however, if any of them believed as he did that the horses had chosen them, not the other way around. Nobody would ever convince him that his opinionated, stubborn, beautiful mare hadn't looked him in the eye and, magically or otherwise, given him no choice but to pick her out of the herd. If anyone was going to work as a therapist now, it was Pan.

"And Apollo," Skylar added. "He's so big you won't know him."

Pan's colt, now a year and a half old. Damien patted Skylar's back and closed his eyes. People, animals, and endless memories bombarded him in a rush, and Skylar's heartfelt welcome lightened his load the tiniest bit more.

"I'll *bet* he's grown," Damien said.

"He's so big. Bigger than Pan. And he's really smart."

"He was born smart. And speaking of grown—check yourself out. You got taller."

She was sixteen now, a young woman, no longer the little kid he'd first met two years earlier. He held her at arm's length, assessing her with a teasing smile.

"Don't you start," she said, her voice as sassy as ever. "Why is it when you turn sixteen you suddenly have to act like an adult and be a lady and all polite?" Her voice lilted in a slightly snarky, sing-songy voice as if imitating someone who'd annoyed her.

Skylar's father, Bjorn, was foreman as his father, Leif, had been before him, and ranch life was all Sky knew. For as long as Damien had known her, the girl had spoken her mind, gotten her way by working out every angle of a problem, and generally kept her parents on their toes. She also had the biggest heart of any kid Damien had ever met. Not that he knew all that many.

"Poor Skylar. Life is tough in Paradise."

"That's a really tired joke."

"I've been gone a while. I don't have any new stuff yet."

"Yeah well, nothing's new around here, so don't worry. You'll still fit in."

He laughed humorlessly at that. He didn't much fit in anywhere right now.

"I'm sure a lot has changed. There's a new baby I haven't met yet."

Her demeanor changed instantaneously. "Oh, well, yeah, Baby Sadie! She is pretty awesome. She's why I'm up here, actually. I'm coming to babysit."

Gabe's daughter had been born a few months after Damien left for rookie training. His old mentor had sent pictures, and the child was as pretty as any baby, Damien supposed, but he knew fewer babies than he did kids.

"And one of the sisters got engaged."

"Grace. She and Ty are getting married just before Christmas. It's still over four months away. Oh, and Kelly is coming home tomorrow. That's what's got everyone's panties in a twist. Guess there was some kind of fire at the restaurant she owns and she took a trip to California and now is coming home for a visit. Remember Kelly? She's the coolest."

His heart gave a little stutter. Or maybe it was closer to a shudder. He remembered Kelly Crockett all right. One of the triplets. The one who'd never given anyone a moment's peace with her chattiness and questions and perpetual sunniness. If ever there was a person he'd found to be oil to his water… Still, a fire? Just what everyone here needed. Two fire victims.

He calmed his racing mind. He was only staying a week. He'd survive Kelly. He'd survive talk of fire. He'd get through as he always did. He took a step back from Skylar and gave her a teasing scowl.

"I remember her. So, in other words, you lied. There's plenty new around here."

"It's just another wedding and another sister." Skylar wrinkled her nose at him. "There are a ton of both around here. I mean, weddings are fun and all, but everyone's doing them."

"Not you, I hope."

She curled her lip as if he'd offered her a spot in a raw liver eating contest.

"I'm never getting married. I'm living with my horses."

"A wise woman."

The border collie had evidently had enough of waiting around and jumped up against Damien's legs, yipping for attention. He gave the dog a cursory pat on the head and pushed it gently down.

"Asta, get down," Skylar said. "You know better. Damien's not a dog person."

"Aw, she's okay. She's just saying hello."

"Sorry. She's always loved you."

"If I were ever to want a dog, it'd be one as pretty and brilliant as Asta."

Skylar grinned with pride, but before she could reply, the front screen door opened and a wave of pleasure swept away all dog and marriage talk.

"Finney!" Gabe Harrison trotted down the porch steps, a wide smile of welcome leading the way.

It had taken Damien two years after leaving Afghanistan before he'd even agreed to start the therapy he'd needed. Getting over the whole damn "soldiers who ask for help are weak" syndrome had plagued him as much as any physical or emotional wounds. Only a year-long, experimental support program, led by an amazing man with a selfless vision, had helped him shed the stigma of asking for help. That man had been Gabriel Harrison.

"Hey, Gabe." Damien took the outstretched hand of his former mentor and closed his eyes in resigned acceptance when the handshake turned quickly into a warm hug and backslap. "Thanks for letting me come on such short notice."

"Man, you never need an invitation, you know that." Gabe stepped back and chided him with the stern look an older brother would have given. Damien had been the recipient of that look many times over the course of their relationship, never in rebuke, but with true warmth. "You're like family, and we love to have you. Why do you think we keep your horses hostage?"

"Yeah, and refusing board payments, too? It's too

much and I can't thank you enough."

"Nothing to thank us for as long as you come on inside before you head to the barn. Everyone wants to see you first. Especially Mia."

Damien smiled at the thought of Gabe's wife. "She's good? And how's Rory?" Gabe and Mia's adopted son would be nine or ten now.

"Mia's fantastic. Rory is...an amazing young man. Turning into a real ranch kid. Attached at the hip to Sky's brother Aiden and Ty's daughter, Lucky."

He hadn't met this Lucky. "Sounds like the family is doing great."

So many people. Damien already felt overwhelmed. He hadn't returned to Paradise looking for family or help from Gabe. Since the jump episode, he was in danger of reverting to his original belief that therapy and all the hype around it was so much BS. He *would* have been happier heading straight for the barn but Gabe deserved to know the truth, and playing the good guest was step one.

As he climbed the porch stairs, threads of nervousness wove themselves inexorably back into Damien's gut. When he'd been lucky enough to land a spot in Gabe's VA-based, experimental group therapy program, he'd been one of eight veterans living in the same apartment building, autonomous and independent, but consistently required to check in, attend therapy sessions, and eat family-style meals twice a week. Without question, he could admit now, he'd been the toughest of the eight to reach—the undisputed king of stubborn vets who didn't believe they needed any touchy-feely shit.

It had taken almost the full year of the program to prove his attitude wrong, but over that year and the year following, when he'd stayed on as a Paradise ranch hand, he'd made a life-long friend in Gabe and found this surrogate family in the Crocketts. His fear now was ridiculous; these people were on his side. Nonetheless, he dreaded the inevitable questions that hadn't yet been asked, as well as the sympathy they'd undoubtedly heap on him when he answered.

"Of course, there's that other new girl in my life," Gabe was saying. "She's really the owner of my heart now."

Damien nodded. "The newest little Sadie."

"Named after Grandma." Gabe grinned. "And the oldest and the youngest are peas in a pod—independent and smarter than the rest of us combined. Scary, but I'm a slobbery fool for them anyway."

That was another thing he remembered about Gabe: the man had no trouble expressing his feelings. It had taken all the guys in the program a long time to figure out that even though their leader could talk about emotions, he was far from a wimp. He was one of the toughest men Damien knew—a lot like Stone.

The dull, permanent pain of shame sent Damien's gaze away from Gabe's eyes, so proud as he talked about his daughter. The two men Damien admired most were the two people he'd most utterly failed. What the hell was he doing here? He checked his nerves and stepped through the door only to be embraced without warning for the third time.

"Damien! You made it. Oh, I'm so glad to see you."

Becoming a mother had only made Mia Crockett Harrison more beautiful, and that was saying a lot. Thick chestnut hair flowed past her shoulders, and her eyes now bore contentment—an emotion they hadn't always held.

He remembered when Gabe had introduced her—Doctor Amelia Crockett—the night she'd accompanied him to help an injured buddy. Once upon a time, she'd been a highly regarded New York City surgeon, used to a high-pressure life. She'd brought her own brand of tough kindness to Gabe's mustang program, helping Damien and all the vets learn to deal with their new horses. Now, she was a family practice doc at the VA outside of Jackson, and the toughness was tucked away beneath happiness.

"Mia," he murmured. "Thanks for letting me come."

"Letting you? I'd have been furious if you hadn't called."

"Who's that I hear?"

Damien released Mia and looked toward the hallway leading to the kitchen. Delight he couldn't contain lifted his sore spirits, and he had no trouble granting a smile to the elderly woman who entered the room. Grandma Sadie's steady gait was aided by her iconic black cane covered in bright red poppies that was as much a part of her as her wise, penetrating eyes.

"Hello, Miss Sadie." Damien bent to hug the ninety—wasn't it something like ninety-six now?—year-old matriarch of the family. She patted him firmly on the back.

"It's good you're back. This is a healing place, Damien."

Leave it to Grandma Sadie to touch instinctively on the real reason he'd come. Yet she said nothing to embarrass him.

"Something drew me back—" Damien murmured to her. "Most likely it was you."

He turned his smile into a wickedly teasing grin.

"Don't you play the flirt with an old woman who knows more than you do," Grandma Sadie admonished him with a shake of her head and a smile of her own.

"I'd never play when it came to you."

"Devil child." She kissed him on the cheek.

"Ahhh, here she is!" Gabe beamed as Mia's sister Harper emerged from the kitchen carrying a plump child in pink overalls. For a kid who wasn't quite a year old yet, she had a surprisingly full head of curly brown hair and eyes that searched Damien over, quizzical and unafraid.

"Hi, you!" Harper called. She handed the little girl to Gabe and moved close to offer the sixth hug. "Welcome home. Cole will be here in a few minutes. He, Leif, and Ty just got back this afternoon from moving cattle to the second summer pasture."

More memories assailed him. Harper and her husband, Cole, ran Paradise Ranch with the help of his brothers-in-law and Skylar's father and grandfather. With six Crockett sisters, four of whom were married or nearly so, the family was large, but there was work enough on the biggest cattle ranch in Wyoming for all of them and more. Damien had enjoyed his one and only cattle drive. After slapping the saddle for two solid days, he'd had the sorest ass of his life, but he'd also felt freedom he'd never known existed.

He didn't expect to find that again this visit. He only planned to stay long enough to say hello and get his bearings before heading east to Sheridan, where he would surprise his mother. Another person he had to call and disappoint.

"Meet the ruler of the house." Gabe took the baby and bounced her high up into his arms. "Sadie the Younger. Our presiding miniature queen."

It was no surprise the baby was beautiful. With parents like Gabe and Mia, it would have defied the laws of physics and biology for her to be anything else. Still, Sadie the Younger proved herself a benevolent and friendly queen by holding her plump little arms out to Damien and laughing. Reluctantly, he took her and let her study him with innocent, blue eyes.

"Hullo there," he said.

She reached to grab his nose, and Mia laughed apologetically as she took Sadie's hand. "Oooh, careful, sweetie."

"It's fine," Damien replied, normally no more comfortable around kids than he was around dogs, but oddly okay with this one. He smiled at the baby's answering babble. "A sign of acceptance, right, Sadie?"

He didn't totally understand the relief he got from holding her, except that maybe she was a person who didn't give a graham cracker crumb about his past, his failures, successes, or future, and who wasn't going to ask him a single question. Or hug him.

"You're good with her," Mia said.

"Nah, I just know enough not to pinch her." He wrinkled his nose at the child, who exposed three sweet, white baby teeth with a wide grin.

Gabe gave a fatherly snort. "Good to know. Come and sit. Long as you aren't going to torture her, you can hold her as long as you want, but then Skylar's here to take her while we all catch up. The rest of the family will be here soon. Nobody wanted to miss your homecoming."

Damien's stomach dropped. "The family" could mean a dozen or more people, and while the Crocketts owned an iconic, hand-built, unusually enormous table in the dining room that would easily hold twice that number, Damien didn't think his acting skills would hold up to a Crockett kind of party. He'd come to say hello to his old friend, ride his horse for a few days, and go on to Sheridan, where he'd discover whether or not he had to relocate there permanently and find a job in a nice safe office somewhere. He held back a sigh.

"Can't wait to see everyone."

Liar.

"We'll eat in a couple of hours," Mia said. "You have plenty of time to get settled and visit with your ponies. When Grace and Mom get back, we'll find you. You knew Grace moved back to Wyoming, right?"

"I did. Skylar told me she's the next to be married."

"So exciting!" Mia gave Harper a quick, happy high-five.

Damien pictured Grace and the other two triplets. Grace, Kelly, and Raquel had been named for their late father's two favorite actresses. He hadn't seen them often, since they lived in Colorado, but they were identical enough to fool anyone they wanted to fool—which made them, he'd been told, statistically one-in-a-million. He'd never kept them straight by looks, but it hadn't taken many meetings to learn to identify them by personality. Kelly, with her outgoing nature, Raquel, quiet, brilliant, and a little intimidating, and Grace, kind and spiritual. There'd been a momentary, never-spoken-of crush on Grace—the one who'd seemed to match his temperament best.

He carried Sadie into the cathedral-ceilinged living room with its comfortable blue, rust, and red sunset color scheme. Mia shooed a huge, fluffy cat off an overstuffed armchair and laughed.

"Remember Rory's ragdoll cat, Jack?" she asked. "Lazy, beautiful old thing."

Damien laughed and sat with the baby while Jack

curled at his feet. "My kind of chill guy. Sorry, buddy." Jack yawned and licked his paw, unperturbed.

Sadie babbled and stared at Damien again. She patted his cheek with clumsy baby taps, and he blew her a little raspberry before turning her around, setting her on his thigh to face outward, and jiggling his leg until she bubbled with laughter. Hers was the kind of conversation he wished he could keep to all evening.

"Are you sure you have to leave us after just a few days?"

Grandma Sadie's question surprised him. He planned to talk with Gabe eventually and tell him his whole story, but nobody else had to know. Grandma, however, was astute as a guru on the mountain and never asked questions just to make conversation.

"I want to surprise my mother while I'm on leave," he hedged. "She's been asking me to come back to Sheridan ever since I moved to Jackson Hole before joining the army."

"I've been there many times. Sheridan is a nice little community." Grandma Sadie, not an old woman who liked granny dresses or baggy pants, crossed her jeans-clad legs and fixed him with a kind but firm gaze. "Would you ever want to live there?"

He *wanted* to live in wide-open spaces and be based in Montana during fire season. He let a sigh flow from him like air from a deflating balloon.

"Is there a reason you ask?" he asked.

"There is. We all think you should visit your mother, then come back for the rest of your leave and work on the ranch."

His mouth literally opened and closed so that he felt like a grouper. He stole glances at the faces in the room.

Gabe watched him, assurance that this was not an intervention of some kind in his eyes, his elbow braced on the arm of a sofa, one hand loosely over his mouth in his thinker's pose. Mia and Harper's features held nothing but surprised interest. Skylar stood in the doorway. What the hell was he supposed to say?

"Work and do what?" His question came out slightly sharper than he felt.

"I told them you had a month off," Gabe explained. "You're strong, experienced, and we're starting a new cattle project this month. Cole always needs help even with Ty around now. Full pay and benefits until you have to go back to Montana."

Damien stopped bouncing his leg, and Little Sadie threw her head back to look at him. He started jiggling again, but Skylar intervened and swooped up the baby with an expert grab.

"Come on, you. Let's go play and let the big people talk."

"Thanks, Sky," Mia said.

"No problem."

With his distraction gone, Damien felt the world closing in around him. "Gabe, this is a generous offer," he said. "But I don't know…"

The phone rang in the distance and Harper stood. "Sorry. Be right back."

"You don't have to decide right now," Gabe said. "But think about it."

"I promise I will."

Gabe was a straight shooter, but his earnest request gave Damien more than a little pause. The man was astute, too. If Grandma Sadie had suspicions, then so did Gabe. This smacked of his old mentor wanting to keep an eye on him, but escaping analysis and head-shrinking was the very reason Damien hadn't asked to come and stay in the first place.

"That's all I can ask." Gabe nodded. "As for the next few days, just make yourself at home. You've got the guest suite upstairs, and you're to come and go as you like, raid the fridge, be social or not. The place is yours—there are so many of us we won't notice you anyway."

Fat chance of that. The Crocketts noticed everything.

"Thank you. I appreciate this more than you know."

Harper returned, her features a combination of disappointment and concern.

"That was Kelly. Her flight from San Francisco has been delayed by four hours. She won't get in until eleven. Poor kid sounds exhausted. It's not like her. I guess she and Rocky are still at odds over what to do after the fire. She admitted she's coming home because she isn't ready to deal with Raquel and the financial stuff yet. The fact that the two of them are fighting is the most worrisome thing of all."

"We'll take care of them," Mia said and turned to Damien. "I'm so sorry. When you have a big family there's always some kind of drama. My sisters in Denver had some trouble at their restaurant, so Kelly will be here for a little while, too."

"Skylar told me. A fire? Was there much damage?"

"I don't know all the details, but yes, a fair amount. The fire started in the building next to theirs, but they have structural damage and part of the restaurant kitchen was destroyed. We'll find out more when she gets here."

Murmurs of sympathy, understanding, and shared frustration swirled around him, and as they escalated, Damien made up his mind. He couldn't stay longer than he'd originally planned. Paradise Ranch was big, but it didn't need two houseguests broken by fire. And he didn't need more reminders of how broken a fire could leave someone. The Crocketts needed to circle the wagons around one of their own—and he'd let himself be fine with that.

Chapter Three

EVERY TIME KELLY sat on a horse, she forgot why she'd ever left home, much less stayed away for almost ten years. Although she'd been back at Paradise for only seven hours and spent four of them tossing fitfully in a vain attempt to sleep, ten minutes with the soft squeak of saddle leather and the sway of the horse's back beneath her erased all traces of sadness and exhaustion. Horses always met a person wherever she was at. If a day proved to be a challenge, the sisters liked to joke that there was an App for that. If, like Kelly did that morning, someone needed comfort and familiarity, a horse could be a best friend and confidant.

After saddling up in a barn still empty in the early morning, she rode Jellyman, a quick and handsome half-Arab bay gelding, out of the ranch yard at a leisurely pace, with the pink and gold sunrise barely beginning at the horizon off her right shoulder. Even though "Kelly riding Jelly" was a source of great, infantile amusement, he'd been Kelly's favorite ranch horse the past few years.

Friendly, eager, and versatile, he was happy to mosey away from his pasture, but he'd jump out of his walk at the touch of a heel. She looked forward to testing his speed, but for the moment Kelly made for Wolf Paw Peak, Paradise's very own small mountain, happy to be riding farther from Denver. Farther from the problems a single accident had caused—or maybe problems that had already existed and the fire had simply exposed. Either way, Jellyman carried her temporarily away from her real-life mess toward the spaces where, little by little, her breath came back, her back and shoulders loosened, and her optimism rose.

Half an hour after setting out, she reached the changing landscape that marked the beginnings of the Teton foothills. At fifty-thousand acres, Paradise was not only the largest ranch in Wyoming, but it was also home to eighty-six square miles of beautiful, incredibly diverse scenery. While there were miles of waving pasturelands, there were also canyons and a river, and the start of the mountains. Ahead of her, still three miles off, was the ranch's own icon, Wolf Paw Peak—a three-thousand-foot aberration in the surrounding rolling hills.

From the right angle, Wolf Paw Peak looked like the head and paw of a wolf emerging from its den. The tiny town ten minutes north of the ranch had taken its name, Wolf Paw Pass, from the lone mountain, and both peak and town were central to Paradise and its history. Kelly continued to her first destination of the morning: a long, flat path a little over half a mile long that created the best racing spot on the property. Every one of the six Crockett sisters had won and lost many a bet on the outcome of a challenge between favorite horses.

Jelly knew the spot even though he'd only been at the

ranch since the girls had grown and participated in fewer races than some of his older equine buddies. As she passed the tall pine tree marking the head of the straightaway, Kelly laughed at her mount's anticipatory jigging.

"Dork," she laughed. "You guys don't forget a good run, do you? Or has Skylar been taking you here on the sly?"

Sky had all but been born on a horse. She had her own stunning appaloosa named Bungu, but she could and did ride any and every piece of horseflesh that arrived at Paradise. She was second only to Mia when it came to whispering with horses. Jellyman snorted and Kelly trotted down the start of the naturally-occurring track, her heartrate rising in happy anticipation.

"Are you ready, then, boy? Okay, take us flying!"

Mia had wanted to use Jellyman as a regular mount for Mustangs for Veterans, her part of Gabe's VA rehabilitation program, but the gelding had proven a little small for some of the bigger men and a little too mischievous for guys who needed a steady-Eddie mount in order to get comfortable. In addition, Jelly was turbo-charged and nimble as a Ferrari if given the right cues — even accidentally. Kelly shifted her right heel back behind the cinch pressed on purpose, letting out a whoop as Jellyman jumped out of the trot. In four strides, he was at a full gallop.

The wind in her face blew away the last thoughts of anything but the staccato hoofbeats and driving muscles bunching and releasing beneath her like the pistons of a perfectly tuned engine. She bent over Jelly's neck and kissed at him. Even with nobody to push him, he raced as if for Derby roses — as if he knew he could outrun Kelly's stress and worry without being asked. Then she did the thing her mother hated more than anything else — she closed her eyes and gave over full control to the horse.

The rush of adrenaline, exhilaration, and a frisson of fear made her understand real freedom. It had to be close to truly flying. Or leaving her body. Undoubtedly, the blind run was as careless and foolish as her mother had always told her it was. But they'd all done it at some point — pushing against their fears, testing their limits. Kelly was simply the one addicted to the surge and the mental test; she was pretty sure her sisters had outgrown the need for this kind of speed long ago.

The sightless tear lasted only ten seconds or so — her record was twenty — and she opened her eyes, lifted her head enough so Jelly's thick, black mane swirled around her face, and then started to slow him as the path began a slow curve around the base of a large grass hill. She let him wind down slowly, breathing in the scent of heated horse and laughing at his disappointed snort that the race was over.

"Good boy. What a good boy." Half breathless but fully exhilarated, she cooed out her praise and leaned forward to scrub along the side of his neck.

Maybe she'd just put up a tent next to the path, live here for the next ten years, and stay away from the conflict. Away from decisions and castle-in-the-sky dreams. Raquel seemed to have all the answers. Kelly would be perfectly happy letting her sister implement the solutions on her own if she herself could live in the stunning scenery surrounding her now.

She straightened in the saddle and inhaled deeply of the sweet, early May air as she walked Jelly around the base of the hill. The Teton mountain range came into view in the distance, and it along with the scent on the breeze laced with fragrant spring green and the cool tang of the nearby Kwinaa River added to the first peace she'd felt in a week. It was hard to stay angry or stressed in the presence of Grand Teton. Although it was eighty miles distant, it had always felt like Paradise's personal guardian—its spirit a constant calming reminder that nearly all troubles were small compared to the majesty of the mountains.

Jelly startled before Kelly saw anything, his snort and sideways jump catching her off guard. Years in the saddle kept her seated, but she looked up after calming her horse and saw the mounted figure far to the outside of the path, watching her carefully. That horse, a sturdy, steel-gray mustang, was instantly familiar and Kelly took in the rider with a sharp intake of breath.

She'd heard he was visiting Paradise, but the last time she'd seen him, he'd barely gained the skill to canter around a small arena. Now he sat on Panacea's back—she knew the beautiful grulla mare well—with the confidence of a born ranchman, and his features, placid and starkly handsome, were unreadable.

"What in the world?" she asked, her heart rate slowing after its shock. "Damien Finney?"

"Kelly Crockett." His features remained neutral save for one brow cocked slightly in teasing response. "I saw you coming and moved as far to the side as I could. Sorry, we didn't mean to scare you."

"Jelly saw you first and he's not the bravest with gremlins, real or imagined, but I admit I didn't expect to see you here. I didn't expect to see anyone this far out so early in the morning."

The angles of his face softened, almost as if he was relieved to find he wasn't in hot water. She remembered him as a laconic but sarcastic tough guy from Gabe's first group of veterans in the mustang program. A practical joker. They said he'd changed a lot once he'd gotten his horse, and she didn't see any of the cynicism she remembered the few times she'd met him. She didn't remember the classic good looks. Or the fascinating, opaque blue eyes that gave nothing away.

"Yeah. I thought we'd beat the crowds. See the sunrise."

"It was beautiful."

"It was that." He scratched the back of his neck, his mouth crooking slightly as he decided whether to speak. Finally he caught her eyes and allowed the slightest of smiles. "I might have spooked the horse a little, but you're the one who scared a few months off my life."

She stared, still unable to read his face. "And how's that?"

"Seems potentially suicidal for a person on a horse to run hell-bent for Hades with her eyes closed."

"How in the world could you even tell that?" Bubbles of laughter inappropriate to his legitimate concern rose from her chest and she breathed heavily to hold them back.

"It was an educated guess. Your face was buried so deep in your horse's neck that if your eyes weren't closed, they were clearly not on the path. I kept waiting for the horse to hit a hole or for a marmot or pika to pop out and send you ass-over-shoulder into the rocks."

Her laughter broke in one burst—a choked snort born of a failure to hold it in. "Sorry, but you sound like my mother."

"There's a reason they're called mothers."

"I suppose there is; I get it." She sighed but shrugged,

not willing to allow any daughterly remorse to mar her moment of freedom. "And I'm sure you're both right, but don't tell her. We all used to dare each other to be brave by keeping our eyes closed as long as we could—I always won."

"And so far you've lived to brag about it."

"So far." She tossed him her cheekiest smile. "I heard you were visiting."

"Just a few days. Visiting the horse mostly. Then going to visit *my* mother."

"Nice. You're a wildfire fighter now, right?" she asked, genuinely curious about this man who seemed so changed from the year before. "That's really impressive, Damien—good for you. Getting a little R&R time before the main fire season? I hear there've already been a few in Idaho."

If his eyes had been impenetrable before, they went all but shuttered now, their blue dulling to a no-trespassing gray. His loose, comfortable posture in the saddle stiffened and Pan reacted, shuffling beneath his tighter frame, interpreting the change as a cue to move on.

"A few," he said simply, gently quieting his mare and ignoring the compliment and other questions.

"Well, sorry I missed you last night." She didn't push, but she studied him until he looked away.

"Yeah. I knew I was getting up early and I heard you were arriving late."

"It *was* late. But who's sleeping much these days?" She forced herself to blow off the reckless comment with another laugh. She wasn't about to tell him of her sleeplessness. "I can never wait to get back on a horse when I come home."

"And now that you've won your deal with the devil

you can continue, eh?" Dark humor returned to his eyes.

"Bite your tongue. This boy is sure-footed as a Rocky Mountain Bighorn. I needed no agreement." She scrubbed on Jelly's neck again. "Right, guy?"

"Everyone has a favorite way to mainline adrenaline." He shook his head good-naturedly. "It was good to run into you, Kelly Crockett. Guess I'll see you back at the ranch, as they say."

He'd fully relaxed again. His even tone gave testament to his reserve, and maybe a well of emotion he kept in check. Still, it was impossible to ignore the way he looked completely unlike a fireman and more like a mountain drifter, with a perfect blend of sculpted shadowed features, the intriguing, changeable blue eyes, a slightly crooked nose, and a day's scruff of beard. She had to admit, his whole persona fed more than her than curiosity.

"Are you really done riding already? You can't have been that much farther along than I am. I'm heading to Ancestor Canyon. You could ride along if you want."

He hesitated, took his turn to study her, and shook his head. Still, the furrow developing between his brows hinted that he weighed his options. At last, he shrugged.

"No. I don't want to interrupt your first ride back at home."

"If I didn't prefer company, I wouldn't have invited you. It's always more fun, not to mention safer, with more people." When he continued to hesitate, she smiled. "It's perfectly fine to say 'thanks but no thanks, I'm on my own.' I wouldn't be insulted."

For the first time, he allowed a small laugh. "I've heard about Ancestor Canyon but never gone that far."

"It's worth the trip."

At that, he acquiesced, and Kelly led the way in silence that only grew the farther they went. She hated silences—they were never comfortable. She tried to remember more about Damien from his earliest days in Gabe's program and the four or five times she'd met him. He'd been less uncommunicative then—clearly, conversation from him now wasn't going to be a gift. On the other hand, she thought back to the trouble he and his buddies had caused with a slew of practical jokes they'd pulled. Damien had been the de facto ringleader. Given that, there had to be a funny bone inside of him somewhere.

"You're pretty impressive on that horse of yours now," she said finally. "Last I saw you, and it was a long time ago I admit, you were still most comfortable in the arena."

A glimmer of pleasure escaped his quiet gaze.

"Last year Skylar designated me her summer project, and we went trail riding a lot. She acted like a trail boss crossed with a drill sergeant. It's more than a little motivating to be yelled at by a fifteen-year-old."

"Skylar." Kelly laughed. Everyone always ended up loving the outrageous teenager, but to say she took people aback at first meeting was an understatement. "She doesn't always have a filter on that mouth of hers, but she gets away with it because of her kind heart."

"Yeah." He gave a half-laugh. "Her heart is biggest for animals, but I like the kid. Smart like a little fox and works like a demon for something she's taken a shine to. Teaching me to ride was more of an obsession for her than for me, but I'm glad. I guess."

"You should be. Whatever she did worked."

"I'll take that as a compliment."

Silence descended again. The sun poked in and out of marshmallow-soft cumulous clouds, and the morning heat began to rise. Kelly soaked up the sunshine.

"So you're really leaving in a day or so?" She tried starting the conversation again.

"My mother lives in Sheridan. I haven't seen her in a few months."

"I bet she's eager to see you."

"She will be when I tell her. I'm giving her a call when I get back from the ride."

He hadn't told his mother he was coming to visit? It made no sense to Kelly's brain since four of her sisters had already moved back to the ranch and she or Raquel called home nearly daily from Denver. And she was living proof they came running to their mother the instant they needed anything.

"That will be a nice surprise for her then," she said, although she had no idea if that was true. "Moms crave having their kids come home. Even when there are dozens of them, like in our family."

She sent him a smile of camaraderie, but he didn't return it.

"She'd love it if I stayed in Sheridan. But I haven't lived there in six years."

"Would you? Live there again?"

"No."

Well, that was unequivocal, she thought, surreptitiously watching him focus straight ahead. But something told her not to press the issue.

"Have you ever considered staying here? Cole told me he'd asked if you wanted to work here for a few weeks."

"He did. I thought about it briefly." A shadow Kelly

couldn't decipher crossed his face.

"What made you turn him down?"

The shadow turned into disapproval. "Is there some particular reason you need to know that?"

She shook her head, used to the reactions caused by the inquisitive nature she so often forgot to check. "I'm sorry. There's no reason at all. Nosey Nettie, my dad called me. Most people just tell me to mind my own business." She aimed her most brilliant smile at him. "You can, too, but I promise I'll keep quiet now even if you don't."

"Can you?"

"Can I what?"

"Keep quiet."

She checked to see if the teasing in his voice reached his eyes. It did not. "When forced. It's been known to take duct tape."

He merely shook his head and, finally, allowed a smile. "Even with tape, I'll believe it when I don't hear it."

"I always deserve that." She grinned. "'Kelly, take a breath,' 'Kelly, it's Grace's turn to talk,' 'Kelly, I don't need every detail.' Believe me, I've gotten every admonishment adults can give. What can I say? I have a gift."

She'd learned long ago she had to make fun of herself for being able to converse with a hitching post and have a great time. She couldn't help it; she got energy from talking to others, and she got ideas and a mental camaraderie she couldn't explain to a quiet or shy person. What she didn't always admit was that immersing herself in someone else's world also allowed her to temporarily set aside her own issues.

A wave of melancholy wrapped its frosty, uncaring arms around her. That's exactly what she was doing now, wasn't it? Nobody seemed to know for sure, but the rumor was Damien Finney's world was as out of whack as hers. If that was the case, she would much rather spend time learning about his troubles than trying to sort through her own.

"I didn't mean you had to totally stop talking. Sorry."

His voice warmed her, and she lifted her gaze to his. For the first time, she imagined she could see the tiniest glimmer of fire in the depths of the carefully controlled blue eyes.

"You don't have to be sorry. I talked before I could walk."

"Truth to tell, the distraction isn't a bad thing."

The similarity to her own thoughts surprised her. "Sometimes I think I live for distractions."

"That sounds deep."

"Nah," she replied. "I just have squirrel syndrome. Every piece of a story is a nut to gather."

At last, he let out an actual, full-voiced laugh. The music of it sifted into her, lifting her spirits from the gloom she'd almost fallen into.

"You never say the expected, do you, Kelly Crockett? You're definitely refreshing."

Her cheeks heated with pleasure, and the words soothed even though she wasn't convinced he'd intended them as a compliment. For once, she didn't reply except with a smile. They rode on, the quiet this time filled with the peaceful sounds and smells of the mountains. A warm, gentle breeze rustled the scrub grasses, and the scent of lodgepole pine from the shallow valley to their left drifted in the air. Kelly relaxed into the saddle, chancing a glance now and then at her unexpected companion. His body language softened, too. The tense hollows below his cheekbones eased and his mouth released its wary lines.

As his calm grew, a sense of relief blossomed within Kelly's chest. Maybe there was hope for the day.

Slowly, the landscape changed further as they neared a shallow valley. She led them down a rocky path toward its floor, and the trees thinned, giving way to sagebrush and boulders. Right before reaching the bottom, Kelly guided Jellyman around the end of a rocky wall and couldn't miss Damien's audible intake of breath when the valley floor with its winding braided river spread before them in front of the entrance to a narrow box canyon.

"Jiminy Christmas, Easter, and New Year's," he said.

"Pretty, isn't it?" she asked, laughing.

"How is it Skylar never showed me this place last summer?"

Kelly shrugged. "Sky likes the higher places. This is a low spot, and depending on the season, it can be much more barren than it is now. It also floods periodically, so this is the very best time of year to come. It's not a Shoshone holy place, but their people used to gather here for meetings or trading. And they say the spirits of the elders still protect the spot.

My great-great-grandfather probably bought this part of Paradise from someone who'd claimed it like all Indian land was claimed—by force. By then, the Native population had been moved to the reservation, and Grandfather, being from the generation he was, didn't think better of it. Today we don't use this space for more than visiting and maybe a little self-renewal. It's very poor recompense, but it's as respectful as we know how to be. We've offered it back, but even the Shoshone think it's isolated and not a good place to live. It's also difficult to access. So, for now, Ancestor Canyon has been allowed into our care."

"It has a good feel but..." His eyes darkened again, focused far off in thought.

"But you aren't a hundred percent certain?"

"I'm looking at it from that viewpoint of protection. Is there a back way out of the canyon?"

"Not really. That's the nature of a box canyon—one way in, steep walls all around. A haven."

"How wide is it?"

"Come on down. I'll show you."

Chapter Four

KELLY IRRITATED, FASCINATED, and attracted him in equal parts. The endless questions and the pathological chirpiness she couldn't seem to help were exactly what he'd remembered about her. He'd never known someone who could ask three questions on three subjects all in one breath. The last thing he'd needed—and definitely the last thing he *wanted*—was to notice her light brown ponytail or the way her smile turned her cheeks into the prettiest round puffs and her eyes to a sparkling golden brown. He shouldn't be fixating on the natural way she sat a horse—as if her body had been created to move and sway with the rhythm of any gait without conscious thought.

He'd wanted to stare like a rude schoolboy, all the while wishing she'd give her tongue more than five minutes of rest at a time, and he'd followed her across the windswept valley floor with no clue as to why he was happier in her company than anywhere he'd been in the past two weeks.

Pan picked her way expertly through the rocky maze of rocks, dirt, and scrub, leaving him no need to guide her. Maybe it wasn't Kelly at all but being with his horse again that made him content in the moment. He'd pinned a lot of hopes on the tough little mare being able to soothe him, and she hadn't disappointed. She had the healing power he'd remembered. She'd always had it. He relaxed. That was it. Kelly just happened to be along for the ride. Literally. The feelings were all Pan. Beautiful, one-of-a-kind Pan.

The scenery they rode through was at once beautiful and surprising. The softer silhouettes of pine trees were juxtaposed with jagged granite outcroppings as the land started its rise toward the Teton mountains. Stark colors and shadows, the green of trees, grass, and bushes touching the gray, yellow, and red of ancient stone, and the silver-brown ribbon of water created a western-hued rainbow in front of him, and as they drew closer to the canyon mouth, the world around him took on ever greater majesty. He'd jumped into forested areas burning with color, but he'd never ridden into an immersion of color so slowly he became part of it.

"Unofficially we call this Angel Valley," Kelly said. "From the air, it looks like a snow angel. Her skirt lies right in front of the canyon entrance. You and I rode down one of her wings to get here. The halo is a small pool at the mouth of this little creek about half a mile that way."

"Your family is nothing if not imaginative."

"That's my mother's influence. Who else names her modern, log ranch house Rosecroft after an English cottage? She's the one who pointed out the angel from an airplane one year. We also have a Dinosaur Valley and a Manatee Valley."

"You make my point."

Damien gazed around Angel Valley and, as they reached its floor, finally felt his chronic depression succumb to the peacefulness. "I never remember the immensity of this ranch until I get out here."

He tipped his head upward. The walls were perhaps eight or ten feet high at the canyon's entrance but rose to twenty or thirty feet as they stretched out on either side like granite arms embracing the boxed-in space. As they rode into Ancestor Canyon, he continued looking up, feeling like Frodo Baggins passing the Argonath. Silly, he knew, but the passage seemed momentous.

As soon as they were through the opening, the landscape changed as suddenly as if they'd been transported to the other side of the world. Rocky soil became fertile green carpet, and scrub brush bloomed into emerald mounds of big leaf sage and grasses splashed with orange paintbrush and purple lupine. Damien sighed.

"I could build a house right there," he pointed to a flat spot in front of a rock wall, "and live like a hermit."

"I know what you mean." She turned her golden-brown eyes on him. It took his breath away. "Be warned, though, you might not like it as well down here in January."

"Killjoy."

She grinned and he returned it, his smile coming easier at last. Once they were in the canyon, however, his firefighter's brain kicked in. Clearly, if something were to block the entrance, there'd be no way out. He pushed away the thought. The entrance was twenty yards wide, and the canyon itself stretched for two football fields. It wasn't huge, but a small herd of cattle could forage for several days. This was not a trap.

"What the...?" Kelly pulled up short and pointed. "Look there."

He followed her finger and did a double-take. In the shelter of a semi-circle of boulders, the clear and tidy remains of a campfire lay in stark contrast to the wildness around it.

"Do people regularly camp here?"

"Not that I know of. We did once in a while when we were kids. Unless Skylar has been using it...but I don't know why she would. I wonder how long this has been here."

Without answering or waiting for her, Damien swung out of his saddle. His thighs protested, gleefully reminding him he hadn't been on a horse in months. He looped Pan's reins around a low scrub pine branch and walked to the fire site. Palm down, he hovered his hand over the middle of it and frowned. A second later, Kelly squatted beside him. She brought with her the scent of spring flowers, and the hair on the back of his neck lifted in a tingle of pleasure.

"There's still heat," he said. "Whoever lit this fire didn't fully put it out."

Her brows squeezed together. "That's disturbing."

"I don't think this is hot enough to spark anything now," he said. "But you're right. It should never have been left like this."

"Unless the person is still around somewhere." Kelly checked the surroundings. "Not that we'd find him or her if they didn't want to be found. There are a lot of places you could take cover in here. Whoa, wait..."

She stood.

"What?" He followed.

"The person came on horseback, look at the droppings."

Damien almost laughed. He'd gone from being Frodo Baggins to Sam Spade in the course of five minutes. He strode past the manure pile Kelly had found and scoured the ground. A few yards away he found more manure and continued on. Within a large circle, he found multiple signs of horses.

"If he did ride in, he came with a whole bunch of horses."

She joined him and nodded. "You're right. There's been a herd in here." Then, as if the idea fully registered, her frown disintegrated, and she gave his arm a soft slap of excitement. "A herd! A wild herd. Do you know how cool that is? They rarely, rarely come down here. They stay farther up in the grassy foothills where there's lots of running room and escape routes. Oh, man, I'd love to see them. I can't wait to tell Mia—she knows all the bands."

Her focus had switched completely away from the mystery of the fire, and he couldn't keep his eyes off the bright beauty of her features. She looked like a kid on Christmas morning.

"How could a fire pit possibly be related to the horses?" he asked.

"Good question." A flash of dark humor made her laugh. "Horses sure didn't start it. Come on, let's look for clues as to who did."

He followed as she led them back and forth across at least a third of the canyon floor, searching for further signs of the horses or the mysterious person who'd left the warm fire. She pounced on each pile of droppings like she'd found treasure. All he could do was laugh.

"You are a very weird girl. What exactly are you

finding so thrillin' about this search?"

She returned his laughter. "I know; it is weird. It's just clear the horses were here recently. Some of the droppings are no more than a day old, maybe fresher. Since the fire pit is still holding heat, it seems the camper might have been here the same time the horses were. I think we didn't miss them by much."

"It isn't easy to get here. Wouldn't someone have to have a strong motivation to find it?"

"For sure. But leaving a warm fire, especially with reports of fires not that far away...it's unforgivable."

"Agreed." Damien looked to his saddlebags on the back of Pan's saddle. "I have a water bottle. It's not full but we can dump what I have on the coals."

"I've got one, too, and the stream is close if we need more."

Damien picked up a thick stick and, once they reached the fire ring, poked it into the ashes. Steam rose, and his gut clenched in anger.

"This wasn't a one-night fire," he said. "Look how deep the mound of ash is. Lots of fuel got burned."

Kelly's lips pursed into an angry knot. "You know, we've never been stingy about allowing people onto the land. It's such a big spread that as long as they check with us, we're happy to let them. Maybe someone does have permission from Harper or Cole or someone, but even if they do, none of my sisters would have time for this."

"Yeah."

They retrieved their bottles and Kelly poured her water onto the center of the old fire, making hiss and steam rise from the ashes. Damien added what remained of his and gave the still-thick pile a thorough mix.

"One more round?" he asked, and she nodded.

They rode together to the shallow stream two minutes from the canyon entrance, speaking little while Kelly dismounted to fill the bottles. He watched her efficient movements, remembering how he'd never been able to tell the triplets apart the few times he'd seen all three. He wondered if he'd now be able to pick Kelly out. Did all three sisters have the same quick flash of a grin that could turn serious in a snap? Could they all make the mundane feel like a treasure hunt? Did they charge the air around them like a lightning storm?

He had no clue. He did know that this morning at least, Kelly's slightly manic cheerfulness had made him forget he had only four weeks to get his shit together or be done as a smokejumper. Eventually, the respite with Kelly would end, and he'd have to face the black hole that had brought him here in the first place. He'd dreamed twice about the disastrous non-jump, but the cause of his fear remained unidentified, and he didn't know how to find it. In the past two years, he'd let people probe his brain so hard his amygdala still hurt. There couldn't be anything left to find.

"Okay, here's yours."

He shook his head and met her eyes as she held out his filled bottle. Their sweet brown spark again calmed the disquiet he'd allowed back into his thoughts. If Pan was his healer, Kelly's chronic cheeriness was a balm—one that could mask pain, however temporary the effects. He took the help, although she had no idea she gave it.

They returned to the fire pit and finished drowning the ashes so that when Damien stirred the muck all they heard was a safe, cool slurp.

"I think we've killed it," he said.

"Good job, partner." She lifted her palm for a high five

and their hands met with a satisfying slap. "This is why experts are good to have around. Thanks."

At the reference to expert, he couldn't stop a wince. "I'm no expert. You'd have put this out just fine all on your own."

"I don't know. You thought to check the heat. Gabe says you went through some kick-ass training. That's kind of the definition of an expert."

"Training taught me to respect fire, that's all."

He immediately heard the flat finality in his own voice, and a thoughtful light rose in her eyes as if she'd had an insight. One he didn't really want her to have.

"Is everything all right? Did something happen in Montana?"

Bells, warnings, klaxons even, went off in his head, all alerting him to shut down, keep his distance. He didn't want to talk about this—not with her. He didn't know this woman. He didn't even know if he liked her beyond finding her attractive. Yet the question was filled with concern and empathy, not invasiveness, and it plucked at the temporary bandage he had on his wound. He considered for a long moment until he shook his head and evaded the question.

"We all need breaks after tough jumps."

Her shoulders rose on a long, thoughtful inhale, and nodded.

"I get that. And just so you know, you never have to talk about anything you don't want to around me, even if I am obnoxious and nosy. I guess I'm a little fire obsessed right now because we just had one in Denver that damaged our restaurant. It's kind of a fluke that we're here at the same time and now we find yet another fire."

He didn't like flukes—they were accidents. He liked

planning and precision.

"I admit I pressed Gabe last night to find out what you were doing here." She bubbled on with her cheerful admission. "But all he said was that you're taking a break. I don't have a single preconceived idea of what you do or should do, so if you ever want someone who'll just listen, I'm here. I actually *can* listen without an opinion." She hesitated. "Well, sometimes."

She finished with a twinkle in her eye, and he had no idea how to respond. How she could be so sincere in such a fluffy way baffled him. Cap had offered an ear as well, but his chief couldn't listen without bias. To Stone Rayburn, sympathetic leader though he was, mental illness still held a touch of stigma. "Pull yourself up by your bootstraps, recruit," was part of his motto. Until whatever was causing Damien's issue was fixed, by his own strength or with help, it was mental weakness.

Only the lessons learned through Gabe, both here at the ranch and living in the nearby tiny town of Wolf Paw Pass, were saving Damien now. It had been drilled into his head that people like Stone were wrong. Traumatic brain injury was just that—injury. Not weakness. For the most part, Damien could believe it—as long as he wasn't standing on the lip of an open plane door at altitude, creating an abyss that didn't exist.

Now here came a woman who would barely reach to Stone's breastbone, trying to tell him she could listen without judging. Damien didn't know her nearly well enough to trust that promise, but something inside him wanted to trust somebody. And Kelly Crockett, it seemed, could already pick at his emotions and change them like a country fiddle player. From down to up and from depressed to happy. He'd end up exhausted if he spent too much time with her, but for this moment she soothed and smoothed out his life.

"I appreciate the offer. I'm fine."

She picked up Damien's stick and sat beside the stone ring to stir the ashes, crossing her legs in front of her.

"You could always be a cowboy. Cole did tell me he'd offered you a temporary job. Harper wants to experiment with a few organic beef cattle. You'd be a welcome hand."

He was tempted to tell her how much he wanted to take this easy route and stay. But he'd already decided that going to Sheridan would help banish a few other minor demons, like owing his mother a little of his time. He hadn't spent enough time with her since his father had died, and in some ways, he was looking forward to surprising her—although explaining what had happened would disappoint her.

"Cole was more than generous," he said. "I don't know that I'd make a very good full-time cowboy."

She nodded and, somewhat to his surprise, she didn't argue. "You have to do what's right for you."

"I kind of wish I knew what that was," he said and regretted the words immediately. Hadn't he just decided not to spill his guts to her?

"I know the feeling."

That surprised him again, enough to switch his selfish focus from himself to her. "What do you mean? You have a dream job. You're a chef's chef, according to Mia and Harper."

"That's what sisters are supposed to say. The truth is, I make ultra-creative sandwiches and fun desserts for my current restaurant. I just got done spending time with an old teacher, and believe me, I learned that a real chef, I am not. At least, not at the moment."

"And that's what you want to be? A real chef?"

"I went to school for that purpose."

It didn't escape him that she hadn't answered the question, but he followed her example and didn't press. Instead, he sat beside her while she rubbed self-consciously at the corner of her mouth, unsuccessfully trying to hide a rueful twist of her lips.

"I've always planned to start a real restaurant, not just a small coffee-and-short-order cafe. But, in the six years we've been open, I've forgotten a lot. During my time in San Francisco, I visited restaurants and talked a lot with the chef I worked for right out of school. He let me help for three days. Ha! I worked my tail off and he spent three days telling me I'd lost my edge and my instincts were rusty."

"Doesn't sound like a very good teacher to me."

She shook her head adamantly. "On the contrary. He's the best. It's Landon O'Keefe."

The name meant nothing to Damien and he shrugged. Kelly's eyes lit with a spark of disbelief.

"Seriously? Bayvio Restaurant in San Francisco? Three Michelin stars?"

"Sorry. I'm a maker of zero-star sandwiches myself."

He didn't tell her how many things besides sandwiches he'd made in fire stations over his early career. The last thing he wanted was to hint this was a comparison.

"He's one of the world's top chefs and I'm lucky to have him as a mentor. He's tough but great. My goal was to go back and sous chef for him again, but he doesn't have an opening right now. I'd be welcome in a year, or he knows of another three-star chef looking for an intern if I don't want to wait."

"I'm going to bet you don't want to wait."

"I don't, but the fire has put everything in jeopardy. My sister believes once we rebuild, we'll have used all our reserves and won't have the capital to start a new place. She's also even more critical of me than Landon O'Keefe is. She all but told me she no longer has faith in me or our original plan."

She seemed genuinely saddened by her words, but there was an underlying touch of self-pity, too. Since he had no way of reading her motives, he stuck to the cliché.

"I'm sure that's not true."

She lifted one shoulder and smiled, still sad but resolute.

"Hey, I'm sorry for blathering on like that. You didn't need my whole story."

"Sometimes life decisions are hard—you need an ear. Don't apologize."

Her smile returned in the quick, effortless way he was starting to recognize. "Thank you. I love Triple Bean for what it is. All I want next is to have people see what I'm good at."

"Then here's to deciding what's next. For both of us."

She plucked a long grass stem, popped in her mouth, and leaned back on her elbows, searching the clear summer sky. While she let the sun bask her face, Damien caught himself admiring the slender line of her silhouette. This time he didn't shy away. If he was perfectly honest, it was nice to feel like a normal guy, attracted to a pretty woman. He wanted nothing to do with commitment, relationships, marriage, or kids but he liked leaving the PTSD-riddled dude behind for even a short while. And when Kelly caught him staring, she proved her outgoing reputation correct with a flirty wink that sent a satisfying trill through his belly.

"You'd make a real handsome cowboy, Mr. Finney," she drawled. "You should consider it, you know. But, regardless, thanks for the company today."

The compliment pleased him far too much. In his current state of mind, the joking remark felt good enough to hold him for the entire upcoming, grim month.

"It's been a good distraction."

Good job, Finney. Exactly the kind of compliment every woman loves.

She didn't seem to notice his ham-fisted reply. "I suppose we should think about heading back," she said. "It's pushing noon, and I didn't bring any food, did you?"

He shook his head. "I wasn't planning to find a perfect companion and be gone this long."

There. That was better.

She laughed again. "A perfect point. Well, come on, perfect companion. It's an hour-and-a-half ride back. Have you been to my sister's new restaurant yet? We could go there for late lunch."

His confidence rose back up a notch. At least he hadn't completely turned her off if she was asking him out on a date.

"I haven't been there."

"She supposedly has a new chef. Her fourth since opening three months ago."

His brows quirked in surprise. "Four?"

Kelly shrugged. "She thinks this one's finally a keeper."

He hefted to his feet and held out a hand, letting her slender fingers wrap his palm as he pulled her up. The top of her head reached his bottom lip, yet she didn't seem tiny. Vibrancy filled every inch of her, making her larger than life, like a celebrity.

"Okay, deal. Let's scope out the new chef."

The horses, tied to a couple of pine trees, were happily grazing, looking too content to disturb. Sort of like himself. He didn't want to ride back to reality, but Kelly dusted off her pant legs and her seat, getting ready to ride.

"I'd better find a bush before we mount up. Better than trying to hold it or stopping on the trail." She grinned. "Real cowboys, which I guess we can agree we're not, have iron bladders."

"Some firefighters."

Her brows rose in surprise. "Isn't there an obvious joke about watering a forest fire…" Her head wagged in a quick rejection. "Sorry. Fire again. Not funny."

"No, it's a saying. 'You might as well piss on a wildfire.'"

She stared at him a moment.

"It's a little funny," he added and laughed at her rather cute little giggle as she walked toward a protected spot.

Following her example, he searched out his own secluded sage bush and kicked at it to make sure nothing deadly lurked near the base. His toe rammed against something large and soft-sided. Bending to part the thick, fragrant branches, he found the object—a black backpack of the kind most kids carried to school. He hoisted it free of its hiding spot and looked for an ID tag.

He spun the pack around to assess every side and frowned. When Kelly's head popped up from behind her screen of scrub brush, he held up the pack.

"Hey," he called. "What do you make of this?"

Chapter Five

AT THE SIGHT of the bag in Damien's hands, Kelly threw glances around the canyon, as if after the half-hour they'd been sitting in plain sight, the owner would suddenly decide to show himself. Common sense returned and she stopped searching. The backpack's owner didn't want to be found or they'd have found him. But he—or she—had to be nearby if the backpack was here. Why the person was hiding, however, she had no clue.

"Do you recognize it?" Damien asked.

"I don't. I guess our camper isn't gone like we thought. He could be out exploring. I suppose he could be watching us…"

"Creepy. But if it was a murderer or highwayman, we'd be victims by now." Damien grinned when she shivered visibly.

"Stop, that's not funny. I live in a big city. According to papers, crazy mass murderers don't follow any logic."

"And we're trapped in a box canyon. Not good." His voice lowered in a teasing warning and she glared.

"You're cruel."

"No. I'm not worried. This place gives off a safe vibe."

"If I really ever needed a safe place on Paradise Ranch, I'd flee to the other side of Wolf Paw Peak." She looked to where the tip of the ranch's lone mountain was visible just over the far canyon wall. "Tucked behind it is one of our outback cabins. It's secluded and only easy to find if you know how to get there."

"The perks of having fifty-thousand acres at your disposal."

"Right?" She wiggled her brows.

"All that aside, our non-murderer actually found an effective hiding place for the pack," Damien said. "Finding it was pure luck. What should we do with it?"

Kelly searched the hiding spot and let out a squeak of surprise when she spied a small, worn, tan leather pouch. She picked it up and stared at the decoration on the front of the two-inch bag, a chevron shape of intricate beading in bright colors from turquoise to red. Four inches of leather fringe hung from the bottom of the pouch, and a thin leather strap on top was long enough to slip over an adult's head.

"Whoever this belongs to will definitely be back," she said.

"What is it?"

"A medicine bag. Usually, these are very important to the owners and rarely leave their necks. I can't imagine why it would have been left behind." A terrible thought came to her. "I hope nothing happened to this person."

"Should we just leave it?"

Her mind whirled with uncertainty. She understood

privacy, but she also knew that in wild country like this, a person could easily end up lost or hurt. Paradise couldn't be monitored or posted as private property in every corner. It would be impossible to monitor every wanderer, but a chance to confront this camper about his dangerous fire behavior would be satisfying. Aside from that, fifty thousand acres was also home to dangerous wildlife. If someone got hurt, nobody might ever find out.

"I hate to dig through someone's property," she said. "but there are mountain lions and rattlesnakes in this area. If the person who owns this is hurt..." She grimaced. "Let's open the backpack and see if there's any ID."

The bag had decent weight to it, and something inside rattled slightly. Kelly knelt, unbuckled the front flap, and flipped the top open. Her search revealed a rain jacket, a fleece pullover, several dehydrated meal packets, and a simple, collapsible backpacker's stove. Matches in a waterproof container, a heavy plastic pencil case filled with various artist's pencils, and a geological survey map of the Jackson Hole basin were nestled in the bottom of the pack. Finally, wedged against the back, was an eight-by-ten-inch sketchbook.

"Interesting," Damien said. "An artist, but no wallet or ID? I suppose we could sit here and wait until he or she comes back."

She blew out a half-laugh. "Which one of us would starve first?"

"I would."

She shot him a quick grin. "And we used all our fresh water on the fire. No, I think we take the medicine bag and leave the backpack with a note. If the medicine bag is as important as it could be, they'll come to claim it. Then we'll know he's okay and wasn't injured or attacked."

"Fair enough." Damien squatted beside her and reached for the sketchbook. "I'll look through this; that way we're partners in the crime of backpack invasion."

"If you were smart, you'd go on record as strenuously objecting."

"No. I'm okay with having a way to know the person isn't dead."

He flipped open the sketchbook and gave a low whistle of astonishment. The first page was full of perfectly rendered horse sketches—grazing, grooming each other, one alert with head high and ears pricked.

"Looks like something Skylar could have done," Kelly said. "That girl can draw, did you know?"

"Yeah, she did several drawings of Pan last summer. She wants to be an artist like Harper is. She was taking a lot of classes from Harper at the community center when I left."

"I wonder if there's a chance this is Sky's stuff and she's got it stashed so she doesn't have to carry it on horseback when she comes out." Kelly's voice rose in hope. It would be a huge relief to know the interloper was part of the Crockett extended family and not a stray.

"But what would she be doing with a medicine bag?"

Kelly's shoulders dropped. "Right. Good question. She loves Native American legends and history, but she's not obsessed with it. Certainly not enough to make a medicine bag that isn't part of her heritage."

Kelly flipped another sketchbook page, and then another and another. Her amazement grew with each new drawing. Every page was filled with mustang horses in different poses and groupings. In addition, there studies of horse markings: face stripes and blazes, socks and stockings, dorsal stripes and shadings. But what astounded her most was that every single horse clearly shared Pan's striking gray-and-black coloring. The proof was in the labels: "grulla mare, Whimsy" "grulla foal, Sugar" "grulla foal—no white, Smokey."

"Check it out." She looked closer at some of the full-body drawings. "They're all named. Here are more: Mac, Dancer, Eeyore."

"This is beautiful and strange at the same time."

Damien stared at the drawings with her, standing so close his upper arm pressed to hers, skin against skin, and his spice-soap, male scent filled her senses. The hyper-awareness shocked her. When the pictures begin to blur and the pleasant valley air turned August-sultry, she dropped her hold on the sketchbook, leaving it in Damien's hands so she could step away. She *knew* how to handle herself around men—how to make the situation what she wanted it to be. She was good at smiling and flirting. She was good at dates. She was even good at sex when the chemistry was perfect. But this was different. Out of the blue. Out of her control.

"What?" he asked, making her shake her head to clear it. Damien quietly closed the sketchbook. "Did you think of something?"

He didn't seem to notice that her reaction had been to him. Thank goodness.

"Nope, nothing," she replied. "It seems this person loves gray horses."

"Maybe she's following a bunch of gray horses around."

The off-hand remark got her to look up, and she bit her bottom lip, forcing herself to consider his words and not the impact of his eyes or what the heck had happened to her in the last fifteen seconds.

"Following a herd..." she said slowly. "The herd that's been in here, maybe?"

He stepped back. "I can see your mind spinning, trying to connect the mystery dots."

"It's exciting and yet makes no sense. Grulla coloring is not unique but it's special. Drawing nothing but that color horse seems almost fanciful. I just don't know what to think."

She flipped to a blank page and tore it out, then dug in the backpack again for the pencils. She wrote quickly and after several minutes handed the paper to Damien.

"This okay?"

He read aloud. "Dear Backpack Owner. We found your pack in Ancestor Canyon on Paradise Ranch land. I have left it for you but have taken your medicine bag for safekeeping. If you find this note, you can pick up the medicine bag anytime at the main Paradise ranch house. I want to be sure you're safe and not injured. Text me at this number or come to...blah blah..."

He read silently to the end where she'd signed her name and then he nodded.

"Sounds good. I hope they contact you."

"I do too. But whatever happens, let's pack this back up and head out. I may or may not want to meet this person in a secluded canyon."

By the time they reached the ranch yard, Kelly had been re-introduced to the Damien Finney she remembered from the previous year. What chattiness and camaraderie she'd drawn from him the past two hours had reverted to quiet nods of agreement and carefully chosen words. He possessed a sense of humor as laconic as his personality — quiet with unexpected clever comebacks as she laid out all the outlandish scenarios she could conjure about the mystery backpack and its person: a writer researching the landscape; a backcountry scavenger hunt for a bunch of kids; aliens who'd landed in the remote area and thought the horses were the planet's prevalent life form. She chattered away, used to people who didn't talk much. And although she had to work harder than before to draw him out of a protective shell, he was attentive company.

And damn fine-looking company to boot.

Once back, they spent a solid forty-five minutes caring for their horses, and Kelly let quiet prevail so she could study the attention Damien paid to Pan. His solid frame should have looked awkward around the little mustang, but instead, they were made for each other. He clearly knew every spot where she loved to be scratched or stroked. He took his time with the curry and body brushes, rubbing out each saddle mark, brushing until Pan gleamed like a silver loving cup and her black-and-gray mane flowed like molten pewter down her neck.

Kelly hadn't had her own horse for years. Since she was at Paradise so infrequently, she was content to ride whatever horse was available. Jellyman was always a pleasure, but he belonged to anyone who needed a good mount. Damien's obvious adoration of his mare gave Kelly a twinge of envy. She missed the bond and the partnership of a horse she knew as well as she knew herself. The loyalty that could be as unconditional as a dog's love.

"Well, darlin', it was good as I hoped to be back with you." She overheard Damien's low murmur into Pan's ear. "I missed you even more than I knew. Thanks for the great ride."

Her heart melted a little. It wasn't unusual for a man to talk to his horse, but Damien meant it with the deepest passion. For a second, Kelly considered asking Mia if she could join the Mustangs for Vets program just so they'd help her find a horse. At the thought, she snorted out loud without meaning to. If she ever wanted to get a new restaurant off the ground, there wasn't time for bonding with a horse. There hadn't been time in years.

"What?" Damien's voice, aimed now at her, popped her head up.

He leaned on Pan, his hip cocked against the horse's flank, his arms crossed so his long fingers wrapped the front of each bicep just beneath the sleeves of his T-shirt. She sighed and pushed away flutters of appreciation. Why did every move he made suddenly affect her entire body?

"I was just thinking how nice it would be to find a horse of my own again."

"I get that, although a year ago I wouldn't have understood. A horse is the last thing I ever thought I'd own."

"You have a special way with her."

"I have to admit it wasn't automatic. She taught me a lot. I'm grateful."

"She's a beautiful girl."

He turned slightly and ran his hands down her shoulder like a sculptor smoothing his clay. "Mia told me it was dangerous to choose a horse strictly for color, but that's exactly what I did. The instant I saw her, she lifted her head, looked me straight in the eye, and took a step forward. Something inside shifted." He looked at the ground as if suddenly embarrassed. "It sounds ridiculous, but it's still true. I figured even if I never got to ride her, it would be okay as long as I could be around her. Riding has been a bonus."

"It doesn't sound ridiculous at all. I can sense your

connection. Mia did a good thing coming up with the mustang program."

"She did."

They let the horses back into their pastures and watched them amble off to find their friends. After leaving the barn they headed up the winding driveway toward the house and Kelly dangled the medicine bag from her fingers.

"I'll have to find a safe place for this until it's claimed."

"Can you look inside?"

"No. Whatever's in here is personal to the owner; it won't mean anything to us."

"What could be in there?"

"Hard to say. Anything meaningful to the person who filled it. I've been feeling through the leather out of mild curiosity. There's maybe a stone or gem of some kind. Could be an animal tooth or a bone. There could be plants or herbs like sweetgrass or sage. Whatever it is, the owner believes it has protective and healing powers."

"I kind of like that," he said.

"I do, too," she replied. "I don't personally believe objects have power, but a medicine bag is like having a tangible object to remind you someone or something is watching over you. That's sort of tweaking the true native belief, but it's still comforting." She sighed and let her hand with the bag drop to her side. Doubts about having it at all plagued her anew. "I don't know. I'm worried now that I shouldn't have taken it."

"Look at it this way: it's safe and the owner will know immediately where it is."

A simple electronic tone sounded and then pulsed three times from Damien's pocket and he grunted.

"Sorry."

"Not at all. Take it."

"It's just a text." He pulled out the phone and touched the screen, studied it for several seconds, and shook his head. "Well, damn it."

"What's wrong?"

"It's a boarding stable where I was hoping to bring Pan for the month."

"Wait. You're planning to take her away?"

He frowned. "I want to keep her near when I'm in Sheridan."

"You really are going?"

"My mother..." He hesitated. "She's been on her own for a long time, and she hasn'tbeen the same since my father died a few years ago. I've been away handling my own things too long, so I need to check on her for the next month. If I go back to Montana, I'll ask Mia and Harper about bringing Pan back."

"'*If*' you go back?"

His frown turned to a scowl aimed directly at her, and Kelly held up an apologetic hand.

"Sorry. I promised not to be nosy."

"You did." He sighed. "I just don't know exactly what my plans are."

"Fair enough. What did the text from the stable say?"

"At first they had room for Pan for two months, but it seems they've changed their minds. Says they made a mistake and the 'boss' says there isn't room after all."

"Prejudice," she said simply.

"Excuse me?"

"It's insane, but a lot of ranchers and stable owners don't like mustangs."

"Oh, come on. I thought that went out with the last

century."

"Yeah," she snorted in derision. "So did all prejudice, right? But don't you know that mustangs are wild and unpredictable? They overuse land the ranchers need for cattle. These people honestly believe wild horses should be eliminated."

The word he muttered under his breath made it clear what he thought of "these people," and he stalked on, his big strides carrying him momentarily ahead of her as he stepped off his clear frustration. When he slowed, he glanced back with a flat apology in his eyes before averting them again.

"I'm sorry. I stop thinking rationally when I get pissed off. Is that invitation for late lunch still open? I'd kind of like to forget about medicine bags, campfires, and stupid people for a little while."

His colorless voice had lost all its normal, lazy friendliness. When she tried to catch his eyes, he had them focused straight ahead and didn't meet her gaze.

"Of course it's still open," she said, and caught up to him, her brain searching for the right comforting words. In the wake of his heavy silence, she found none.

She'd named it Peas Porridge.

A year and two months after Grace had walked away from Triple Bean, Kelly still couldn't deny how much losing her sister's partnership still hurt. Grace had always been the sister who'd most seemed to share Kelly's dream of creating a star-level restaurant. But even though her leaving had felt like treason at the time, the major rifts had healed. Maybe there was a twinge of personal slight skulking deep inside, but when Kelly stood with Damien before the lovely establishment her sister had created, she had to admit Grace's defection looked like one smart move. Peas Porridge honestly was a great, fun name for a family restaurant. Good ideas had always been Grace's strength. And there was no envy. The new place was wonderful, but it wasn't the kind of establishment Kelly wanted.

"Wow," Damien said, his eyes finally lighting back up with interest as he took in the refurbished old cabin. "I remember seeing this place when I lived here in town. It was so run down I thought it should be demolished before it fell on top of someone. Skylar told me how Grace discovered the building actually belonged to your family."

"I certainly never knew it was ours when we were growing up. It was just the old library, then the place the Elks and the Lions stored their old stuff. Turns out it held a lot of Paradise Ranch treasures—letters and my great-grandfather and grandmother's history. Now it's all Grace's, and I'm glad for her."

They climbed the three brick-laid steps to the porch, where several benches cushioned in teal and lavender lined the house front, and two small game tables awaited chess or checker players. The main door had been set at an angle on the front right corner, and the porch railing wrapped around it then widened into a space containing two rustic bench swings and a gas fire pit. They entered the restaurant beneath a charming green wrought-iron sign filigreed with grape leaves and roses, and bearing large script letters reading "Peas Porridge."

"Nice," Damien said.

"Grace and Ty designed all of it. Grace was always our visionary, and we still miss her terribly, but Raquel and I never fully understood that this is what she wanted until we saw the plans. I've seen it as she progressed, but this is the first I've seen it completely finished."

"Does Grace cook, too?"

"She can, although it's never been her favorite. Her menu is pretty simple, and the choices are super eclectic. I'd go a *little* fancier, but she's serving things she considers comfort food that anyone will like. Plus she caters to kids, too, which is cool. Now if she could only find her forever chef."

"There's a lack of chef talent in Wolf Paw Pass?"

Kelly had to laugh even though she felt for her sister's ongoing plight.

"She's going through chefs the way the Bachelorette goes through roses. But, fingers crossed, she has a new girl who sounds promising."

The main dining room greeted them with rustic-chic decor: pine logs on the two end walls and creamy paint everywhere else to lighten the ambiance. Grace had found a beautiful wildflower border wallpaper to hang around the many windows, and the chairs and tables were a burnished honey oak. Simple blue cloths covered the tables, but every place had a different floral napkin, and each table had a unique teapot filled with flowers.

But not everything was feminine. Bold picture frames set off gorgeous Wyoming landscapes and animals. Kelly's favorite was one Harper had painted—a mural-sized sunset behind a band of mustangs. A separate room to the left was set up as Grace's beloved experiment: a well-supervised children's restaurant and play area where kids could order their own food from a menu selected by their parents.

To the right were restrooms, each one filled with fun posters and sayings on the walls, where people were known to stay for much longer than their business took.

Her sister had more than outdone herself.

"Kel?"

She pulled her gaze away from its visual tour to see Grace hurrying toward them, nearly skipping. The worries and the unknowns of her current problems melted away at the sight of her other mirror-image best friend, and she held her arms wide to catch Grace in a wild hug.

"Oh my gosh, Gracie! I am so glad to see you!"

"I heard you got back last night, but too late for us to see you. I'm off tonight and I'll be there for dinner, but I was still sad—it wasn't soon enough. I'm so thrilled you've come in."

"I had to, didn't I? Plus I went for a ride this morning and found Damien—or he found me, I guess—so I brought him along."

Grace released her and lifted her eyes. "Damien! I heard you were visiting, too." She offered him a giant hug as well, and Kelly watched pleasure seep into his smile as if he'd been worried she wouldn't remember him.

"Good to see you, Grace."

His gaze bounced between them and Kelly laughed when he raised his brows in apology for staring at the matching pair. "We're used to it," she said.

"And we're vain about it, too," Grace added. "It's so much fun to watch people's faces."

"It is amazing. You have to look pretty close to find differences."

"She's the pretty one," Grace said.

"She's the gorgeous one," Kelly replied.

They hugged again, and when they parted, Grace beckoned for them to follow. "Come on, sit at one of our back-garden window tables—very coveted spots these days." Her brow rose teasingly. "You can see a super-stunning view of the construction on the walkway around the pond."

"You've got it going already?"

"Just started two weeks ago. In for a penny, you know. It'll be fun once it's done—people will be able to stroll and even take a picnic lunch or dinner to spots along the walkway. We got a grant from the Ecological Society here in Wyoming so it's being subsidized. Let's git 'er finished, I say."

"It's all beautiful, Gracie. I'm so proud of you."

She blew out a breath. "Thanks. I do love it, but you, better than anyone, know how hard it all is. The day I get you in here to solve my kitchen issues is the day I'll truly have it made." She patted Kelly on the cheek. "I could use a little of your kitchen diva-ness."

"Diva? I'm not a diva." Kelly made a face.

"She kind of is, though." Grace winked at Damien. "The thing is—it's totally justified. She's that good."

"I've heard rumors." He smiled, and a flush of surprised pleasure rippled through Kelly's stomach when the smile was aimed at her and not her sweeter sister.

They followed Grace to a table in the back corner of the dining room, where the view was, indeed, of construction vehicles and workers busy as ants, carrying planks and tools out to a boardwalk taking shape around the water. Grace handed them menus she'd surreptitiously grabbed along the route.

"Anything you want," she said. "This one's on me. No arguments."

"Oh, Grace, you—"

Grace held up her palm. "What did I say? Oldest sister rules."

Kelly hid a grin and bowed her head. "Yes, ma'am."

"I'll be back. I'll tell Greta, my waitress, I'll take care of you myself."

"Royal treatment," Damien said. "Guess we picked the right place for lunch."

"You definitely did." Grace laid a hand on his shoulder. "And I'm so excited to see my sister that I haven't even asked how you are. Promise we'll catch up tonight?"

"I'll look forward to it," he said, and maybe it was the self-deprecation in his eyes, but Kelly even found the nod of his head attractive.

She banished the thoughts, as she'd done multiple times the past two hours. Men were her weakness; she knew it. This above-average fascination, however, was out of place after spending only a few hours with him, and she turned her goal into simply getting through lunch without saying something stupid.

Grace ducked back into the kitchen, hidden behind the wide, floor-to-ceiling wine rack just beyond where they sat. Kelly glanced at Damien surreptitiously over her menu. He'd continued his taciturn quietness on their drive to the restaurant, and though she knew most people would allow him to sit quietly until he was ready to talk, her nature made that impossible.

Just nothing stupid, she reminded herself.

"You doing okay?" she asked. "You're awfully quiet."

His shrug was barely perceptible. "Sorry. The text about the horses threw me. Sure. I'm in a great restaurant. I got fresh air this morning and had a full-blown mystery fall into my lap. I'm livin' the dream." He gave a half-smile and wiggled his brows.

"And your dream is...?"

His silence deepened and she couldn't read the

emotion that fueled it. His features held no tension, no anger, but also no real joy or pleasure. Whatever he was thinking about her question was none of her business. Neither was an answer. But something in her desperately wanted to know his truth. Know what had really happened to bring him here. Draw him out.

Given time and the chance, she knew she could get to his heart; it was what she was good at. But all her life, her family had tried to pound through her head that despite her gift of hyper-social extroversion, despite her mostly harmless ability to flirt and be anyone's new best friend, there were lines, and some people's lines were drawn further from their toes than others'. She tried to take the advice to heart this time. She didn't want to step across Damien's line this soon. Giving a dismissive wave, she picked up the menu Grace had set before her.

"Your dream is whatever you—"

The heavy, horrible crash rang without warning from the kitchen like a gunshot crossed with a car wreck. Kelly bounced in her seat and Damien's face tensed, on high alert. When a cry followed, they simultaneously pushed back their chairs, leaped to their feet, and ran for the kitchen.

Chapter Six

THEY RAN STRAIGHT into a bona fide disaster. Flat on her back on the floor, one hand fluttering to her head, lay a twenty-something woman in a white chef's jacket. Grace squatted beside her.

"Dana? Can you hear me? Don't move yet," she said.

Damien took in the mess with a trained eye. The woman on the floor was moving and starting to murmur apologies, so she was breathing and Grace was keeping her still. Good. Three cookie pans lay upside down on the floor, their fully-baked, chocolate-chip contents strewn halfway across the kitchen in crumbled lumps. In front of a combo stove and griddle, two cast iron fry pans lay atop one another, and flour drifted like snow beneath the stove. Worse, an ugly pinkish-brown substance oozed lazily into the white powder and an unpleasant, all-too-familiar odor wafted into the air.

Mixed with the acrid smell of what had to be vomit was the seared scent of grilling hamburgers. He blocked it all out and knelt beside the fallen woman.

"What happened?" he asked gently, and the young woman's eyes fixed on him. They were filled with mortification and the start of tears but otherwise looked clear. "Miss—Dana is it? Are you hurt? Did you hit your head?"

"I'm so sorry." She blinked and squeezed a tear from the corner of her eye. "I got so very dizzy and then nauseated. I grabbed for the counter to steady myself and everything got pulled down at once."

"Did you pass out?"

"No. I…I'm not sure exactly what happened. I think I slipped on the oil and fell on my back. When I tried to sit up, I'm afraid I—" She made a slight gesture toward the mess on the floor and then closed her eyes as more tears trailed down her temples. "God, how embarrassing. You can't throw up in a restaurant kitchen."

Kelly coughed beside him and he looked at her, stifling a laugh at her wrinkled nose and watering eyes. He placed a reassuring hand on Dana's shoulder and turned to Kelly.

"Suck it up, buttercup," he whispered, and she punched him in the upper arm.

"You're a guy. Guys gag at this. Why aren't you gagging?"

"Bah, it's a teensy bit of puke. You see a lot of it at fires and even more in the army."

"Call me impressed," she replied. "What can I do? The grill is turned off and the hamburgers are off the heat."

"Thanks, you got the important things." He turned back to Dana. "How do you feel now? Can you move everything? Toes and fingers?"

She moved her extremities and nodded. "Nothing

hurts. I feel better."

"Is it all right if I help you sit up?"

She nodded miserably and let him raise her first to a sitting position and, when she nodded that she was fine, help her slowly to her feet.

"I'm so sorry," she said again. "I think I need to get to the bathroom."

"I'll take you." Grace gave him a grateful half-smile and mouthed, "Thank you."

The two women headed for an employee washroom at the end of the kitchen. Damien turned to Kelly, who looked slightly like Gretel lost in the woods as she stared at the chaos.

"At least she missed the cooking surfaces," he said, deadpan, even though for some unprofessional reason he still wanted to laugh.

"That is true," she replied, pinching the bridge of her nose. The flour wasn't exactly neutralizing the smell. "What worries me is that she's obviously got some kind of stomach bug and that means virulent germs. It'll take a major cleaning effort to get this floor sanitized and the room aired out. Meanwhile, customers are probably waiting for those," she waggled her thumb at the meat, "and we can't use them. Although I suppose we could ignore that and market them as Ralphburgers."

That did it. A full belly laugh won out and Damien couldn't stop it. With his hands on his thighs, he tried to apologize but couldn't wheeze out the words. When he finally got control, he looked to Kelly again only to find her wiping her own eyes.

"We are awful," she said. "Poor girl. She must be mortified on top of being sick. And here we are, complete loons."

"What can Grace do now?" he asked against the hand he had fisted against his mouth.

"I have to close down and clean it all up." Grace appeared. "Even though it's just the floor, I have to disinfect all surfaces."

She stood stock-still, like a punched boxer, arms straight at her sides, hands cocked at the wrists as if she wanted to lift them and hit something back but couldn't summon the will.

"Aw, Grace, it's not that bad," Kelly said. "It won't take that long."

Grace's paralysis ebbed away and she shook her head.

"The good news is that Dana is not sick with some kind of flu bug. It turns out she's eight weeks pregnant and hasn't told anyone except her husband. She's had severe morning sickness, but really needed a job so didn't tell me when I hired her. She's handled the sickness so far, but today she got blindsided."

"Poor thing," Kelly said.

"Yes. Well, the bad news is, she realizes she can't tolerate the kitchen smells. The food is making her queasy and the raw meat does her in. She has to quit."

"Shouldn't it only last a few more weeks?" Kelly asked.

"It should, but who knows? I can't wait another month to find out. My part-time assistant cook can't handle the dinner menu alone."

"Who's the assistant?"

"Liam Hanson—remember him from school? He was two years behind us. He usually works from noon until about five, and then he goes to another night job. He just happened to have taken today off for a kid's school thing." She held up her hand. "I know, I know. For a restaurant this size I need a bigger staff, but I can't even keep one chef."

Silence fell and Damien watched as the two sisters sank into discussion. They really were uncannily identical. After studying them, he decided Kelly had a rounder, softer eye, but the biggest difference was that his heart didn't warm when he looked at Grace. When Kelly caught his gaze, it felt like someone had lit a fire under it.

"What do you think, Mr. Finney?" She turned to him. "I'm staying a while. I can give you my keys so you can go back and Grace will bring me home later."

"No, no, I will stay and do whatever you need. I know how to scrub a kitchen. I can even wield a chopping knife or follow a recipe. Tell me where to start."

"Wield a chopping knife?" Kelly peered at him.

"Or make a mean pot of chili." He shrugged, slightly sheepish. "When the occasion calls for it."

"You're a cook?"

"Not a trained one. I, uh, was the station cook in Sheridan for about fifteen months before I went to Afghanistan. I learned a few things, but certainly have no culinary school education like you do."

"Are you telling me I have *two* chefs standing in front of me?" Grace asked, her eyes bright with fresh hope.

"One chef." Damien held up one index finger. "I'm a cook by default. When Keebler left, nobody wanted the job."

"Keebler?" Kelly asked.

"Jim Elfmann, our original fire station cook. *He* was talented, but his forte was dessert, so Elfmann—elf— cookies, Keebler." He shrugged. "Firefighters have a weird logic."

"I don't care what kind of logic they have," Grace

said. "If you two can bail me out today, I'll figure out something for the rest of the week and I will owe you."

Kelly gave him one last amused look and shook her head. "A man of limitless surprises. Okay then. Gracie, how busy is the restaurant today?"

"We're just past the big lunch rush, but you saw. We're still about half full. I could close and claim a kitchen malfunction."

"As I recall from English class many, many years ago, that's called a euphemism," Damien said.

"Thanks, Captain Obvious." Kelly shot him a cute little smirk, and he wrinkled his nose.

Grace rapped her knuckles softly on Kelly's forehead. "Now is not the time to flirt with handsome guys. This is crisis mode time."

Damien laughed. "I like your sister, Kelly. So practical."

She smiled again. "Memo to self. He likes practical women."

"Oh, and, well, crap," Grace said suddenly, interrupting the humor. "Today aside, I totally forgot I have a catered event scheduled for tomorrow evening. A hundred people using the private room and patio starting at six. Dana could have handled it along with Liam and me, but I can't get someone else ready in one day. This stupid chef situation is beyond hopeless."

The words seemed to light a fuse beneath Kelly. Every inch of her rocketed into hyperdrive.

"Nope. Absolutely nothing's hopeless. Here's what we're going to do. Gracie, you go out to the dining room and tell everyone waiting on their food that there's been a temporary equipment issue in the kitchen. Sadly, it will take about an hour to fix, and you're so sorry for the inconvenience. Offer each person a free drink. Tell them they can wait, or they can enjoy their drink, and then we'll send them down to Dottie's Bistro or the Basecamp Grill with a voucher for a complimentary meal next time they come in. That costs a little but gives back a ton in goodwill."

"Agreed." Grace thought a moment. "I have gift certificates. And I have some old carnival-type tickets leftover from our grand opening."

"Perfect. Damien and I will start to clean up this mess." She grinned, and despite the slightly unpleasant task, his heart did a small quick-step. "Since you're so good with puke and all."

"Ha. I'll hand you the bleach."

"We'll scrub and disinfect the floor, counter, stove, and grill within an inch of their young lives. We'll have to season the grill again, but we should be ready to cook in an hour or so. I'll need about fifteen minutes to study the menu and check out your pantry. Damien can be a sous chef if he's willing. And if you can get Liam in for tonight, we'll set up for him."

"Oh, Kel!" Grace threw her arms around her sister. "Thank you! I know you didn't come here to cook."

"Hey, it's like the pilot of the plane passed out, and I'm the passenger who knows how to fly." She clapped her hands twice. "Chop, chop. Let's do this!"

She was amazing.

Damien had been attracted to Kelly before the kitchen disaster, but he fell in unabashed respect for her as they put things back in order. It wasn't exactly a Herculean task, but she led him and Grace through the clean-up as if they were prepping a sterile environment for surgery. She found pairs of Nitrile gloves, sent Damien after buckets of the hottest water he could manage, and set him to work with sponges, rags, and industrial cleaners to scour every inch of the stove and griddle. Grace cleaned up the cookies and pans, and Kelly herself went after the contaminated liquid and flour from the floor, finishing up with bleach water.

To top it all off, she sang. And she got Grace to sing. Starting with the ancient Disney "Heigh Ho" song from *Snow White and the Seven Dwarves*, followed by Garth Brooks' "Friends in Low Places." He was in no way a singer and didn't even attempt to join in, but the carefree silliness buoyed his spirits for the second time that day. Only when they got to Beyonce's "Single Ladies" did he start to laugh and hold up his cleaning rag.

"Hey now," he called. "One of you *has* a ring on it and the other doesn't know me well enough to be singing about putting one on it. I'm right here, you know."

"You could sing along," Kelly teased.

"Nobody wants to hear that."

"Then get to scrubbing and stop complaining. It's free music after all." She offered her most winning smile, and he responded with a smart salute.

"His mama raised him right." Grace nodded in approval. "Sarcasm in that salute aside."

"Yeah. He's okay."

"Darn right," Damien muttered and turned to his task to hide a grin. "Solve a mystery. Clean a kitchen. Be a sous chef. You two have no idea what a treasure I am."

"Solve a mystery?" Grace asked, laughing.

"Long story," he replied.

"And it's not exactly solved yet," Kelly said.

"This I've gotta hear."

They told her about the fire, the backpack, the

medicine bag, and sketchbook as they scrubbed, and once Kelly declared the space clean enough to meet her standards, there wasn't a surface Damien wouldn't have eaten off himself. Above all, she accomplished everything with a smile and enthusiasm he and Grace caught without realizing it. By the time Grace brought out the detailed menu listings for Kelly to study, Damien believed he could spend his life in the *Peas Porridge* kitchen with her and be forever free of depression. She hadn't cooked a morsel yet, but he knew Kelly could accomplish anything she wanted if she put her mind to it—and sang "Heigh-Ho" to her staff.

"I have no idea what to say or do about your mysterious backpacker," Grace said, hands on hips as she surveyed the cleaned kitchen. "But there's no mystery about how much I owe you two—it's a lot. I can't thank you enough."

"Bah," Kelly dismissed her. "You're welcome."

"Damien?" Grace asked. "Would you take a break and do me two favors?"

"Anything."

"Run out to the front and ask Greta to take final drinks orders and get ready to hand out menus in ten minutes. Then take a spin out back and tell the construction foreman—James in the red shirt—that their coffee and cookies will be coming in half an hour. He's cutting me a deal if I supply break snacks while they work."

Damien grinned. He'd forgotten all the funny little bartering that went on in a small town where everyone knew everyone. Wolf Paw Pass pretty much defined living in each other's back pockets.

"On my way. If I help them can I get a cookie, too?"

"Yours is already well earned, my friend. Thanks."

He left as the sisters put their heads together over the menu. After passing on the message to Greta, he wandered through the restaurant, noting that even after an hour, more than a quarter of the tables were still occupied.

He opened the door to the patio, crossed the wooden decking, and stepped down to a flagstone walking path that led to a knot of construction workers and their equipment near the pond. None of the busy workers paid him any mind until he identified James and relayed the cookie news.

"That Grace—she's one of a kind," James said, laughing. "I would never have bet I'd agree to work for chocolate chips and lemonade."

"Hell of a deal. I'd agree to it," Damien said and waved the crew back to work.

Knowing it would be a few more minutes until he was needed back in the kitchen, he found the access to a weathered dock jutting into the calm, blue-green water of a pond he guessed was maybe three or four acres in size. Sitting heavily on a built-in bench, he gazed across the lily-strewn pond surface. The moment of solitude cooled like a soothing balm on a burn. As if by magic, his shoulders released tension he hadn't realized they held.

He would have said he'd been having fun; now he realized he'd been fueled by effort and adrenaline. Even the rise and fall of voices from the work site, and the occasional ring of a hammer, were peaceful compared to all the talking and listening he'd done in the past six hours.

How did he reconcile attraction to this woman with the exhaustion that came from being with her? For three-quarters of a day he'd set aside his worries, but at the cost of now longing to close his eyes in quiet for the rest of the day. Instead, he was about to head willingly back into the pleasure of Kelly Crockett's presence. Maybe mental exhaustion would end up being a benefit when it came time to sleep tonight.

He gathered his energy while studying the jigsaw-puzzle shoreline of the pond and the roughed-in path around it where a boardwalk would be built. It would be a great addition to the restaurant property. When he finally checked his watch, the time surprised him. His breather had felt like only a few minutes, but nearly fifteen had passed. He stretched his shoulders and stood, then turned to a chipper, chirpy call.

"Hey, Watson! You okay?"

Kelly, a plate in her hands, made her way toward the dock.

"It's so peaceful out here I lost track of the time, sorry. What do you mean 'Watson?' The name is Holmes. And how does the menu look?"

"It's straightforward—no problems. I thought you'd given up and gone to find a better joint for supper since you never got to eat."

"Nah. Got hooked on watching the dragonflies."

"Wow, how nature-boy and twenty-first-century sensitive of you." She reached the deck and handed him the plate, the contents of which made his mouth water like a Pavlovian dog's. "This is a pretty spot, isn't it?"

"It is. And it doesn't move underneath me to remind my adductor muscles how sore they are from gripping a saddle."

"Adductor muscles? He's scientific, too."

"Anatomy. Basic EMT training. I pull the vocab out occasionally to impress."

"I'm impressed for at least the hundredth time today.

I cede the name Holmes to you."

He lifted the plate. "Crime solving aside, what's this amazing thing?"

"Absolutely nothing fancy, I'm afraid. It's a club sandwich, some sweet potato fries, and a brownie. I'm so sorry we missed our official lunch, and after all your help cleaning up, you deserve gourmet. I promise I'll make you something better when I have time."

From anyone else, the words would have sounded easy and teasing, but her eyes were genuinely apologetic.

"Kelly, what the hell are you sorry for? This looks like food from the gods."

The sandwich, on golden toasted bread, was thick as a fist.

She laughed. "Hardly."

"Hey. A peanut butter sandwich would have been fine. A 'can I get a rain check on lunch?' would have been fine. You've worked your tail off stepping in to help Grace with barely a blink."

"I'm a chef. I know how to run a restaurant kitchen."

"Clearly. What about you? Have you eaten?"

She nodded. "I grabbed a roll and a handful of fries. I'm fine. Come on, you have dispensation from the owner to eat before you come back. And I'm on an official break. Go ahead. Try it."

He lifted half of the hefty sandwich and took a bite. The bacon was perfectly crisped, the tomato sweet and bursting with juice that mixed with the creamy, eggy goodness of the mayo and an extra flavor he couldn't identify to fill his mouth with heaven.

"Oh, lord, I wasn't lying. This is delicious."

Pure pleasure lifted the corners of her mouth. "Thank you. It's my signature sandwich."

"There's a really unique flavor mixed in there."

"A dash of chipotle seasoning and a pinch of cinnamon. It's subtle. Sweet and savory."

"It's genius."

She grinned. "A little better than peanut butter and jelly."

He took another bite and then held the plate with the other half sandwich out. "You try it."

The shock on her face was comical, as if he'd offered to let her sneak food from the king's plate. "I'm not eating your sandwich."

"Why? Boy cooties?"

"What? No! Because it's your lunch."

"I want you to share it with me. The chef here is pretty good; you have to try it."

"Damien, I—"

"Just take a bite, Kelly."

She sighed. "Why, to prove I didn't poison you?"

"What? Did you?"

She leaned toward the sandwich, her gaze filled with confused humor. "You're weird. I made it; I know what it tastes like."

"Not standing on a sunny deck with water lilies in front of you and a fellow crime fighter beside you, you don't."

"Got me there, dude."

She opened her mouth and sank her teeth into her own creation. With a gentle little slurp, she sucked all the component ingredients safely into her mouth and caught a drip of tomato juice at the corner of her lips with her forefinger and a giggle.

"I guess it's—" She started to talk over her full mouth and then stopped herself and closed her eyes, chewed, and swallowed. "Wow, that's good."

He couldn't help but laugh. "I knew you were hungry, too."

She gave a resigned little whimper. "Starving."

"Eat it." He handed her the half sandwich. "You can't cook on an empty stomach."

"But I don't want—"

"Yeah. You do. And, like I said, I know the chef. If need be and I begged, she'd make another one."

"It's always good to have friends in low places."

"I see what you did there."

She smiled, took another bite, and sighed. "Thank you. *Do* you want another? I can go make one now."

"Nope. Sit."

"I—"

He recognized the personality type all too well. Firefighters were notoriously work-driven, always had to be doing something, and one of the first things a smart firefighter learned was how to grab downtime.

"Nobody in the restaurant will starve or get angry if we add five minutes to our break. You, on the other hand, will die much younger than necessary if you work on constant high alert. So sit. Breathe. Enjoy the food you made."

If he hadn't known better, he'd have sworn she looked puzzled. Slowly, she sat and looked around as if she expected guards to come and haul her back to the chain gang.

"Deep breath," he continued.

She actually took one. Then she looked down at the half-eaten sandwich. "I really don't mind helping Grace, but honestly, you don't have to stay. I'm pretty sure you didn't come here to work in a restaurant."

"Hey. I said I'd help and I meant it. You're the one who should slow it down—for your own sake. You don't relax much, do you?"

A furrow formed between her brows. "Of course I do. I went riding this morning for five hours."

"And you talked almost nonstop about plans and history and horses and then the mystery of the backpack. You were like a tense little squirrel ready to spring off after any nut that fell in your path."

"Oh really."

He shook his head at the indignity rising in her eyes.

"Don't be offended. None of that is bad. I wish I had some of your love of life. I just remember how hard it was for me to learn to take any moments of downtime I could find."

She said nothing, but the irritation drained from her face before it had time to take hold. She slumped a little on the bench while she took another bite of the sandwich. Chewing thoughtfully, she stared out over the lily pads, then swallowed and sighed.

"I get antsy if I sit too long. I feel like I'm missing things if I'm alone too much. My guess is you're the opposite."

"I like working on my own," he admitted. "But firefighters have to be team players, same as cops, same as soldiers. Lives depend on it. So, you learn the skills. If I can learn extroversion, you can learn introversion, chef."

"I feel a little like I'm in therapy here."

"No, just stuck with a stranger passing through. Sometimes strangers notice things regular folks don't."

She polished off the last of her half of the sandwich and dusted her palms together.

"I think you're just strange," she garbled through her

mouthful. "Will we see you at dinner tonight?"

His stomach jumped uneasily. So much for a quiet night. He'd managed all right with a smaller contingent of Crocketts the night before. There'd be twice as many people tonight, including Skylar and her whole family. He gritted his teeth and nodded.

"I promised I'd come."

"All right then. It's settled." She stood.

"One more minute."

He caught her hand and tugged her gently back down. The perfect fit of her hand in his jolted him. The touch was presumptuous and he let her go though he didn't want to. He broke the large brownie on his plate in half and handed her one. She shook her head.

"You really are trying to get us fired the first day."

He took great pleasure in watching her relax once more and take a bite. He did the same and allowed a happy groan as the warm, gooey treat spread chocolate ecstasy through his mouth.

They watched the pond in silence until movement flashed in front of them and a pair of shimmering turquoise dragonflies flew past, one atop the other. Without warning, Kelly burst into laughter.

"I'm telling my mother on you. On our first date, you took me to see dragonfly porn. Shocking!"

He choked on his chocolate and stared at her. "I don't want to hear another word about who's weird around here," he said.

She placed the tiniest of kisses on his cheek, sighed, and stood.

"Okay, Holmes. Time to quit screwing around."

"Talk to the dragonflies."

She almost seemed to dance back up the hill beside

him, as if the time sitting still had filled her with too much energy to handle. He shook his head, both delighted and tired already. Mostly, however, the touch of that meaningless kiss on his cheek lingered, and he decided mindlessly chopping vegetables would be a good thing to do to numb his brain. Although it would be more effective if Kelly Crockett wasn't next to him.

Chapter Seven

"OKAY. WHERE'S MY knife?" Kelly narrowed her eyes at Damien, who didn't look at her but kept stirring the pot of beef stew he'd made, following Grace's recipe.

"Last I saw, it was next to the stove. You carried it there."

"I did not. I never carry my knives around."

He shrugged. "You keep saying that and yet it's the second time you've mislaid the thing."

She swore his shoulders gave the slightest shake, but she couldn't tell definitively from the back that he was laughing again. Cooking with Damien Finney was proving to be an experience unlike any other. There'd been a lot of laughter, actually, along with quite a lot of goofing around. And yet, the work area remained spotless, the scents were delectable, and the man hadn't lied. He knew his way just fine around a recipe. It couldn't have been a more different atmosphere from Landon O'Keefe's serious, properly run, three-star kitchen. Here, the recipes weren't anywhere near as exacting, and there, the coworkers not nearly as distracting.

"Oh, come on," she said, exasperated at her forgetfulness. The man creating the stew had her discombobulated.

"Did you drop it?" he asked, calm and helpful.

"Of course not." But after checking every surface again for the missing utensil, she squatted to look around the floor. Beneath a rollcart next to her counter, she caught the glimpse of ebony and silver. "What the heck? This is ridiculous."

She'd left it in a compost pail half an hour before.

"Just wash it and finish the onions for the meatloaf. No big deal." Grace shook her head, her own eyes narrowed as she swung her gaze suspiciously from Kelly to Damien and back. Exactly what she suspected, Kelly didn't know, and she didn't have time to ask. "It's close to four and prep for the evening is almost finished. I think we've done it."

Kelly retrieved the big-handled chopping knife and took it to the sink. Despite her lapses, they had gotten a lot done. Grace had an easy menu to prep, and she'd managed to get her temporary cook, Liam, to take off from his other job and bail her out for the night. Crisis averted for one day.

She turned held out the knife and lifted the faucet handle. A steady blast from the hand-held sprayer caught her full in the face. Her screech of surprise echoed through the kitchen. When she'd managed to get the water turned off, she turned around, her face dripping and her light blue T-shirt darkened across her stomach and breasts with a giant water stain.

This time there was no mistaking Damien's ear-to-ear grin, despite the fact that he tried to hide it and laughter behind a judiciously cupped hand.

"Wet T-shirt contest is in the bar," he said.

"You." She pointed and growled at him.

"What?" He dropped his hand, but the grin didn't disappear.

"You had me fooled all day with that quiet, suffering-man act. You who once wrapped a VA official's car in cling wrap."

"Hey, I had plenty of help. And there's no cling wrap here."

"You who tried to bring a cow into the lobby of the VA?"

"That is just a rumor."

"It is not. Mia has told the story a hundred times — one of your buddies got kicked and foiled the plan." He only continued grinning. She turned to study the sink sprayer and found the malfunction — a short, thin piece of black electrical tape holding down the sprayer handle. "What are you, nine?"

"And then some."

"You hid the knife, too. Twice."

"Did I?"

"Hey, you two. You're *both* like children." Grace's voice acted like a ruler rapping their knuckles. "There's been nothing but banter and silliness all afternoon. I think I'm done with you for the day."

"I'm sorry, Grace; we shouldn't be treating this like a joke just because you're my sister." Contrite, Kelly met Grace's eyes only to find her wearing a grin to match Damien's.

"I'm joking, Kel. I haven't enjoyed my kitchen so much since I opened it. And look at the prep work. You two worked a miracle. Even if you are both infantile and immature."

"At least one of us is." Kelly breathed a sigh of relief and leveled a stare at Damien.

"Look, Liam will be here in half an hour and I can get him going," Grace said. "Damien, you finished that stew and there's nothing more to start now. You two go on home."

"Order up!" Greta called and placed her slip on the carousel near the counter.

"How about I stay and help you until Liam gets here? Damien can take my car. I'll ride home with you."

"You'd trust me with your car?" he asked.

"Anything to avoid riding with you. You're mean." She stared, trying to match her voice to her words. In truth, she wanted to start a water fight with him and keep him smiling. She much preferred jokester Finney to reserved Finney.

At that, he laughed out loud. "I'm not mean. I'm hilarious."

"Narcissistic. Go home without me."

He checked his stewpot one more time and then moved to her and placed a hand on each of her shoulders. "Sorry," he said. "I don't know why you brought out the worst in me. I'll make it up later. Are you sure you don't want to go home with me?"

With a forgiving sigh, she nodded and smiled. "Orders are coming in. You go ahead and I'll see you at the ranch."

He almost looked relieved, and her heart went out to him. He'd made the very most of a long, weird, crazy day.

"Okay. But just so you know. You were pretty funny, looking all over for that knife."

***

As Damien navigated the small county roads back to Paradise, he couldn't remember a time when exhaustion had been so weirdly blended with a cheerful high. On one hand, he wanted nothing more than to escape unseen to his room and flop into sleep. Unfortunately, he had the Crockett family dinner gauntlet to run because he'd promised to be at the table. Like "one of the family." On the other hand, he'd come as close to letting his walls down as he had in two years. Not since he'd been free to cut loose with his fellow vets in Gabe's program had he even thought about little pranks and schoolboy laughter, much less participated in both.

And Kelly had been the perfect cohort, laughing at herself and striking back. He'd liked the dynamic between them in the kitchen—all fun, no serious talk of troubles or questions about the future, his attraction buried. He wasn't sure that version of himself was completely honest; it was like a costume he could put on for safety. But it was familiar and friendly—the way it had been during his time with Gabe and the guys.

He frowned to himself at that unexpected thought. That was wrong. He hadn't been playacting back then. The program had been serious with a lot of talk about serious things. Of course, he'd been honest. They'd simply known how to have fun, too.

Kelly had let him remember how to find it tonight. Her laugh, so throaty and full it hung in the air like musical chords, had been addictive, and the endless, genuine optimism she exuded had temporarily overpowered the pessimism and depression that had brought him to Paradise. He was grateful.

And more tired than he'd been since the day he'd passed the fitness pack-out test during smokejumper training. His hundred-and-ten pound pack, carried three miles in less than ninety minutes, hadn't exhausted him any more than keeping up with Kelly for a day. A grin slipped its way onto his lips. He had to leave. As much as he'd enjoyed one day, he'd never survive her full time.

The high lasted until he pulled into the ranch's driveway and caught sight of the neat, perfectly laid out ranch yard beyond the house, with its corrals, office, sheds, and barns. The sight of the old horse barn, with its rough cedar siding and navy-blue trim, flipped the switch on his good mood. He remembered the text from the owners of the stable he'd planned to bring Pan to early the following week. That Kelly might be right and the sudden cancellation was a matter of prejudice against mustangs infuriated him. Sure, he knew of the decades-old fight between ranchers and mustang proponents over grazing land, but since everyone on Paradise was so pro wild horse, he'd considered the problem solved.

His mood sank as he pondered what steps to take next. Most good facilities had waiting lists for boarding. He could leave Pan right here at Paradise, but in every fiber of his being he knew he needed to be with her for the next month. He'd heard the Native people believed in spirit animals. Part of him believed that was what Pan was to him. She was the reason he'd come here before going anywhere else, and even before telling his mother he was coming back.

After parking his car in the spot Gabe had designated for him, Damien checked his watch. Four-twenty. Dinner was at six. With luck, he could snatch a shower and take ten minutes to call his mother. She deserved a few days' heads-up. Cowardice over admitting his failings was an unacceptable excuse for waiting any longer. Besides, if he didn't call Sarah Finney soon, she'd call him, as she did anytime more than two weeks passed without talking. It had already been that long. She would apologize for bothering him, make sure he was all right, and tell him news of his small family—an aunt and uncle and three cousins. Then, in the quiet way she'd had since Damien's father had died, she'd promised to keep him in her prayers and ask him to stay safe.

So much for that. Well, he was safe enough, he guessed.

Still ill at ease letting himself into the big house unescorted, he opened the unlocked front door as quietly as he could and closed it behind him, relieved at the soundlessness of well-oiled hinges. As his mother had drummed into his head, he toed off his boots and picked them up before heading for the stairs in his stocking feet.

"You know we don't stand on any ceremony here, right?"

His breath caught at Grandma Sadie's voice, and he looked to his right, into the sunny sitting room his mother would have called a parlor. There sat the beautiful Crockett matriarch, ensconced in a worn rocking chair beside the front picture window, knitting needles in hand, a rich maroon and blue flow of knitted softness cascading over her lap and down her legs. Damn, if she truly was ninety-six, he'd eat his boots. She would always be mistaken for twenty years younger.

"And what ceremony would that be?"

"Taking your shoes off. Unless they're full of wet, smelly stuff, you can walk through the house. It's pretty but it's not a palace. Folks live here."

"Tell that to my mama." He smiled. "She had a basket of slippers at the door for any and all. Hard soles were for hard surfaces outdoors."

Grandma Sadie shrugged and nodded. "That's all right then if it's what you like. Me, I always wanted to be ready to run outdoors if need be. As much as I grew up a country tomboy, I was never fond of going barefoot. A rattlesnake bite when I was nine did it, I guess."

"You got bitten by a rattler?"

"Hurt like Beelzebub himself had hacked my foot off, but I got treated in plenty of time. I've had respect for the little demons ever since."

"The things we don't know about people."

She made a dismissive scowl. "A rattler bite doesn't make me special. This flooring isn't special either. For your future consideration, if you care. How was your ride?"

He stopped and allowed a thoughtful breath. The ride had happened a lifetime ago. "Way more interesting than I ever could have imagined."

She finally looked up from her work and gave an amused smile. Patting the arm of a green and pink floral armchair next to her, she nodded again. "You can't give me a line like that and not come tell me the story."

He laughed and shook his head, more relieved than he wanted to admit for the temporary excuse not to call his mother.

"All right. I'll tell you the story of a ride to Ancestor Canyon, a warm campfire, a mysterious hidden backpack, and a pregnant woman."

"My word, sounds like we could fill the rest of the afternoon."

He lowered himself into the chair, which looked antique and too fancy to be comfortable, only to find it cradled him as if custom-made for his shape.

"I think I could sit here the rest of the afternoon. My

legs definitely aren't in cowboy shape."

"Regale me," she said and picked up the knitting again.

Grandma didn't have to look up once to let him know she listened to every word. She made exactly the right comments and asked for exactly the right amount of extra detail. But when he told her about the medicine bag, she put down her handwork and took him in with her wise, corner-crinkled eyes.

"That's important," she said.

"Kelly thought so, too. We worry a little that something might have happened to the owner because it seems odd that he or she left it behind. So, we kept it and left a note telling the person how to find us. We didn't see any signs of that person, but we didn't detect an accident either."

Grandma Sadie chewed thoughtfully on her lower lip and then nodded as if to herself.

"You could talk to John Red Wolf. He might have an idea of what's going on."

Damien's heart tripped. He was happy to let the bag's owner come to them, but he considered his Sam Spade moment over. He didn't have any desire to go digging up information.

"Who is John Red Wolf?" he asked reluctantly.

"A Shoshone elder—much younger I am, only in his late seventies, but he's very much respected."

"A medicine man?" Damien lost his reluctance to curiosity.

"No, no. Just a man who's lived a lot of life. I think, a lot of people think, he has gifts of sight and understanding. As for John himself, he's unassuming and kind. He's still asked often for advice, by both his people and non-natives alike. He lives east of our ranch border just outside the Wind River Reservation on about two hundred acres with his horses."

"He raises horses?" Damien's apprehension dissipated at hearing that information.

"I don't know exactly what he's doing these days. Over his life, he's raised almost everything at his place — cattle, sheep, chickens and, yes, always horses. He's an interesting man, embracing the good of two worlds. He used to have a beautiful tipi in his backyard and would live there for a lot of the summer. He's kept well-versed in the traditional ways of his people. To this day he makes his own moccasins, even though he buys his boots in Jackson at a place called Teton Boot Factory, where they custom make them."

Damien had to laugh at the twinkle in Sadie's eyes. She clearly thought highly of this elder statesman.

"You seem to know him well."

"I've known him all my life. He lived on the reservation until middle school and then came to our white school with us because it was closer to his home and he wanted to play baseball. I played at his house with his sister a few times and liked his family. His wife passed away a few years ago and his children have mostly moved away, although one son lives in Jackson. He likes his solitude, but he also likes a good game of poker. You should ask Gracie's Ty. I think he's met John Red Wolf a few times across a table."

"So, do you think your John Red Wolf might know who was camping in the canyon and drawing pictures?"

"I really don't know, of course, but if anyone has heard anything, it would be John."

"I'm pretty sure Kelly would be interested in finding

out more."

Despite everything, he couldn't fight his own growing fascination with Grandma's story of the man.

"Why were you led to this mystery? Why did John Red Wolf pop into my mind when you told me about it?" She gave a nearly imperceptible shrug over her knitting. "I don't know, but I believe there are always reasons. Kelly might benefit in many ways from talking with John Red Wolf. But I believe you might benefit even more."

A shiver descended with uncomfortable slowness through his body and landed in his stomach.

"I believe another thing," she added, glancing up and fixing him with kind, unwavering eyes. "And since I'm a very old woman, I'm giving my opinion without permission or apology. You should take Cole up on his offer of a job. This is a good place for you at the moment. The right place."

Her "opinion" landed on his heart like a boulder. He'd finally found time to tell Gabe what had happened and, true to his nature, his former mentor had been concerned but otherwise so understanding that he had, though Damien knew better, only fed his guilt. Still, nobody else knew the one other reason he had to go to Sheridan—that he was required to meet with a therapist Stone had called, who specialized in firefighters' PTSD. He bucked at that idea as hard as he was resisting calling his mother. The idea of going back to therapy angered him. As much as he acknowledged everything he'd learned from Gabe, all the talking and analysis had proven useless at the door of that cargo plane. Digging deeper wouldn't help; his war was over, and the demons of Afghanistan had been exorcised. What remained, whatever it was, was his problem. Yet here sat Grandma Sadie, not even his own grandmother, filled with wisdom and something that felt an awful lot like judgment-free grandmotherly love, and he couldn't help but tell her the truth.

"I have to go to Sheridan. Whether I want to or not."

"Your mother needs you."

"I tell people she does, but that's not why. My captain in Montana is requiring me to contact a counselor there. If I don't, I could lose the chance to return and rejoin the company."

Grandma Sadie didn't blink an eye. She also didn't ask why he needed the counselor. "You could see someone here."

"This is a person who specializes in working with firefighters. Stone, my captain, knows Gabe, likes him, but he believes I need to work with someone who doesn't already know me."

"Ahhh." Grandma Sadie murmured in understanding and sat quietly. "So something did happen in Montana."

He leaned forward, resting his elbows on his thighs, and looked at the floor.

"Something did."

"You've told Gabe."

"Yes."

"All right then."

"But…" He straightened and rubbed his palms along his thighs, lightening his voice. "I'll be here a couple of extra couple of days, assuming it's all right that I stay. The place I had set up for Pan for the month fell through. I want to see if I can find somewhere else."

"There's a reason for everything."

"Well, I wish sometimes the reason was clearer."

"Don't we all, darling boy? How about you settle for

telling me the end of today's story? Someone is pregnant, did you say?"

He laughed and pushed the secret he hadn't fully disclosed to the back of his mind, and continued with the story of Grace's plight and her chef's morning sickness. He ended with a recounting of acting as sous chef for Kelly.

"She's amazing," he said. "Every girl in this family seems to be amazing."

"Good genes." Grandma gave him a saucy wink. "And I'm glad. Kelly needs a way to reconnect with her sisters," Grandma Sadie said. "She's searching, too, but she seems to have the horses and now cooking in common with you. I see something in that unlikely mix."

Damien grinned. "You're a wonder, Grandma. Thank you for your ear."

"No. Thank you for the news. Old women love stories."

"You'll never be old."

"A happy thought. Only the good die young."

"I'll definitely talk to Kelly about John Red Wolf."

At the sound of footsteps, they both turned.

"John Red Wolf? What about him? I love John!"

The new voice belonged to one of the Crockett sisters he hadn't yet seen, and Damien stood with a huge smile as Joely Crockett Morrissey entered the room, a permanent limp from a severe automobile accident now much less pronounced than it had been two years earlier. The special bond he had with Joely went back to the day Apollo had been born, when she, just starting her veterinary training, had been the one to help the distressed foal into the world. The memory still brought swift and happy emotions. Now she was a newly minted, full-fledged Doctor of Veterinary Medicine.

"Joely!"

"Oh, Damien, it's so good to see you at last. I'm sorry I wasn't here when you arrived yesterday."

She wrapped her arms around his waist and he folded her into his hug.

"Nonsense. I didn't require a welcome party. It's good to see you, too."

They parted and Joely bent to hug her grandmother as well. "Whatcha workin' on, Gran?"

"An afghan for Grace. Have to be ready for that wedding."

"We're so lucky to have you to make us special things! Now, what's this about Red Wolf?"

"Damien and Kelly found a lost item today—a medicine bag. I thought maybe John could help identify it."

"If anyone can, John can." Joely reiterated her grandmother's earlier words. "I caught his name being mentioned because, weirdly enough, I'm going out to see him tomorrow. I can talk to him if you like, see if he wants to meet with you."

Maybe there was something to Grandma Sadie's insight that everything happened with a purpose.

"Sure," he said. "It's possible by then someone will have come forward to claim the bag anyway."

"Happy to do it. I guess John has a mare that's limping, so I'm heading out first thing."

"Talk to Kelly. She's got the medicine bag."

"I'll do that. And, I just talked to Mia. Dinner is still on for six. I talked to Gracie, too, and heard about the fiasco at the restaurant. Sounds like you and Kel are heroes."

"Kelly maybe."

"She is a kitchen genius," Joely said. "I'm kind of glad she's working with Grace again. Even for a little while."

"My thoughts exactly, sweetheart," Grandma Sadie replied.

Joely gave her grandmother's back a soft, circular rub. "'Kay you two, I'm going to go stick my nose in Little Sadie's business for a few minutes. Ty's bringing Rory and Lucky in a little while." She rose on tiptoes to became the second sister who'd kissed his cheek. It didn't buzz through him the way Kelly's had, but it was nice just the same. "I'm really glad you're back with family, Damien."

He shook his head. The Crocketts definitely did sweep in and gather up everyone around them.

"Thank you. I think I'll shower off the day's dust before dinner so I won't offend everyone at the table."

"Can't blame you. Sounds like you managed to keep awfully busy your first day back."

If that wasn't an understatement, he'd never heard one. He offered a smile but said nothing more.

Chapter Eight

IT HAD BEEN ages since Kelly had joined her family for a huge, raucous meal. The sheer volume of noise from around the huge oak table her grandfather Sebastian had built was enough to drain the fatigue from her muscles and mind. Plentiful chatter and frequent laughter always energized her. She might have experience as a chef and cook, but her own restaurant was an oiled machine after six years. The amount of work it had taken to organize the kitchen at Peas Porridge had been off the scale. Grace was a fabulous idea person and a good manager—but she'd left the kitchen setup to each of her three failed chefs, and nothing was efficient.

It was slightly more so now, but there was work that could still be done.

As much as she had no desire to become long-term help in another small-time restaurant, it had been fun to work with Grace again. And Damien had been an astonishing bonus—stupid kitchen pranks aside. Nonetheless, having two restaurants in dire straits bordered on exhausting.

She looked across the table to where he sat, back to being the silent presence again. She still found him handsome enough to make her pulse flutter, but his mercurial mood was hard to get a handle on. She never knew which of her selves to be around him.

"So, no luck finding another place to bring the horse?"

Cole switched their end of the table's attention to Damien, whose brows furrowed at the question.

"I, uh, well I called two other places and they were full. I got two more names."

"This is Wyoming." Ty Garraway was the strong, wiry man who'd won sweet Grace's heart, and if for no other reason than that, Kelly knew he had to be one of the really good guys. He rested a fork next to the half of a steak left on his plate. "It shouldn't be that hard to find a place for one little horse."

"Right?" Damien nodded.

"I understand you have obligations back in Sheridan," Cole said. "If you have to leave, you know the horses can stay here until you find a place. We can bring 'em up later."

"Bring 'them'? You're not taking Apollo, are you?" Skylar piped up from four people away. "Doesn't matter. You can't have him."

For an instant, the entire table of seventeen people went silent. Then, as if they collectively remembered it was Skylar speaking, everyone laughed as one.

"Way to go, dumb butt," Skylar's older brother Marcus said. "You can't tell the horse's owner what he can't do."

Skylar didn't waver. "I know who Apollo belongs to, but he loves me. He's so smart and he's learning so much.

I'm not done with him yet."

"There are trainers in Sheridan," Mia said gently.

"Oh really? From what everyone is saying, there aren't even barns in Sheridan." Skylar's flip, and adamant, retort marked the first moment of petulance Kelly had seen in ages. The girl was always cheeky but never disrespectful.

"Skylar!" her mother, Melanie, admonished, and then lowered her voice. "That was uncalled for."

"Sorry," the teen murmured, the stubborn set of her features not remotely matching the half-apology. She studied her plate and then stuffed a forkful of baked beans defiantly into her mouth.

"Hold on, hold on." Damien's voice got Skylar to look up. "She's spent a lot more time with the colt than I have."

Sky's face filled with hope. "I've been working with him almost every day."

"You cannot keep a horse that belongs to someone else," Melanie said and then turned her stern eyes on Damien. "And don't you think of giving her a horse. She earns things around here just as everyone does."

Damien smiled. "I'm not giving her anything except the job of continuing to work with him. Besides, I was never going to move him anyway. I don't have time to work with him, nor do I have the expertise."

Skylar scraped her chair back so quickly it rocked for a moment on two legs. She sprang up like a little model rocket and launched herself at Damien, four chairs down from her, to throw her arms around him from behind.

"Thank you!" She squeezed her eyes shut. Damien's face lost every ounce of gravity and he grinned while he patted the arms forming a human scarf around his neck. "Even if you should have said all that before I got in trouble with my mom."

"Hey, lesson learned, my friend. Don't get in trouble with your mom any time," he said.

"Dumb butt," added Marcus.

"Butt face." Skylar made a face at her brother.

"That's quite enough," Melanie warned.

The exchanges brought more laughter.

"This is Apollo's only home, why would I make him leave?" Damien pried the girl's arms free. "Go sit down now. You're embarrassing me."

Sky did a mini happy dance behind his chair before heading back to hers. "You don't get embarrassed, but nice try. You promised you're going to come and see what he can do, right?"

"Yeah, of course, but it'd better be impressive after all this."

"Oh, it is."

Kelly could clearly see the friendship the two had forged over the previous summer. She couldn't help but believe it was a good thing for both of them—a mentor for Sky and a mentee for Damien, yet they were so easy with each other their relationship was almost equal, as if he were just a much older brother. The connection was important; she knew it in her depths. She just didn't know why she also believed it went beyond the training of a little colt.

Had Skylar gotten her way, she'd have dragged Damien to see Apollo the instant everyone pushed away from their plates, but Melanie put the brakes on that by putting Skylar and Marcus in charge of their younger brother, nine-year-old Aidan, along with Lucky and Rory, in charge of clearing dishes and tidying the kitchen. Kelly liked Melanie—she was a mother who brooked no nonsense but loved her kids more fiercely than a bear sow, moose cow, and wolf mama put together.

"Right after we're done then." Skylar gathered up a load of plates with a face that said she might as well have been asked to clean her room with tweezers. "It won't be too late, right?"

"Sure." Damien nodded, and Kelly's heart went out to him. He looked like he could fall asleep on his feet.

"Horses," Melanie muttered, following the adults out of the dining room. "Everything is horses with that one."

"I remember from first-hand experience." Damien laughed and waggled his brows at Kelly, losing a little of the exhausted dullness in his eyes. "Does she know yet if she wants to be a horse whisperer like Mia or a veterinarian like Joely?"

"Or an artist, like Harper," Kelly added. "She's awfully good."

"I always got a kick out of the ways Sky found to rebel without turning into a delinquent. The kid has learned how to pick her battles," Damien said.

Her mother snorted. "She has the soul of a cunning old jackal, that one. She might rule the world someday with that combo of sweetness and sass."

"I totally believe that." Damien grinned.

It took forty-five minutes for the kids to finish and earn release from KP duty. Skylar took no time assembling a group to see Apollo, and she led the way down Paradise's long curving driveway to the ranch yard with the air of a parade grand marshal. They made a plenty decent parade at that, even though most of the men opted to stay away from the ranch where they'd worked all day to watch a baseball game. Kelly joined Joely, Grace,

Harper, Damien, Lucky, Skylar, and two dogs-- Sky's Asta and Joely's enormous Irish Wolfhound, Rowen. Mia promised to bring Little Sadie after she'd changed the baby's diaper. The ratio of girls to guys left poor Damien outnumbered, but he didn't appear distressed. She surreptitiously watched him as they reached the main yard and he swiveled his head slowly side to side, taking in all the details of Paradise's working heart—from the original two-room cabin that now served as an office, to the linked series of cattle pens, the two twenty-acre pastures for the horses, the horse barn, and the machine sheds. Kelly's father Sam and her grandfather Sebastian had done their planning well. It was not just a functional ranch; it was an attractive and efficient working organism.

"You've seen Apollo this trip, right?" Sky asked.

"I gave him a treat in the pasture this morning," Damien said. "He's almost as big as his mom. And just as pretty. Handsome," he amended when Skylar wrinkled her nose.

"It's not uncommon for a grulla to throw a grulla—like buckskins and palominos, the genetics are complicated. But, still, you were lucky to get two."

They reached the gate of the geldings' pasture, and Sky put two fingers to her lips, letting out an impressive whistle.

"Dang." Damien looked at her. "How did I not know you could do that? I've never been able to master it."

"Lucky taught me."

They all looked to the angelic, strawberry-blonde seven-year-old who surveyed the world like Merlin's owl Archimedes.

"I'm good at whistling and spitting." She shrugged.

She was good at everything, the little prodigy. Ty

claimed to have no idea where his daughter's genius-level brain had come from, though Kelly knew he was far more brilliant than he ever gave himself credit for.

"Both useful skills," Kelly said. She bumped Damien with an elbow and pointed as an avalanche of sound bore down on them from behind a clump of trees. All the boys, with flashy, fourteen-month-old Apollo in the middle of the pack, thundered into view, and a grin erupted on Damien's face.

"I always feel like a dad when I see him," he said. "One of those obnoxious ones who takes credit for everything the kid does. As if I had anything to do with him."

"You helped bring him into the world," Kelly said. "I heard about how Pan needed a little help with the birth."

"Joely did that." He nodded at their resident veterinarian. "She literally pulled him out. I bawled like a lost pup."

"Way more than that. Maybe there were some tears, from all of us, but you added much-needed muscle power." Joely said.

"Deep down, you're nothing but an old softie, aren't you?" Kelly poked Damien with her elbow again.

"You tell a soul outside this ranch and I'll never eat your club sandwiches again."

She laughed as Apollo snorted his way to a stop ten feet from the fence. Even though he wasn't yet two, the little mustang was developing his first muscles and was impressive as a gleaming racehorse.

"Have you considered leaving him a colt, not gelding him?" Kelly asked. "If he could throw his color, you'd make a small fortune on stud fees."

"We're talking about it," Joely said. "We'll see how he

looks and goes when he's fully two. And see whether he keeps his sweet personality. It'll be up to Damien, of course."

"I will bow to the experts," Damien said. "Although no man worth his salt is going to readily ask you to, um, change him."

Harper shook her head and Kelly nodded, laughing. "Not a full-fledged cowboy yet. Hasn't had to deal with a horse once he discovers he's a boy who likes girls."

"I'm a boy. I like girls. Is it that much different?" He lifted his brows in an innocent question aimed directly at Kelly.

"Well, now, I guess I really don't know, Mr. Finney," she drawled back. "That would require more knowledge than I currently have."

"I'll have to remember that." He turned to watch the horses, the corners of his mouth twitching.

Apollo showed off his baby machismo with exaggerated blowing and snorting. His pasture mates jostled for attention from their unexpected audience but left Apollo to find Skylar and snuffle her hair, shoulder, and hands. Suddenly, with a genuine impish twinkle in a naughty eye, he grabbed the baseball cap off her head and shook it like a rag doll.

"You little poop!" Sky climbed the fence and reached for the hat. Apollo lifted his head toward the sky and snorted again. "Gimme that."

"I thought you said you've been training him." Damien laughed.

"Yeah, and he knows I'm here to show him off so he's being a turkey." She went over the fence, pried the cap from the colt's mouth, and slipped on the halter she carried. "Gotcha now, you little butt head."

"Aw, he's adorable," Kelly said. "He obviously likes people."

"He loves people. He's like a big dog," Sky said. "And as long as he stays respectful—all hat stealing aside—that's good. Maybe he can be a well-mannered stallion someday."

"Hear that, boy? Take heed." Damien climbed the gate beside Sky and ruffled the colt's forelock. The young horse didn't object.

"All right," Kelly said. "Show us what he's got."

For Sam Crockett's six girls, Paradise had never been about the cattle that were the ranch's lifeblood; it had always been about the horses. Even in the modern age of using four-wheelers to guide cattle from areas that would take days to reach on horseback, there were always places a motorized vehicle couldn't navigate. And for cutting, chasing down a wayward cow, or pure ease of exploration, nothing was more valuable than a really good horse.

Kelly had grown up like Sky, breaking the colts and fillies and knowing exactly what they needed to learn to be working cow horses. Memories of her favorite equine partners over the years filled her thoughts and, for the second time that day, made her wonder why she'd gone so many years without horses in her life. Sky's confidence and obvious bond with the colt turned Kelly's longing into a pang of regret.

Then there was Damien, watching his horse work as proudly—and seriously—as Penny Chenery must have watched over Secretariat's training. For a man who two years earlier had been the first one to pooh-pooh the idea of adopting a mustang, he had turned into a horse-lover's horse lover. The longer Kelly watched him, the more his focused features intrigued her. She didn't know how, but she could see he was a man who felt and loved with every bit of his heart and soul but kept those deep emotions hidden until he forgot people were watching. More than ever, she wanted to know his whole story. There seemed to be a hurt he was still hiding.

Apollo quickly figured out he was supposed to be performing his best tricks. He did nothing a non-horseperson would find extraordinary, but for a baby just a year-and-a-half-old, he was advancing remarkably well. He stood stock-still while Sky had him raise each hoof for inspection with just a touch on his leg. She rubbed him over every possible ticklish spot with rags and a long lunge whip, and the young horse never flinched or fussed. She set blankets on him and then flapped them around as she took them off. Apollo ho-hummed like he was hitched to a line of dead-broke dude horses waiting for something to do.

"Super impressive ground manners," Kelly said.

Sky accepted the compliment as her own and grinned as she led her charge toward a large round pen in the ranch yard. Once inside the enclosure, Apollo showed how he could be led at a walk and a trot and stay in perfect time with Sky. Then she sent him cantering off in a circle around her and he obeyed every voice command to change gaits, paying no attention when Asta joined him in the circle and followed him as if trying to convince everyone she was doing the driving.

"Isn't he a good boy?" Sky asked once she'd called Apollo and Asta to her side. The horse shook his haltered head as if to agree that indeed, he was.

"He was just a big ol' baby when I left last spring," Damien said. "He was friendly, but now he's disciplined."

"He's still a big old baby," Sky said and scratched his cheek. "And these are just simple things. He still has a baby brain."

"What's next, then?"

"Yeah, what's next?"

Kelly turned to where Gabe had settled against the fence, appreciative eyes on Apollo. Next to him, Mia held Sadie and perched her on the top railing. The baby human squealed in excitement, and Apollo pricked his ears.

"I'd like to take him on a trail ride—lead him behind another horse and get him familiar with the outside world," Sky said. "We could go through some water and some brush. Super simple stuff."

A hint of wistfulness showed in the way Damien's gaze settled on his horse. "Sounds good."

"Are you sure you really want to leave?" Gabe asked quietly, raising his brows for gentle emphasis.

Kelly watched the two men, Damien shuffling in place until he rested one booted foot on the bottom rail eighteen inches off the ground, and Gabe, not three feet away, staring into the pen as if he wasn't expecting an answer.

"I'm not sure at all," Damien said, "but the dice are pretty much cast."

Gabe nodded, but behind his smile, mild concern turned his handsome eyes smoky.

"How'd you get so good at this?" Damien quickly changed the subject and lifted his eyes to Sky's.

"Mia," she replied. "She's the real horse whisperer."

"Don't discount for a second your own natural ability with horses," Mia called.

The only member of their party who had been silent chose that moment to let loose with a bark that resounded like Paul Bunyan's voice in a canyon. Rowan, who on all fours stood higher than Sky's waist and on two legs could tower over six-foot-two Cole, jumped up beside Damien, his front paws scrabbling against the top fence rail. A large, rodent-like animal scurried across the far end of the pen and Kelly stared in surprise.

"That's a marmot!" Mia said. "You don't see one of those this far from the high rocks very often."

Rowan woofed again, adding a whine because she couldn't get through the rails to reach the infiltrator. She licked pleadingly at the cheek of the closest person to her...Damien.

"Gah!" He pushed back at the wolfhound, throwing her off despite her size, and took three rushed steps backward. "Get away, stupid dog. I didn't do anything to you."

"Sorry, sorry!" Joely pulled the dog away in seconds. "I wasn't paying close enough attention. She thought she could convince you to let her in the pen and her manners were terrible. I'll watch her more closely, Damien. I really am sorry."

"It's not a problem." Damien swallowed, allowed a wan smile, and gave the dog a cursory pat. "She surprised me is all. I'm not usually a dog's best friend."

Joely scratched the huge beast behind the ears and kissed the top of her long-haired head. "Come on, you horrid thing. I swear you need a new round of obedience classes. And you definitely don't need to go after marmots. He'd probably bite your nose off."

She held Rowan's collar and turned the dog away from the round pen while the others watched the groundhog-looking creature waddle off into tall grass and a stand of trees.

"Cool!" Skylar said. "Wonder why he was down here?"

"They wander sometimes," Mia said. "I'm sure that's all it is. Although..." She turned to Damien. "I heard there were reports of new wildfires in southern Idaho. Have you seen anything about that? Might they be headed in this direction? If wild animals sense danger, they'll migrate from their habitats."

Kelly studied Damien's reaction, baffled when his lips tightened the same way they had when Rowan had jumped on him.

"I haven't heard about any near here," he said. "The last fires I crewed were in northwest Montana. You should definitely check the Forest Service website."

He turned back toward the pen, clearly putting an end to any fire discussion. It didn't make any sense. This was a man whose career was to fight fires, yet more than once now, he'd shied away from the subject like he'd been asked about kicking puppies.

In fact, he didn't seem to like puppies much either. Or at least dogs. She sidled next to him.

"Hey there, you okay?"

"Fine." His voice was several degrees lower than warm, and he didn't turn his head or even glance her way.

"I guess you aren't a big fan of dogs."

"Dogs are fine. It was just a big dog that moved fast."

"That is a true statement. And I came over in case you want a protective shield should that marmot critter return." She grinned, hoping her joking would ease the steel tension in his shoulders.

"I don't," he snapped. "Let it go, Kelly."

She could see his jaw starting to clench, and she stepped back, surprised at his annoyance and, if she was honest, stung by his tone. Her own mouth firmed into a frown. "Sure," she said. "No problem."

He still didn't look at her.

"Kelly!"

She turned away to find Grace half-jogging toward the round pen, mild panic on her face. Kelly met her ten feet from the group and caught her shoulders.

"Hey, hey. What's wrong?"

"I just got a call from Liam."

"Liam who's working the restaurant right now?"

"Yeah. One of his kids just got rushed to the hospital with appendicitis. He has to leave and he can't work this weekend. I have to go back to town."

"Gracie, I'm so sorry."

"I know this is your vacation, but I have to beg. Is there *any* way you could help me more than tomorrow night, just for this weekend? I'm so sorry, I—"

"Grace!" It was so unusual for her, the calm one with all the faith, to be panicked over anything, that Kelly nearly laughed despite her sister's distress. "I'll help. Of course I will."

Grace threw her arms around Kelly's neck and squeezed. "Thank you. I mean really and truly. I don't know what I'm doing wrong. Three chefs in six months. Dana lasted less than two weeks. And now Liam."

"You're not doing anything wrong." She gave a haughty sniff and a teasing wink. "People like me are very hard to find."

"You mean arrogant, super-talented Gordon Ramsay types?"

When Raquel had invoked Gordon Ramsay's name, it had been an insult. This time, with Grace grinning in her face, it felt much more like a high compliment.

"Exactly! Come on, we'll go make plans. I'm done here."

She glanced over her shoulder. Damien still stared at Apollo, but now Gabe stood beside him. Still bemused by his mood, she started to return and announce that she was leaving, but as she approached, she heard Gabe speak.

"You know, my friend, dice can always be re-rolled."

She changed her mind and left the two men to wherever that comment led. With a quick good-bye wave to Joely, she turned toward the house with Grace to plan her weekend as a temporary chef. It was a relief to be needed and a boon to her pride to be appreciated. She'd come from San Francisco wondering if working in a high-end restaurant again was worth it. Leaving Triple Bean for most of a year was nothing to take lightly. But if the thought of helping out in a simpler restaurant like Grace's had her stomach dancing with excitement, how much greater would working with haute cuisine be? She threw a glance back at Damien. The man certainly had problems to figure out, and she still wished she knew what they were. But it was time to put this crazy day aside, stop flirting with Damien Finney's life, and concentrate on her own. Maybe her decisions would come to her more clearly if she simply re-rolled the dice, too.

Chapter Nine

DAMIEN LAY ON his bed in the dark with the window open to the sounds of the night. He'd hoped the drone of cicadas, the breeze through the pines behind the house, and the periodic yip-yowls of far-off coyotes would lull him like white noise, but he'd had no such luck. His mind had run aground in the muck and mire of the day's events and in the failure of his plan to slip mostly unnoticed into Paradise Ranch, collect his horse, and ease off to Sheridan. Instead, he'd been drawn full force into the whirlpool of Crockett family dynamics—especially those of one talkative, questioning, well-meaning but nosy Kelly. He couldn't get her out of his thoughts, although he wished he could. The same way he wished he could ignore his guilt.

He'd been a giant ass that afternoon when all she'd tried to do—as usual—was be friendly. And caring. His reaction to her was only more proof that when it came down to it, he was simply no good at caring. Especially not if it involved personal feelings.

The damn wolfhound had just been being a dog. Once upon a time, Damien had loved dogs. He'd had a favorite one growing up, and all dogs had once seemed to have a special affinity for him. But ever since that fire, during his time with the Sheridan Fire Department and long before heading for Iraq—when he'd been injured and woken in the hospital to much relief and praise from his station crew members, the things he liked and disliked, along with the vision of his future life had changed. Life had taken on a more serious meaning at that point, and he still didn't understand his relentless commitment to going the future alone or his strong need to live up to his father's example of sacrificing himself for the world. Not that such an altruistic vision mattered anymore, since at the moment he was failing every commitment spectacularly.

Like the episode with Rowan. One large, friendly dog shouldn't have ruined the day with Kelly—the first day in weeks he'd been able to set aside the boulder of failure he was carrying for even a few hours. She'd disappeared without a word after he'd turned his cold attitude on her, and he hadn't seen her again all evening. Someone told him she'd gone back to the restaurant with Grace. A silly twinge of jealousy dogged him over that. He'd have gone to help, too. He'd enjoyed being at Peas Porridge.

But the idea was ridiculous. He had no reason to help out no matter how much fun it had been earlier in the day.

The circular thoughts continued whirring in his brain until he finally quit fighting them and just let them play. The jumbled movie of memories calmed him more effectively than the cicadas had. The calm brought him to the lip of the open cargo plane door, where he stood suited up with a hundred and ten pounds of gear, listening to Stone read off their names one by one.

"Ready Shark?"

He looked down and there was the black hole, a swirling abyss now as familiar as his reflection in a mirror.

"Can't, Cap," he replied calmly. "There are too many dogs to save."

He looked to his left and was shocked to see Apollo, wearing a halter, his lead rope dangling. He looked to the right and saw Rowan, crouched as if she was about to jump on him again. He reached for the colt's lead rope, but Rowan grabbed it in her mouth and, without warning, leaped not at him but out the door of the plane. "Don't look down," Apollo called and followed the dog. "No!" Damien cried and grabbed the colt's tail. For one instant he tumbled into freefall with them, until he jolted awake, breathless and junkie-high from pumping adrenaline. Scrambling to a sit, he gulped in calming air and released it in a slow stream, letting his head sink to his bent knees.

This was it. Dogs and talking horses pulling him out of planes. He had gone irrevocably mad.

It took long moments for the dream fog to lift and the dream itself to fade. It was a new twist on a recurring theme, all featuring the black hole that had appeared out of left field and attached itself to his memories. He wasn't insane. The stacked-up events of his weird first day in Paradise had simply turned crazy thoughts into a nightmare cocktail.

The therapist expecting him in Sheridan *was* a specialist. He had to remember that. Few people had as much experience dealing with the unique trauma of firefighters. Stone had made seeing her a requirement for returning to the Montana crew. And he was returning. He wasn't going to let his mother or the memory of this father down again.

That meant he had to apologize to Kelly and then get out away from the ranch.

The thought created its own kind of black hole.

Slowly he lay back down, still tense but at least able to focus on his weak plan to apologize to Kelly. One thing he'd learned about her during their hours together was that, for all her endless chattiness, she appreciated sincerity. Fine. Then he'd be more sincere, damn it, than Linus Van Pelt's pumpkin patch. If he had to beg, he'd get her to believe his apology.

The black hole didn't reappear when he finally drifted off again. Instead, the dream was kinder to him for a change—an image of soft, brown eyes, a beautiful mouth that smiled as easily as it opened to let out a smoky, sexy low voice, and sweetly rounded hips rocking mesmerizingly in a saddle. They would feel so right between his hands...

It wasn't sunshine pouring through his still-open window the next morning that woke him, but his phone, buzzing away in the pocket of his jeans, draped over the chair beside his bed. He squinted at the clock on the bedside table and frowned. How could it be 8:00 a.m.? He never slept past six. It had to be the very nice dream...

The phone.

He scrambled from the sheets into a morning-fresh room, grabbed the pants, and dug his phone from the pocket. He saw the displayed name, and his heart dropped guiltily. She'd beaten him to the punch. He tapped the answer icon.

"Mom? Hi."

"Oh, honey, thank goodness. I'm so sorry it's early, but I've been worried about you and I finally had to call.

Is everything all right?"

"Yes. Yes," he lied, his habit of protecting his mother's feelings an old one that surfaced even as his heart pounded with the knowledge that he'd have to tell her the truth. "I am so sorry. I should have called days ago. It's been a crazy couple of weeks."

"As long as you're all right it's fine. I should have called before this, too. How is Montana? I've read about the fires there. Have you been staying safe?"

For a moment his breath caught. The moment he'd dreaded was in his face and he had no idea how to start.

"I am safe. I'm not in Montana at the moment. I'm in Wyoming. At Paradise Ranch."

"My goodness! Damien, are you on vacation? I'm so glad."

"I'm here for a few days but then I'm planning to come see you. Maybe stay for a couple of weeks. I was waiting to settle a few details before letting you know."

"Honey..." A long, hesitant pause followed her endearment. "I would just love that..."

He heard a definite, unspoken "but" in her voice. "Mom, is everything okay with you?"

"Of course, of course, everything's wonderful. But one of the reasons besides my normal overbearing worry I wanted to get hold of you is that I've had a wonderful opportunity come up and needed to let you know."

"Okay. What's up?"

"Do you remember the river cruise in Europe I was planning last year that got canceled?" Her normally quiet and unassuming voice held the excited anticipation of a ten-year-old talking about visiting Disney.

"Sure."

"Bonnie found a fantastic new deal and has reorganized the whole thing."

Bonnie—his mother's jet-setting, tornadic sister—was his favorite aunt. Nice but always on the move, and slightly flighty. A frisson of concern shimmed through him as he felt his solid plan from hours earlier shudder. "That is wonderful, Mom. When are you going?"

"Well, now I'm a little disappointed. We are planning to leave next Tuesday and we'll be gone three weeks. But that means I'll miss your visit."

This marked the second big obstacle tossed in front of his plans. At least his mother wasn't dying or depressed from worry.

"Don't you dare be disappointed. This is on your bucket list, right?"

"You are far more important than any bucket list."

Another thought occurred to him and buoyed his spirits. Slightly. Maybe he could postpone worrying her about his issues until she was back and the problems were solved. "I'm a big boy and as much as I'll miss checking up on you, I'll survive for three weeks. I can see you when you get back."

"Checking up on me?" The surprise in her voice was genuine.

"I've hated being away from you all this time and leaving you alone after Dad died." He made his made-up reason for their newly aborted reunion sound plausible.

"Sweet boy. I can say the same as you—I'm a big girl. I'm just fine and I've *been* just fine. But it's always nice to think you're keeping tabs on me."

She was gracious as always. Checking in by phone wasn't the same as seeing her and supporting her. Still, relief at the postponement fueled more guilt. Because he didn't have enough.

"You'd better let me keep tabs on you while you're gone, too. Do you promise to keep in touch regularly so I know you haven't drowned or had an ancient ruin fall on you? Or, worse," he teased, "met some tiny, forgotten country's widowed king who'll talk you into staying."

Warm laughter flowed through the connection.

"Oh, darling, no king and no amount of money will ever entice me. I raised two men, that's plenty for me. This trip is purely about selfishness."

He pondered her words and the confidence they exuded. She sounded good, he realized. Different than he always remembered her.

"How about if I come earlier to see you off?"

"Sweetheart, no, don't change your plans." Her voice remained firm. "I will be running around getting ready for this trip since it's so last minute, and I'd be terrible company. How about when I get back, I come to see you. I'd love to see your base in Montana if you're back at work."

There was no option; he had to be back at work.

"Yeah, sure, Mom. We'll talk about it."

"Good." She hesitated and he waited out the short silence. "Are you really all right, Damien?"

He almost told her no. He almost let her be the mom who could soothe away the nightmares. But he wouldn't put that on her shoulders before this trip. She was right. She hadn't done anything for herself since his father had died. This had to be about her.

"I'm fine. You don't have to worry about me."

"As if those words give me any more comfort than they ever did."

He knew she was thinking about all the nights she'd lain awake worrying about his dad. As it had turned out, cancer had been a worse devil than any fire.

"I'm on vacation, too," he said. "No fires here at Paradise."

"I don't know if I've ever said so out loud, but I've always been grateful for that place. I know you love it there. And I love you, son. I'm sorry I ruined your plans."

"Stop it. Nothing's ruined." *Confused them but not ruined them.* "You have a great time, got that? Just call me whenever you can. I love you, too."

He hung up after their good-byes and flopped onto his back, stymied over the frivolous actions fate was taking. He'd had everything planned out; nothing should have been difficult, right down to knowing the time of his first appointment with the specialist next Thursday. Her name was Dr. Amanda Goodrich and, as with all the other parts of his story, the only one who knew the appointment had already been scheduled was Gabe. Now that he had no place for his horse and no mother who immediately needed his visit, that appointment was his only anchor to Sheridan.

The thought of going back there for no other reason than to bare his soul to someone he didn't know held more dread than purpose. If he didn't go, however, he didn't go back to Montana. Long ago, Damien had decided the Universe enjoyed screwing with him. Having his current plans start falling apart only proved it—the foul luck of the past half-decade was not simply imaginary.

A door down the hall closed, softly but clearly, and footsteps so quiet they had to be Kelly's made him sit back up in bed while his heart gave a hopeful jump. Maybe he could get to that apology immediately, and the rest of the day would be free of the burden and anticipation of tracking her down. He dressed in moments and made his way downstairs, only to find that Kelly had already left with Grace for Peas Porridge. Harper, Mia, and Joely had also left for work, and only Grandma and baby Sadie and Bella greeted him in the kitchen. Bella stood at the stove and turned, the corners of her eyes crinkling in pleasure when she saw Damien.

"Good morning! Hope you slept well. Are you ready for some breakfast?"

Little Sadie, ensconced in a high chair, wielded one baby spoon while her great-grandmother attempted to feed her something vanilla pudding-colored with another. The baby spouted continuous joyful burbles and laughed when Damien waved at her.

"Di-di-di-di," she called.

The simple scene and warm welcome eased the agitation that had settled throughout Damien's body since talking to his mother.

"Did one of you come from upstairs just now?" he asked.

Grandma and Bella exchanged glances. "No," Bella replied. "We've been here since six-thirty. Why?"

"Someone came out of a bedroom and walked down the hall five minutes ago. I was pretty sure. I suppose it could have been my imagination."

Doubt shadowed Bella's face, but before she could speak the front door opened and, seconds later, closed

"That was not my imagination," Damien said, and he turned toward the kitchen doorway.

"Suspicious." Grandma Sadie popped another spoonful of food calmly into the baby's mouth. "Maybe one of the boys came back for something?"

"They would have used the back door. Or, at the very least, they'd have come in to say hello." Bella moved toward Damien but he held up a hand.

"Stay here. Whoever it was probably went out, not came in."

"Probably, but we don't know for sure." Bella changed direction and disappeared into a large butler's pantry.

Damien didn't wait to see what she was after. He slipped quickly through the dining room and then slowed through the living room taking in every corner like a police officer checking for clear passage. He found nothing out of place by the front door. Wrenching it open, he hurried onto the porch, saw nothing to the right but then, to his shock, saw a figure disappearing around the far corner of the house to the left. Adrenaline surged and he took the three big porch steps to the yard in one leap.

"Hey!" he called.

"What?" Bella appeared behind him, a ten-inch, cast iron frying pan in her hands. Damien nearly lost it with laughter. "Who are you, Daffy Duck?" he called as he broke into a run.

"Don't you laugh," Bella shouted back. "These things are more lethal than most weapons."

He rounded the corner of the house and stopped, his eyes darting back and forth looking for what should have been an easy target. There was no sign of any life other than Bella's luxurious gardens flowing around the foundation. Growling in frustration, he forged forward. Fifty feet of lawn stretched between the gardens and the woods surrounding the back and side yards. Those woods were far enough off that the person even at a run wouldn't have had time to enter them. Damien was tall but he'd always been nimble, and one of the fastest members of any crew or unit. The intruder couldn't have outrun him.

He continued to the garden, searching behind peony plants and arborvitae. Along the back of the house stretched the family's massive deck, and Damien peered under the posts and behind more greenery. Nothing and nobody.

He finished his check of the back yard and met Bella coming around the other side, frying pan still at the ready.

"Damn," he said. "I don't think I'd want to meet you and that thing in an alley. Those suckers are heavy and you're wielding it like a fly swatter."

Her loaded hand and arm fell to her side. "Adrenaline," she said. "I don't like the thought of someone who wasn't invited being in my house."

"You didn't see anything?" He took the pan from her and she smiled gratefully.

"No."

A swish of brush and crackle of twigs made them both turn toward the wooded area south of the yard. Damien dropped the pan and started off, but six rustling steps later the sounds disappeared and he stopped.

"Whoever it was hid like a shadow in plain sight," he said. "I'll never find them in a wooded area with a million places to disappear."

"What on earth is this about?"

Bella's voice shook ever so slightly. Now that her adrenaline had ebbed, she looked like exactly what she was—a worried mother with a household to protect. Damien picked up the frying pan again and put an arm around the woman who'd raised six girls to perfect, brave adulthood. She had every right to panic, and yet she'd gone after a potential danger with a close combat weapon.

"I don't think we're in danger."

"You don't?" She wrapped an arm around his waist

and gave him a squeeze.

"I think it has to do with that backpack Kelly and I found. Kelly left her contact information for the owner, so my theory is he wants the medicine bag we took for safekeeping. What I don't know is why they didn't simply knock on the door. Why break in and try to steal it back?"

"I still don't like it."

"I can't blame you for that."

Bella released a long sigh. "Well, it's not very empowered, Damien, but I admit fully I'm glad you were here." She hugged him again and he let her go.

"Bah." He laughed. "You were better than a hired assassin."

She blushed. Bella Crockett might have been in her early sixties, but she was walking proof that sixty was the new forty. "Grabbing a frying pan is a little silly."

"Mama Bear tactics. That was what my mother used to call it." He flashed back to the conversation with his mother not fifteen minutes earlier. Vulnerable as he always portrayed her, she *had* often stood up for him and with him. Maybe not with a frying pan, but definitely with words and deeds. He'd always seen her as a modest, almost a reticent person, but she would have protected him and his brother at all costs. "We chased off the threat, and that's the important thing," he said to Bella.

"I hope they found what they were looking for. I guess I'll be locking the doors for a while. It's too bad. I've never worried about that."

"Let me find out if Kelly still has the medicine bag. If she doesn't, then the owner found it and won't be back. If she does, we'll double our efforts to find him."

"Do you think the footsteps you heard this morning were this person's?"

He hated to acknowledge that the person had not only been in the house but in the most private of spaces, but it seemed obvious. He nodded. "I'm guessing so."

Bella shuddered. "I really, really don't like that."

"I'm going to go check on my horse," he said. "Then I'll go into town and talk to Kelly. We'll solve this."

"Thank you," she said. "You really have said all the right comforting things."

"Well I'm glad," he said. "But words are easy."

He took half an hour with Pan, doing nothing but groom and scratch her favorite spots and murmur the morning's story to her. He took Apollo from his pasture as well and did the same, giving the colt at least a little time to get to know him better. Calmer once the pair of gray horses had given him back a sense of control, and the feeling that he wasn't a screw-up at everything he tried, his deep-seated conviction that he couldn't leave Pan behind this time was reinforced. He made one more call to a stable near Sheridan, but even if he wasn't a failure at everything, the universe still took no pity nor did fate open a spot for his horse there either.

By the time he headed into Wolf Paw Pass to talk to Kelly, he was calmer if no closer to knowing what to do next. The heart-pumping rush from the intruder chase still unnerved him, but mostly because he had no idea how to find the person without waiting for him or her to return. What were they all supposed to do? Sit around the living room drumming fingers until that happened? H wracked his brain for options the entire twenty-minute drive to the little town, perturbed with his lack of ideas and sorry he no more to offer Kelly than upsetting news. The grand apology that had originally been the reason for seeing her today paled in comparison. Despite yesterday's good times, this morning felt like a step backward.

The intricately carved "Welcome to Wolf Paw Pass" sign, with its watchful black and gray wolf peering over a snow-capped mountain peak, sent a welcome moment of warmth through him and boosted his discouraged mood. He'd spent a year in this tiny town and, in truth, good things had happened here. He'd met friends, he'd been part of some quite excellent practical jokes, he'd been befriended by Gabe and then the Crockett family, he'd eaten good food and certainly drunk a little too much Wolfheart Lager, the local microbrew, which, at the memory, he suddenly craved like water.

He'd also found Pan.

The thought of Sheridan once again doused the mood that was moving up and down like an old-fashioned mercury thermometer. He parked at Peas Porridge at twelve-thirty-five, knowing his lunchtime arrival was probably terrible timing. Kelly would be cooking for the mealtime crowd. For a moment he considered going to have that Wolfheart—or three—and a burger at the Basecamp Grill, and ignore the whole morning's mess…

He knew better. A nice buzz could easily erase the realities of a bad day, but drinking had never been his escape of choice. Anger. Practical jokes. Back in the day a joint now and then. But temporary escape wouldn't solve any of his current issues.

Instead, he determined to spend no more than two minutes interrupting Kelly to ask her about the medicine bag and make his apology. Stepping into the restaurant, he felt the warmth and friendly embrace of the room, just as he had yesterday. It had the vibe of a venerable old building that would last for a very long time and welcome anyone who entered. The crowd was impressive for an establishment that had been open less than half a year, and it smelled delicious. A rich riot of food scents mingled into a feast for the nose. Despite the good breakfast he'd had after the intruder adventure, Damien's stomach rumbled.

"Just one today?"

A young man wearing tight black jeans, a black shirt, and a red vest greeted him with a friendly smile and a flop of purple-tipped hair across his forehead. His nametag read Charlie.

"Yes," Damien replied before he could stop himself. He hadn't planned to sit much less stay, but the atmosphere and aromas overpowered his resolve.

"You're in luck, we have a new chef today," the man said. "Everyone's been *raving.*"

"Yeah?" Damien smiled to himself.

"I've heard the club sandwich and the Reuben are better than ever. And the soup of the day—some kind of minestrone."

Damien's stomach growled harder than ever. He could have born witness to the club sandwich's quality, but he followed Charlie to a table on an inside wall without saying anything. Why ruin the young man's promotional speech?

"Greta will be right with you," he said.

"Thanks."

Greta showed up, another young person, perhaps twenty, with a gleaming black ponytail and a ready smile. She took Damien's soup and sandwich order, added his requested sides of onion rings and a Coke, and was about to turn away when he stopped her.

"Would you do me a favor and ask the owner if I could speak to her?"

Worry lines formed on Greta's forehead. "Grace?"

Damien nodded. "Sure. Is there a problem? Anything I can do?"

"No, no, not at all. I know her and just want to say hello."

The worry lines disappeared and her smile returned. "Sure. I'll go find her. What's your name?"

"Tell her Finney wants to make sure his food is top-notch."

Greta laughed as she walked away. Damien pulled his phone out of a pocket to check messages. The exercise was only out of habit; nobody had cause to send him messages. And, as expected, there was nothing. He settled in to wait but to his surprise, Grace rounded on his table grinning like she'd found a lost winning lottery ticket.

"Damien! I can't tell you how happy I am to see you. How happy Kelly will be."

He grimaced, doubting that statement.

"I'm happy to see you, too. I wasn't planning to stay but the atmosphere of your place is like a siren's song. I had to come in."

"I guess that's very gratifying. But if you weren't planning to come in, does that mean you're in the middle of a busy day?"

"Hardly. I'm on vacation, remember. I'm loafing."

"Then please, please, *please* would you let me hire you? Again. Until this evening? You can see how swamped we are and I desperately need Kelly to start helping me prep for the event tonight. I'll feed you first. I know Kelly will make you something magical."

Grace's earnest request dashed away all the morning's discouragement. Before yesterday he hadn't cooked in ages, and he'd had a genuinely good time. The thought of spending time in the kitchen with Kelly was more than a little enticing. If he could smooth the waters with her.

"I would be more than happy to help out," he said. "I don't need anything magical. But I do have a quick request first. I have some news for Kelly; could I take her away from her duties for five minutes? Can you spare her?"

Grace nodded. "Of course. She's so efficient; she can make her own break time. How about I have her bring out your lunch order? She can talk with you and you can both come back to the kitchen when you're done."

"That would be great. But change my order to a simple soup and any sandwich. I don't need the greasy burger and rings if I'm going to come back and work."

She smiled again and nodded. It was strange looking into Kelly's face on another person—and yet, he was pretty sure he could see differences now. Grace's eyes lacked the inner fierceness of a woman born to compete, and her voice lacked the bubbly animation that spilled into Kelly's the moment she opened her mouth. Grace was the embodiment of calm joy.

"Have you found a place for Pan yet?"

He shook his head. "Another strikeout this morning."

"I'm sorry." She placed a comforting hand on his shoulder. "It's hard to wait when the Good Lord takes his time coming up with a plan. But he will."

He didn't remember asking for a plan, but he nodded again. He'd heard about Grace's solid spirituality, and he had to admit, her confidence felt good even if it came with a side of God-has-a-plan.

"Yeah, things always work out," he said in the voice he'd used countless times with his mother to convince her he'd be fine, though he hadn't truly believed those words in a long time.

He sank deep into thought after Grace left. He honestly didn't mind helping in the kitchen; it was a great excuse for putting the morning as well as the immediate future out of his mind. It wasn't going to find him a stable in Sheridan nor an itinerant camper looking for his medicine bag. They could call the sheriff and find out if anyone else had seen a wanderer in the hills. Maybe the bag had been reported missing. He shook his head. The owner wouldn't break in if he'd gone to the authorities. And the bag wasn't missing—Kelly had told the owner exactly where it was.

He ran a hand across his mouth and chin, sighing. This lack of insight was costing him his investigator status, that was for sure.

"Hey, Mustang Man."

"Hey, Cowgirl."

She set the sandwich on the table—some kind of chicken salad, it looked like. Then she unloaded two bowls of soup, filled to the rims with vegetables and little white shells of pasta. His mouth watered.

"I hear you're back as sous chef," she said.

"I guess that depends on whether I pass muster with the master chef."

"Why wouldn't you?"

"I was kind of mean to her yesterday."

"Oh, that." She placed the empty serving tray on an unused chair and sat across from him. "I think I can probably find some way to make you pay once you put on an apron. Unless you're too scared of revenge."

She held back a smile, but Kelly was no good at all at masking emotions in her eyes, and hers were wide with humor.

"Oh, believe me, I am."

Chapter Ten

SHE LAUGHED AT him and, once again, his mind dove into comparison mode. So shallow of him, he knew, but being around two identical women was still a unique and somewhat wondrous experience. Same features, same full lips, same strong, lovely cheekbones. So why did *Kelly's* face, so identical to Grace's on the surface, send his heart into a happy dance and his breathing rate into the stratosphere?

"Earth to Finney. You don't really have to act afraid of me, you know."

A self-conscious grin erased his thoughts. "Sorry. In truth, I'm just glad you're here. I really did come to apologize. I didn't mean to be a jerk yesterday."

"You weren't a jerk, Damien."

"Yeah, I was. I snapped at you when you were being nice."

She appraised him for a few long seconds and finally shrugged. "I admit at the time I was miffed. But that was stupid. It was a long day. All's forgotten."

He shook his head and gave a short breathy laugh. "Nice of you to lie for my benefit. It wasn't the worst thing, but it was rude. My mama taught me better."

His hands rested, folded, on the table. With a gentle movement, she covered them with her own, sending warmth radiating through him.

"The dog triggered something. Maybe sometime you'll tell me what it was," she said.

"I wish I could. I used to like dogs, and maybe that's what got me so upset. I don't know why they annoy me so much now. It kind of pisses me off."

"When did that start?"

"Eight years ago, before I went to Iraq and then Afghanistan. I was a regular-issue firefighter in Sheridan County."

Kelly's fingers tightened over his. "I thought you'd once told us you drove a truck before going to the Middle East."

"I did, for part of the year before. I was injured in a house fire right before that and by the time I was fully healed, I'd decided to enlist. I don't remember much of the incident that injured me; I was told I fell through a floor and broke a leg, an arm, and a rib. Oddly, mercifully, I wasn't burned, but I woke up twenty hours afterward in the hospital.

"It took weeks for any memories to surface, but I've never remembered the accident itself. I remember the two-story older house and how quickly it burned. And I remember the family lost two pet dogs I think I was trying to save when the floor gave way. It seems that affected my feelings about them."

He shook his head. The familiar old, piecemeal memories were less troubling in the daylight with Kelly's soft hands over his, but he still didn't like the discomfort they left in his chest. "The thing is, that kind of memory is part and parcel of a firefighter's job. We live with loss. It shouldn't have been an issue then and it definitely shouldn't be an ongoing one—not after some of the ugly things we saw in the Sandbox. Those I've worked through fine. Thanks to the time with Gabe."

"I'm really sorry," she said. "Who can explain the things that lodge in our minds? My guess is seeing dogs now triggers the memory of the ones you couldn't save. It makes sense to me. And hey, not to make light of this, but if dogs are no longer your favorite animals, so be it. You have Pan and Apollo, and that means you have animals in your life. That's the important thing."

He wasn't sure what to say. Her words touched him, and they made perfect sense even if they didn't quite touch the spot inside of him that made dogs such a ridiculous issue in his life. Exhaustion made his head ache. He didn't talk this much. He hadn't told the dog story to anyone in years. It had never seemed relevant.

"I do have Pan and that's enough. Still, the story seems silly," he said.

She rubbed the knuckle and lower half of his thumb with the pad of her own. Little shivers of comfort filled him. He smiled gratefully.

"I don't think it's silly at all to be uncomfortable with dogs. If all you ever do is stop and pet one once in a while, your traumatized self will be reminded each time that it isn't Asta's or Rowen's fault you went through the floor. That's enough. You never have to do more than that."

Her simple analysis took him aback. Her busy, chatty nature had made Damien sure she'd try to take on the role of fixing him. Her lack of judgment left him relieved.

"Well, I thank you. And, I'm sorry again. That story wasn't meant to be an excuse."

"Hey." She squeezed his hand one last time and released her hold. "I know you didn't really want to tell it. It's safe with me. No more apologizing, okay?"

"Okay."

"Are you willing to come back and cook with me?"

"I am. But there is one more reason I came. Can I ask where you're keeping the medicine bag from yesterday?"

Her brow furrowed. "I have it in my purse, why?"

"It's generated a bigger mystery than we thought it would. Something pretty weird happened this morning."

The story about the mysterious person in the house clearly shook her.

"You think this person was actually in my room looking for the bag?"

He shrugged. "I don't know that for certain but I think so. I'm convinced I heard the door and the footsteps, but I didn't actually see anyone in your space. I only got suspicious when you were already long gone and we knew it hadn't been you."

"You're right, it has to be the medicine bag." Kelly didn't panic, but Damien watched excitement grow in her face and demeanor like a time-lapsed video. "I didn't directly put the ranch's address on the note, but it wouldn't take much to look me up or find out I'm one of *those* Crocketts."

"The problem with knowing you're keeping the pouch on your person is that it means the owner didn't find it and might try again."

"Depends on how deeply he dug around looking for it. He'll only come back if he thinks there's more to explore."

"Like the rest of the house?"

She drummed her fingers on the table. "That's a little scary. We'll have to make sure everything stays locked for a while."

"Already done. And, by the way, your mother wields a mean frying pan. So that's at the ready, too."

Kelly snorted. "Figures she'd grab the nearest weapon of mass creativity. And Grandma Sadie barely raised a brow, right?"

"Never missed a beat of the baby's feeding." He grinned at the memory.

"They're both brave and so strong, but they have different ways of showing it. Mom reacts and then worries. Grandma accepts and plans."

"Which one are you?" he teased.

"Mom. Totally. Although, I'm not worried. I just want desperately now to go search through that woods and find a trail."

"Tough to do since we're about to go work."

"And I'll be here late tonight." Her mouth twisted in regret. "You should follow it when you're done here."

"Kelly, the person is long gone. And based on how easily he hid from us in plain sight, I doubt there'll be much of a trail."

"We can't do nothing." Her fingers drummed even faster. Damien laughed and stopped the frenetic motion with his hand. "Sorry, I'm thinking. Maybe we should publicize this—put up "Found" signs, like you would if you found a stray animal."

"How about simply reporting the break-in to the police?"

She shrugged in potential agreement. "They'd want more detail than you gave me."

"There isn't anymore."

"And that would be my point. Still, I suppose that's the smart thing to do even though I feel a teensy bit bad because I'm the one who took the bag in the first place. I'm sure they only want it back."

"They could patrol more...maybe make everyone feel safer."

"They might add an extra run out there, but they'd have to be lucky to see anything. How about this? Tomorrow morning we should ride back to Ancestor Canyon and see if anything's changed."

"I'd bet my last dollar there's nothing there anymore."

"Probably not. But, hey, you know from experience it's a nice ride." She arched a brow in invitation.

"It is." He fidgeted with the handle of his mug, hoping the sudden, anticipatory fluttering in his gut didn't show in his face. "Okay, I'm up for that. Meanwhile, we can call your mom and grandmother regularly while we work to make sure they're okay."

"I like that plan." She stood and brushed her hands together. "All right then, let's go to work. But just so you know, I've hidden the electrical tape so don't even think about sabotaging that sprayer again. I'm the chef; I can fire you."

"But you won't." He sent her the most beatific smile he could muster and added a wink of confidence.

"Oh, brother."

To Kelly's delight, it was evident within the first ten minutes back in the Peas Porridge kitchen with Damien that the previous day hadn't been a fluke. Cooking beside him was like participating in a master class called Fun

With Food. She showed him how to chop an onion twice as quickly as he normally could—without losing a finger. He dealt out twelve slices of bread with the skill of a Bellagio card dealer and showed her how to butter the entire dozen almost at once. Since firefighters could scarf up three sandwiches apiece in less time than it took a horse to eat an apple, he told her, hyper-speed bread buttering had been a priceless life skill.

They laughed. They split duties effortlessly since Damien preferred taking orders to giving them. He forgot to be worried and quiet, and showed off a funny, complimentary side Kelly wanted to wrap up and keep with her because it made her forget to worry about future plans, too. They made it to five o'clock before she knew it.

"Hey, you two." Grace entered the kitchen, her smile easier and her step lighter than Kelly had seen it anytime in the past day and a half. "Believe it or not, there's a before dinnertime lull. You guys kept up with everything and Harper just called. She's on her way. Damien, I hereby declare you are officially finished with your shift."

"Seriously?" Kelly caught Damien's eyes and found her surprise reflected in the arch of one thick, perfect brow. "The time just flew. Dang, Finney. It's been a while since I've lost track of time in a kitchen. Good trick."

"I didn't do a thing."

"I remember the days before we really got rolling with Triple Bean having to use an air horn to blast you out of the zone when you were cooking." Grace laughed.

"Yeah. It's fun to do new things. You have some great basic recipes, Gracie; it's a nice menu. We should talk about ways you could make a few of these dishes really special."

A flash of uncertainty crossed Grace's features but

then she nodded.

"Maybe so. *After* the party tonight."

"Of course."

"Are you sure you don't need me to stay?" Damien asked. "If you want more hands I sure could."

"Seriously, you've been more help than you'll ever know," Grace said. "No. You go take care of your own stuff. I know you're leaving soon. I'll let you know if—"

The buzz of Damien's phone interrupted, and he fished it from his pocket.

"Huh. It's Gabe," he said.

"Take it," Kelly urged. "Maybe he has news on another stable or something."

He shrugged but smiled and answered the call. "Hey, Lieutenant Harrison. What's this? A surprise check-in call like the old days?"

She vaguely heard Gabe's rich laugh through the phone, and a few of the words as Damien turned. "Nope, just an old friend meddling. Got a second?"

"I'm at Peas Porridge helping Grace, but I'm about finished. Meddling, you say?"

He shot a look over his shoulder and Kelly grinned.

"Gabe meddles," she whispered.

He shook his head and turned so the phone's speaker was fully muted to her. But despite not hearing Gabe's side of the conversation, Kelly couldn't miss the slow straightening of Damien's spine, nor the rigidity that overtook his shoulders. Then he spoke.

"I wish you'd told me first instead of contacting Stone Rayburn." His tone, low and suddenly hard, was measured as a metronome.

The tightness in his posture didn't ease as he listened. Kelly frowned at Grace, who pulled her around to face the prep counter.

"Don't eavesdrop," she whispered. "Start on the onions for those fish tacos."

Kelly nodded and moved to the pantry where she pulled out a container of ten onions. Still, she couldn't fully obey Grace's order to stop listening.

"I know you're trying to help. I'm sure he's a fine doc," Damien said. "But I want a straight path back to Montana, Gabe. Without multiple people standing along the way cheering me like I'm attempting a marathon. And there'd be no keeping things private. Around here, everyone knows what you're going to say before you say it. You know that."

Kelly bent her head over the first peeled onion, starting the dicing, trying to turn off the curiosity that always got her into trouble, but unable to get past the words "fine doc," and "no keeping things private." Grace had moved to the other side of the kitchen, out of earshot—a much more virtuous choice than Kelly's—but suddenly she didn't care. Worry crept into her mind, even though she had no idea what the conversation was about. Fortunately, Damien took care of her eavesdropping for her.

"Look," he said quietly. "We need to talk about this later, not here or now... Yes, that's fine... Yeah."

The call ended abruptly, without a closing good-bye, and for a long minute, Damien didn't turn around. It took every ounce of Kelly's weak willpower to keep from spinning to him and begging to know if he was all right.

Well, he wasn't. Or things weren't. Literally minutes earlier he'd been a different man, one who'd been happy, one who'd sneaked a tight seal of cling wrap onto the top of a mixing bowl so the chopped tomatoes she'd scraped into it had bounced off the surface and back onto the counter. That man now stood like a defeated athlete avoiding the crowds.

She gave herself a hard mental shake. None of this was her business. Nosey Nellie had to steer clear and she needed to say nothing until Damien allowed her closer again—if he ever did. But her heart ached in a deep, unfamiliar empathy, and her arms longed to comfort him. As if she had some reason to think there was a connection between them.

At last, he turned, his face a mask of forced nonchalance.

"Sorry. There should never be personal calls at work. Like you said, Gabe meddles."

"But everything's all right?" She feigned ignorance.

"Bottom line is, he's working the angles to try and get me to stay."

"Good for him."

"Kelly." He stopped and the nonchalance dropped away. "Your family is amazing. But I have a journey I need to take on my own."

"Can you tell me where you're going? Other than just to Sheridan?"

He actually laughed. "Hardly. I have no clue myself."

"Then maybe it is just a journey to Paradise Ranch."

He scratched the back of his head and then untied the apron at his waist. With a half-smile, he didn't take the bait. "Well, it's time to journey back there for the moment. I told Gabe I'd meet him as long as I was done here. I had a great afternoon. You're an amazing chef."

He wasn't going to let her back in. Sadness shafted through her. Through his smile, she saw no happiness in his eyes, just a new, deep-seated worry.

"It was fun. Again."

"You'll be here late, right? I probably won't see you when you get home."

"But we're still riding to the canyon tomorrow?"

He hesitated, and she realized he was going to bow out. Her heart plummeted to the base of her stomach, and then he shocked her.

"Sure. What time should I meet you?"

She stared, slightly discombobulated by the unexpected, and the smell of onions, pungent and strong, hit her eyes. She usually chopped so efficiently onions didn't bother her. She hadn't cried over them in years. "Ah…eight? Eight-thirty?"

"I'll see you at the barn." For one instant, Damien-of-the-kitchen returned. "Aww don't cry."

Grabbing a clean towel, she swiped at her eyes. "Like I'd cry for you."

One last flash of a grin and a hug for Grace later, he was gone. The lack of a gesture for her stung, and she chastised herself. She wasn't a jealous thirteen-year-old. She wasn not allowing the attraction to grow either. The man was passing through. And he might be hotter than a deep fryer with hair made for touching and a laugh made to drown a woman, but that didn't matter. It was the vulnerability, the wounded animal inside of him she wanted to rescue. The fun and funny man she wanted to draw out and nurture until it stayed and the darkness receded and the whiplash emotions stopped.

She wished to heaven she wasn't falling for the whiplash.

Chapter Eleven

"I THINK THAT'S what you call a successful night."

Grace leaned back against the locked front door at Peas Porridge and closed her eyes. Kelly sat atop the table closest to the exit, her legs dangling, her feet swinging back and forth. For the first time all evening, her shoulders relaxed, dropping from where they'd hunched the past five hours in the vicinity of her earlobes. Grace looked as exhausted as Kelly felt. The last of the guests from the corporate party were gone, Harper had said she'd meet them back at home, and they were officially closed. There'd been zero fires. Grace had received rave reviews all night.

"You planned a great evening for them," Kelly said. They'll spread the word; they'll be back."

"I hope so." Grace straightened and covered the several steps to Kelly's perch, opening her arms to embrace her in an enormous hug. "It would not have happened without you. I don't know how to begin to thank you."

"All I did was cook."

"And reorganize the entire kitchen so the workspaces flowed and the prep times were cut in half. I should have had you here at the beginning to set it up. Maybe I wouldn't have lost so many chefs. Maybe that's been my problem all along—I have a tough kitchen to work in."

Kelly stood. "Hey. A week without near disasters or crises in a restaurant would signal the zombie apocalypse. We did this together. And we had lots of years of experience under our belts to draw from. I had fun."

That was the truth. She'd had more fun memorizing Grace's menu and improvising preparation than she'd had for quite a long time at Triple Bean.

"That idea you had for the overstock of cod—mini fish tacos?" Grace shook her head. "Genius."

The "genius" compliment when it came to cooking was one Kelly always craved like a junkie craving drugs. She longed to create unique dishes that would get noticed and make her a name. To be known for the only thing she was really good at? Wasn't that everyone's dream? She loved Triple Bean; it was her first solo cooking endeavor and a beautiful child she and her sisters had created. But culinary school had been a long time ago now, and she wanted to use the expertise she'd gained there.

Like finding a unique way to use ten pounds of fresh cod unexpectedly delivered ten minutes before a huge event. The look of gratitude on her sister's face when spicy fish tacos had been ready to pass around as appetizers to the corporate crowd of nearly one hundred was gratifying. It proved she could be more than the flirty middle sister who had the ability to whip out items on a short-order menu.

"They were pretty good, if I do say so," Kelly said.

"Who knew fish that wasn't deep fried could be comfort food?" Grace patted her stomach. "I stole too many."

Kelly grimaced. "I did, too. In the name of taste testing."

"Want a glass of wine to celebrate?"

Kelly thought a moment and then grinned devilishly. "When's the last time we broke into Dad's Scotch reserve?"

Sam Crockett had always told his daughters that if the Good Lord had seen fit to give him girls and not boys, that was fine by him, but he'd by gosh teach them any skill he'd teach a son. And passing down his connoisseur's taste for Scotch—be it a triple-distilled Auchentoshan, a peaty Talisker, or a classic Glenfiddich—had been one of his most successful lessons. Any of the Crockett girls could hold her own drinking with the men.

Grace returned the impish smile. "Let's finish cleaning up and head home. We can drink at midnight, right?"

"Hail Jimmy Buffet. It's five o'clock somewhere."

They reached the house fifteen minutes before midnight and made their way quietly into the kitchen, hanging their jackets in the large mudroom and groaning with relief as they toed off their shoes. Kelly made it to the dining room first and turned on the light, heading immediately for the wall unit holding a built-in oak bar. The Scotch collection was still kept well stocked, and a dozen bottles gleamed amber beneath the cabinet lighting. She chose a twelve-year McClellan and two Scotch glasses and set them on the table. Grace joined her with two of the fancy printed paper napkins their mother loved to collect—these were white covered with sprays of forget-me-nots—and they pulled out the heavy dining room chairs to sit kitty-corner from each other. Grace did the pouring, expertly filling both glasses to exactly the same three-finger depth.

"I love that our very own Church Lady could easily be a sommelier." Kelly laughed and raised her glass. "To success and sisters and excellent Scotch."

"And to Dad."

"May he watch over us as we drink."

Giggles spilled from both of them. It was good, after four years, to be able to laugh with the ghost of their father, whose unexpected heart attack had taken him far too early at age sixty-eight. The stern taskmaster they'd all adored but never wanted to work for had drawn all but two of his girls back home since his death. He was missed and still revered.

"So how is it working out, having three of you and your families living under one roof?"

"It's going well. Mom and Grandma have their wing. Gabe, Mia, Rory, and Sadie got the basement finished, and it's an absolutely lovely big space. Harper and Cole love the main floor master suite, and all the bedrooms make great offices and guest digs for whomever. I stay mostly with Ty and the house we rent from Cole. Except now that I'm spending time with you."

"Ty doesn't mind?"

"Not at all. He and Lucky say they're planning our honeymoon and it's a surprise."

"Lucky? You're taking her with you?"

"For part of it. Like Mia and Gabe did with Rory. In a way, I'm marrying her, too, so I want to celebrate with her."

"We haven't talked about the wedding at all, Gracie.

I feel like I've totally ignored that and it's only a few months away. A Christmas wedding! It's so exciting?"

She flushed with pleasure. "Super exciting."

"You're so calm."

"I have three sisters, a mother, and a grandmother on every detail, and now I have you as well. There's very little for me to do except say yes or no to things and, believe me, that's fine. You're the one who's had your wedding all planned since you were twelve. I'd be happy with a simple service in the chapel in town. But Lucky wants a pretty party."

"Good for Lucky, I say, and you know I'll help however I can."

"Thank you. I do know." Grace sipped her Scotch.

"Then there's Joely and Alec living right outside of Wolf Paw Pass." Kelly lifted her glass and followed Grace's lead. "It's amazing that you've all come back and stayed. And that you love it like we did when we were kids."

"So? Maybe it's time for you and Rocky to join us?"

She had no time to make her argument against the idea. The back door creaking open made them both start, and heavy, male footsteps filled the rear hallway accompanied by deep, quiet voices.

"Who the heck else is coming home at this hour?" Grace whispered.

"I can't thank you enough for your help." They heard Cole first. "Sorry it got so late."

"Not a problem," Gabe replied. "We do what we have to do."

Kelly and Grace remained still, eavesdropping while the men entered the kitchen. They didn't sound worried, but only a crisis would have had them working until after midnight.

"Proof I'll need another hand when we bring in that new herd of Harper's."

"Her organic cows," Gabe chuckled. "It's a good idea but, yeah, a lot of work."

"Definitely until the rodeo season is over and Alec is back—whoa! Hullo, ladies!"

Cole stopped in his tracks at the dining-room door, and Kelly grinned.

"Hullo, boys," she said, lifting her glass "You're up late."

Cole's shock eased into a warm, handsome grin. "Two women. Two filled glasses. An open bottle of McClellan's. Hope we're not drowning sorrows."

"Just the opposite—celebrating a successful event at Peas Porridge tonight," Grace said. "We've only been home fifteen minutes ourselves."

"Got room for two more drinkers?" Gabe asked.

"You know we do." Kelly patted the tabletop.

When the men were seated and their Scotch poured, Cole sighed and stretched his legs out under the table.

"Everything all right?" Grace asked.

"It is now," Cole said. "We found a micro-herd of forty head wandering next to the horse pasture. They'd busted through two fences and decided to mix it up with the ponies. Took us two hours to coax 'em back into their space. Then we had to replace some boards and some wire in the dark."

Gabe, across the table from him, raised his glass. "Take over a ranch, they said. It'll be fun, they said."

"I'll drink to that!" Cole answered the toast and they all sipped again, Kelly tipping her glass for her last swallow. "More?" Cole asked.

"No. Better not. I'm getting up early to ride back out to Ancestor Canyon. See if there are signs that our trespasser has moved on. As you might recall, this day started with a break-in."

"Jeez, that's right," Gabe said. "A little disturbing."

"I wish I hadn't taken the medicine bag," Kelly admitted. "But now I think someone needs to confront this person. All he had to do was call the number I left, but instead, he's not only camped on our land but broken into our home."

"We'll find him," Cole promised. "Meanwhile, doors and windows locked."

"Absolutely. I'm sorry about all this. I'm planning to ride back to Ancestor Canyon in the morning. If there's any sign the person is still there, I'll leave the bag and be done with it."

"Is Damien going with you?" Grace asked.

"He said he would."

Gabe scratched his earlobe self-consciously. "I'm afraid I overstepped into his personal life a little today trying to get him to stay. I'm sorry I did but, damn, I wish I could convince him not to leave. Especially since he told me his mother is leaving on a trip and won't be in Sheridan. I'd rather he stay with us and not hang out there alone."

"I sure wouldn't mind having him around to help with those new cows," Cole added. "He could stay right here or even move into one of the ranch bungalows for privacy. Two are empty now." He curved his lips into a half-smile and cocked a brow. "Maybe I should make him an offer he can't refuse."

"I wouldn't push him," Kelly said before she could stop herself. Three pairs of eyes turned on her quizzically, and her face heated. "I just mean, I get the impression he needs space and time to make up his mind."

"You seem to know a lot for having spent less than twenty-four hours with the man." Grace gave her the "triplet look" —one eye shut, head cocked, arms crossed. It meant 'spill the beans 'cause we'll get the scoop anyway.' Kelly blew her off with a dismissive puff of breath.

"You know I'm the party girl. I pretend to read people as a hobby. Damien's a good guy. He hasn't told me a single thing about why he's on leave, but it's not hard to figure out he's struggling with some big decisions."

The only one who didn't nod in quick agreement was Gabe. Kelly studied him while she ran a finger around the rim of her empty glass. From the thoughtful, downward cast of his eyes, she could tell he knew more than any of them. Minor envy lodged in her heart. She was growing to like mercurial and stoic Damien Finney. She longed to help him whether his issues were her business or not.

"I won't push, but I may still make him one more offer." Cole drained his glass. "But not tonight. I'm going to head in and try for five hours of sleep before the fun starts all over."

"Same here," Gabe said. "Have to try and sneak in and pray Sadie doesn't wake up. If she does, she might decide Mommy and Daddy's bed is better than her crib."

They all stood. Gabe stoppered the Scotch bottle and put it away. Cole stepped between Kelly and Grace, wrapped an arm around their shoulders, and pulled them into a hug. He'd grown up on the ranch neighboring Paradise and Kelly had known him all her life. To have him as an official big brother was, she always told him, better than chocolate.

"Don't you two worry about the break-in. We've got this. We're family."

"Thank you," Kelly said.

They said their final goodnights and Grace headed up the stairs. Kelly rinsed the Scotch glasses, closed up the cupboard, and turned all the lower level lights off. Despite Cole's confidence, she dragged her feet up the stairs, swiveling her head and checking every shadow. She hadn't let herself think about the break-in all day, but now that the deep night enveloped her, she was unnerved.

The upstairs hall was lit with only a dim nightlight, and she glanced at Damien's closed door. No light shone from beneath it, and her stomach fluttered as she passed. The attraction to him was inevitable, she supposed, although the funny joker was a persona he only slipped on when they focused on the restaurant and the real man was one she'd normally find far too serious and internally-focused for her taste. It had to be his brooding good looks and the plastic wrap over the bowl.

She gave his door a last look, wondering just what Gabe had done to overstep his boundaries. Three steps further down the hall, a shadowy figure stepped out from her room. Her thoughts slammed to a halt, and claws of fear dug into her heart.

"Boo," he said quietly, and she screeched before she could stifle it.

Chapter Twelve

DAMIEN COULDN'T HOLD back a low, self-satisfied chuckle as Kelly pressed her hands hard to her chest.

"What the hell is wrong with you?" Her whisper croaked with residual fear.

"I am really sorry," he said, not meaning to find it funny. There'd already been a real intruder in her house. "I wanted to surprise you not scare you."

"Yeah, well, you failed."

She shot him a dirty look and they heard a bedroom doorknob turn down the hall.

"Grace!" Kelly rasped and moved like The Flash, pushing her door fully open and shoving Damien, stumbling, into the dark within seconds.

"Everything okay?" He heard Grace's concern.

"Fine. Sorry. I stubbed my toe on the door." Kelly lied like a seasoned grifter. "Sleep well, Gracie."

Damien backed farther into the room, and Kelly followed him, closed the door behind her, and only then flipped on the light.

"Listen here. I just talked myself out of a corner because people think I'm up to my old good-time girl tricks with you."

"I know."

"All I need is for Saint Grace to see me meeting you in a dark hallway after midnight."

"Saint Grace is living with a guy," he whispered back.

"Yeah. But it's the first time in her entire life, and she's going to marry him..." As if her brain caught up with her mouth at last, she stopped. "Wait. What do you mean 'I know'?"

"I heard."

Her eyes widened and she poked at his chest. "You were eavesdropping."

The conversation he'd accidentally stumbled upon had lifted his spirits, and he couldn't summon any guilt at her accusation. "Only the last few minutes."

"You heard us talking about you."

A gorgeous blush fanned across her cheeks, and his heart melted. For all her chattering and bravado, she had the tenderest of hearts. For better or worse, right or wrong, he'd stopped pushing away the attraction flaring within him. For two days it had been no more than a smoldering ember, but something about her filled the hollow spaces inside he was trying to run from. He stepped in front of her and brushed a dark blonde lock of hair behind her ear. When she didn't flinch or back away, he left the strand wrapped like a satin ribbon around his finger.

"What I heard was you standing up for me even though for all you know I'm running from the law."

"Right, sure." She met his eyes. "You aren't running from the law, that much I do know. And I've told you I respect that your business is your business. But I wish I knew more of what you are running from so I could help."

"You help more than you know, by getting into people's thoughts without even trying. Your only problem is that you start caring before people know how to accept it."

"That's nice of you. I like 'you start caring' much better than 'you're nosey.'"

"You're a little nosey." He smiled and touched his fingertips to her cheek, watching her eyelids drift closed. "Mostly, underneath all the talking, I see innate kindness."

Beneath his fingers, her skin heated, and for the first time he could remember, she remained silent. Reluctantly, he pulled his hand away, but the heat stayed with him, spreading deeper and lower into his body. Getting further away from her was not what any part of him wanted.

She opened her eyes with a shy smile that wasn't like her at all, then took a tiny step back, swiveling her head to search the room. A moment later, animation returned to her features and her smile turned to concern.

"I can tell someone's been in here." The words felt ominous in the quiet room.

"You can? How would they know this is your room?"

She pointed. "They knew from the dumb name signs we all still have on our walls. The desk chair is pulled out, and the top drawer is open three inches. The dresser drawer isn't shut." She opened her purse, which she'd tossed on the bed upon entering, and fished out the small, tan medicine bag. "Nothing is missing that I can tell, so I'm ninety-nine percent certain they came looking for the bag. Maybe I *don't* need to know the owner. I should have just left it alone."

Her voice made "ninety-nine percent" sound more

like "seventy-five," and he wished he could wipe away the uncertainty. He much preferred confident Kelly, who sputtered indignantly at practical jokes and then pulled her own. But her home had been invaded and she blamed herself for causing it. He took her hands and squeezed them.

"You didn't make a wrong choice," he promised.

Her small, soft fingers curled gently around his palm and the distress in her eyes softened. A slow, warm shiver of desire rolled unbidden through Damien's stomach and although he told himself to fight it, he ignored the warning.

"I'm fine," she said softly. "This person isn't dangerous. I'm thinking about you now. Tell me what happened in Montana? It doesn't take a Holmes or Watson to see this is more than a month of vacation for you. Or that Gabe upset you."

A wave of last-minute panic rolled through him. He'd come to her room and waited so he could tell her exactly what she'd asked, but instinctively his flight response kicked in. He didn't want her to feel sorry. Pity didn't mix well with attraction. He tried to drop her hands, but Kelly grasped his more tightly and refused to let him go.

"No judgment, Damien. Tell me to let it go if that's what you need."

"No." He released a deep sigh. "If you have to spend time around me, you deserve to know." He told her simply before he could change his mind. "I froze before a fire jump."

"I...don't know exactly what that means."

"I stood at the door of the plane, ready to parachute out, and I froze. I couldn't make the jump. It happened several more times when I tried to practice on the training grounds. Before I can go back, I have to figure out why it happened."

"Oh, Damien, I am sorry. So sorry that's what you're dealing with."

He steeled for a barrage of questions and searched her eyes, looking for judgment even though she'd promised he wouldn't find any. People judged. That had always been a fact of his life. But Kelly remained silent, holding him close with sincerely caring eyes and giving him the courage to continue.

"The real reason I'm supposed to go to Sheridan is that my captain found a therapist there who specializes in the PTSD of firefighters. I guess we're different even than soldiers. Fewer people want to deal with our shit."

"I'm sure wanting to deal has nothing to do with it. But I have no trouble believing that your pressures are unique and that it's probably really hard to find somebody a firefighter could believe knew what he's talking about."

He stared. She got it.

"Gabe found another expert here. While it's great of him to want me to stay, he already talked to my captain."

"Ahhh. I get it. He should have asked you first."

"I wish he would have."

"And you were going to see your mom, anyway."

"Well, that's not an issue anymore. She's taking a vacation. She called this morning to tell me. She didn't yet know I was in Wyoming."

"You maybe can't even answer this," she said. "It might be too soon for you to know. But what do you want to do? Where do you want to go?"

He smiled wanly. "Other than back to Montana, you mean?"

To his surprise, she finally released one of his hands

and set hers against his cheek. "Yeah. Other than back to Montana."

The warmth from her fingers only added to the heat in his belly, even as his emotions—sadness, worry, confusion—warred within him.

"I've spent a lot of time with therapists over the past three years. I spent a long time with Gabe. I'm not angry with him—he's always gone above and beyond when trying to help his friends. But I'm living proof that years of therapy isn't necessarily enough. I've come to believe that if I'm going to figure this out, I have to do it for myself. Nobody else has a magic bullet."

"You are figuring it out. Look how far you've come since I met you two years ago. One stumble—"

"One that could cost me my career."

She dropped his hand and brought hers to his chest. "To keep that from happening, would it be so horrible to see one of these therapists?"

As they stood, mere inches apart, it took all his willpower not to wrap her in his arms.

"I don't have a choice about seeing someone. It's a requirement for going back," he said. "But honestly? Pan has been a better therapist than any human I've ever talked to."

She took a step closer and he could have buried his nose in her hair if he'd wanted to. She smelled like a buffet of comfort—sunshine and bakeries, a touch of cinnamon and the faintest underpinning of flowers. Her body didn't touch him, but she radiated heat and *his* body responded in pure desire.

"I don't know if Gabe is right—that you *should* stay here," she said. "But I want you to."

"After knowing me two days? Why?"

"So I can know you for three days. So you can stay here with Pan where she's happiest. So I can be here to cheer when you figure out how to get back to your crew."

Whether it was the emotional safety her sincerity and understanding evoked, or whether he was simply falling like a shallow teenager for a beautiful girl, he suddenly wanted her against him. He wanted to touch her face, her scented hair.

"The problem is, I'm not convinced there's anything to find in my memories except a guy that's scared to jump into a fire. A jump crew is an extremely close group that depends on each other, and they don't have time to coddle a coward."

They stood so close he could see immediately the blaze of irritation when it flashed into her eyes. It shocked him after the pure empathy that had been there.

"You are what you believe you are, so stop telling yourself you're a coward. I've been around Gabe and heard plenty about the men he helps. Firefighter. Soldier. There is so much you all deal with that I couldn't begin to handle. You were injured, Damien. In multiple ways. That is not cowardice. Whether this latest injury—and that's what it is—stems from fighting fires or still from fighting in the Middle East, it doesn't matter. For God's sake, give yourself a break."

It was hard to comprehend that she was riled up because she was defending him. The group he'd been part of that year with Gabe had been full of affirmations and justifications along with the tough love. But it had all come from other servicemen or therapists. Kelly didn't even know him and yet she'd been standing up for him all night. As humbling as that was, her Nosy Nellie/Kind-hearted Kelly, buttinsky personality felt like clear air he needed to breathe.

"What makes you so sure you should defend me?"

"You love your horse. You love your mom." She grinned then, her irritation vanishing. "What else matters?"

He gave up and rested his forehead against hers.

"People who love their moms have turned up as murderers."

"Not you. If you were a creep, I'd know it. Told you, it's my superpower."

The last words turned to physical touch against his lips—puffs of breath faintly scented with Scotch. He stared at her inviting mouth, and hard shivers dove to his belly.

"I—"

Her kiss on the corner of his mouth interrupted the thought, and he turned into her with a groan of surrender. She rose onto her toes and opened her mouth without hesitation, inviting him in to share the lingering taste of alcohol. Sexy as hell. The blood rushed to his head, removing any hope of wisdom banishing foolishness. The willingness of her full lips, the sure slide of the hands ran up the front of his chest and around to the back of his head, and the hard play of her tongue against his shot heat into his groin, pooled in his belly, weakened his joints. He couldn't pull away, nor did she ask him to.

Their tongues danced more eagerly. Seconds turned to minutes, turned to deep exploration. Their hands joined in, sifting through hair, pulling each other closer. He traced down her spine and cupped her butt, pulling her close enough to cause a purely erotic gasp from her but not quite close enough to allow her the full feel of his all-male reaction. When his breath threatened to shudder into an audible moan, reality finally crashed in. He pulled away, holding her cheeks with his palms, smiling in regret.

"I'm sorry," she said before he could speak. "That was my fault."

"It didn't feel like a fault to me. I thought maybe it was part of your superpowers."

"I don't usually wield them this soon." She flushed again, prettily. "Although my sisters think I do."

"You might have noticed I didn't exactly try to fight them."

The tiniest shade of uncertainty crept into her expressive eyes. They changed visibly with every mood, he noticed. Big, beautiful brown eyes...

"I didn't make things weird?"

He chuckled. "I don't know what to make of you. Or of me when I'm with you. It's been a long time since I wanted to do that much with a girl. It wasn't weird, Kelly. It was a damn good kiss."

Slowly he bent again, stroked his thumb outward from the corner of her lips, and slipped another kiss onto her willing mouth. This time he kept it sweet even though she invited him deeper again. He wanted deeper. He wanted to push this brand-new desire onto the thick quilt behind them and into much, much more.

"This is all good enough that we're leaving it at that before we find out good leads to great."

"Great would be...pretty great."

"Kelly Crockett. You're not a bad therapist yourself."

"Oh, no I'm not. I can pry and I can listen, but I haven't helped you solve anything."

"That's not your job. And I don't want to ruin those kisses by talking about me any more tonight."

"Will you still come riding with me in the morning?"

"Sure. There's still a mystery to solve. How about if I don't see you downstairs beforehand, I meet you in the barn at eight?"

"Yeah, perfect."

It was hard to leave her. The fact that he'd opened up and even now that she knew his dark secret she hadn't run in the opposite direction, gave him hope that there was hope.

It wouldn't last, the feeling of redemption. He was thinking with the part of his anatomy that sent endorphins out to addle a man's brain. But even that was healing. It had been a long time since sex had meant anything significant.

"See you in the morning," he said and stepped back. "Just so you know. I think you really might have some superpowers."

"Wow," was all she said.

He closed her door behind him and stared down at the floor, mildly lightheaded. He hadn't lied, she did have some kind of weird power over him. It sure as hell didn't fix the future, but when he flopped onto his bed and stared at the ceiling, he felt normal—uncomfortable at the moment, but close to normal. And if his problems were far from over, his mind was, at least, as easy as it had been in a while.

Chapter Thirteen

THE MORNING WAS cool and slightly overcast with a mild threat of showers when he and Kelly rode out of the ranch yard the next morning. Grand Teton in the distance wore a hat of sulky gray clouds, but Damien believed they'd dodge the rain. He'd gotten pretty good at sensing the weather. Nobody could read it a hundred percent of the time, but when a fire crew had to choose a direction in which to concentrate efforts, the wind, the temperature, the clouds, the smoke all played a part in telling them what was coming. This morning he'd staked his semi-decent prognostication reputation on declaring the sun would shine by noon.

He'd worried the atmosphere with her would be awkward after the previous night, but Kelly proved she wasn't a person who dwelled on the awkward. She'd greeted him with a happy smile and though she didn't mention the kiss, she moved around him with the comfort of an old friend. They readied the horses, joking and teasing, and in the ease, Damien felt as much joy as relief.

It had been a long time since mornings had brought happiness. Better yet, when they were underway, he felt no guilt this time at admiring her swaying riding style or the well-worn, fitted jeans with the hole next to the right back pocket. Even the gentle up-and-down motion of her feet, so easy in the stirrups, was sexy, and the frayed hems of her jeans resting over the tops of her cowboy boots—a faded turquoise-green—attractive. She had on some kind of red-plaid jacket with a short fleece collar, stopping just above her rocking hips, and she'd topped everything off with a brown cowboy hat that was as well-loved as the rest of her outfit. To Damien, the whole picture was perfect, and sexy enough for a fashion magazine.

"You promise we're not going to get wet?" she asked as they rounded the base of the mountain that led to Ancestor Canyon and faced a looming thunderhead that hadn't been visible before.

He studied the thick-bellied clouds and nodded.

"It's all moving southeast," he said, and then pointed to the right. "Look. Watch the thinning clouds over there. Another hour and a half or so and the sun is going to win out. The front is pushing all that in our direction long before the storm clouds are ready to burst."

But as he studied the moving clouds, he stopped and his heart lurched in concern. Behind the thinning clouds he'd just been admiring hung a gray-yellow haze. It was barely noticeable to anyone who hadn't seen that warning sign a hundred times.

"He's a rider, he's a fireman, he's a cook, he's a weather dude… What? Do you see something else? Are you wrong?"

"The color of the clearing area," he said simply. "What does it look like to you?"

"Like hope." She grinned. "I packed a rain poncho, but I don't want to use it."

"I'm serious. Can you see the color—the way the light is yellowish?"

"I guess." She squinted.

"Smoke," he said. "You heard about those fires in Idaho."

"What? They aren't supposed to be that close." Her eyes widened in concern.

"That's not necessarily direct smoke from a fire. But it's drifting haze. It means the closest fires are either growing or changing direction."

"How close are they?"

"Last I read, they're a hundred and fifty miles from here."

"That's good, right?"

"It is. But they're worth watching."

"You're still monitoring the wildfires?"

"It's a hard habit to break. I haven't looked for a day and a half. I'll see what's going on when we get back. I'm sure Cole and Ty watch pretty closely every season. And the VA, where Gabe and Mia are, is even farther west, so they'll be watching, too. I haven't heard that Wyoming is in a fire path. But fires don't read projection maps."

"So we're safe to go on."

He smiled. "We're safe to go on."

They reached the canyon forty-five minutes later and stopped beside the pond outside the entrance. Damien kept his eyes on the sky, which continued to clear but also retained the haziness that mildly concerned him. The smoke drift wasn't thick, but it felt heavier than something that came from hundreds of miles away. Still, there was no scent of smoke and no variation in the color, so it also wasn't close.

He turned to Kelly, who had stopped worrying about potential fire, for which he was grateful, and was eyeing the canyon entrance pensively.

"Everything okay?" he asked.

"Fine. I'm stupidly nervous. I don't know whether I want proof that the camper is gone or to find something that will help identify him. I guess I hope he's gone. I expect he will be."

"I can't imagine they stayed," he said. "If they're looking for the bag, it means they found your note. That would pretty likely have convinced them to move on."

"Yeah, maybe."

They entered the canyon and Damien still felt the majesty of entering the natural walled room. This morning the floor of the canyon was dramatically cast in shadows since the sun hadn't quite moved overhead. The high rock walls threw pointed areas of dark and light across the space and the beauty took his breath away.

They rode directly to the campfire and dismounted, tying Pan and Jellyman to the same tree they'd used days before. They knelt together beside the pit and Damien checked. This time the ashes were perfectly cold.

"This hasn't been used today, at least," Kelly said.

"But it has been used sometime since we were here two days ago. There are pieces of wood here that aren't fully burned." He turned one over with his hands and stared. Crumpled in a hollow between two pieces of wood was a wad of heavy paper. "Hey, check this out."

He took out the paper ball and handed it to Kelly. She carefully opened up the wad. A few scorched edges crumbled to the ground but once smoothed, the content was clear. A drawing of a grulla-colored horse, matching those from the sketchbook that had been in the backpack. This one had a long, black line slashed through it, clearly indicating the artist hadn't been happy with it.

"I don't know if this is totally cool or a little creepy," Kelly said.

"Creepy?"

"Somebody is hanging around here drawing hundreds of pictures of horses, all the same color and type. It's like an obsessed person drawing ghosts—they just happen to be of mustangs."

"At least they're not skulls or bloody dead things. It gives me a little more confidence we aren't dealing with a serial killer."

He laughed at the evil eye she shot at him. "I thought I was being weird."

"The whole thing is weird," he said. "Might as well join in. And here, we can add to the mystery even more. There's this second ring of rocks around the first. This person is not only still camping here, they're improving the site."

"Oh my gosh. You're right."

Kelly stood up and walked slowly around the campfire pit, searching the ground, kicking at tufts of grass. A couple of times she squatted and ran fingers in a patch of dirt. Damien studied her movements, not sure what she was looking for. He could tell the grass was still trampled, but not how recently.

"Here," she said suddenly, squatting about twenty feet from the fire. "Come see."

He moved to squat beside her and she pointed to a set of two hoofprints, one slightly behind the other.

"Horses," he said. "We knew some had been in here."

She took his hand then and placed it over the print

and then singled out his pointer finger. She grinned when he raised his brows at her.

"You could do this yourself. I've been trying to manufacture a reason to touch you all morning."

He swallowed a laugh and hid the shiver from her touch. "Let's just get this out there right now. We kissed. We liked it. You don't have to manufacture a reason."

"Okay." She stroked her thumb along the knuckle of the finger she held. "That's good to know. For now, feel this. There's a deeper ridge around the edge of the print."

He let her run his finger around the outside of the depression, ignoring the tiny zips of pleasure she left behind at her touch. "Yeah. I feel what you mean."

"This horse was wearing shoes. It wasn't a mustang or a herd this time."

"So...you're saying maybe this person is riding a horse?"

"That's my guess." She dropped his hand and rocked back on her heels, resting her arms on her raised knees. "It seems like this is someone who's on some kind of quest. He wants something he's only finding here, and staying until he's done." She glanced at Damien, narrowed her eyes, and bit her lip thoughtfully. "We could solve the whole thing by waiting for him to come back."

"Didn't we once nix that idea because we'd starve?"

She laughed and waggled her brows, then headed to Jellyman and pulled her saddlebag off the back of the saddle.

"Sit," she said and pointed to the ground beside the fire circle. "I'm way ahead of you."

Reaching into one of the saddlebag pouches, she pulled out two plastic containers. One held a rich purple mound of fresh blueberries. The second held half a dozen chocolate chip cookies.

"I got up early," she said.

"You…" Damien went right for the cover of the cookie container, his mouth watering when the fresh-baked scent wafted to his nose. "You made these?"

"I did. So we wouldn't starve."

He sighed as the still-gooey chocolate melted against his tongue. "I swear, you don't need to go to any three-star restaurant to be a world-renown chef. These would make you plenty famous."

Pleasure filled her eyes. "You can't go too wrong with chocolate chip cookies. Although world-famous might be pushing it."

"Who needs more than food you make from the heart? Thank you. I think you made my morning, even if we don't know who's squatting on your land."

"You're welcome."

He finished another cookie and leaned back on his elbows, checking the sky again. The yellow haze had burned off some and he released a sigh of relief before turning back to stare at the fire ring. "So what's here that our mystery person would want?"

"I've been trying to imagine. Grass. Protection. Solitude. Horses—if what we decided the other day was true, that a herd has been in here."

"Maybe he buried a body somewhere. Have we looked for disturbed ground?"

She shot him another dirty look. "Seriously? What is wrong with you? No bodies. No skulls or evidence of evil ceremonies, thank you."

"That cuts out a lot of possibilities."

"Let's hope so. Wow, you're a messy eater."

She touched the pad of her thumb to the corner of his

mouth and gave it a firm wipe. At the unexpected jolt, he froze, letting the electricity flash through him.

"Chocolate." She shrugged. "Slob."

He caught her hand as it trailed away, bent closer to her, and pressed his newly chocolate-free lips to hers. The thrill from the previous night returned, but there was no shock this time. She responded as if she'd been waiting for him, and opened her mouth, slipping her tongue eagerly into his. The sensation built, slowly and steadily, second by heated second, until waves of pleasure dove deep into his core.

She roamed with her tongue—brushing it against his, exploring his inner cheek, deepening the kiss but then drawing back to suck oh-so-lightly on his bottom lip. When she delved back in, the pleasure-building started all over again.

He gave back, relishing their mingled breath and touching her where he could, hair, cheeks, temples, and just when he wished he could get closer, Kelly let escape a demanding groan and broke the kiss. It was only long enough to turn and climb boldly onto his lap, face him, and place both palms on his cheeks before sealing her mouth once more against his. If he'd had any doubt their pleasure was equally shared, she erased all doubt by rolling her hips forward and fitting against him like a perfect little puzzle piece.

The solitude, the wildness of the surroundings, drove away all inhibitions, and Damien allowed the heat in his body to rise along with the pulse of desire that moved deeper, hardening his body, pushing him toward the brink of self-control. Kelly's soft sounds egged him on. The pressure of her soft femininity again his heat made it nearly impossible to stop. But he had to. The next step was not one either was ready to take whether they wanted to or not.

"Hey, you," he said, drawing back, whispering against her lips. He pulled away but allowed her to bob back and feather his mouth with final kisses as long as she could before they were too far apart. "We need to put on the brakes."

"Why would we want to do that?" Her words teased, but she also dropped her head, rested it for a handful of seconds against his chest, and then swung off his lap.

"Wanting to and needing to are different things."

"Yeah." She offered a smile, and he relaxed. She wasn't upset. She didn't regret the moment. She touched his hand and continued. "Look, I don't usually climb onto a man's lap this soon after meeting him. I don't know what... No, I do know. It was nice. Way more than nice. It's felt good to be desired."

Her words burrowed deep into his heart and nestled in as if they'd found a home. She was more right than she knew—it felt very good to be desired. But this desire, between them, was only a momentary shelter from the storm. He couldn't let himself forget that.

"It's very good," he agreed out loud. "But attraction and desire also make good hiding places, Kelly Crockett. You and I both are here to hide, let's be honest."

Her fingers fell away from his hand. "That kind of puts a damper on a pretty great kiss. Damien Finney."

"No. I don't mean to put a damper on anything about that. Believe me, I had to force myself to stop. The desire was—is real. But we shouldn't put too much meaning into it. We shouldn't try and figure out or decide what happens next."

"Don't you tell me we can't do that again some time."

She was staring at the ground between her bent knees, but cocked her head very slightly and eyed him with enough playfulness to show she understood. The way she always did.

"Don't we have a date tomorrow night?" he asked. "I think we're past the point where I have to wonder if I can kiss you goodnight."

"Gives me hope, at least."

"Neither of us lives here, Kelly. I might not stay past tomorrow and you...I don't even know what big things you have planned."

"Neither do I," she murmured.

"That's what I mean. We're hiding out, avoiding decisions. Don't get me wrong. I like hiding with you, even though you talk too much and you're not my type."

He leaned sideways to give her a playful bump. She laughed.

"That's okay. You're mostly too serious and not my type either. Guess we're an imperfect match."

They packed up the food after that and decided the camper wasn't likely to show up if they were sitting by his fire ring.

"I wish I really were a detective," Kelly said as they mounted Pan and Jellyman for the ride home. "At least then I'd have an idea what the next step would be."

"I suppose the person may just knock on the door next time."

"Sure." Kelly snorted. "Let's go with that plan."

Despite the way they'd fallen into too deep an analysis of their kiss for Damien's comfort, Kelly gave no indication that she'd been bothered by their talk. She returned to her talkative self, keeping the conversation animated and unimportant. Part of him wished for quiet so he could get his emotions back in check, admittedly the lively tour guide beside him made sure no demons got loose in his brain. He feared the demons.

Just before one o'clock, they entered a quiet house with an empty kitchen.

"It's nap time for Little Sadie and Grandma sometimes takes one, too," Kelly said. "I'm sure everyone has eaten, so how about we search for something more substantial than cookies and fruit?"

"I'm not stupid. If you're cooking, my mouth is watering."

Kelly had promised to help Grace again in a few hours, but Damien didn't necessarily need to accompany her since Liam was available to help prep. After she rooted through the refrigerator for several minutes, Kelly surfaced with ingredients for a gourmet frittata.

"This will change your worldview on eggs and cheese," she told him.

"Sounds like a pretty bold statement."

"I'm pretty confident."

"So you always are." A new voice startled them both and Kelly turned to the kitchen doorway with a gasp.

"Rocky?"

Kelly was across the room in seconds and had her arms around yet another vision that made Damien think he needed to blink away double vision. Raquel fell into their hug and the sisters held each other for long seconds. When they parted, Damien shook his head. They really were uncannily identical.

"I can't believe you're here," Kelly said. "You didn't warn me."

"Oh, I tried." Raquel folded her arms. "I couldn't get

you to call, so I decided to track you down in person."

Damien couldn't tell if Raquel was honestly as miffed as her words seemed to indicate because she also smiled, although it wasn't the open, happy smile Kelly always wore. He didn't hear more, however, because Bella entered the kitchen and pointed happily at Damien.

"There you both are! Kelly, how do you like your surprise? Damien Finney, you're a wanted man."

"Excuse me?" He stared.

Bella laughed. "Cole wants to see you. He's working in the den and I promised I'd send you in when you got here."

"Called to the principal's office, huh?" Raquel asked and sent him a warm smile. "Hello, Damien, I'm sorry. I've been rude to ignore you."

"You weren't rude," he said quietly. "Sounds like you're right, though. We'll have to catch up later. I've been summoned."

"We'll all go with you," Bella said. "Joely's there, too. I guess she has some news, too."

"Can't be all that dire then." Damien smiled but didn't feel it. Cole was bound to push the question of Damien staying on, and if he was marshaling the Crockett troops...

"Nope." Raquel looped an arm around Kelly's and propelled her toward the door. "Dire comes later when I get my sister alone."

Chapter Fourteen

KELLY SLOWLY FOLLOWED Damien into the impressive, solidly masculine home office of Paradise Ranch and took in the space that had been a comforting haven since her childhood. The dark mahogany wainscoting and ultra-classic burgundy-and-navy-blue décor had been in place since her father had built the house nearly forty years earlier. She remembered sitting in the overstuffed leather chairs or lounging on the huge sofa with books or homework, safely ensconced in the warm, dark space while her dad worked. Once in a while, there'd been time for a game of checkers and later, chess with him. She hadn't been in here since coming home this time, and she smiled at the memories despite the unwelcome nerves still assailing her over Raquel's unexpected appearance. She and their mother entered behind Kelly and waved at Joely, who already sat on the couch.

Cole sat at the massive desk, made of the same mahogany as the wood on the walls, and looked up from the papers before him. As the official ranch managers, he and Harper acted as the heirs to Sam Crockett's legacy, and after nearly four years of running Paradise since Sam's death, Cole had as stellar a reputation as all three of the previous Crockett patriarchs. Their pictures hung on the wall opposite the desk: Eli, who'd founded Paradise, his son Sebastian who was Grandma Sadie's late husband, and Sam, father of six daughters. The portraits made an impressive triad of watchful guardians.

"Welcome!" Cole stood and rounded to the front of the desk. He offered Damien a hearty handshake and Kelly a warm hug. "Did you two have a good ride? Anything new to report?"

Her mother and Raquel sat beside Joely, and Kelly shook her head.

"Not much. Our uninvited camper is apparently still there—the fire pit is more elaborate now, ringed with more rocks and clearly used since we were there last. At least everything was cold this time. There was no sign of him or any belongings."

"Do you think we need to get the sheriff out there?" Cole asked.

"Not yet. I'd rather not scare him away. If we can keep a quiet eye on things maybe we can discover who it is."

"I might know someone who can help with that," Joely said. "It's one reason I wanted to be sure and see you today. I did go to John Red Wolf's place to see that horse I told you about."

"John Red Wolf," he repeated. "The man Grandma Sadie told me about."

"I promised I'd ask if you could meet with him, and while I was there I heard the most amazing story. And the horse nearly shocked me to death."

"Why?" Kelly sat beside Joely. "What's wrong with

her?"

"She had a simple hoof abscess and it'll be fine. Her health wasn't the issue. What got to me is that she is a dead ringer for Pan."

On a more common color of horse—bay, black, chestnut, pinto—Joely's report wouldn't have been noteworthy. Grullas, however, like palominos or buckskins, were more genetically unusual.

"You're kidding."

"I'm not." Joely's eager grin held surprises. "When I say 'dead ringer' I mean this girl's got the same build, same bald face, and that gorgeous, wise eye. Even three white socks and the silvery color instead of the dark, matte gray. She's as like Pan as you're like Grace and Raquel."

"That's freaky," Kelly said.

Damien's brow knotted. "Where's the sketch we found?" he asked.

"Oh, right!" She shifted and fished the piece of sketchbook paper out of her pocket. After unfolding it, she held it out. "When we found the backpack the other day, there was a sketchbook inside of it filled with drawings of horses. Every single one was a grulla. Today we found this page balled up and thrown into the fire pit."

"I swear these horses are following me around," Damien said. "I've started to wonder if they mean something. Aren't there such things as spirit animals?"

"If you have one, I always thought it was Pan," Bella said. "You have such a connection with her."

"I don't know about a spirit animal," Joely sat forward on her seat. "But I might have part of an answer. Or a clue. Maybe. John told me there's been a legend among the local Shoshone for the last three generations about the "Cloud Band." It's supposed to be a herd of gray horses that wanders the great Teton basin. The story handed down is that these are mystical horses with the power to bring healing, joy, fortune, and wisdom when they pass through an area. But they're fleet-footed and stealthy, and few people have ever seen them all together. Some offspring of the powerful stallions leave and mingle with other herds. Old stories also said they're protected by the Great Spirit and kept sacred, and secret, so they can spread their gifts without being hunted or tamed. The only exceptions occur once in a great while when a lucky human bonds with one.

Kelly had grown up hearing stories of the west and legends of the indigenous people her whole life. She'd never put more store in them than she had in morality or fairy tales. All cultures had mythologies that explained the inexplicable. This one, however, gave her chills.

Something true and exciting came through in Joely's telling of it; it was as if her sister actually believed what John Red Wolf had told her.

"So, I'm one of the lucky few."

She studied Damien, who looked, with his fixed gaze and a palm over his mouth, as if he'd seen a vision. She could see he, too, had been affected by the story.

"Could be. When I told John about Pan, he reacted as if we'd found gold in his backyard. He's always believed his horse, Bird of the Gray Sky, is descended from the Cloud Band. He says you have Pan for a reason. He'd like to meet you."

"*Meet* me?"

"And Pan. There's no mystical reason for it. He simply said he's always wanted to meet another Cloud Horse owner."

"When does he want to meet?" Kelly asked.

"Anytime. There are no timelines. No deadlines. Those were his words."

"Sounds like a chill dude," Damien said.

"Very. He's seventy-six years old; he's seen a lot. He's got patience. Also his words."

Kelly could almost see Damien warring with his emotions. Now that the first impact of the story was over, reality was setting in for all of them. It was a lovely image—a band of magical grulla horses with superpowers. But how much credence did you give to a man who'd probably been making up stories for his children and grandchildren for decades? Still...

"You have to go." She reached forward and touched Damien's knee. "Just to see Pan's twin. Plus, think what John Red Wolf could tell you."

"That I have a gray horse who might have the power to heal?" He eyed her with amusement.

"You're not taking this seriously!"

"I don't believe for a second Pan can create a sudden, mystic fortune, but I know she's brought a lot of peace and happiness since I returned from Afghanistan. Is that healing? Sadly, I'm probably taking this way too seriously."

"Seriously enough to change your mind about leaving us next week?" Cole asked. "I have some ideas that might meet all your requirements for the next month."

"Aw, Cole, I don't know..." Damien looked at the floor.

"No pressure. I only want a few minutes for you to hear me out."

"All right." Damien nodded.

Kelly's heart soared. Maybe John Wolf's story combined with Cole's persuasive powers could convince

Damien to stay. Her wish made no logical sense. She couldn't be so school-girlish that two nice—extremely nice—kisses made her want to hang onto the handsome new boy in class. He had plans. He had problems. He was far too mercurial for her to stay with. Then there was her own huge set of issues and the fact that if she got the job at Opus, she would be in San Francisco. And after she finished there, if Raquel hadn't disowned her—which was not at all a sure thing—they could be building a new business anywhere.

Wanting Damien to change his plans was no more than good-time Kelly looking to keep the party going as long as she could. Except, something about this particular party didn't feel like fun and games.

"Come on, Kel, let's leave them to negotiate." Joely stood and smiled at Damien. "Hope you'll get a chance to meet John. I think you'll like him. You'll definitely enjoy his stories."

"Thanks, Joely. I'd like to."

"Before you all go, just one more official ranch thing." Cole sat on the edge of his desk. "I've been watching the fire status reports. I'm guessing you all have, too. Overnight, the fire in eastern Idaho got fanned by strong winds, and it's grown from eight hundred acres to almost two-thousand. It's not contained at this point, but crews are on it."

"How far away?" Bella asked.

"A hundred miles from our northwest boundary— quite a ways from here. I don't expect it to really affect us, but we all need to stay on top of the news."

"That explains the haze this morning," Damien said. "I thought it was from those smaller fires in northern Montana. Guess it was a little closer."

Kelly shared a worried look with him. "Too scary for me, even if they aren't in our backyard. We were right to be paranoid about those warm ashes. Maybe someone should keep watch for the Ancestor Canyon camper."

"I think we need to keep an eye on the spot," Cole agreed. "Maybe a ride down there every day or two until we find them or make sure they've left."

"We'll make sure someone checks it out," Kelly said.

"Thanks," Cole said. "As long as we're all careful and vigilant, I doubt we'll see any action, but it's been dry this summer and we all know that means unpredictability. That's all I have. Report anything you hear. Meanwhile, life as usual."

Bella, Raquel, and Joely each touched Damien on the shoulder as they left. Raquel gave Cole a hug.

"Thanks for taking such good care of Paradise," she said.

"A team effort," he replied. "Glad to have you home for a bit."

Kelly offered a small smile of encouragement as she made to follow her sisters. "I hope he has a really good deal for you, Damien," she said, low enough nobody else could hear. "I'd miss you if you left already."

True to character, he didn't say anything, but he pulled back one corner of his mouth in a quarter smile and nodded almost imperceptibly.

***

Damien faced Cole and shored up what resolve he had left. He'd always liked Cole Wainwright and his direct, easy-going style of management. Of all the men who'd recently become part of the Paradise story, he was the only true working cowboy. He'd grown up on the Double Diamond, a neighboring ranch, and worked it with his father until it had been sold to the Crocketts years ago. Now the Double Diamond was the site of Harper's community arts center, and she and Cole were bringing it and Paradise fully into the twenty-first century, complete with wind and solar power, new ranching methods, and humane animal care. Paradise Ranch was a good operation to be part of as it grew from being a giant player to an enormous one in beef and food production.

Damien, however, had come to this meeting steeled to give a firm no to any offer Cole made. He'd been given a plan and sticking to it only seemed prudent. Suddenly, he had a crazy story in his head about magic mustangs, and although he didn't believe the damn story, he couldn't shake the feeling that he needed to meet this Red Wolf fellow. The same way he couldn't shake the belief that Panacea was not an ordinary horse—not to him. Wasn't the idea that he'd come to let her heal him just as crazy as listening to a story about a herd of horses?

"Thanks for hanging back," Cole began. "I know this family can come on pretty strong, and we haven't given you much of a break since you arrived."

"It's always been good to be here," Damien said. "Everyone's supportive and I do appreciate it."

"Especially Kelly."

He smiled. "She's a force."

Cole sputtered. "Kelly is pretty special. I only wish she knew it. She desperately wants to be famous, but she already is."

The observation struck a nerve. He'd never considered that Kelly didn't see herself as successful. Her hyperactivity had simply seemed to be drive and determination.

"She has goals," he said. "Hard not to admire that."

"Every one of them has a lot to admire, but I'm telling you from experience—once a Crockett woman gets under your skin, she's like a dangerous addiction. I should start this whole conversation with 'get out while you can.'"

"I appreciate the warning. But I don't think a Crockett woman is what will determine me staying or leaving."

He wasn't entirely certain that was true.

"You want to leave."

"I...I don't know. Part of me thinks that might be best."

"Believe it or not, I understand. We run a huge ranch, Damien, but we're a small family. We live on top of each other, and we men—Gabe, Alec, Ty, and I—have learned the hard way that we don't have room or time to keep secrets. So, we maybe know too much about each other...and our friends."

Damien shifted uneasily, but Cole held up a hand.

"I'm not asking for your story," he said. "Gabe has told me enough so I could decide if I even wanted to put more pressure on you. You're working past a fear of jumping, and your crew captain is requiring you to seek counseling. There's no judgment here, Damien, and that information stays with me until you share it. I just know others have repeated the offer to stay at Paradise so I need to make my final offer in person.

Damien's mind churned and his stomach knotted with nerves. He calmed them both with effort and annoyance. A grown man should be able to make his own decisions without this much inner turmoil. When it came right down to it, he owed nothing to Stone Rayburn or anyone but himself. He was perfectly capable of listening to a proposal and accepting or rejecting it.

"All right." He bent his knee and propped one booted

foot atop his thigh with as much nonchalance as he could fake. "What's the offer?"

"We have enclosed a one-thousand-acre section of land that hasn't been used for grazing in the past forty years, and we're expanding our herd by two hundred to give Mia's and Harper's foray into organic beef a try. We also want to add goats and chickens over time. If things work out, we'll eventually hire a manager or dedicated hand for the organics, but in the very short term I need help getting the new herd settled."

"Where is this thousand-acre section?"

"Not far by car—maybe twenty minutes northwest. It's a longer horseback ride—perhaps two hours. It's near one of the seven cabins we have spread across the ranch property. There's a well and a generator so it has water and rudimentary electricity, but no plumbing yet. What I'd like to have is someone willing to stay out there maybe two nights a week and keep tabs on the fencing, waterers, and new babies."

"Babies?"

"We'll have a hundred certified organic steer: fifty cows and around fifty calves. We need to keep an eye on them for any health issues. We need to immediately remove sick or injured animals so we can treat them. If we can no longer certify them as organic, we'll add them to our regular herd."

"What makes you think I have the expertise to handle a job like that?"

"What you need to know about the cattle we can teach you. Here's the honest reason I think it would be a good fit for you. You'll have time by yourself if you need it, but you'll also have a family behind you. Your room here in the house will remain yours until you don't want it. You can easily get into town to check in with professionals the way your captain requires. You'll be close to your horse. And you can stay at Paradise as long as you like or leave anytime."

"You don't want someone who's just going to up and leave you shorthanded in a few weeks." Damien's objections were weakening. The offer wasn't intimidating, and the idea of an isolated cabin wasn't entirely unappealing.

"This is really about you. If you can get back to your Montana crew next month, we'll be happy for you. If you want to stay here for a year? That's fine, too. If you do decide to take me up on this, all I'd ask is that you give me the time until you have to decide if you're going back to Montana."

Damien wasn't sure what to say. The offer was more generous than anything he'd get anywhere else.

"I'll match the salary you were getting in Montana," Cole continued. "Pan and Apollo included."

"I'll continue paying for them."

He caught the slip as soon as he'd said it. *I'll continue to…* As if his subconscious had decided for him.

"You don't have to decide this moment."

"I'll stay."

Cole's brows lifted in surprise and his mouth tilted with pleasure. "You're certain?"

"I'll be perfectly honest since you've been open with me. I don't know what I want. I sure as hell don't know what I need. But your family is the best one I know. Staying here sounds like the smartest option I have."

Cole stood and strode around the desk. Damien rose as well and took the proffered hand.

"I'm not going to lie, this makes me pretty happy,"

Cole said.

"I'll do my best for you."

"That was never in doubt. Just know we'll do our best for you, too. And if we go too Brady Bunch on you, just tell us to back off."

"I can do that."

Cole ran a hand across the back of his neck and gave another laugh. "You know. There is one other thing you could do and your problems would be over."

"Oh?"

"Have a Crockett girl adopt you and just stay with us. Four of us have done it now, and despite what I said earlier, it's a sweeter deal than the one I offered."

Damien must have looked as surprised as he felt because Cole gave a hearty laugh and clapped him lightly on one shoulder.

"I'm joking, Damien. It's my way of telling you that I might have made the job offer, but none of us ever forgets that the women run the place. They're smart and they're fierce in their ways. Mia and Harper made up the force that together first suggested we ask you."

He found himself flattered that it wasn't only the men who wanted him.

"I'll be sure to thank Mia and Harper."

"They'll be happy, too. Do you want to start tomorrow—for the morning? I could show you the new business plan and let you start learning the ins and outs of raising organic, grass-fed beef." He shook his head in amusement. "Harper insists it's gonna make us rich."

"Aren't you already?" Damien took a chance teasing his new boss, but it felt natural. It also felt as if a small piece of his constant inner worry had eased.

"That's what we let people think. The truth is, we

don't hemorrhage money every second anymore. We make enough to buy two hundred organic cows. But I still need a new pair of boots."

"Well, all I ask is you give me a heads up if I'm gonna have to take a pay cut."

"I like you, man," Cole laughed. "I think you'll fit right in around this place."

Chapter Fifteen

"COME OUTSIDE WITH ME."

Raquel gave Kelly no time to process any of what had happened in the short meeting with Cole. Nor did she have time to worry about what might happen when Cole asked Damien to stay. It was stupid to be concerned, for all the reasons she'd already processed. Far better to dread a talk with her closest sister.

"Sure," she said, slipping a bright voice into place. "I'm still so excited you're here."

They moved to the large back deck, and Raquel brought two cups of espresso, handed one to Kelly, and leaned against the deck railing holding her cup between both palms. They'd been best friends since before they'd been born, and the awkward space between them hurt worse the larger it grew. Kelly stood beside Raquel and looked out over the backyard, a huge expanse of brown-green, landscaped beautifully thanks to their mother's deft green thumb, but drier than normal. Cole had been right about the lack of rain this summer.

"All right, this is insane," she said at last. "Are you still angry with me for leaving you behind and going to San Francisco?"

"No."

"Then why are you here ready to lecture me, and why are we on tenterhooks with each other?"

"I'm mad because you've barely told me a single thing about what happened when you were in San Francisco. You haven't even asked how things are going in Denver. And…you haven't told me a thing about Damien Finney."

"Damien?"

"Come on. Mom said you two have been together for three solid days."

"It's just sort of happened. Come on, Rocky, that's not what we're here to talk about."

She looked back out across the yard. "Okay. Right. I'm not here to lecture. I came to ask you to come back to Denver. I found a bank that will give us a small business loan extension above and beyond our insurance payout. The adjusters have gone over the damage and insurance will cover the replacement and upgrade of all the equipment. We can repair Triple Bean and start saving again to make it what you want."

Kelly's breath caught in her chest, but as quickly as the excitement flowed, it ebbed again. If she went back to Triple Bean now, it would end her chance to work at a top restaurant and get back into gourmet cooking. She'd always thought that just expanding their little restaurant would allow them to grow the way she wanted. But after working with Landon O'Keefe, and even after stretching her wings the littlest bit at Grace's restaurant, she knew she needed more time and more training. She had no exact plan, however, and that was the problem. How could she possibly mollify Raquel if she said she didn't want to return to Colorado yet?

"This is great news," she said. "I knew you were our financial genius."

"Not a genius. I found out I was just really angry about the fire. And super stubborn."

"I think there was stubbornness in the amniotic fluid around all three of us in the womb." Kelly laughed.

"For sure."

Their silence settled again, a little easier this time, but Kelly still had to steel herself for the next words. "What if I'm not ready to come back quite yet?"

She made herself meet Raquel's eyes with a calm assurance she didn't feel.

"What does 'quite yet' mean?"

"Landon made a suggestion. Before I venture out with a bigger restaurant of my own, I need to do another internship, but he doesn't have a position right now. He gave me the name of a chef closer to Los Angeles. I'm waiting to hear back from him."

"You'd be gone for months. How is that supposed to work?"

She turned to her sister and took the coffee cup from her, set it on the railing, and grasped both Rocky's hands in hers.

"It could be the very best thing. It's going to be a little while until Triple Bean is ready to open again. During that time, you could work on an 'opening new and better' marketing campaign. We can change the name. We can advertise—"

"We are not changing our name! Kel, that's our brand. That's who we are."

"It's not who we were always going to be. You

remember our plans."

"Your plans."

Just as she had right after the fire, Kelly felt the sting of betrayal, only more definite this time.

"I always thought we were in this together. You, Grace, and me. You knew what I wanted to do eventually."

"And I thought we'd all grown up and found a little reality." Raquel's face set in a determined frown. "We made something unique and very successful, and we all loved it."

"Until Grace didn't."

Raquel stared fiercely at the deck floor. "And until you didn't."

"That's not fair. When was the last time we really talked about the future? Before the fire, I mean. Why would you think I had changed my dreams?"

"You loved coming up with our new dishes."

"Our new sandwiches you mean? They're *sandwiches*, for crying out loud. I know how to riff on Beef Bourguignon or pheasant under glass. I don't want to spend my life upgrading grilled cheese."

Raquel sighed. "You used to say that you loved watching people eat for pleasure. Eat the comfort food, the food that tasted like it was made with love. I thought you'd found your calling."

"I want people to love my food. I want them to be impressed, too. I don't want to be in the shadow of a grill and a line cook."

"Sometimes I think it's all about shadows for you. You don't want to be in anyone's shadow ever, do you?"

The way she said it, with the slightest hint of derision and the barest tinge of anger, brought a sting to Kelly's eyes. She'd known for months an honest talk about the future was imminent, but she'd never imagined they'd have it with such animosity.

"What's that supposed to mean? I'm selfish? For having a dream?"

"I'm sorry, Kel. I didn't mean it that way."

"Then what way?"

"It's like you think you aren't good enough unless you're impressing someone."

"I am good enough, though. I want to impress people, sure, but I wouldn't be telling you my thoughts for the future if I didn't think I could do it. I don't know why you can't see that this is about you, too. I don't want to do this without you."

"I don't want to leave Denver. I like what we built. I like where we were."

"We can work this out, Rocky."

"I'm sure."

"What would I do if I came back to Denver right now anyway?"

"Help design the new kitchen."

"I can do that from here. Besides, have you talked to Grace yet?"

"I'll see her tonight. We're all going to Peas Porridge for dinner. All of the girls."

"That's great. I'll cook for you."

"So they said." She did not sound excited, much less impressed.

Kelly sighed. She hated making Raquel unhappy. She remembered again how hurt she'd been when Grace had left—as if she'd been abandoned and was unimportant. She didn't want that for Raquel. Stepping close, she gathered her into a hug and clung. For a long few seconds,

Raquel's return embrace was stiff and angry. But it thawed, and as the hug turned warmer, the comfort flowed between them.

"I love you," Kelly said. "I'm not trying to abandon you. I want you to come with me on a new ride."

Raquel didn't answer; she just nodded against Kelly's shoulder and then pulled away to lead them back inside.

Grandma Sadie was awake and back in the kitchen with her laughing, burbling namesake beside her in the high chair.

"Sadie!" Raquel scurried to the baby's side and plopped a huge kiss on the top of her short curls. The baby held up a fist full of purply-colored puffy wafers.

"Hello, sweethearts," Grandma said. "We're having some applesauce and rice puffs. That probably isn't on the list of foods you crave, so there are some oatmeal cookies in the jar. Help yourselves."

Her stomach rumbled hungrily, and Kelly remembered she and Damien had never gotten the lunch she'd promised to make him.

"Cookies for lunch is the price I'll have to pay for being slow to cook earlier," she said. "Oh, well."

The family cookie jar was a simple, yellow crockery bean pot. It might not have been fancy, but it was big. And somebody or other in the house always managed to bake some kind of treat to keep the jar full.

"It's a wonder everyone in this place doesn't weigh three hundred pounds," Kelly said as she dipped into the stash and pulled two cookies each for herself and Raquel.

"Want one, Grandma?"

"Sure. I've only had two so far." She gave them a superior smile. "A cookie a day won't keep anyone away, but three cookies sure keep the blues at bay."

"Well, nuts to this then." Kelly held up the cookies she already had and dipped her free hand back into the yellow jar. "One more for each of us."

She set the cookies on a plate, took two clean glasses from the dishwasher, and snagged a half-gallon carton of milk on the way to the table.

"Thank you," Grandma Sadie said. "Little Miss here was making me very hungry." She made a face at the baby, who giggled like she was being tickled.

"I just hate how you torture that kid," Kelly said.

"Yes, cruelty keeps me young." Grandma looked across the table at Raquel as Kelly took a seat. "Everything's all right with you two?"

"Of course," Kelly said a little too quickly. "Why?"

"Chasing down dreams is what we all should do in life. But the chase isn't always easy—on us or on the ones we love."

The woman was so unfailingly, scarily intuitive—absolutely nothing remained hidden from her. Still, Kelly wasn't about to go into details. A rare argument with Rocky didn't need to be broadcast for the Paradise gossip chain.

"Not to worry," Raquel said, smiling at Kelly.

"Good. I hear we girls are all going out to dinner tonight. To celebrate all three of you being home at one time. I told your mother and Mia I'd babysit but that was summarily dismissed. Skylar is coming over to sit."

Kelly's phone rang from her pocket and she smiled when she saw Grace's number and put her on speaker. "It's our better third. Hey, Gracie!"

"I know you're planning to come at dinnertime," Grace said without preamble. "Is there any chance you could get Damien to come along and help again?" Her voice, far too measured and tightly controlled, failed at masking an edge of panic. She was either on a ledge about to jump off or seconds from hysterical laughter.

"I... can definitely ask him. What's happened?"

"Liam just called from the ER in Jackson. This time it's him, not his son. He sprained his ankle and is out for a couple of days. I'm so pissed. Even if my part-time cook doesn't quit, he legitimately can't even be here. I'm fine until five, but it's Saturday, and I don't think you can handle the kitchen all alone. I don't know, maybe I'm wrong. Just thought I'd ask about Damien—he was pretty handy."

"He's talking to Cole. When they're done, I'll see what he's doing."

"Thank you, Kelly. I will owe you my firstborn after all this. You've saved me every day so far."

"Yeah, we'll talk." Kelly laughed. "Don't worry. This is what family does. See you in a couple of hours."

She hung up just as Damien entered the kitchen.

"See what who's doing?" he asked.

She studied him, looking for signs of distress or trauma from his solitary meeting with Cole, but his features were calm and open.

"You. There's a minor disaster at Peas Porridge. Grace has lost another chef Temporarily." Damien winced and Kelly laughed. "Nobody's thrown up in the kitchen."

"What?" Raquel asked.

"New chef was pregnant, got morning sickness, didn't make it to the restroom, we were there for clean-up," Damien told the story in rapid-fire succinctness. "Sounds like this isn't nearly as gross."

"Sprained ankle off-site." Kelly offered a beseeching smile. "Your help was specifically requested. If you're available."

"Hey, Grace knows a great cook when she meets one." Damien spread his hands as if he'd spoken a universal truth.

"Slight correction. A good sous-cook."

"Oooh, ouch. That sounds like grounds for a competition."

"Excuse me?"

"You think I'm only a sous-chef? I challenge you. Firehouse cook vs. Three-star gonna-be."

"I like this guy," Raquel said. "He can stand up to you."

"Why are you in such a feisty mood?" Kelly asked. "This isn't the pessimistic Damien Finney I know and love."

Damien's grin was the easiest she'd ever seen it. He looked at Raquel and then Grandma Sadie. "You heard it here first, ladies. She knows me and she loves me. Let's see if that holds true after I prove my burgers are better than hers."

"Hah! And when would this supposed contest take place?" Kelly asked.

"Tonight." Grandma Sadie surprised them with the pronouncement, and her blue eyes twinkled. "We'll change plans and invite any and all to dinner at Peas Porridge. And we'll all be ordering hamburgers."

"Hey, if Grace agrees, I'm in." Damien raised his brows in challenge.

"You're pretty bold for a guy who's never cooked in a real restaurant."

"You're pretty sure of yourself for a woman who's never cooked for twenty critical firefighters ready to lay into you if they don't like the way you toasted the buns."

He was as happy as Grandma's eyes. Something must have gone right in the meeting.

"Seriously. You're a little too happy," she said.

"Nah. Just feeling relieved that I don't have to pack up this weekend. I'm as pessimistic as ever."

"You're staying!" Kelly had to stop herself from running into his arms.

"For the month. Babysitting heifers and calves, from what I understand."

"He's talked you into helping with the new organic herd."

"He's very persuasive, your brother-in-law."

They all heard the front door open and close at the same time.

"Who's that?" Kelly asked. "And where, exactly, is everyone? I thought Mom was upstairs—she wouldn't go out the front door. And Cole would come through the kitchen to go back outside, too."

"Let's go find out. We don't need any more strangers in here."

Damien led the way to the living room. Kelly instinctively felt in her pocket for the little leather medicine bag; she hadn't dared leave off her person since the break-in. Her fears evaporated when they looked to the foyer and Joely gave a squeal of delight. Kicking off his boots and removing his soft, worn tan hat was Joely's gorgeous husband, Alec Morrissey, who'd been away on tour as a rodeo color commentator for three weeks. He looked dang good in his jeans, boots, and blue chambray PRCA shirt.

"Alec!" Joely called.

"Hey, gorgeous!" He held out his arms and smiled over her head when she was in his embrace. "Hi, everyone."

"I can't believe it! We weren't expecting you for another week."

"I couldn't wait any longer, Jo-Jo. I heard Kelly was here. I knew there was about to be a ton more work to do with the cattle. I only had the week left so I let Sammy take over the announcing and came home to my bride. I mean, you're kind of a good reason to come back, too. I guess."

She laughed in delight as he twirled her once and kissed her soundly before setting her down. With his arm firmly around her shoulders, he turned to Kelly and Raquel.

"It's also good to come back when all the Crockett women are here. This place is at its best when it's full of the whole family. But who did I miss coming out as I drove up?" Alec asked.

"What?" Joely frowned.

"I thought it was Skylar, but I called and she just disappeared around the house."

"Skylar hasn't been here."

"What about me?" Skylar appeared at that moment from the kitchen, followed by Harper. "Alec! You're home!"

"I am, Sky. It's good to be back. Hey, Harper. I saw somebody came down the front steps and head for the back. A girl about your age wearing jeans and a light green baseball cap. Had a braid down her back." Alec thought a moment. "Actually, it was darker hair than yours and the braid was maybe a little longer."

By the time Kelly realized he was moving, Damien was at the door, his features no longer relaxed and jocular.

"Kelly, go check upstairs. I'll see if I can find her," he called.

"What the...?" Alec looked around in confusion.

"Long story," Joely said. "We have a real-life mystery going on."

Kelly took the stairs two at a time. She ran for her room and nearly crashed into the desk chair, totally out of place in front of the door. This time no drawers had been left open, but the closet door was ajar and the clothing hanging inside had been rifled through.

A girl? A teenager?

Kelly stared at her room, violated for the second time in as many days, but felt no fear this time. In fact, the suspected age and gender of the person explained a lot. A girl would be clever and bold, and in a hurry to find her property. Then she spied the piece of paper on the desktop. She picked it up, and her surprise doubled at the sight of another perfect, hand-sketched grulla horse. She had no idea what the drawing meant, except that it confirmed beyond any doubt that the intrusion was a search for the medicine bag.

Dashing back down the stairs, her heart pounding, she ignored the stares from her family and returned to the kitchen. With relief, she grabbed up the leather pouch from the table and curled the leather neck thong tightly into her palm.

"She's gone. Again."

Damien entered through the back door and raked a hand through his hair in frustration. "Damn it. What's going on?"

"I think our theory is completely right," she said. "And now it's positive this girl—at least it sounds like she's a girl—is looking for this. And I think she wants us to know that's what she's doing. Look." She handed him the drawing.

Skylar looked over his shoulder.

"That looks really familiar."

"What?" Damien asked. "Familiar how?"

"I've seen drawings like that. There was a girl who came to a couple of the community classes Harper had last month. She was doing a whole session on how to draw animals. It was mostly for younger kids, so this other girl and I were the oldest. I was practicing drawing Australian animals and she was doing horses. I think she was from the reservation. She said she was Shoshone."

"And do you remember, did she draw all grulla horses? Do you remember her name?" Kelly asked.

"I don't." Sky frowned in thought. "I think it started with a C or a K or something. Cathy? I'm sorry. I'm bad with names. She wasn't very talkative. Do you remember her, Harper?"

"Vaguely. I wasn't as involved with that class. My assistant was teaching it."

"That may be another part of the puzzle John Red Wolf could help with," Grandma Sadie said. "Not that he knows everyone just because they're Shoshone, but there's a small chance he would know of a gifted artist—especially a young one."

"She is that." Damien stared at the pictures again.

"You know what? I do want to know this bold little person. I think, tomorrow after you're done with what Cole needs you to do, we should go see a man about a horse."

Chapter Sixteen

THERE WERE, INDEED, far more than just the Crockett women at the restaurant that night. Grace quickly gave up trying to monitor the contest that went ahead exactly as Damien had challenged. She also gave up trying to stifle the laughter and joking between him and Kelly. He hadn't felt this free of uncertainty in a very long time, although he wasn't naïve enough to think it would last. Not a single important problem had been solved, but Kelly was a better distraction than anything he could have designed, and he was feeling better and better about his decision to work for Cole.

The perfect storm keeping him away from Sheridan had blown through. He'd stay and he'd see the counselor Gabe had found and fulfill Stone's requirement. He had less confidence that he'd figure out what was wrong with his head, but if he could feel this good about cooking in a kitchen, maybe he could get himself straight enough to make a jump. That was all that mattered in the end.

"Do you have your recipe finalized?" Kelly asked.

She was patting out burgers already. He'd finished putting his last ingredient into the meat mixture.

"Don't you worry about my recipe."

"Just remember, nobody will know whose burger is whose, so you'd better be on your game. Everyone can taste both, and those sixteen Crocketts and Thorsons out there know good food. So, it's a fateful vote."

"No worries. Can you count to zero?" He grinned at her.

"You're kind of awful when you're in a competitive mood. Mean even."

He loved the teasing. He loved that she took nothing seriously but dished out just as much crap as he did. "I fed firefighters, remember? They taught me to be confident or get booted. And nobody wanted Ronald to cook. He was the only other possibility."

"Ronald?"

"We called him McDee because he ate more fast-food burgers than any other kind of food. Had he been the cook, he would as likely have ordered out as really done any grilling."

"Yuck."

"Right?"

They finished making up their sliders and each chose a side of the grill. Kelly spread her half with olive oil. Damien chose the fat from bacon he'd fried up earlier. He knew exactly what he was going to serve, had known it since the moment he'd first challenged her. It had been a firehouse favorite—hamburger with crumbled bacon mixed into the meat along with a hint of chili powder and garlic. He fried it in the bacon fat and then garnished it with barbecue sauce and onion rings. He'd also whipped up a batch of chili. While he would have normally soaked real kidney beans, he was happy to use the canned ones he'd surreptitiously picked up at the store on his way into Wolf Paw Pass. For a salad course, he had romaine lettuce and kiwi topped with a zippy lime vinaigrette to offset the heavier bacon and chili. It was an old favorite and surprisingly loved by the company.

He hadn't been able to determine exactly what Kelly put into her meat mix, but it was a frou-frou gourmet spice of some kind along with shallots and Dijon mustard. She'd grated some Gruyere cheese and added it as well, then served it on crusty pretzel rolls. To his mind, pretzels were for dipping in cheese and eating with salt, and they had no place surrounding a good hamburger.

She'd made some kind of tomato soup for her side dish and made up a family-style salad bowl of arugula lettuce, mozzarella cheese, and cornbread croutons. It all sounded way too new-age for Damien. But, damn, he admired her creativity.

Grace took the finished burgers out to the table on two large platters. Damien followed carrying Kelly's soup in a family-style tureen, and she brought out his chili. Once the food was in front of everyone, Grace announced the rules.

"There are three categories of dishes here," she said. "The burgers. The sides. The salads. Kelly and Damien here are not necessarily carrying out their own creations, but they might be. You don't know who made which burgers. When everyone is done eating, I'll give each of you a paper so you can record your votes. The criteria is simple – which was your favorite? Greta and I will be the vote counters."

"What does the winner get?" Cole asked.

"The winning dish in each category goes on the menu for one month. We'll see how it sells."

"Oh, man, that's like a real prize!" Skylar said.

"It's no contest," Kelly said. "I've printed up the menus with mine already."

"Wasted money." Damien shook his head.

"For the record, these two are the most obnoxious cooks I've ever had, so do not vote on personality in any way." Grace feigned annoyance well. "Chefs, you may now leave the area. Judges, dig in. Talk amongst yourselves. You can lobby for one food or another. You can try to guess who made what—but in the end, you'll be better off simply choosing your favorite."

Damien was surprisingly nervous as he followed Kelly back to the kitchen. It was a silly competition that meant absolutely nothing but fun. And it was fun. She was fun. And she shocked him when they reached the preparation area by turning to face him, and swiveling her head quickly back and forth to make sure they were alone. With a gleeful giggle, she did a little run in place and put her hands on his cheeks. Without hesitating, she pressed her lips to his.

He needed no encouragement to respond. Wrapping his arms around her, he dragged her body into his. The zing through his blood was instantaneous, but she pulled away almost as quickly as she'd come—fortunately smarter than he was about getting caught.

"This is amazing," she said, her voice almost a little-girl squeal. "You might be a mean old competitor but you're so much fun. I never would have thought of this in a million years."

"Honestly? I have no idea how we got to this point. I was joking this afternoon."

"You made the mistake of joking when my family was around. Nobody lets a gauntlet drop, however softly, in this place without someone picking it up."

"I'm finding that out. There's no shortage of people to make plans for you. But it's turning out all right."

"Yeah. We've been pretty good at finding things to occupy our time, haven't we?" She gave him the smallest of coquettish smiles. "I admit, I'm really glad you said yes to staying. How did Cole convince you? Or is that none of my business?"

"I've been thinking of it as the perfect storm. Somewhere in the universe is a power telling me not to go to Sheridan. I mean, my mother hasn't traveled more than fifty miles from home in half a dozen years. Why did that change the moment I'm on her doorstep? Why did three places I checked into for boarding turn me down? This is Wyoming—everyone has a place for a horse. Why is Harper's new cattle herd arriving a week early three days from now?"

"Good questions, all," she replied.

He searched her face, looking for a little extra boldness. "Why did I meet you my first morning here and fall into a mystery that I care about?"

"A mystery you care about?"

He looked around the kitchen again. Grace still hadn't returned. Stepping back close to Kelly, he touched her chin and tilted her face upward.

"I'll rephrase. Why did I meet you and decide I care about that?"

"You care about meeting me?"

"You annoyed the heck out of me that first morning."

"I know."

"I must care or I'd have turned down the offer to help both here at Grace's and at the ranch."

"You're a victim of the universe."

He heard Grace's voice and put space between them. "I have always been a fun football for the universe to punt around. It's just, for the first time it feels like I might be being aimed in at least the general direction of the goalpost."

He could see she wanted to laugh, but she didn't.

"What's really stupid about that is, I understand what you mean. Tonight is giving me some ideas about what I want to do next. Nothing is clear, but maybe I have some suggestions for my sisters. Maybe I can at least see a possible goalpost, too."

"A girl who can make sports metaphors with me. Be still my heart."

"Yeah, don't put too much stock in that."

"Hey, you two!" Grace breezed into the kitchen, her face alight with fun. "They are exclaiming about your burgers and sides. I think it's going to be a close contest."

"Did I ever thank you for being willing to do this?" Kelly asked.

"You don't have to thank me, but you do have to take a look at the orders coming in. The other tables are filling up. A few customers have even asked about what's going on because they're overhearing the groans of pleasure. Can you make more?"

"Sure," Damien said.

"Of course," Kelly agreed.

"Let's get cracking, then."

"So, Gracie, when we're all done tonight, this has given me a couple of ideas for the future. Mine and yours. And Rocky's. This kind of contest could be a great promotional tool. There are all kinds of possibilities for upgrading the menu. And you can help me get a leg up on an interview or audition with the restaurant in San

Francisco if Landon gets me an in. Could we talk later?"

Damien saw the flicker of a shadow cross Grace's face. Kelly seemed so animated she didn't notice that Grace's nod was slow.

"Of course. We can always talk, Kel. Just keep in mind that I love my menu and it has a purpose. I'm not interested in changing a whole lot."

Kelly brushed the comment aside with a physical gesture. "Totally not. That wouldn't be my intention."

But Damien wasn't so sure. He didn't know Kelly perfectly at this new point in their friendship—their whatever it was they were growing—but he did know a fevered brain and its idea when he saw one.

Forty-five minutes after the sliders had been served, Grace brought Damien and Kelly out to the restaurant dining room and placed them at the head of the table with great fanfare.

"The first and probably only Peas Porridge hamburger showdown is now completed. Votes are tallied," she said. "Which dinner creation has won? Is it the Chili Bacon Burger or the Cheese Slider Supreme? Cole, drumroll please."

Cole rapped two soup spoons on the tabletop in a terrible rhythm that made everyone boo. When the laughter stopped, Grace held up her hand a final time.

"By a vote of nine to seven, the winner is the Chili Bacon Burger! Who is our winning chef?"

A ridiculous shot of pride flashed through Damien's chest. The happiness didn't come so much from winning or even from having the best burger—he'd most certainly won the kid vote; what nine-year-old wanted arugula and gruyere cheese when they could have chili and bacon? The warmth came from acceptance. From being part of the great family game. He lifted his arms over his head and jogged in place while he made Rocky fists. Hoots and clapping erupted. Harper let out a short, two-fingered whistle.

"Bravo!"

"Way to go, Damien!"

He stopped his grandstanding and made a slight bow, then he turned to Kelly, suddenly mindful that this could be totally awkward. She was the real chef, after all. At first, she shocked him, with her arms crossed and her mouth tightened into a thin line.

"How did you manage to rig this?" she asked.

Then he saw the twitch in her stern frown, followed by the twinkle in her eye.

"I did not cheat," he said. "I only took a poll and found out that Rory, Lucky, and Marcus here all like chili."

"You did not!" Lucky called.

Damien grinned. "Nah, I didn't." He leaned closer to Kelly's ear and whispered. "But having the kids vote was to my advantage."

"I realized my mistake too late," she agreed. "Congratulations. You're a worthy competitor, Mr. Finney."

"It was a lucky win," he said. "The bar was set very high. But guess what? I get my burger on an actual menu."

"Gloat away," she said. "I'll get you next time."

His winner's high grew even bigger with just that simple line, and he found himself hoping for a future where there would be a next time.

They finished at the restaurant before midnight and drove back to Paradise together, the way they'd come. In just a few days, the change in Damien's life could barely be quantified. He'd gone from hopeless to hopeful, jobless to way-too-busy, and nowhere man to family celebrity. His gratitude for the change couldn't be denied. If he'd been packing for Sheridan, he'd have been doing it alone, full of worry. Tonight, with Kelly beside him, the worry had been temporarily buried.

"You're really not upset that you lost?" he asked.

"I don't consider it a loss," she said. "I consider it unsophisticated taste on the part of the judges."

"I see."

She gave a soft laugh in the dark. "For one instant, it was maybe what it feels like to get cut from *Iron Chef* or *Chopped*. And then, I was actually kind of proud of you, Finney. You learned a thing or two in that fire station kitchen."

"Miss Crockett, I am beyond honored."

"I wish I could talk Grace into making something like that a regular feature in the restaurant. Imagine a new dish for the menu voted on every few months. She could have a really popular place if she'd open up her mind a little about the menu. We'll keep talking."

"Don't try to change her too much," he said gently. "This is still a new baby for her. Once she's established, she'll be more receptive to change."

"And how do you know her so well?"

"I don't. I know what it's like to think you can't live up to someone else's standards."

He could sense her staring at him.

"That sounds a little like personal experience."

"I told you my dad was a fire captain's fire captain. Everyone's hero. I wanted to be just like him when I was a kid, but I was never like him."

"Is that why you wanted to be a smokejumper?"

"I tried that because it was different than what he did.

I liked being a firefighter, but I didn't want to compete with him anymore. I'm not the people person he was."

"I don't believe that. You're fun around people."

"I react to people. I don't generate the fun."

"You're too hard on yourself."

"Maybe. But Grace is hard on herself, too."

"Oh my gosh, Grace is perfect!"

"Then show her you think so, too."

She said nothing, and the silence held long enough that Damien feared he'd insulted her. Finally, she sighed.

"I think you just found a way to lecture me, but I can't quite decide how."

"No. No, Kelly, not at all. You just need to know that you're an amazing talent and Grace knows she's different from you. She wants you to be proud of her."

"I am so proud of her. I wish I were nice like she is. I wish I was brave like she is."

"You're all those things."

"No. I'm focused on what I want, but I'm not brave." She shifted in the seat. "That's got nothing to do with tonight. Tonight was about burgers and laughter and you winning. Anyway, we have a mystery to solve tomorrow. Cole said he won't need you after noon. I think he agrees that finding out about the girl, the campfire, and the drawings is equally important as cattle to Paradise Ranch business. We can go see John Red Wolf after lunch."

"You really do know how to pack a day, don't you?"

"Party-time Kelly. That's me!"

"Then let's hope Mr. Red Wolf has information that will solve all this, and you can throw a Thank God That's Over party."

"You are a weird dude, Finney, but okay. Amen to that."

Chapter Seventeen

"HEY, NEWEST RANCH hand. Cole says I can take you away now."

Damien's head popped up from the journal article he was reading and smiled at the welcome rescue. Kelly stood in the doorway of the tiny, hundred-year-old cabin that had been turned into Paradise's farm site office, pretty as a mountain wildflower, smiling and relaxed. His head, spinning from a flood of information he would never have guessed he'd need, cleared at the sight of her. He lifted the copy of Organic Ranching magazine and wiggled it at her.

"I'll never look at ground beef the same way again."

"Into organic now are we?"

"If it's truly raised the right way? Maybe. It does seem like a really expensive way to get meat to your table. And all the debate about cattle and the environment? The research makes my brain hurt."

"Yeah. We've had so many discussions about this with Harper. In the end, I don't think she's trying this idea to help the environment. Cattle pollute, there's no way around it, but since people aren't going to stop eating meat, how can Paradise experiment to raise it as humanely and healthily as possible?"

"Raise Amazon rainforest trees and skip the steers. Sell the oxygen they produce." Damien made a face and set the magazine down.

"Hey, if you can figure out a way to do that, I will personally back you a hundred percent."

She entered the room and looked around at the twenty-foot square space. Damien scanned it along with her. Only the back wall still showed the original, age-grayed pine logs, but they'd long ago been fully caulked and sealed. The rest of the room was finished with utilitarian furniture—the desk and a Navajo rug along with a short wall of filing cabinets, and a large map of the ranch. Damien had found it a peaceful cave in which to study, but he was happy to be done for the day.

"Cole said you can only absorb so much at a time, and it sounds like he's right. Ready for a drive to Mr. Red Wolf's farm?"

"I was ready hours ago."

The drive took forty-five minutes. Damien soaked in the landscape from the passenger seat like a kid on a field trip. He loved the rolling country that made up the foothills of the Teton range and the mountainous vista alongside them. Kelly headed south along Paradise's eastern border, then turned away from the Rockies toward the hilly grasslands. She chatted almost endlessly, the way she always could. She had stories about every rock and turn, and he absorbed her knowledge of the area, allowing himself to imagine he could be as much a part of the place as she was.

At last, on a rutted carnival ride of a dirt road, she

slowed and peered to her left.

"Keep an eye out for a drive that's marked with a four-foot boulder."

"This land isn't part of Wind River Reservation, right?" Damien asked.

"Right. I understand his late wife's family gave them about two hundred acres and a small house as a wedding gift. He built his ranch and never moved. I was only there a couple of times when I was young. He used to put on a fun horse show every year for the kids in the area. He always had a lot of horses and trained them for a while. Now he does wood carving and sells pieces in local galleries. He's a quiet, gentle man by all accounts. I saw him but never knew him the way my older sisters did."

They found the boulder and turned onto a dirt path surprisingly smoother than the road they left. A minute later the house came into view—a simple but sprawling white rambler with dark gray trim and a fieldstone chimney. Across from the house, separated by two hundred feet, was a story-and-a-half red wooden barn, its double doors open wide. Behind the house stood a simple tipi, unadorned but of impressive height. The setting was peaceful and welcoming.

They parked beside the barn and walked first to the house. When nobody answered Kelly's knock on the front door, as rich a brown as a chocolate bar, they turned for the barn. Before they reached it, the person they sought emerged and raised a hand in greeting. Behind him trailed a short-haired black Labrador and a fluffy-coated, mottled cream-and-brown collie mix, their tongues lolling in friendly welcome.

"I thought I heard a car arrive. Hello. You must be Kelly."

Damien had no idea why he'd expected the exact opposite of the man who approached. He'd pictured a wizened older man, content on his porch, perhaps watching the world with wise eyes. The only part he'd gotten correct were the eyes, for they definitely imparted wisdom as they assessed the visitors.

"I am. It's so nice to meet you, Mr. Red Wolf."

"But we've met before, I believe," he said, taking her hand to shake it, even before greeting Damien. The gesture impressed him. "Many years ago, at one of our summer horse shows, I think you celebrated the accomplishment of besting your older sister in an egg-and-spoon race. You rode a small black quarter horse, as I recall."

"Oh my gosh! That was Rollie! How in the world can you remember? It was at least a dozen years ago."

John Red Wolf chuckled. "It's not truly all that impressive. There were three of you who looked alike at that horse show, and it was close to one of the last I held. I remember you."

"Those horse shows were highlights of the summer. So many fun classes."

"They were fun. My wife was the driving force. When she passed on, I held them for two more years and then let them go. Made time for other things. But...that's not why you're here." He turned to Damien at last and offered his hand. "Welcome. You are Damien Finney."

The man's handshake was firm enough, but then he placed his second hand atop their clasped palms and held it tightly as well. The undeniable flow of calm energy almost rendered Damien speechless, but he forced away the surprise.

"I am. It's good to meet you, Mr. Red Wolf."

"Both of you, please call me John. I am happy to meet

you as well. I understand from Dr. Joely that you are the owner of a Smoke mare." His smile was self-deprecating. "Officially known as a grulla, but to a small number of my people they will always be Smoke horses if they come from this region."

"It certainly describes her color," Damien said. "Joely says you have one as well. Almost a twin to mine."

"Please, come and see for yourself. The horses are not rare except in legend. And the legend of The Cloud Band, a herd entirely made up of Smoke horses, is a purely local one. That herd, if it exists, truly would be rare since even horses who carry the dun gene that allows the color do not pass it on automatically—everything has to be genetically perfect. Still, over the years, there have been a handful who claim to have seen the Band."

"Have you?" Kelly asked.

John hesitated. "I thought I did, once when I was a boy. Running in the distance. I never saw them again and chalked the vision up to my wishful imagination until I was in my twenties. Come. Meet Bird."

He turned for the barn, and Damien sought Kelly's eyes. They were round with the same fascination and anticipation he felt, along with the wish to possess their host's calm, unworried air and easy, unhurried gait.

John Red Wolf approached six feet, a well-built man, slender but muscular, and handsome in a craggy, life-well-lived way. They said he was in his mid-seventies, but he could have passed for ten years younger—if you didn't count the timelessness in his demeanor. He wore jeans and a red-and-blue plaid shirt rolled to the forearms, along with a black cowboy hat. Black hair curled from beneath the back of it and rested lightly on his shirt collar.

The two dogs trotted ahead of him like tour guides

and disappeared into the barn.

"I hope you'll forgive us for coming unannounced," Kelly said. "We're excited to hear your story, but we don't want to interrupt your day."

He slowed and fell into step between them.

"I'm happy to share my story with anyone who's interested. It's not particularly exciting to any who aren't. And I have all the time I need, so you cannot interrupt. I expected you both to come at some point, and I'm glad it is today."

The barn was small and tidy with eight box stalls. It wasn't new and bore a few worn or chewed boards, but every stall was sturdy and painted brown like the house trim. Just as with the man, his barn evoked a feeling of peaceful calm. Damien had the sudden, inexplicable thought that any animal in this space would never feel trapped or unhappy.

The stalls were empty except for one, and as soon as Damien saw the head that hung over the stall door, his breath caught. Joely hadn't exaggerated—the horse really could have been Pan.

"Bird of the Gray Sky," John said, stroking one hand down the horse's pearl-gray neck. "She is the third Smoke Horse to have chosen me."

"Chosen you?" Kelly asked.

"Part of my horse story. But first." He looked to Damien. "Tell me how you found your mare."

"I think…she did sort of find me. I noticed her at the Wild Horse Sanctuary purely because of her coloring, but when I approached her, I saw more. I thought her eyes were full of sadness and maybe a little fear, and I was feeling the same way at the time. Then, when I touched her, there was a kind of peace I hadn't felt in a long while."

John simply nodded.

"I was warned against her," Damien continued. "Kelly's sister, Mia—"

"The one you lost the egg-and-spoon race to." John grinned at her and she shook her head, her eyes telegraphing wonder at his memory.

"Mia told me never to choose a horse simply because it was pretty, but I couldn't explain why it was more than that. I didn't understand it myself. I had gone to the holding facility to look at the horses because we were required to do it for a mustangs-helping-veterans program."

"I've heard of this program," John said. "Based at Paradise Ranch, correct?"

"Yes, exactly. I was determined not to take part. I didn't want to buy into the whole 'horses would help me' nonsense. Then Pan appeared and it was all over."

"It sounds like she might have chosen you."

"More like we chose each other."

"Ah…a good answer. My beginning with these horses was similar. I made myself believe there was no band of smoke horses until I was twenty-four years old and fighting my way down the cliché path of Indians and alcohol. I'd lost two jobs and was well on my way to throwing my life into the gutter. One day I was wandering in the hills just outside the reservation not all that far from here. I walked with no purpose; I had a flask of cheap rye in my pocket, so I guess I was looking for a place to sit and drown my sorrows. That's when I came across a group of four mares, all the same coloring. To me, they were as exciting as unicorns.

"I stood in the clearing where I'd stumbled on them and we stared at each other for a full ten minutes. In that time, I knew without a doubt they'd been put there to change my life. I knew they were from that band I had seen twelve years before, and I still believe it. Although I rarely say so anymore. People are quick to label a person as crazy."

"After so many years convincing myself they didn't exist, I would have believed it, too." Kelly stroked Bird and let the mare nuzzle her.

"I'd seen grulla horses over the years, but these were different—so alike. Silver smoke. I finally tried to approach them, and one did not spook. I asked her for permission to go closer, and she allowed me to run my hands over her entire body. I stroked her head and ears. I felt her legs and pulled several burrs from her mane and tail. All the while I told her my story."

"That's amazing. A wild horse let you do that?" Kelly asked.

"It's even more amazing to me now than it was at the time," John said, his voice quiet and almost reverent. "Mostly because that moment led to a long, amazing life. I wanted to take her home with me in the worst way, but I knew I could not do that. She was not my horse. I thanked her, and I left her. But I knew I had to go back home and do something to make me worthy of that moment of friendship."

The man could tell a story. Damien listened, transfixed. Given his life, from his father's stern expectations to the moments of human horror in Afghanistan, to the backbreaking work of getting through smokejumper training, Damien would have traded blows with anyone claiming he'd fall for an old Native woo-woo story. But John was sincere as a tax collector, and Damien hung on every word.

"I know what happened," he said quietly, and John raised a brow. "She followed you home."

The older man smiled, his eyes holding far-off memories. "Not immediately. It was the next evening near sunset. I found her standing next to our lean-to shed."

"She chose you." Damien met John's eyes.

"She did. But don't think it was easy. The story isn't that fantastical. She was a wild horse. For many months, perhaps close to a year, she came and went as she pleased. But, over time, we grew to trust one another and, in the end, we were best friends. I named her Stands in the Mist. Misty lived with me for twenty years. She was never confined and could always come and go. Mostly she stayed.

"When I finally had to put her down, we figure she was close to thirty. I had her head, heart, and legs cremated — it is a white man's tradition from horse racing, but I like the symbolism. I brought the ashes out to the spot where I'd found her, and I spread them across the meadow. When I was done, I looked up. Two smoke horses stood less than a hundred yards from me."

"Oh my gosh, I just got chills down to my heels!" Kelly put her hand over her mouth.

"I think this now qualifies as fantastical," Damien added.

He wanted desperately to find the whole story unbelievable, but he couldn't shake his shivers of pure excitement, nor his need to believe.

"You can see now why I don't tell this story often. Some of my people still believe. Even some young people are willing to study and learn of the connection all creatures have to each other and the Earth. They accept the responsibility we have to revere all life. Others look at stories like mine as ramblings of an embellished memory. To them, I am simply getting old and love to paint my word pictures." John shrugged philosophically. "It's all fine. They're not entirely wrong. I am old. Clearly, I love to talk."

"But it really happened." Kelly frowned.

"I learned how to train horses, and I've had many animals pass through my life over the years. You'd be surprised how many people see that as a lifestyle that would leave a man a little nutty. Especially since I live alone and seem, on the surface, to avoid people."

Damien laughed. "I heard you went to a vocational school. That's not avoiding people."

"I went back to school after I married. I studied mechanical engineering and even did a one-year apprenticeship. I didn't like it much. I missed the horses. I was gone from Emily for too long at a stretch. We decided we didn't need many material things, and I turned to training and woodcarving. That's pretty much my life story. It's worked out all right. Although I do miss Emily."

"Do you have children?" Kelly asked.

"We were never so blessed," he replied. "But we fostered many children over the years, and I'm proud of every one of them. I still see those who live in this area, and I hear from the others. I also have nieces, nephews, and grandnieces. One loved to listen to the horse stories."

"So, the second horse. She came to you, too?" Damien asked.

"I thanked the two who came that morning, for allowing me to share their sister. I said she would be sadly missed because she was my guide and my great friend. Then I approached the pair, and one stayed. I did the same thing I'd done with Misty—touched her, stroked her. But this time I asked her if she wanted to come home with me right then. She was much younger than Misty had been, only four or five. I cupped my hand under her chin and she did follow me."

"What was her name?"

"Fawn of the Smoke. She had faint white spots on her haunches, like a baby deer. My Fawn. She stayed for nearly twenty-five years."

"And Bird?" Kelly asked.

"You'd like to hear that it happened a third time." John smiled.

"Of course!"

"I expected it to. But...it did not. I spread Fawn's ashes, certain the spirit herd would send me another replacement, but the day was cold and rainy and no horses appeared out of the gloomy day. It was nine months later I met Bird at a random visit to a home on the reservation to see an injured horse. She'd been found wandering alone with a cut on her leg. The finder treated the wound, but then kept her in a small, backyard lot as a pet for his young children and fed her just enough to keep her from starving. She was thin and pretty dirty. When I first looked into the pen, I didn't even see her. She was the same color as the sky that day. Although the children fed her treats now and then and pet her, she was broken in spirit. I took her off their hands and she's been with me for five years."

Damien heard no recrimination of the family who'd neglected her. Only calm acceptance of what was now.

"She definitely doesn't look broken anymore," he said. "You do have a way with them."

"Because she knows she can go anytime she wishes. She's only in the stall today because of the abscess Joely drained from her hoof yesterday. She'll be out tomorrow.

Bird is of the smoke band. I know because we have that special connection that after almost fifty years I still don't understand. I've had other grullas come through my barn, and they are beautiful, too, but they are not of the true Cloud Band. I can't explain it, and I don't know why these come to me. Perhaps it's not for me to know but to simply accept. So I do, humbly."

"You've never seen the whole herd again?" Kelly asked.

"Not in the flesh. But what is strange to me is that I've seen them in my dreams the past few months. I hadn't dreamed of them since I was a boy. Now they come frequently, and it's always the same. They are running toward me with billowing smoke behind them, and I know at some point they'll stop, and then I'll know what they want me to know."

"Sounds a little nightmarish." Damien looked for the first time deep into the eyes of Bird standing beside him, and something jolted inside. It was the same jolt he'd gotten the first time he'd seen Pan, and he laid his palm flat between Bird's eyes. She pressed into his touch and a silent sigh flowed through him, followed by a warmth he couldn't explain.

"Not at all nightmarish," John said. "But important. I'm content to wait and see where the dreams take me, but I think, perhaps, that the waiting is almost over."

"Why?" Damien turned to the man, his heartbeat accelerating in anticipation.

"Because of Joely's visit yesterday. And now yours. To learn that I'm with the owner of another smoke horse is exciting. To learn that someone is out in your land drawing pictures of smoke horses is thrilling. It all means something."

Just like that, John had connected his mystical past horses to the very real present, and Damien could almost feel the pull of the legend.

"Look." Kelly reached into the purse she'd carried with her and pulled out the folded drawing from the fire pit. "We found this yesterday."

John unfolded the sketch paper and went still as he studied the drawing. For several long moments, only his eyes moved back and forth across the pencil lines.

"I have seen a drawing like this." His eyes shone. "I cannot say for certain, but I know one girl who has drawn horses in this manner since she was a child."

"We believe this was drawn by a girl."

"The one I know would be about seventeen now."

"Yes, exactly," Kelly said.

"I mentioned I have a great-niece who loves the legends of the smoke horses. She is the one who used to draw pictures. Kaiah. She is the granddaughter of my brother. I haven't seen her for several years; she went to live with another relative for a while. I hadn't heard she was home again."

"Do you think she could own something like this?" Kelly took the medicine bag from the purse as well. "I don't like keeping it with me, I'd rather have it somewhere safe, but I don't want to leave it behind anywhere."

She handed it to John, who straightened the leather neck thong and ran a finger over the beadwork as if reading a page of braille. He tilted his head and nodded.

"This is not an old piece, but it's authentic and the craftsmanship is excellent. It could be something given to the owner by a relative or it could even have been purchased at a shop where local women sell their handmade items. Have you looked inside?"

"No." Kelly shook her head. "I didn't want to be disrespectful."

John smiled. "Thank you for the courtesy. It seems likely that this belongs to a young person. The beading pattern is modern and the leather still new. It feels like there's a coin inside, but it could be any kind of amulet."

"Could you find her?" Damien asked. "If we leave this with you, perhaps she would be more comfortable coming to get it here. I don't personally need to know her."

"Oh, but I think you do."

The simple statement socked the wind from Damien's chest like a physical blow. He had no skin in this game as far as he was concerned. He didn't own the land where the girl trespassing. He wasn't of native heritage. He felt no need to see what was in the pouch.

"How could it possibly have anything to do with me?"

"This bag is somehow connected to the horses—if only because its owner is fascinated with them. You, too, are connected to the horses because of your Pan. The puzzle is to figure out why it matters."

"It could all be a coincidence."

John only smiled. "It may be something very simple. But nothing happens for no reason."

"Do you think the horses have some kind of spiritual meaning to Damien?" Kelly asked. "He does have a very special connection to his horse. We wondered if horses are his spirit animal."

"A person doesn't choose a spirit animal. That's not how they manifest themselves. And not everyone has one or will necessarily ever have one—you aren't born attached to a certain creature." John studied him closely. "No. I don't think the horse is your spirit animal."

With a ridiculous sense of disappointment, Damien felt as if something had been ripped away from him—something he'd come to believe without reason.

John smiled almost impishly. "I sense a bigger connection to dogs."

Reflexively Damien's eyes darted from John, seeking out his dogs. He spied them lying on a couple of old blankets near a door. The lab raised its head as if it had been called. Damien's thoughts almost froze at the weirdness of John's statement, and he shot Kelly a stern look when a smile twitched at the corner of her mouth.

"Absolutely not dogs," he said. "I'm not a dog person. I don't even particularly like them."

"Liking them wouldn't be a requirement. If they have something to tell you, they will. As I said, we do not get to choose our guides—if they come." As if he could sense growing discomfort, he placed a hand on Damien's upper arm. "Let's go to the house and get something to drink. It's getting warmer."

Kelly, who'd sobered dutifully, nodded agreement. "That would be nice. Thank you."

John led them to a flat, circular area outside the tipi behind his house. The patio-like area was covered in natural birch bark and had a large fire pit in the center, and they all sat on surprisingly comfortable, low-slung Adirondack chairs made with rough-hewn half-logs. John fetched old-fashioned, multi-colored metal tumblers and a thermos of iced tea and passed around a plate of store-bought shortbread cookies. Damien and Kelly must have hidden their surprise poorly because John smiled with pleasure and swept a hand toward the canvas structure with a proud hand.

"This is a tradition that has been in my father's family

for three generations. During the summer months, we live as close to the old ways as is practical, and we teach the skills when anyone is interested. I have done everything from tanning leather for moccasins and ceremonial clothing, to smoking fish and preserving meat. I sleep out here most nights, although now that I'm old I do go to the house during the worst storms. And I no longer enjoy being cold so I move out when the temperatures dip. I also doubt my ancestors had chairs and nylon hammocks, and there are some niceties modern times have given us." He indicated the tea. "Like ice coolers."

"To modern insulation." Damien lifted his glass and grinned.

It faded when John's dogs sauntered toward them from the back of the tipi. The collie sat at John's feet, but the lab continued to Damien, sat in front of him, and thumped his tail on the ground. With a sigh, Damien gave the head a stroke, noting the gray muzzle and slightly saggy eye skin.

"That's Tug," John said. "He's older than I am in dog years. Almost thirteen in human years. I'll call him off if you want."

Damien scratched the dog's ear. "No, but even though I don't want to ask, tell me why you think I'm connected to dogs."

"As I said, spirit guides, animal or human, are not chosen by us for ourselves or each other, unlike popular western culture likes to say. But sometimes guides choose us for reasons we don't know—to help or to show us things. Why I sense that dogs play a part in your story isn't clear to me."

While Damien continued to fondle the dog's ears, Kelly patted her thigh to call the other one.

"And who are you?" she asked, taking the dog's happy face in her hands and kissing the nose.

"Honey," John replied. "She's not a spring chicken either, but she is only eight."

The conversation drifted naturally away from dogs, spirit animals, even horses, after that. John asked about Kelly's interests and her sisters and, especially, her grandmother. Sadie, he told them, had been one of his favorite people when she'd been more involved in charitable organizations years ago. Although they were twenty years apart in age, he'd always thought she should have been born into the native community. She reminded him of a wise Indian leader.

"Women are the heart and true leaders of our people," he said. "Far wiser than men. We used to look to them with more reverence than we often do now, but those who understand know the truth." He chuckled. "It certainly was true when Emily was alive. I still have a hard time not running every decision by her."

"Sounds like she was a lucky woman to have a husband who saw that," Kelly said.

"Maybe. But she used to tell me that nobody, woman or man, is wise in a vacuum. Everyone needs a village. Every village must listen to collective wisdom." He turned to face Kelly, now serious on her behalf. "Don't be afraid to claim your wisdom, but especially don't be afraid to listen to the village. You are fortunate to have one where the women are still revered."

She was silent, a mix of surprise and awe in her features.

"How do you know these things? Is this Native elder magic? And I don't mean that disrespectfully."

John's laughter rang with pure enjoyment. "No. There

is only age and listening to the lessons it has brought. And a little paying attention. Your family is well-thought-of. It's no magic."

They finished their drinks in easy conversation and it was only when he and Kelly were ready to leave that Damien thought about Apollo. He hadn't mentioned the colt and neither had John.

"You know, I never told you that Panacea has a colt, born last year," Damien said. "I don't know why I didn't mention him before."

"And does he have the color?" John's face lit up with renewed interest.

"He does. She was in foal when I got her; I didn't know it. He looks a lot like her but with different white markings. Same silvery color."

"It's rare enough that you have a mare of the Cloud Band. Damien, if you also have a future stallion, you truly are a chosen one."

"Oh, I don't know if my belief can be stretched quite that far."

"Okay, now that's pretty cool now that we know the story," Kelly said.

"I don't know if he's stallion material," Damien said. "We've talked about leaving him a colt for now. He's smart and still well-behaved. The young lady who's working with him is doing a great job. She wants to start taking him on the trails—ponying him behind another horse so he starts to see what his job might be in the future."

"It should be his mother that he follows," John replied. "She would know the ways of the trails. In two ways. You should bring them here. It might even be Pan would know the place. At the very least, they will travel where their equine ancestors called home."

"Is that a real offer?" Kelly asked.

"It very much is." John looked thoughtful. "When you told me of the colt—"

"Apollo," Damien said.

John nodded approval. "An Olympian. The god of prophecy, leader of the muses. And of healing, as is his mother. Very fitting. I have a strong feeling. There is some important reason they should come here, your Pan and your Apollo. This is not a premonition or a directive. It's only a feeling. But you would be most welcome. I'd love to meet your Smoke horse, and I'd love to ride the hills in the company of three Cloud Band descendants."

"I would like that." Damien gave Tug a final pat and he and Kelly stood. Strangely, he was reluctant to leave. Answers to his questions felt closer here. When they all reached the car, he held out his hand to John and welcomed the man's return clasp.

"I can't thank you enough," he said. "I didn't come here expecting to find anything. I think I've found more than stories. There's a lot to think about."

"There is always a lot to think about." John laughed. "My advice is to let the next thoughts come to you. Don't dwell on what I've said or even on the stories. Perhaps they're just fanciful, the things of dreams. Or maybe these stories will lead you to find more stories. Either way, they are simply yours to hold. I know we'll meet again."

"Can I give you a hug?" Kelly asked, and the older man smiled happily.

"I would be moved and honored."

They embraced. Damien saw the same reluctance to leave in Kelly that he felt.

"Are you sure you don't want to keep the medicine

bag?" Kelly asked when she straightened.

"It came to you two. It should stay with you until it's claimed. I'll see if I can find Kaiah's parents to learn more."

"All right. I'll keep it safe."

They drove away in silence. Damien had no idea how to put any of his feelings into words. Kelly's hand drifted from the steering wheel and covered his, giving him a warm jolt.

"That," she said, her voice low and awe-filled, "was mind-blowing."

That, he thought, was exactly the word.

Chapter Eighteen

SLEEP SHOULD HAVE been easy and sound. His mind should have been filled with peace. Instead, he found himself once again high above the swirling black abyss, so familiar now it didn't terrify as much as it filled his dream-soul with exhaustion and despair. He needed to see beyond the black and there seemed to be nobody, not even John Red Wolf, who could clear it away.

This time he wasn't on the plane. He stood on the edge of a bluff, the wall below his feet a vertical drop into Ancestor Canyon, only in the middle of the valley, just to the side of the whirlwind of darkness, stood John Red Wolf's tipi. And it wasn't Pan beside him on the ledge, but Cole.

"Why are *you* here?" Damien asked.

"Don't look down," Cole replied.

"Look at the drawing." Skylar suddenly appeared behind Cole and pointed down.

"Okay. Where is the drawing?"

"The artist jumped out of the plane with it."

"We aren't on a plane."

"We're always on a plane," Cole replied, his voice even, cold, like a robot.

"If you want to save the drawing, you have to go after her," Sky insisted. "You have to go after Kaiah."

Two loud barks beside him pulled him up and away from the cliff. He looked down from where he levitated and saw Tug and Honey. John's dogs? In sudden horror, Damien watched helplessly as one after the other, the dogs leaped off the bluff.

"No. I can't save you if you jump." He shouted and jerked awake just as Cole's last words reached him.

"You have to save them. But don't look down. It's way too scary."

In what was now his normal post-nightmare ritual, Damien sat up and hugged his knees, calming his respiration that puffed like a wind storm, settling his thundering pulse. He looked at the clock. It was only one in the morning.

As the dream faded, his irritation rose. Irritation, he supposed, was better than depression. He had an appointment with the therapist in thirty-six hours. He was going to have a field day with these dreams—and Damien resented the thought. With a growl of frustration, he threw off the sheet and stood. Grabbing his jeans from the floor, he stabbed his feet through the legs and yanked up the denim. Bare-footed and bare-chested, he opened his door and peered into the dark hallway. Silence greeted him, and no lights glowed from downstairs. Carefully, he closed his door, padded to the stairs, keeping to the right where he'd learned they didn't squeak, and headed for the kitchen.

She was there.

His heart fumbled a beat in his chest and he tried to turn before she saw him. He failed. Kelly turned, took him in, and started to smile. Then her brows furrowed.

"Hey," she said so quietly he almost missed it. "Are you okay?"

"Yeah."

"You don't look okay."

"Gee, thanks."

"No, no. You *look...*" She did smile then. "Pretty delicious. And I'm a chef, I should know. But you also seem worried."

He looked delicious? That was a new one.

"I've always said, trust a chef. I'm not worried. An insomniac looking for sleep aids."

"Hmmmm. Must be going around. Are you thinking about all the crazy stories from today?"

"Wish I was." He regretted the admission immediately because her smile faded again.

"That's not going to fly tonight, Mister. I'm making some cliché hot cocoa, and you're getting some, too. We're going to sit in the living room on the soft cushy couch and tell each other stories until we fall asleep."

"More stories."

"However many it takes."

Two minutes later, she handed him a mug of chocolate and added a generous slug of Bailey's. Even though it was August and not remotely cold, the warmth from the ceramic cup comforted him. He followed her into the dark room, and she turned on a low light next to the couch where ragdoll Jack was curled in a gargantuan pile of fluff. Kelly picked up the cat and nuzzled him before transferring him to a different chair.

"Movin' you, bud," she said sweetly. "Sorry—that's

your lot in life."

In the glow of the lamp, he looked at her closely for the first time. Her features, so kind with the big, soft cat, melted him. She wore a buttery yellow T-shirt adorned with a huge purple flower that hung soft and loose over her torso. It wasn't see-through, but the fabric caressed her breasts in a way that made his Adam's apple bob in an involuntary swallow. Her lightweight purple and yellow plaid pajama pants clung in the same draping way to her legs. She sat in the corner of the thick-cushioned blue and rose sofa and looked like a garden fairy in her sexy pastel colors.

He sat in the corner opposite her and she laughed. "I'm not going to bite you, Damien. If I decide I want a good night kiss, it'll be hard this far apart."

"You don't beat around the bush, do you?"

"I guess not tonight." She pulled a lightweight afghan from the back of the couch and shook it open. "Here, put your feet up."

He swung around and stretched his legs along the back cushion. Seconds later, their legs were interlocked beneath the blanket, and her warmth and the intimacy of her touch infused him. The dream and the questions it raised faded further away.

"What gives you insomnia if it's not dreaming about Smoke horses?" she asked.

He didn't want to talk about his insomnia, but after almost a week of knowing her, he'd learned it didn't matter what he wanted. She would bring out the story because she was Kelly Crockett. She'd learn about the dreams because he'd eventually tell her.

"I dream about a black whirlpool I can't see into," he said simply. "It's what my brain saw that day I failed to jump. And it isn't the unknown that bothers me; it's the inability to figure out what that unknown is. The dreams are ridiculous—Pan jumping into it from a plane. Tonight it was John Red Wolf's dogs. And Sky was there, telling me the girl with the drawings had jumped as well. Everyone is jumping into this void except me. Nonsensical. My warped brain."

She studied him and he found he didn't mind her scrutiny. She moved her foot slowly down his shin beneath the blanket, and he knew it was unconscious because it was so slow and thoughtful her face didn't show the least bit of interest in the movement.

His groin tightened warningly.

"I don't think it sounds warped. Remember what John said today? That he thinks the dogs have something to tell you?"

"Dogs," he scoffed. "How can animals I avoid possibly show me anything? It's the only thing he said today that didn't make sense."

"I admit horses make more sense—they at least bring you happiness."

Her foot traveled back up his leg and over his knee. This time, though, she knew what she was doing. Instead of stopping her, as he should have, he copied her and cocked his knee outward so he could run the sole of his foot up the side of her thigh. He didn't miss the widening of her eyes and smiled to himself. If this was dream analysis, he was ready to dive fully into the session.

"They do," he agreed. "I'd much rather go searching for a mythical band of wild horses than follow a couple of dogs anywhere. Do you think he was really serious about taking us riding into the hills around his property?"

"I think every word out of John's mouth was sincere,

if not always serious."

Her foot made a slight turn off of straight and curved over his knee and onto his inner thigh. This time she didn't even pretend it was a casual move. Her eyes met his and the challenge was easy to read. *Do you like this?*

He matched the movement, pressing his toes into the soft flesh near where her thigh met her body. Any higher and he'd unquestionably be overstepping gentlemanly boundaries.

"John is a sincere guy," he murmured.

Her foot slid higher, and if *she* went further, she'd find out how quickly he'd forgotten the nightmare and allowed ancient male responses to replace it. Slowly she massaged his leg with her toes until the rough denim between her skin and his seemed to melt away under the heat she generated. The tightening in his belly turned to hard desire. The breath in his chest could barely escape with each exhale. Beneath his foot, her body tensed, even as she seemed to sink into his touch. Hard and wanting, he tried to convince himself to stop playing. This was fire, and he'd known the woman a week. That was not enough time. And still, he didn't listen to himself.

With a groan, he threw off the afghan, reached for her foot, and moved her leg gently over his, away from her path of exploration. He grasped her hand, pulling her up and then forward to lie on top of him. She offered not a shred of resistance but settled against him, her knees embracing his thighs, her breasts through the soft knit top crushing against his bare chest. She gave a squeaky little moan of pleasure and sealed her lips against his, thrusting her tongue into his mouth. Bold and sure, she delved in and pumped against his tongue, mimicking the action with her hips.

He wrapped her in his arms, slipping one hand around the swell of her bottom, pulling her tight, and riding along as she rocked with him. All he wanted in the world was to reach between their bodies and yank open the snap on his pants, drag down the zipper, and join with her. The desire was already theirs for the taking. The motion, the pressures were new but so right—as if they'd known each other far longer than days. Her kiss drove him deeper into pure need. It teased and it comforted. It thrilled and sent heat into his core, yet it calmed and made him want to take his time—to live in the moment she offered. That he was taking.

Cold truth doused his desire like ice water. Taking. He was only taking comfort.

With hands as gentle as frustration would allow, he threaded his fingers through her hair and pushed her head away, halting the kiss, making her groan.

"I know," he said. "Kelly, I'm sorry. We have to back off."

"We don't *have* to anything."

"We do," he corrected and stroked her hair back from her face—her beautiful face that hung over his now, eyes brimming with disappointment but no anger. "We have to stop but we don't have to want to."

"You make no sense."

"I agree."

She dropped her head until her forehead rested on his. "Why can't you just be a typical man who only thinks of sex and getting his way? A bad boy instead of one with some kind of scruples?"

"My mother filled me with scruples?"

He tried to smile, but her body still pressed against the heat of an erection he was soon to regret big time, and smiling didn't fit the moment. He didn't want her to move, but he was going to have to make the break or risk becoming the bad boy she claimed to want.

"This is really a terrible time to invoke your mother."

"Oh, I don't know." He took a deep breath before pushing her up and away. "It might be the perfect antidote for me at the moment."

She huffed in frustration and gave him the lightest of fake punches to the shoulder as he managed to sit, uncomfortably, and pull her to curl against his side.

"I'll tell you what the antidote was."

"I agree. But we'd be wrong."

She didn't say anything, but she laid her head against his chest and wrapped an arm around his stomach.

"I am sorry," he repeated. "I know this was rotten, but I can't do this just to chase away nightmares. That's not fair to you."

"I know why you stopped." She rubbed her hand in a comforting circle on his chest. "But don't talk about fair. I also knew what I was doing."

"Yes. Yes you did."

"Don't go upstairs yet. Maybe I was using you to chase away fears, too."

"Were you?" He craned his neck to peer at her. He could see her long lashes resting against her cheek. Feel her shoulders lift ever-so-slightly in a feeble shrug.

"Nothing bad. Just a lot to think about."

"Tell me?"

"Nothing to tell yet. Just deciding how to get where I want to go without ruining everyone else's life."

"You aren't going to ruin anyone's life, Kelly."

"Maybe. Maybe not. I need to talk to my sisters tomorrow. After that, I'll have a better idea of which it is.

Meanwhile, I promise to behave if you'll just...not go back to bed yet."

He finally smiled and dropped a kiss on the top of her head.

"Yeah, sure," he said. "I owe you that much."

They sat quietly for several minutes and the tension slowly drained from Damien's body. He closed his eyes and let himself simply appreciate not being alone. He hadn't wanted this kind of company for a very long time.

"Damien?" Her voice whispered through him.

"Hmmm?"

"If I talk Cole into letting you go, maybe next week for a few days, will you help me arrange a ride to John's? With Pan and Apollo?"

The idea warmed him further and stirred up the excitement he'd felt when John had first suggested it.

"I'd like that."

"I would, too." Her voice was slow, sleepy—sexy. "Thanks."

"No thanks needed," he replied. "I think I owe Pan that much."

Chapter Nineteen

THREE HOURS OF sleep in her own bed, after two hours curled with Damien on the couch, after the frustration of what could have but hadn't been, should have left Kelly drugged from exhaustion. Instead, six-thirty saw her wide awake and hopeful. Somehow, in the midst of the fragmented night, talking with Damien, she'd formed a plan. Implementing it might annoy Raquel and Grace in the next half hour, but she had to trust they'd forgive her—and they'd take care of multiple issues with one outing.

She threw on her riding jeans and a clean T-shirt, grabbed a pair of boot socks, and headed for Grace's room, glancing at Damien's closed door with a wistful smile. She would miss riding with him this morning, but he was now a working cowboy. Raising her knuckles to the door, she rapped soundly.

"Gracie," she called. "Get up."

The door opened almost immediately. Her sister wasn't dressed, but she hadn't just awoken.

"What the heck?"

"You don't have to be at the restaurant until eleven. We're going for a ride."

"We are?"

"All three of us. I'm getting Raquel and we're going to Ancestor Canyon. Let's see if we can catch our little camper in the act. And I have some ideas to run past both of you."

At that Grace hesitated, but her features cleared almost immediately and she nodded. "Yeah, okay. But you are the one who's waking Rocky. I'm not getting my head bitten off because it isn't nine yet."

Kelly laughed.

"She went to bed early so I'll take a chance. See you downstairs."

Grace's prediction wasn't far off.

"Kelly, what the hell is wrong with you?" Raquel's sleep-wild hair and squinting eyes greeted her from the middle of her double bed. "It's barely six-thirty."

"Six-thirty-six," Kelly chirped. "And you're getting up."

"I don't think so."

"Yup. We're going to Ancestor Canyon."

"Have fun."

"Seriously. I need your help."

In the end, Raquel dragged herself out of bed and, after a requisite amount of grousing, actually agreed it would be fun to try and surprise the young girl who might be camping in the canyon. A weight lifted from Kelly's shoulders, and optimism showed its head for the first time in a long while at the thought of spending time with both her sisters. They'd been apart from Grace for so long that this reunion felt like a tiny miracle.

They rode out before seven-thirty. The morning was fresh, still only hinting at the deep summer heat a few hours away. Kelly studied the early morning light for signs of smoke haze, but the pale blue sky shone clear and cloudless. Jellyman, fresh as the weather, jigged alongside his companions—one a little bay mustang Mia had been training for the past two years named May that Grace claimed felt like driving a little sports car, and Joely's newest horse, a taller quarter horse gelding named Jack Flash. They hadn't ridden together since their father's funeral four years earlier.

"All right, I admit it. This was a good idea." Raquel bent forward to give Flash a long stroke on his neck.

"I forget to come and ride," Grace said. "I should be able to make time for this, but I'm always finding excuses to keep busy with other things."

"We all know what it takes to make a business successful," Raquel said. "You don't have to feel guilty about riding."

"Once I can get my hands on a chef who'll stay…" Grace trailed off.

Raquel laughed. "Yeah, what's it been?"

"Four now," Grace said. "Until Kel and Damien stepped in. It figures that the perfect combo in my kitchen is the most unsustainable."

"It's been fun."

"Damien is a big surprise," Raquel said. "I remember him as a tough guy who liked to cause grief with Gabe's first group of jokers."

"Yeah," Kelly said. "The joker still shows up. First day in the kitchen, he taped the handle of the sink sprayer down."

"I've been wondering how to ask about that little

shine in your eyes when you talk about him." Raquel gave a knowing smirk.

"There's no shine."

Grace made an un-ladylike snort. "Try again, Kel."

"There's no shine! I like the guy. And to head you both off at the pass, I've kissed the guy."

"What!" Raquel and Grace exchanged a look of glee.

"Like you're even surprised. He's a good guy. A little tortured for me, but hey. Party girl, remember."

"I've seen the party-girl eye shine," Raquel said. "This is not that. This is a Damien Finney shine."

"Okay, that's enough." Kelly forced back the start of an embarrassed flush. "I didn't organize this to talk about me. I want to find out about the girl who might be related to John Red Wolf."

"Nice deflection," Grace said. "Fine, you're off the hook for now but not for good. Tell us about your visit with Mr. Red Wolf."

They reached the canyon forty-five minutes later and Kelly felt as if she were coming home at the sight of the braided stream and the pond outside the canyon entrance. Rivulets of pleasure assailed Kelly thinking of Damien filling his water bottle there, and that led inevitably to thinking about Damien the night before. But then they reached the mouth of the canyon itself and nervous anticipation replaced the pleasure.

"The fire pit is to the left," Kelly said.

"What do we do if she's there?" Raquel asked.

"We treat her carefully and get answers," Grace replied. "Whatever we do, we don't want to scare her."

"A little scare wouldn't be a bad thing." Kelly scowled. "She's given us a couple."

"And we're not her. Besides, you did take her

medicine bag."

It was a fair point.

They entered between the high walls and Kelly's heart pounded with anticipation. She had such a strong feeling…

The fire ring was abandoned.

As far as Kelly could tell, it looked no different than when she'd been there with Damien the day before. The same piece of half-burned wood lay in the center of the ring, and nothing in the area had changed. All three girls dismounted and searched the surroundings for clues or stashed items, but the only horse droppings were older, and there were no new hoofprints.

"Dang," Kelly said. "I honestly thought she'd still be here. It doesn't look like she spent the night."

"I'm sorry," Grace said. "I know you want to find her."

"We may never identify her if she's moved on. Damien and I think she's on some kind of search."

"We know she wants that medicine bag back," Raquel said. "Sooner or later, she'll have to knock on the door or find you somewhere."

"I can't figure out why she doesn't simply do that," Raquel said.

"If she is a young girl, then that answers itself." Grace chuckled. "Teenagers don't want to talk to anyone they don't have to."

There wasn't much else to do in the canyon except explore for fun, eat the cookies Kelly had packed for a mid-morning snack, and prepare herself for the discussion she knew would make the ride home far less easy-going than the one they'd been having. However, once they were underway, Kelly didn't have to broach the subject of

Triple Bean. Grace opened it for them.

"You said you have ideas you want to talk about, Kel. What kind of ideas?"

Kelly swallowed. This was what she'd dragged them out of bed to talk about, but faced with reality, it suddenly felt like a dangerous idea since their track record on discussing the future stunk.

"Ideas for getting us all back on the same track going forward. I've hated avoiding the problem, so if we can come up with an actual plan, maybe things won't seem so bad."

"What do you want to do? I mean really want to do?" Raquel asked. "Everything you've talked about so far is ethereal. Things that could be if all the stars align properly."

"I got an email before bed last night." Kelly focused on the trail, hoping Rocky would accept the news graciously. "Landon said Mark Lansbury will contact me in the next day or so. On Landon's recommendation, Lansbury is willing to let me apply for his sous chef internship even though there are already a couple other candidates. I'll need to create a sample menu and some kind of application package that will show off my qualifications, and he'll decide. If I get it, it'll be six to nine months and then I'll be free to do what we want."

"Six to *nine* months now?" The disbelief in Raquel's voice came as no surprise. "The time keeps growing. What am I supposed to do for nine months?"

"I've thought about it. What if we give Lauren my head cook position at Triple Bean while I'm gone? She knows the menu and she's very good. She could keep things running."

"Lauren is a line cook. She's never expressed any

interest in taking the head job. And even if she did, you'll come waltzing back after your vacation and what? Un-promote her?"

"No. We assess. If she wants to, she keeps Triple Bean going while we start the new restaurant. If she wants to leave, we find a new cook. Either way, we keep Triple Bean and still keep growing."

"A new restaurant *and* the old one? Just where are we going to get that money? Everything we own is tied up in the current place, and the small business loan would only be enough to expand, not start a whole new restaurant."

"There would be options to discuss, I know."

"I don't understand why you want to abandon everything we worked so hard to build." Raquel's tone didn't hold one smidgen of warmth or understanding.

"The same reason you don't seem to remember that this was our plan all along."

"No. This was your plan after about two years when you discovered how much you like to be successful."

Kelly's optimism from the early morning stalled fully. She turned to Grace, pleadingly.

"You remember. You know I always wanted to have a starred restaurant somewhere. We started in Denver because we all went to school there and we knew the city, but is there really anything sacred about Colorado?"

"Kelly, I'm the last one who should get in the middle of this. I'm the first one who defected."

"You went after your dream and you're realizing it. You've done great."

"Except that I lose chefs the way babies lose mittens. Yes, okay, I followed a dream and I'd do it again. But it's been super hard."

"See? Rocky? We can make changes and it will work

265   *Lizbeth Selvig*

out."

"And I told you. I have dreams, too."

"Tell me!" Kelly asked sincerely. "Seriously, Rocky, you are the most brilliant person I know. Your brainpower blows all of us out of the water, and I include our three big sisters in that. Triple Bean took off because you know numbers, you know budgets, you know marketing. It can't be enough for you to manage one little restaurant all your life."

Raquel rode silently and Kelly reined Jellyman in beside her, matching her pace until finally, she spoke.

"I love Denver. I'll never love it as much as I love Paradise, but it's my home now. I like the area where we live. I like the neighborhood where the restaurant is located. I'm worried about everyone abandoning it. You know what I want? I want to bring it all back. I want to weather the rezoning storm and overcome the bookstore fire. It needs to be an area that attracts everyone, not just people with money for high-end restaurants. I want bookstores and toy stores and..."

"You don't want an expensive, three-star restaurant." Grace didn't say it like an accusation, but like a realization. "A fancy eatery doesn't fit in the vision."

"I want Kelly there. I want her expertise and her talent. But I don't want to start over trying to maintain something big and pressure-filled."

"Wow." Kelly honestly had nothing else to say. This was not Raquel simply dragging her feet. This was Raquel saying Kelly's dream had no place in their future together.

"I haven't known how to tell you that," Raquel said. "I don't want to squash your dreams. I don't want you to leave. I want you to want what I want." She followed with a rueful laugh. "I'm as selfish as the next person."

"I don't see why over time there can't be a compromise," Grace said quietly. "Who knows what can happen now that you both understand each other."

"Understand?" Kelly's heart ached. "I don't. Why do you want to bang your head against the wall in a dying area? You tell me I'm only out for myself and glory. Well, I think you're scared to leave what you know."

"I think you're scared to fight."

"Hey." Grace rode between them, physically separating the anger that hung almost visibly in the air. "You do know you're both trying to make these decisions after a really traumatic experience, right? This isn't actually about what to do in the future. This is about nearly watching our dream go up in smoke. Killing a living dream is far scarier than making plans for those that aren't born yet."

Grace. The wise one. She'd been playing Solomon ever since their first triplet fight at age two. Kelly released a breath she didn't realize she'd been holding.

"You're right. It was scary. It does make me want to leap away and create something safe. Something that won't burn."

"And it made me want to fix it and make sure it would never burn again," Raquel said.

"Aren't those two ends of the same dream?" Grace asked.

There wasn't much to argue with except that the distance between those two ends was longer than Kelly could measure at the moment.

"I think you should do what you have to do."

Raquel sounded tired and resigned. Kelly still didn't like being the cause of her unhappiness, but something kept her from giving in, even though going back to her old restaurant would make her comfortable and probably successful enough.

"It isn't what I have to do."

"Fine. What you want to do. Go. Go to San Francisco."

"Rocky, come on. What I want more than anything is your blessing."

"Fine. You have it."

If ever there'd been a listless response to a question, this was a prime example.

"And you have mine." Grace smiled. "I think you should go and learn as much as you can. Maybe you'll find your bliss the way I did. Maybe you'll get homesick and find out you want to come back to where you've always been happy."

"Thank you." Kelly would have hugged her if they hadn't been on swaying horseback. "Will you help me? When I find out what I need to prepare for Chef Lansbury, can I experiment in your kitchen?"

"What does 'experiment' mean?"

"Create a menu. Maybe try it out on the family? Or do a promotion of some kind."

"You are bound and determined to see me change my menu." Grace's smile was a little less warm and fuzzy.

"No! I swear. It would be the equivalent of a bookstore bringing in an author to sign books. A guest cook. One time and done."

"To showcase you." Raquel didn't look at her.

"No." Anger picked at the edges of her calm again. She couldn't figure out why Raquel was so unbendingly mad. "To *help* me. To figure out what I'm best at. I told you, my culinary school skills are rusty."

"Our fault for keeping you at a little coffee bar and lunch spot."

Even Grace looked askance at that. "Come on, sis, that wasn't fair."

"You're right. Sorry." Again the apology was more automatic than sincere.

"I won't change the menu, Grace." Kelly ignored Raquel's pique.

"Okay, Kel, here's the deal." Grace's voice was calm but firm. "I'll let you experiment in the kitchen and serve your dishes in the dining room under two conditions."

"Name them."

"You will not play around with my menu. I know it's not creative enough for you, but it's what I want. No suggestions. No plans."

Kelly pushed back her resentment. Grace was right. "Okay fine, and the second?"

"Raquel does a marketing plan for this. Like you said, this is me having a guest chef in. Raquel figures out how to promote that. You two will work together on this or not at all."

Raquel scowled at Grace. "And how are we going to pick out replacement equipment and fixtures for the remodel of *our* restaurant if we're stuck here?"

"Rocky, think about it. This is a great idea," Kelly said. "I would love your help, and you'll do a better job for Gracie than I ever could. As for Triple Bean, we don't have to be on site to design it. We can do that anywhere."

They rode on, each considering the plan, such as it was.

"Fine, but I have my conditions, too," Raquel said. "These jobs are separate. Grace runs the restaurant. Kelly makes up her dishes. I run the promo. We're not going to get in each other's spaces, because right now that seems safest for us."

They'd never been three separate entities before. It had always been the Musketeer cliché with them: all for one. Kelly hated the division, but Grace's idea was the best they'd come up with, and at least it was a step forward.

"All right," she said. "Let's do it. I'll find out soon what the details are. I...thank you both. I appreciate the help."

Help but not full support, she thought. It would have to do for the moment.

Chapter Twenty

DAMIEN WAS SURPRISED and happy when at the end of dinner the next night, Kelly arrived home early from working at Peas Porridge. Liam had returned to the restaurant, his foot in a walking boot, and she'd been able to leave after helping prep for the evening shift. Her presence gave Damien's very long day a welcome boost.

After she ate, Kelly insisted on taking care of dinner clean-up since her early night was bonus time. And, she claimed, she'd use the time to start planning the gourmet menu she needed to prepare for the chef in San Francisco. Despite that, she welcomed Damien's offer of help.

"You look tired," she said when they had the dining room cleared and she was filling the dishwasher. "First full day before the cows arrive?"

"We went back up to the site and checked the caretaker cabin. We rode the fence line and then came back here to do some repairs on one of the big corrals. I had to take time off to go meet with that therapist Gabe found, and I still managed some more fascinating reading about raising organic beef. The day was plenty long."

"I knew you had your appointment. Did it go well?"

She didn't ask specifics. She didn't hound him to tell her anything. So, of course, he told her everything.

"He's a nice guy. He does work primarily with firefighters, but also with victims of fires, both domestic and combat-related. I don't knock his credentials. But I still think he's a waste of time."

"Oh?" She leaned sideways against a counter, dishcloth in her hands her eyes sympathetic. "I'm sorry he didn't give you more hope."

"He was interested in my history with the Sheridan Fire Department. He was far less interested in the things I thought helped me the most. I told him about the horses and about John Red Wolf. He's of the opinion that I shouldn't delve too deeply into John's stories and theories. He doesn't want me to "bury the problems" deeper by chasing after fantasies."

"I really am sorry," she said. "I'm sure you'll work things out with him, but I agree. I'd think he'd be interested in anything that might help you tap into your thoughts or memories."

Damien shrugged. He'd been through so much counseling that today had not been a surprise. Disappointing, maybe, because he had such a limited time in which to find answers, but nothing he hadn't expected or been asked fifty times in the past.

"I'm okay. I fully intend to follow where the horses lead me no matter what this doc says—even if it's just down a rabbit hole. Maybe I'll like living in a nice, comfy burrow."

After a glance to be sure they were still alone, she walked into his arms and hugged him. He reveled in her touch and in the tacit approval it gave.

"I say the biggest rabbit hole we go down is a horseback camping trip that takes us to John's, and I also say we take some others with us. I think Sky has to come if we're bringing Apollo. The colt knows her best. And some company for her besides us—Marcus maybe, or a friend. Actually, anyone who wants to come could. There are usually a lot of rabbits in a burrow."

He grinned and squeezed her. "I like how you take a metaphor and run with it."

"Or hop with it." She buried her head in his chest and laughed. "Okay, sorry, I'm done. How about after we're done here, we go talk to Sky? If she wants to do this, we'll start planning in earnest."

He bent to kiss her hair. She was short and slight but felt fierce and focused in his embrace.

"I didn't realize how much I needed some kind of plan. Thank you."

They found Skylar in the barn, grooming her own horse, Bungu. The name was a Shoshone word for horse, and in his own way Bungu was like Pan—more than a mere horse. He was Sky's best friend, a beautiful black appaloosa with a blanket of bright white rump spots. Sky wasn't alone. Rory, handsome and tall at ten, and Lucky, an extremely precocious seven, each groomed their horses, too. Rory's quarter horse, a solid bay mare with no white markings named Largo, was one of the most experienced horses on the ranch. Lucky's pony was a mischievous palomino pony named Bugaboo. Lucky had developed an obsession with horses that rivaled Skylar's, and had taken Damien's place as Sky's trail-riding protégé.

"You guys heading out on an evening ride?" Kelly

asked.

"We're going to the river and see if we can spot the osprey we saw the other day," Sky said.

"We hope she's nesting around the big bend of the Kwinaa," Lucky added. "I want to do a report on ospreys, so I hope I see her and can get some pictures."

"What a fun trip," Kelly said. "I'll cross my fingers. Sky, can we ask you a question before you go?"

"Sure."

"Come on over here a second."

When they told her a much-shortened version of the Smoke horses story and then presented the idea for several-days-long camping trip with Apollo to John Red Wolf's ranch, Sky's reaction was exactly what Damien had expected. Aside from her love of trail riding, now that she knew the artist behind the horse drawing might be involved, she was all in for the sheer mystery of it all.

"When can we go?" she asked.

"Yeah! When can we go?"

They all turned to see Lucky, kneeling on a hay bale in the aisle, listening in as only a gifted eavesdropper could.

"Whoa, hang on," Damien said. "This isn't a trip for kids, Lucky. Sorry. This is a long ride into country you don't know well. I'm pretty sure your dad wouldn't be too interested in having us take you into unknown territory."

"He would," she insisted. "He knows what a good rider I am."

"I'm a good rider, too," Rory said.

Damien's heart fell. He hadn't intended to involve the younger children. He couldn't imagine their parents being pleased with this idea, but Kelly surprised him.

"Hold on, let's think about this. I won't promise

anything, but when we were kids we always used to pack up the horses and take an end-of-the-summer camping trip. Maybe, if we plan this right, and get enough chaperones, we could convince your parents you're all old enough to go on one."

"Yeah!" Rory pumped his fist. "That would be so cool."

"Don't start packing anything yet." Kelly waved the kids back to their horses. "I'll let you know if we can do anything. Just go on your ride and have fun."

All three scurried back to their grooming, buzzing like cicadas with ideas for a potential camping trip despite Kelly's warning.

"Are you sure that would be a good idea? Taking kids camping?" Damien asked.

He certainly wasn't sure.

"Seriously, we used to do it all the time from a pretty early age," she replied. "We would pack up a little camp stove. Dad would pony along a pack horse with food and water, and a couple of tents. We'd each bring our own bedroll and rain gear. It was great fun and helpful for building outdoor skills. It could be good for them. Plus, what kid doesn't need a great mystery to follow? They all love horses."

"What about John? Will he take kindly to a bunch of kids tagging along?"

"That's the big question after we get the parents to sign off. But you heard how he ran those horse shows for years. I think he'd be okay. If he's not...we won't do it. Of course."

As always, Kelly's optimism left no room for his I-have-a-problem-for-every-solution attitude. The way she talked about her early horse camping trips almost made him excited to try it. Almost. He was still Damien Finney, after all. It didn't do to show too much enthusiasm for a new idea right off the bat.

She took him aback when she clapped him on the arm and read his mind.

"Come on, Finney, take a chance. And if all the kids come, you won't be stuck with me jabbering in your ear the whole two days."

Yeah. How did he explain that the idea of such a fate no longer put him off? What a difference eight days could make.

***

Gabe and Mia agreed whole-heartedly to letting Rory go on the camping trip. Joely had little trouble convincing Alec it would be a good experience for Lucky, too, and both offered to chaperone. All that remained was to get Melanie and Bjorn's permission for their kids and receive John Red Wolf's blessing for the entire idea. But despite the positive end to a long day, Kelly tossed sleeplessly that night, dwelling not on plans for an exciting trip, but on the morning ride eighteen hours earlier with her sisters. They might have come up with a truce, but the plan was not a comfortable one.

She was the odd sister out this time—roped and tied by Raquel's and Grace's rules. In some ways they were fair; she was the one who wanted a change, and she remembered how hurt she'd been when Grace had announced she was leaving their partnership. On the other hand, she was only following a course she'd set out for them all from the beginning. Wasn't she? They'd known all along what she'd wanted to make of her culinary training.

After staring into the dark for half an hour, she turned

on her bedside light and tossed off her covers, hoping to find an old book on the shelves. Before she could find her literary escape, however, the door opened just down the hall, followed by footsteps that were too heavy to be Grace's or Raquel's.

Damien.

A thudding started in her chest, and for several minutes she fought with herself. She shouldn't go find him. She needed to pull up her big girl panties and deal. He needed his space as well.

Yeah, she told herself at last. Forget that.

Following the thin trail of light emanating from the kitchen, she found him searching the refrigerator and her heart lightened. She cleared her throat.

"My turn to expose the night thief."

He turned, a slow smile spreading, his eyes dark and opaque in the room lit only by a small light over the sink and the refrigerator open behind him.

"Caught dead to rights," he admitted and held up a bottle of orange juice. "You want some of this, too? Easier than cocoa."

She reached into a cupboard and pulled out a small bottle of vodka that she waggled in front of him. "Add a little of this to party it up, and it sounds like a plan to me."

"Party. Right. I am not surprised. What if I told you I'm glad? That I didn't try to be quiet tonight, hoping you'd hear me get up?" he said. "Sound enough like a teenage boy's stupid plan to get a girl?"

"Nah. Sounds like a grown man who maybe had another stupid dream?"

His smile dimmed. "I should be used to them now, but they still bug the hell out of me. You're supposed to go back to sleep after a dream when you're a grown-up."

"Nope. I declare that's not a rule. Tell me about this one."

"Pretty simple actually. I was on that plane, ready to jump. This time Hermione—she's one of the crew members who was with me that last day—handed me the picture she always carries of her boys when she jumps. She told me to keep them safe. Then she looked behind her and there were five horses, all of them grulla but none of them Pan or Apollo or even Bird. She climbed on the back of the first one and they jumped out of the plane."

At the end, he smiled.

"That doesn't sound simple to me," Kelly said.

"What it sounds is ridiculous. Maybe I should be going to some fortune teller-slash-dream interpreter instead of a therapist."

"Just for the record, again, I think the therapist is missing an opportunity. He should be asking you about this."

"I don't know." He took a generous drink of his screwdriver.

"Come on. Let's go back to our sofa where it's comfortable."

Damien shook his head. "I want to sleep with you."

She must have shown the shock that rocketed down her body at the bold admission because he set his glass on the counter and grinned before taking her glass and putting it next to his. With his hands on her cheeks, he bent his head and whispered against her lips.

"Just sleep. Like taking a teddy bear to bed for comfort."

"Sure. Right. And I have a mountain to sell you."

He kissed her softly in exploration, his lips asking nothing except for her breath to mingle with his. He requested no entry into her mouth and, instead, let his mouth play magically, teasingly on hers, opening but then merely closing gently on her lips. He roamed to the corners of her mouth, first one side, then the other. When he trailed his kisses across her cheek and landed in the soft depression below her earlobe, she shivered and failed to stop a guttural moan. With eyes closed, she reached up into his hair and gripped, pulling his head tight to keep his lips to their task.

When he pulled away, she shook her head at him.

"Those were some hundred-proof goosebumps you raised."

"Just sleep with me," he repeated. "I'll be good."

"If you are, I'll be disappointed."

She questioned no more and followed him back upstairs and into his room. They finished the drinks, maybe for courage, maybe just for the taste they could share at the next kiss.

"Why were *you* still up?" he asked. "This isn't all about me, you know."

"I had another argument with my sisters," she admitted. "But we're working it out. I just feel like we're adrift. We've never been so at odds, and they think it's my fault. Maybe it is."

"It's nobody's fault." He smoothed the hair away from her face. He was so handsome she wanted to melt like a silly teenager herself. "Life throws curve balls all the time. And don't forget, however messed up I might be, I do know how traumatic fire is. Don't discount the fire you went through."

"You sound like Grace. She says this is me reacting to sudden change."

"See how it all plays out. Don't worry about what we

all think."

"I have to create a four-course dinner that will impress a chef in San Francisco. It's like an audition. A test."

"Do you know what you're making?"

"Not a clue. Yet."

"Come on." He led her to the soft double bed. "You can keep my nightmare at bay and I'll try and inspire you."

They crawled in as nonchalantly as if his promise to be good was a true one. But her heart wasn't going to believe it until they fell asleep. Still, at first, they followed their rule, simply wrapping into each other's embrace, letting the warmth and comfort of their bodies snuggled together be enough. In his arms, Kelly could believe her world would right itself and she'd know how to pursue her goal without losing her sisters. And she believed Damien could find the light to illuminate his internal darkness.

He changed the rule first, using one long, strong finger subtly, slowly tracing the line of her spine to the top of her seat. He drew the line up again and then down, and she shivered. This time he burrowed past the waistband of her pajama bottoms to find the cleft of her bottom.

"Soft," he said.

"You're breaking your promise." She kissed his neck.

"Say the word and I stop. I won't break that one."

She said nothing, just followed his lead and ran her fingers across his shoulder blades to his spine and then kneading downward until she could squeeze the taut muscles of his seat. To get closer, she threw one leg over his hip and wriggled in. Her eyes widened in pleasure when she felt his clear, hard reaction.

"Well, part of you is glad to see me."

"Pretty darn glad."

He covered her mouth with a kiss again and this time there was nothing chaste about it. Alarm sirens of pleasure and wayward chills of delight spun through her body. Liquid sluiced to her core as his tongue probed for her response and she gave it, groaning into his mouth, pushing him onto his back and climbing onto him, pressing into the heat and hardness that, tonight, wasn't constrained by jeans.

"I honest-to-God truly was not going to do this," he said, breaking the kiss for each word.

"I never believed that for a minute." Her words were equally breathy and broken.

He placed his hands on her hips, and in one fluid motion, slid her pants down her legs. Arching over him, she helped finish the job and kicked them off beneath the sheet. He flipped them over so he hung suspended over her. She pulled at his bottoms, too, and they soon joined hers on the floor. Tops went next, her camisole top and his plain white T-shirt. Skin to hot skin they sank back into the mattress and he slid down to take one breast into his mouth.

"Oh, yeah, Damien," she murmured, and her stomach clenched in pleasure as he nibbled and kneaded so gently it was exquisite as lovemaking.

She held his head to her as he made long work of each breast. Finally, he moved down, kissing over her sternum, teasing the soft skin of her stomach with his lips, and swirling his tongue at the skin around her navel. She waited, trembling, for him to move even lower but, instead, he touched her, his hard-tipped fingers, slipping through the moist folds where he stroked her gently, over and over until she was so close to the edge of release she begged him to let her fly.

He stopped.

At her moan of distress, he grinned and slid back up her body, rough against soft. Teasingly, he kissed her, slow and torturously.

"You said you were going to be good," she whispered. "You're so not. You're evil."

"Let's just see about that."

He took ten seconds to grab a foil pack she hadn't noticed on the side table, tore it, and let her help slide it on. They joined in an easy movement, so perfect she only felt the pure hot pleasure of Damien Finney deep inside of her, making them one, taking them to a place where neither of them could wound or be wounded. They moved together, in rhythm, in a perfect climb to the exact place where he'd let go of her moments before. This time, however, as she rose right back up to that edge, he was with her and he let her fly. He called her name and she flew into beautiful pieces in his arms.

Chapter Twenty-one

KELLY AWOKE IN a happy fog of memory and stretched luxuriantly only to find herself alone in the bed where hours earlier she'd fallen asleep wrapped in Damien's arms. In an instant, her eyes cleared, and her senses went on alert until she sat and found Damien across the room, quietly slipping on jeans.

"You're leaving without saying good-bye?" she asked.

He turned his head and smiled, but it held none of the joy from the previous night. Her throat tightened.

"I would have waited for you to wake up."

"But…you are leaving."

"I have to be at the ranch office in forty minutes. I'm a working stiff now, remember?"

"Is everything all right?"

He zipped his jeans and returned to the bed. He sat sideways and seemed as though he forced himself to capture her eyes.

"You're amazing."

"Thank you?" Her chest tightened.

"Last night was amazing."

"Yes. It was."

"It was a mistake." He shook his head to ward off her protest. "Not you, Kelly. You aren't a mistake and neither are my feelings for you. But we slept together for all the wrong reasons."

"How could anything about that have been wrong?" Her heart sank at the cliché of this aftermath, and the back of her eyes burned with sorrow.

"You were depressed. I was depressed and afraid of the dark. I used you."

"Hey, excuse me. I was a full participant. Don't treat me like you owe me an apology—I made my choice."

"I know that. But be honest. We used each other, not for love but for comfort."

"Love *is* comfort, Damien. I finally felt safe last night. Like I would be able to figure things out because you were there to take my side and to give me a haven."

"I will always take your side. But I am not in a place to be anyone's haven. I have too much to figure out and I'm not sure I'll ever get there. As unbelievable as it sounds, based on what we shared, I did not intend to have sex with you last night. I really did want to sleep with you, in the strictest sense of the word. I just didn't stop myself when it went further."

"And I don't regret that for a single second."

He reached for her hand, and if it solved nothing, it did reassure that he wasn't fully walking away.

"I haven't met anyone who's climbed over the fences I build around myself as fast or as easily as you have. I don't know how you do it and I don't know why I let you in. I don't want to lose that. But we can't do this again until

I know I'm fully there for you."

"I think you're being silly."

"Because you have a different way of dealing with the world. You think everything can be fixed with fun and laughter. With a contest or a new idea. Don't misunderstand; I envy that. I'm working on getting there. But I'm not there."

"You're closer than you think, Damien. Don't fall backward; we can keep going forward."

He pulled off a smile that looked genuine.

"I can compromise. We can go sideways. Because I do need to find out how to fix this before going forward. Not with something like whatever this might be."

She wanted to tell him she knew exactly what "this" was—to her, the night before had been real and beautiful. A start. But in her heart, she knew she'd promised never to push him.

"Fine. Go to work, cowboy," she said. "I'll give you the space you need for this, but don't expect me to give up on a kiss now and then. That horse has left the barn."

"I think I can handle that." He stood up, looked momentarily uncertain, and placed a soft kiss on the crown of her head. "I'll see you tonight."

Damien's sudden distancing kicked off one of the strangest few days of Kelly's life. It was as if the entire world decided to take a break from her. Nobody seemed angry. Everyone looked busy. But the Crockett family seemed to have dispersed into individual lanes and there they ran, waving at each other and exchanging news at dinner, then heading off to the next tasks.

Kelly only needed to work at Peas Porridge three nights, since mid-week was slow and Grace managed with

Liam the other three. Kelly scheduled herself to work the busy weekends, and that seemed to satisfy her sister. Raquel disappeared into a world of telephone calls and planning for promoting Kelly's chef audition. She actually seemed happy with the task, but she refused to give any details. It seemed like overkill for one little night, but Rocky was happy, and that felt like a minor miracle.

Once the new organic herd arrived, the men were outrageously busy getting the cattle settled. Damien spent two nights at the remote site, keeping watch as the new moms and babies adjusted to their space. He did return relaxed and happy, saying that the solitude had been healing, and Kelly couldn't deny the knowledge stung. She chastised herself for believing she should or even could be the best one to help him find his way. Thinking he was right, that they weren't ready to be a couple, only put her in a gloomier mood as she went about her own tasks, wracking her brains and combing old favorite cooking sites for ideas that would give her the perfect, high-class, three-course menu Mark Lansbury had requested for her application.

Grandma Sadie turned into her closest companion. She gave her opinion on every dish Kelly suggested and made no bones about handing out a thumbs-up or a thumbs-down.

Her mom played the ultimate cheerleader and, for the most part, agreed with Grandma Sadie on choices. In the end, the job of deciding on her three courses turned out to be a lonely and nerve-wracking endeavor. She found herself wishing for Damien's opinion—irreverent as it would certainly be—but he remained distracted.

The happiest parts of her days were listening to the kids plan the five-day camping trip that had been sanctioned and blessed by all parents and enthusiastically welcomed by John Red Wolf. After all family members were polled and schedules checked, ten people planned to ride out two weeks later, after Kelly's special-menu night at Peas Porridge. After three days of poring over recipes and menus from restaurants across the country, Kelly couldn't wait to implement all the kids' plans and get out into the open with a tent and a pack of easy meals to cook.

At the end of the week, she finally armed herself with seven potential recipes and made plans to take them to the restaurant so Grace could give her opinions on what sounded best. She'd wanted Raquel to join them, but she'd disappeared without a word, and even Grandma Sadie, Paradise's version of the town gossip who knew everything, didn't know where she'd gone.

Finally, when she was pulling into the parking lot at Peas Porridge, her phone signaled a text message. She pulled it up as she walked into the kitchen, to find Grace reading her phone as well.

"From Rocky," Grace said.

"Yeah, I got one, too."

"Sorry I left without warning," Grace read. "Had to run to the airport. I have an idea and a surprise, so make sure you're both at the restaurant tonight. Kelly, I hope you've got something big up your sleeve. Grace, I took a big liberty. Hope you'll both forgive me."

Kelly squinted at the message again and then turned a quizzical frown on Grace.

"What on earth is she talking about? I don't have anything up my sleeve except seven pieces of paper that make me very nervous because they aren't good enough ideas. And taking a liberty? She's making no sense."

"I'm lost," Grace agreed. "I thought she was dead set

against all of this stuff we're doing, but this week she's been sequestered like she's on some kind of life-or-death deadline."

Kelly laughed. "Raquel takes every deadline like it's life or death. She makes up for my lack of seriousness."

"Always has. Thank goodness one of us has focus."

For the first time in a long while, Kelly took the jibe as good-natured camaraderie. All their lives, they'd been able to capitalize on each other's strengths. Only lately had their differences had been divisive rather than unifying.

"Well, I have no focus, for sure. I've got myself so confused. While we wait for Rocky, would you please look at these recipes and give me your opinion about a sample menu?"

Grace laughed and gave her one last squeeze.

"Of course. We have time before we need to prep the chicken for tonight."

Forty-five minutes later, they'd narrowed Kelly's choices to Cornish turbot with garlic, lobster ravioli with braised leeks, or Beef Wellington with roasted cauliflower and fennel. For dessert, she thought either a Grand Marnier crème brulee or chocolate petit fours. Kelly wished she were more certain of her choices. She had no idea if originality really mattered or whether Mark Lansbury simply wanted to see if she could look like a real chef. Either way, it had clearly been too long since she'd created gourmet food.

She was just tucking the recipes and her new notes away when the main door opened and the restaurant dining room, still in its pre-dinner lull, filled with laughter. One voice stood out and brought relief—and anticipation.

"Rocky!" Kelly said.

She headed for the dining room with Grace beside her, but halfway there they both stopped short. In pure disbelief, Kelly nearly ran smack into Marley Beckham and Lauren Waller, her co-chef at Triple Bean. She shrieked with surprise and stared at Raquel, who stood in the mix wearing an ear-to-ear grin.

"Hi sisses! Surprise!"

"Surprise? What an understatement. Lauren? How did Rocky ever get you to leave Denver?" She threw her arms around her friend and fellow cook.

"She told me she had an opportunity that would boost my career in a really special restaurant."

"She said that? Raquel?" Kelly's brows shot up and Raquel shrugged.

Grace, dumbfounded to that point, finally broke her silence with gushing words. "Marley Beckham? You're Marley Beckham, here in my hole-in-the-wall restaurant!"

Marley, gorgeous and put-together as always, held out her hand. "You must be Grace. I've heard nothing but wonderful things about your place. And when Raquel contacted me to let me know Kelly was taking a next step in the aftermath of the fire in Denver, I had to come here and see if we can add to the feature about The Crockett Sisters."

"It's wonderful to meet you," Grace took her hand, gaining her composure but still wide-eyed with excitement. "I've gotten so many ideas from watching your show over the years."

"I'm honored, Grace. And Peas Porridge is lovely from the moment you walk in."

"Thank you so much."

"Kelly." Marley stood in front of her, offering a sidelong, conspiratorial wink to Raquel. "This idea you have for trying out a gourmet menu so you can apply for the sous chef position at Opus with Mark Lansbury? I know him well; this is brilliant. When Raquel called to tell me, I absolutely had to come and follow it with my crew. I hope you're all right with that. And I want to film you in preparation over the next few days, leading up to the big night."

She didn't know what to say. Raquel had gone so far beyond what Kelly had imagined. She'd thought there'd be a few posters around town, some social media buzz, a fun slogan perhaps. But Marley Beckham and *Undiscovered Gourmet*? That wasn't a promotion. That was an advertising blitz.

"I hope you aren't too mad I didn't okay this with you first," Raquel said. "I didn't know if you wanted this made public. And it won't air before you present your menu to Mark Lansbury. But..." She gave a sheepish shrug. "I wanted us to make a grand gesture if we're going to do this. It will help us all, whatever happens. And Lauren is out of a job until the renovation is done in Denver, so I thought, while I help Grace search for a permanent cook, Lauren could take up the slack here. With your help, Kel."

"This is so much," Kelly said. "I'm blown away." She gave Marley and then Raquel a huge hug. "Thank you. Both."

"Okay, then." Marley dusted her hands together. "First things first. I'm starving. Let's try out the menu here and then get the lay of the land. Might as well hit the ground running."

In just one day, Kelly felt like the world had exploded around her. It didn't take long in a town the tiny size of Wolf Paw Pass for word of Marley's presence to circulate.

Peas Porridge turned into meeting-place central, and Kelly decided it was a very good thing Lauren was part of the crew. Between the two of them and Liam, the kitchen kept up with demand, but barely.

At first, Marley spent long periods with Kelly, asking her questions about what she planned to make for Chef Lansbury and when she was going to practice. But it soon grew obvious that the TV host was also enamored with *Peas Porridge* itself and with Grace's vision for the restaurant she'd built. She adored the children's restaurant idea and had her crew film a segment interviewing the kids who got to eat and order on their own, getting adorable footage of mini-humans ordering like grown-ups, so proud they beamed.

Marley handled the story of Grace's rotating kitchen door of chefs with supreme sympathy and fun, playing up the angle that it was extremely difficult to entice talented chefs to a tiny town in the mountains of Wyoming. Despite the ups and downs, however, Grace had managed to keep the reputation of her restaurant growing. And the Crockett triplets were right there to make sure she succeeded.

By Sunday afternoon, as the rush was starting to build, Kelly could clearly tell Marley's focus had switched. She loved the small-town restaurant, and she interviewed Kelly and Lauren both about the uniquely uncomplicated menu. Didn't they think it was a brilliant strategy to bring all types of diners through the doors?

The high Kelly had felt the first day of Marley's arrival, slowly disintegrated into frustration. She didn't begrudge Grace's moment in the spotlight, but if Raquel's purpose was to help Kelly and add to the story about Triple Bean going in new directions, then things were off course. Kelly's plans were once again secondary and neither sister noticed the direction change. Had she said one word, however, it would have made her the glory-grabber once again, so she said nothing and kept smiling. Or she tried.

"Hey, Chef, why the grumpy face? Someone put sugar in the salt shaker? Tape down the sink sprayer?"

Her head popped up from mixing a batch of biscuit dough to see Damien leaning against the freezer door, feet crossed, arms folded. He was scrubbed and shaved and the kitchen grew immediately brighter with his vibrant energy.

"Hi, you!"

"Whew." He said the word purposefully as he smiled and straightened, then glanced at Lauren, who had her gloved hands deep in meatloaf mix. "I can't tell you how happy I am to see that smile. I've hardly seen you the past four days, and I thought maybe you'd think..." He stepped closer so he could lower his voice. "You'd think I was avoiding you on purpose. I honestly haven't been."

"I knew you were at the remote cabin with the new herd. But in truth? I did miss you."

To her relief and delight, she saw the spark of desire in his eyes. Despite his vow after their night together, he hadn't drowned the fire. For a long, quiet moment she simply stared back at him until, finally, she shook her head to clear it.

"Uh, Damien, this is Lauren Waller. The awesome cook who works with me in Denver. She's here to help Grace for a week or so."

"Hi, Damien! I'd shake your hand but I'm elbow-deep in ground chuck."

"Nice to meet you," he replied. "Carry on. It looks to

me as if the meatloaf is in capable hands."

She laughed in delight. "I'd like to think so."

He turned back to Kelly. "How goes the haute cuisine planning?"

"You know what? It's really hard. But I think I have it narrowed down to turbot."

"What the heck is turbot?"

She pulled back in surprise. "Fish?"

"I don't know. I asked you."

"It is fish. A flatfish from the Baltic Sea and the northeast Atlantic. Light, tender, has both eyes on the same side of its body. You know, like a flounder or a halibut."

"I'm floundering to express how horrifying, or maybe just sad, it is to have both eyes on one side of your head. Makes it tough to swim. They'd say 'watch where you're going,' and you'd be doing this." He circled his finger in the air.

Lauren snorted with laughter.

Kelly shook her head. "You're so incredibly peculiar."

"Sometimes that's all a person has—saying things just for the hal—"

She whipped up her hand and slapped it over his mouth. "Don't you *dare* make a halibut joke. That's beneath even you."

His eyes widened above her palm, and she finally laughed and removed her hand. He scowled playfully.

"Very few jokes are beneath me."

"That's way sadder than turbot eyes."

"Right. So. Why turbot?"

"It's mild and exotic, and you can do a million things to dress it up. I just have to decide on a sauce and a side."

"Mac and cheese and baked beans." He grinned at the

stare she leveled in his direction.

"Oh, my lord. Stop talking now. Here." She tossed him an apron. "I've just volunteered you for KP. Peel me five pounds of potatoes—over there." She pointed. "Then you can put them through the slicer and make us some French fries. That should keep you quiet."

He nodded. "Yes, Chef. But I have to tell you. The guys at the station would never in a million years turn up their nose at mac 'n cheese and beans."

"Then they haven't tried my verjus and raisin sauce. Or my beurre blanc."

"Has anybody?"

"It was my specialty in culinary school, so yeah. Don't knock it."

"Never. Just wondering how beurre blanc could compare to bourbon barbecue." He shrugged and dropped the apron over his head.

"Do I hear another gauntlet slapped down, Finney?"

"Can you really afford another loss, Crockett?"

They laughed together and fell into their kitchen routine as easily as if they'd been doing it for years. Lauren spent the next hour laughing, but what Kelly didn't know until later was that Marley had followed Damien to the kitchen when he'd arrived and, along with a cameraman, surreptitiously listened in on their banter.

"Do you know how hilarious you two are?" she asked when she finally revealed herself. "You play off of each other like an old comedy couple."

"It's a good way to ease the tension of keeping up with a busy restaurant," Kelly said. "And Damien, here, is a practical joker from way back. He takes nothing in this kitchen seriously yet, somehow, he manages to throw together good food. I don't understand, but neither do I question."

"You're a fire station cook?" Marley asked.

"I was. Some firehouse cooks are pretty talented. I'm mostly a meat-and-potatoes guy. I could make something out of nothing, but I didn't go in for truffle sauces and beurre blanc." He shot Kelly an exaggerated wink.

"Well, I've been watching you both, and I have to say, you wield a mean chef's knife, Damien. And Kelly, you run a tight ship despite all the laughter."

"She always has," Lauren added. "She'll make a great high-end chef someday."

"When she doesn't have jokers to herd in her kitchen," Damien said. "Things will be much more sedate and she'll actually get to make her turbot."

"Turbot?" Marley asked. "Is that a hint of what's to come?"

"Still very undecided," Kelly replied. "Getting a rare fish here to a land-locked place might be prohibitive, but I'm researching it. A fish entrée fits in well with what Opus already does, but we are in beef country, so that might make more sense."

She'd had that insight while fielding Damien's teasing about European fish. She'd been willing to splurge to get her hands on the expensive turbot, but he'd chided her about the plentiful beef right on her own ranch. Why didn't she just make her gourmet hamburgers? She couldn't do burgers, but maybe he had a point.

"Would you two give me permission to add a little footage of you in the kitchen?" Marley asked. "It would make a fun little spotlight."

Kelly exchanged a look with Damien. It took a moment, but he finally shrugged.

"I suppose it's all right. It's not like I have some kind

of non-compete clause with the Sheridan fire department."

"Great!" Marley gave her camera guy a thumbs-up. "Thank you. This is turning out to be a bonanza trip. I can do a whole show on what's going on here in Wyoming."

"Gotta say, I didn't see that coming." Damien raised his brows. "Personally, I think if you're stuck having to feature us, you need something big to happen in Restaurantlandia, and soon."

Marley patted him on the shoulder and smiled. "Oh, I think we can define 'soon' as right around the corner."

Chapter Twenty-two

"HE LOOKS GOOD.

Damien rested a booted foot on the bottom rail of the round pen, wiped a bead of sweat from his temple, and watched Skylar send Apollo into a trot around her. The colt punctuated his movements with snorts and head tosses, but he floated like a circus liberty horse, his strides even and rhythmic. He was a handsome boy, and Damien watched him with new eyes since John's stories. Did they really have a future prepotent stallion on their hands? Was there a real chance Apollo could consistently produce horses of color given the chance? What did a person even do with that if it were true?

Damien understood so little of equine genetics even though Joely had tried to explain how the dun genes that caused the grulla coloring worked. He got the gist of the science, but retaining the myriad details of alleles and gene pairs was like expecting him to memorize a full Shakespeare play. Wasn't likely to happen. He wiped at his forehead again and wished for a little breeze. August had turned up the late summer heat beyond normal.

"I'm going to take him on a couple more short rides behind Bungu before we go on our camping trip," Sky said. "He's getting pretty good at being ponied, but I want to be positive he won't turn into a basket case when we show up with his lead rope and halter and drag him off in two days."

"You're the trainer," Damien replied. "Just keep being careful."

"Always. You and Pan could come, you know. We can go now, if you want."

"Love to, but I have to get down to the office in a few minutes. Cole's going over the breeding records for the new herd. You're doing fine with him."

She did a happy little shimmy in the middle of the ring "I can't wait for this trip. It's going to be a blast, and the little kids will love it. Tents are fantastic. Sleeping under the stars is even better."

"Yeah, I heard about this under-the-stars thing. Still assessing that." Damien laughed.

"You can't call yourself a cowboy until you do it."

"I've never called myself a cowboy."

"You work with cows and you're a boy," she said dismissively and clucked at the horse.

"Can't argue with that," he muttered and rested his folded arms on top of the fence. He set his chin atop them and closed his eyes briefly as memories from the past week, remnants of his constant dreams, and what were turning into circular discussions with the counselor, played through his exhaustion. The only times he wasn't tired were when he sneaked into Wolf Paw Pass to help Kelly and Lauren for a few hours. He'd done so three times since Marley the television host had first discovered them in all their irreverence the past weekend. Irreverence had become an addiction.

Not that Kelly wasn't stressed more than he'd ever seen her. She worked long hours after Peas Porridge closed every night, perfecting the version of Beef Wellington she was creating since abandoning her plan to use way-too-expensive turbot. He had no doubt that tonight when she served her specialty meal to the public at last, she'd do herself proud. But if he was honest, he couldn't wait for the weekend to be over. Kelly was nervous, thin-skinned, periodically short with everyone, and had lost the uber-confidence he'd grown to admire. She'd be so much better off once this audition was signed, sealed, and delivered, and she could stop worrying about whether it was good enough.

He went to the restaurant for his own distraction, but also because in the few hours they spent together Kelly turned back into herself. There was satisfaction in feeling like he helped her relax a little. He would much rather have helped her relax—and, without a doubt, helped himself forget his own issues—in a much more intimate place. But that wasn't going to happen. He'd meant what he'd decided about making love for all the wrong reasons.

He settled for being so proud of the event the Crockett triplets had planned. Raquel had sold seventy-five meal tickets for the one-choice menu, and all the proceeds would go to the local food shelf. It was brilliant, and something Kelly could add to her application package. She'd be a shoo-in for the sous-chef position in San Francisco, although the thought of her taking it left him hollow. He completely understood why Raquel didn't really want her to go either, but he never said so out loud.

They were both selfish to want her to stay. Kelly

deserved to follow her dreams. But being with her was the only way Damien seemed to be able to stop living with his unwanted ones. He hadn't told her the dreams were continuing, growing stranger every time. Now he was often riding Pan at breakneck speeds, following wisps of smoke. And often, when he looked into the familiar black abyss, there were dogs peering over his shoulder staring along with him. At his worst moments after returning from Afghanistan, he hadn't felt this crazy. He thanked the Good Lord every day for Cole, who'd talked him into taking a very distracting job, and for Grace, who'd started a restaurant where he could escape reality for short times.

He heard an unfamiliar woman's voice calling his name and had to blink to realize he hadn't fallen asleep on his feet. He turned and stared, shocked at the sight of the tall, lithe brunette he'd only met once before—on a plane he was trying desperately to forget.

"Hermione?" He shook his head. "Anna? What on earth are you doing here?"

"Shark," she replied, and her lips curved into a warm smile. "You're a tough guy to track down. But seeing you makes it totally worth the effort, I must say. You look good."

"I—"

Blown away, he could only stare at his fellow jumper while his brain tried to make sense of her presence.

"I know. There's no logical reason for me to be here."

"None," he replied, but finally held his arms open for a hug. "But it's amazing to see you, too. Why did you spend *any* time finding me?"

"Everyone wants to know how you are."

He scoffed out loud. "Nobody knows me. Certainly not in your company. Everyone knows *you*."

"You'd be surprised. You made a big splash when you joined your team. A decorated veteran, a man willing to overcome tough issues. The four jumps you made gave you a reputation as a damn hard worker and a smart firefighter."

"One who lost it when it counted most."

"Damien." She searched his eyes. "Everyone knows that if this can happen to you, it can happen to any of us. We're rooting for you. We want you back. I just came to see for myself that you're hanging in there and still planning to return."

He released her and offered an uncertain smile.

"I'm just looking for answers," he said. "They're not easy to find."

"I tell my kids all the time that the easy answers aren't what teach you the most important lessons."

"You came all the way from Grangeville to tell me that?"

"Nah. Five of us from the base there are headed to West Yellowstone. Fires are flaring up all around the area there and we're supporting. Five from your base in Missoula are coming over, too. I ragged on your captain until he gave in and told me where you were. I have to report in tomorrow morning."

"I'm flattered, Anna. You barely know me."

"You're one of us, Shark. I know you. And I've always felt bad because I knew you were struggling that day we were jumping together. I don't know how. Intuition? The sound in your voice? But I didn't have the words to help. Not then and not even now. But I thought maybe I could be an emissary to let you know you're not the only jumper to go through this. You'll figure it out."

His emotions swirled at the words. There'd always

been camaraderie among the crew, but he'd still felt like a lone man with more hidden wounds than the others. He'd never realized how deep and real the bond was between all of them in the profession, and it had certainly never occurred to him, despite all the lessons learned during the past two years, that others might share his fears.

"That means more than I can say."

"Why did you become a jumper?" she asked, her curiosity genuine, not judgmental.

"My father was a firefighter—a tough, dedicated one. And he was critical. I'll never be the man he was, but I always wanted to try. I'd have liked him to be proud."

She studied him a moment and then nodded very slightly.

"I get that. We all have someone whose approval means everything. But can I give you a little advice? When you come back, forget about your dad. Be the man you are—that's more than enough. It's enough for any of us."

The words comforted him in a soul-deep way. Others had said them before. Even Kelly had told him not to compete with his father. But coming from someone who truly understood, an equal who had the moral authority to correct his thinking, gave the words weight.

"Thank you," he said simply.

"You're welcome."

"Where are you staying tonight?"

"A little B&B in Wolf Paw Pass."

"Do you have dinner plans?"

"I do not. If you're asking me out, just don't tell my husband."

Damien laughed. "I don't mess with husbands, no worries. But since you're stuck in our miniature town for the night, I might as well give you a tour of Paradise and then, have I got a meal deal for you."

***

In all her days as a cook and even right out of school when she'd landed the plum job working for Landon O'Keefe, Kelly had never let nerves overpower her the way they were doing tonight. Ridiculous. This was one night. One meal that meant nothing but a good dinner for the patrons who'd paid thirty bucks a person for the privilege of being guinea pigs. It didn't even mean life or death for her. If people liked the meal, she'd send an account of the event and pictures of her dishes to Lansbury. If the night flopped, nobody would know but a few people in a tiny Wyoming town. And her sisters.

Raquel would be proven right: Kelly should stay at Triple Bean as a talented fish in a little pond. Grace would know and would sympathize, but be reassured that she'd made the right choice in leaving Triple Bean and striking out on her own.

She wouldn't flop, damn it. She was good, and she knew these recipes inside out and sideways after the work she'd put in. She regretted banishing Damien—kindly—from helping her tonight. The light atmosphere he'd have brought would be welcome, but she needed to focus like a top chef. Lauren knew her style and forgave her nervous shortness. She was thrilled to have Lauren and Liam as sous chefs.

Service started at six-thirty and everything went smoothly for the first two hours. Damien and her family had reservations at eight-fifteen, and as their arrival time approached, Kelly's stomach, already battling nerves that wouldn't calm until the last diner left, added dive-bombing butterflies to its unsettled state. Damien would praise her no matter what, but she wanted to know without question she'd genuinely impressed him. She needed to have him say, 'wow, this is the best food I've ever tasted." She'd never let a guy get to her deepest self this way. She didn't *want* to need his approval this much. But what she didn't want didn't seem to matter.

It was when the Crockett entourage entered, and she followed her plan to personally serve them, that she dropped her first plate of food. Damien sat at a table for six with Harper and Cole, Joely and Alec, and a slender, attractive brunette Kelly had never seen. Although she knew full well there was a logical explanation and she'd get a full introduction, the sight of him with a woman slammed into her aching stomach like a tidal wave. The only thing that saved her from absolute mortification was the fact that she was still in the kitchen doorway when a salad plate slipped from her shaking hand and shattered on the tile.

Everyone in the dining room looked up, but only a few could see what had happened. Grace was at her side in a flash.

"Shit," Kelly whispered.

"It's fine. It really is. Lauren, grab another salad. I'll clean this up. Deep breath, Kel, and go on out with the rest of the plates. This happens."

"Not in a three-star restaurant, it wouldn't."

"Well, this is only a two-star joint." Grace grinned. "It's nothing. Go."

As soon as she reached the table, a spontaneous round of applause greeted her, and it took her a second to realize it wasn't sarcastic clapping for her faux pas, but honest congratulations. She also saw immediately as she served the salads that the woman next to Damien wore a beautiful diamond wedding set on her left ring finger. Relief filtered through the butterfly-flapping in her belly, and she introduced her first course, hiding her embarrassment with a professional smile.

"Belgian endive salad with pear and ginger vinaigrette," she said, shaken by how much everything that had to do with Damien Finney threw her for a loop.

"How's it going, Chef?" he asked. "This looks mighty fancy."

"A fancy salad for a fancy night," she quipped. "Not as comfort-food good as iceberg lettuce with French dressing, but passable."

"Ahh, you know my true heart, don't you," he teased. "Chef Kelly Crockett, I'd like to introduce Anna Swenson. She's a fellow smoke jumper based in Idaho, heading for West Yellowstone to help with the fires there. I talked her into coming for something special before she has to go to work."

"He didn't have to talk very hard," Anna said. "This looks delicious, Kelly. I'm so glad to meet you."

"Welcome. It's good to meet you, too. I hope you enjoy dinner."

After that, the disasters were minor, but still present: gravy drops on the table cloths, a mix-up in a vegetable order for a customer who couldn't eat nuts—caught in time, but inexcusable. A spilled glass of wine. One order cooked far too long. Most customers likely noticed nothing amiss, but Kelly jumped on the others and fought constant low-level panic. Knowing Damien had a colleague with him—an amazing woman with a job most men couldn't handle—only added to the tension. It was Raquel who finally took her aside.

"This isn't you, Kelly," she said. "You can do this with your hands tied behind your back. Just stop fretting. Stop with the Gordon Ramsay outbursts. Enjoy this!"

The Gordon Ramsay comment rankled, echoing the slight Raquel had made right after the fire in Denver.

"I'm fine," Kelly snapped.

"Yes. You are. Now finish out the night with a smile. Forget you know anyone out there and just do it."

She did it. Barely. Damien zipped into the kitchen before he left, to thank her and give her a quick kiss of congratulations on the cheek.

"Well done, you," he said.

"Did you like it?"

"It was great," he said. "You did yourself proud."

He didn't exactly rave.

"Thanks. I'll be happy when it's over."

"I'll bet. But I'd certainly give you a job if I were hiring."

"That's very good to know."

"You'll be ready for that camping trip day after tomorrow."

She hadn't even thought about the trip for the past three days. And she was too tired to show proper enthusiasm.

"Something different will be most welcome."

He noticed the dullness in her voice. "You all right?"

"I'm great. I am. I think the adrenaline is finally ebbing. I might sleep until we have to pack up the horses."

He chuckled. "Good idea. Sleep in tomorrow. You deserve it."

"Thanks, Damien."

And he was gone. An hour and a half later, so was the last customer. Kelly slumped into a chair in the empty dining room and stared, waiting for the spark of elation inside to grow. But the joy wasn't for the success of the evening. And it had been a fair success. It was for the fact that she was done.

"Wow!" Grace pulled up a chair beside her. "That was amazing. Well done, sis!"

"You think it was okay—all the muffs aside?"

"There were no muffs! One dropped plate. Bah, everyone loved it."

"Thanks."

Raquel patted her shoulder. "I'm proud of you."

"I'm sorry I Ramsay-ed you. Thanks for the pep talk."

"That's the nature of haute cuisine, right?" Raquel shrugged. "It takes much more focus than whipping up club sandwiches."

Kelly closed her eyes and smiled. A stupid club sandwich sounded pretty good. "That's the truth."

"I got some great pictures," Raquel continued. "And Marley was here; she filmed a little of everything. I think you'll have a great presentation."

Kelly smiled again and, finally, a small sense of victory started to kick in. With relief, she closed her eyes. She'd do as Damien said and sleep in. She'd tackle getting her info together tomorrow.

Tonight, she was simply happy to be done.

Chapter Twenty-three

SITTING AROUND A perfect campfire, in the company of nine of her favorite people, Kelly couldn't believe what a difference thirty-six hours had made in her outlook. Miles from Peas Porridge, twelve hours after sending an e-mail portfolio package filled with descriptions of her menu and pictures from the night at Grace's off to San Francisco, she was nervously optimistic about her chances with Mark Lansbury but more thrilled to be helping Aiden Thorson and Lucky Garrison wrap raw dough, popped from a store-bought canister, around twigs so they could be roasted and eaten with cheap hot dogs. And Damien's favorite baked beans.

She glanced at him across the fire from her, his stick bearing its hotdog held expertly over the coals, sizzling with juicy pops. He smiled at her and went back to chatting with Alec and young Rory, who was hopped up on the hope of seeing a mountain lion or a coyote.

They had come only as far as Ancestor Canyon and were using the fire pit their mystery girl had created. All the kids had insisted they wanted to stay in the place the mystery had begun, and since it was as much their trip as the adults', nobody said no even though they'd have a long day getting to John Red Wolf's. Damien and Alec were the ones with a schedule to keep. They needed to be back in time for the new calf castration and branding day. Cole would pick him them up at John's and the others would have two days' ride home. But Damien would get to explore the land of the Cloud Band, and that's what he cared about.

It was always a wonder to see Damien's face change when he talked about the grulla horses. He became the kid who still believed in Santa and the boy who'd never been touched by sorrow. If such a thing as magical realism existed, Damien would find it.

When hot dogs had been roasted and devoured, bean fart jokes had been exhausted, and the first night's requisite number of s'mores were consumed, Skylar and Asta, who'd refused to be left behind, took Marcus, Aiden, Rory, and Lucky off to explore the canyon floor. Kelly, along with Raquel, Joely, Alec, and Damien stretched their legs out around the fire and reveled in the fact that there was nothing to do. Two lightweight, four-man tents had been pitched. Food was ready to be packed into a canvas bag and hoisted into one of the few trees for overnight safety, and there was not a cow to be herded, a fence to be mended, a piece of paperwork to be dealt with, or a tractor to be fixed.

"I think I'm going to sleep outside tonight after all," Damien said, crossing his hands behind his head and leaning back against his saddle. "I told Sky I wasn't crazy about the idea, but I've changed my mind."

"It's not the most comfortable bed, but it's the most

beautiful," Joely said. "We did it for two nights on our honeymoon." She wrinkled her nose at Alec, who shook his head.

"Never marry a ranch girl," he said.

"That seems counterintuitive." Kelly laughed. "I mean, we're pretty expert campers, I know, but there are things you want to do on a honeymoon that don't mix well with hard ground."

"You'd be surprised." Joely giggled. "Ranch girls are creative."

"TMI!" Raquel put her hands over her ears. "This is mixed company. Some of us are too innocent for that."

Alec fake sneezed the word 'bullshit' into his hand and Damien laughed.

"I agree. There's nothing innocent about these Crockett girls."

"Yeah, but grab one quick, Damien. They're going fast," Alec said. "Worth the trouble."

"Hey!" Kelly plucked a grass stem and tossed it at him. "Trouble? Bite your tongue."

"I call 'em like I see 'em." Alec leaned over and kissed his wife. "And I love what I see."

"You are well trained already," Joely laughed. "I am so good."

"How are you liking ranch work?" Alec asked Damien, neatly changing the subject and removing the need for him to respond to the 'grab one quick' comment, for which Kelly was grateful.

For a week, there'd been nothing physical between her and Damien except for the quick kiss after the dinner two nights earlier. She wished she could say it didn't matter, but the memory of their one night together hadn't remotely faded. All she had to do was look at him and see those long legs, toughened and honed by the training he'd completed to gain his position on the jump crew, to have her insides melt like hot chocolate and her desire flare like the fire that separated them. She wanted nothing more than to crawl around the fire pit and curl up next to him the way Joely curled with Alec. But he remained adamant that he was not ready to get closer again.

Alec and Damien chatted on—in the spare, efficient way men talked—about the ranch and the amount of work associated with its upkeep. Kelly let them talk and looked down the canyon to search out the kids. She could no longer see them and although there was nothing to worry about, she used them as an excuse to get up and stretch her legs.

"I'm going to go see if the kids have found anything worth noting," she said. "Rocky? Need a walk?"

"No thanks, Kel. I'm liking this fire just fine."

Raquel didn't look at her. She'd been supportive at the end of the special dinner event, but ever since Kelly had sent off her formal application packet, she'd gone back to being aloof.

"I don't blame you," she replied cheerily. "Joely?"

"I'm with Rocky; I like the view right here." She smiled and snaked her arm around Alec's middle.

"Disgustingly sweet," Kelly teased. "It's been a year already. Aren't you over it?"

"That doesn't happen, sister dear," Joely laughed.

She was beginning to see the truth in that for all her married sisters.

"Okay. I'll be back. Carry on," she said and got to her feet.

She hadn't been gone three minutes when Damien called out behind her and she turned to find him jogging to meet her.

"I can't let you wander off alone. What if Rory's mountain lion shows up?"

"Ooooh. I would definitely need a big, strong chauvinist to protect me!"

"Touché. I clarify my reason for coming. I haven't been alone with you for days, and I wanted to be."

"Much better. I'll take it."

He settled in beside her and matched her stride companionably.

"Are you all right after your crazy week? You still look tired."

"Do I?" The observation surprised her.

"Don't get me wrong, that was not a comment on your looks—always stunning, by the way."

"Again. Well done."

"I, too, am trainable. I just mean, it seemed like last week took a lot out of you."

"I discovered cooking muscles I'd forgotten how to use."

"You did a good job. Was it fun?"

The question rocked her back. Had it been fun?

"I...think it was. It was definitely challenging. It taught me how much I have to learn."

"Did it inspire you?"

She stared at him. "Are you taking cues from therapists now? It's way too soon to say whether it inspired me. I found other dishes I'd love to try making. I don't want to put together a package like this again for a few days."

His soft chuckle filled her with warmth. "I get that. You worked your pretty ass off, that's for sure. I'm glad you get to take this time off."

"I am, too. How about you. Have you been okay?"

"During the day. Nights are still bizarre. I dream more than ever."

"Damien, I'm sorry."

He shrugged. "It's good to be going to John's. He said Pan and I should go—I believe him. But it's good to be with you, too."

"I believe it, too. And I'm happy to be with you. Everyone else, Raquel mostly, is still treating me like I'm taking the puppy off to the pound to give it away. I don't think she'll ever forgive me for wanting to change things up."

"She will. I promise."

He looked around, and in one swift motion, he pulled her into the shadows behind a rock outcropping along the canyon wall.

"Let's make a deal," he said.

Before she could ask, he found her lips with a hungry kiss that left her breathless in seconds. She grasped his shoulders and pressed the length of her body into his, reveling in the heat of his torso where her breasts crushed to his chest, thrilling when she placed one leg between the spread of his. His tongue pulsed against hers, and she pressed back letting shivers overtake her and weaken her knees. He pressed his hips to hers and heat raced to the soft spot between her thighs. The desire was glorious and she moaned happily into his kiss.

"A deal?" she finally asked, when he pulled away enough for her to speak.

"Meet me outside the tents after everyone is asleep."

She licked her lips, loving the lingering taste of him. "We don't dare with the kids along."

"Get your mind out of the gutter." He placed his nose

against hers and grinned. "I haven't changed my mind about anything. I just want to talk to you."

"In what language?" She rocked her pelvis into his again.

"On second thought, maybe you should stay away."

"Nope. No backsies on the invite. I'll be there."

Hours later with the kids divided into the tents, boys with Alec, girls and Asta with Joely and Raquel, Kelly was grateful to grab her bedroll and join Damien as agreed. For a long while, they contented themselves with tending the fire and stargazing. Kelly was impressed with how much he knew of stars and star legends. They found all the major constellations and wished on a lone shooting star they saw at the same time. But the longer they sat, despite being cuddled up next to each other exactly the way she'd wished for earlier in the evening, the more Kelly felt the peace of the night seep away, as if the closer time crept to midnight, the heavier she and Damien grew. She didn't know why until Damien broke the silence and reality crashed in on them both.

"I have just under two weeks before I have to report in to my captain. He'll want to know what I've learned. What I've decided." His voice, unlike earlier, betrayed no emotion.

"Have you decided anything?"

"Not fully. But I'm learning that if I don't go back to smoke jumping, the world won't end."

"True. But will it end a dream?"

"Dreams sometimes end."

"You can't give up yet." She placed a hand on his chest.

"I think, if I stop worrying about having to make another jump, the dreams will stop. Maybe this is all as simple as the Universe telling me this isn't the job for me."

"I can't believe that, Damien."

"Well, maybe you should start." His voice was sharper than it had been, and it reminded her of Raquel.

"I'm sorry. I'm not trying to say you're wrong. I'm saying I know this isn't really what you want. What would you do instead?"

"I still have Sheridan. I know my mother would be happy if I moved closer. You have your new exciting plans. I'll find my place."

"Stay here. Work for Cole."

"No." The answer was so unequivocal she didn't even ask why. "I don't belong here long term."

"What about Pan?"

"Wherever we go, I'll make sure she can always see the land she was born on. Apollo can stay here until we know what his job is."

"It sounds as if you've made up your mind and thought this all through."

"No. I have to have a basic plan, that's all. At the very least, I'll follow your career. Come eat at your new restaurant, whatever it might be." His words were light, but even in the dark, she could sense it was false cheer.

She pulled away from his side and straightened. "Why are you telling me this?"

"Because I keep losing my self-control around you, and I need to be honest about everything. I don't want to hurt you, but I will if I let you think this thing between us can keep growing. You have too much riding on the future."

Heat welled behind her eyes, but she held back the tears. She wouldn't let him see that her future suddenly didn't feel as if anything but loneliness rode there. If

Raquel never forgave her, and he wasn't going to be there, what good would creating gourmet dishes for strangers be?

"We have two weeks," she said finally. "Maybe don't rein in all your self-control quite yet."

His unexpected soft snort of laughter didn't give her much confidence that he'd listen to her request.

They reached John Red Wolf's ranch late the next afternoon. The ride had been long but the kids kept the atmosphere light and fun. They noticed everything and asked endless questions. They begged to race each other and the adults sought out flat, safe stretches to accommodate them. Damien rode most of the time beside Sky, taking turns leading Apollo, and making sure during their rest and lunch stops to groom and praise the colt. Kelly had no time to dwell on their conversation the night before, and no time to worry about the status of her Opus application. By the time John greeted their party in front of his barn, she was ready for a rest, but happily so.

Clearly, John was happy as well. He'd prepared for them as if they were visiting royalty, with stalls for the mares and a good-sized corral for the geldings and Apollo. He had places around his fire and his tipi for their tents, and surprised the five children by showing them he had sleeping mats set up for them inside the tipi itself. Joely and Kelly made sure to lecture each child about the fact that the invitation was an honor. The only way they'd be allowed the privilege of staying there was to understand that the tipi was not a toy tent, it was John's home. They were not to play inside. They were to remove their shoes. They were to respect his belongings. And while they solemnly agreed, they were excited as a troop of little chimps.

They feasted on smoked pork and roasted vegetables grown in John's garden. Tug and Honey accepted Asta without doggy question. Talk was plentiful and stories were abundant. John told the younger kids a fanciful new story about the gray smoke horses, and nobody could wait until morning when they'd head out to search for them in the surrounding hills.

But the best part of the night was watching John's Bird and Damien's Pan meet for the first time. Pan was in a stall with a small run out paddock, when Bird came to the barn after being in John's biggest pasture. The two mares stopped still as stone when they caught sight of one another. Pan, first, let out a whinny Kelly was certain they heard back at Paradise. Bird answered and the two trotted to the fence line and squealed and bucked in greeting. It was like watching a horse in a mirror, the two were so alike.

"As alike as you and Raquel," Damien whispered, watching in awe. "I'm half afraid I wouldn't know my own horse if she got out and ran off with Bird."

"You would," she promised. "She'd be the one who's your soulmate."

It only took minutes for the pair to settle in and stop stamping at each other. Within five, they were sniffing each other. Within ten, they were grooming each other's necks.

"They know they're related," John said. "They'll have fun on the trail tomorrow. We should let her meet Apollo, too, so he doesn't see her for the first time in the morning."

That meeting went almost as smoothly, although clearly Apollo couldn't figure out why the horse looked familiar but didn't smell the same.

"He's still a baby," Sky said. "He doesn't really know what to do with his parts yet. He should be good tomorrow."

The littler kids tittered over such talk but nobody shushed them. Ranch kids learned early enough about the birds and bees – and horses and cows. All in all, between the horses, kid humor, and stories, there was no time for worry or tension. Kelly almost had to believe that John owned a ranch filled with some kind of spiritual magic that eased all burdens. Even when she rolled herself into her sleeping bag, alone except for Raquel and Joely beside her in the tent, she managed to sleep rather than fret about Damien.

They ate porridge, eggs, and pancakes in the morning and declared that nobody was leaving John's place ever again. He promised his culinary skills would wear thin after a while and all the kids would have to do chores if they stayed. Lucky didn't care.

"If you adopt me, I'll do horse chores all day every day," she said.

"Okay, I'll have a talk with your dad and mom," John promised.

They rode out by ten and the mid-morning sun already baked the grass, browned by the hot dry summer. The air sat heavily, and Kelly watched Damien scan the sky over the hills, then speak with John and Alec.

"What's up?" Kelly asked, bringing Jellyman alongside Pan at the front of the group.

"I'm seeing some smoke haze," he replied. "It's faint, but John noticed it, too. It probably doesn't mean anything, but I haven't checked the fire forecast in a couple of days. The closest outbreak was seventy miles northwest and moving away."

"This weather is bad for stopping fires," she said.

"It is. Still, we should be safe enough here. We're heading into the southern hills, going away from any path. We'll just watch the wind."

John led them deep into country as beautiful as anything Paradise had to offer. They lunched by a rushing river and found a box canyon much smaller but similar to Ancestor. The pine-covered foothills of the Wind River mountains and Bridger-Teton National Forest were greener than the flat grasslands, and the wooded trails smelled of spruce. Or, as Aiden said, like they were getting close to Christmas. Finally, they reached a valley between two hills that opened before them in a light brown carpet. John held up a hand and studied the landscape.

"Horse have been here," he said.

"The Smoke Horses?" Lucky asked.

"No way to know that," he replied. "You can see where they've eaten, where they've left their droppings. It wasn't a large herd, but at least we can be sure some horses know this place."

Kelly watched Damien search with keen eyes. She watched Pan and Bird, desperately wanting to believe that they would sense if their distant relatives were near. But short of flicking their ears at blackbirds landing on tall grass stems then flitting away as the riders approached, none of the horses paid any mind to their surroundings.

They'd ridden nearly ten miles and explored several valleys and a hidden cave by the time they returned home. A cloud of disappointment that they'd found no horses hung over their group. The kids were tired and quieter than they'd been the past two days, and even the border collie collapsed by her tent and didn't move. Horses were cared for, and a pensive group gathered around the fire where John had set a hearty stew to simmer over the campfire, and a reflector oven baked cornbread.

Lucky, who'd fully adopted John as her temporary grandfather, clung to his side like a shadow. Rocky and Joely bent together, in a deep discussion Kelly wasn't privy to. Alec pulled a piece of wood from his pack and began whittling. Skylar pulled out her sketch pad. Damien sat slightly apart, staring into the fire, as quiet as he'd been when he'd first arrived at Paradise. Ever since he'd admitted his fears about never going back to smokejumping, he'd turned in on himself.

John walked by him on the way to stir the stew and stopped to place a hand on his shoulder. "I'm sorry we saw no horses today," he said. "But stories have reasons for being told. Have faith."

Damien offered a grateful smile that disappeared as soon as John had passed. Quietly, Kelly moved to his side and sat. She knew the horses had taken on some kind of greater life meaning for him, right or wrong.

"Things are as they should be," she whispered, even as she looked at her two sisters, who were making no attempt to include her.

"I know."

She had to believe the words. Somewhere in the universe God, or the Great Spirit, somebody had to know what was going on because she sure didn't.

Chapter Twenty-four

DAMIEN AWOKE AFTER a fitful night in the tent. The sun was just rising over the hills and the morning, already hot, shone a shimmery, gray-gold. Nobody was up, not even John, who had been sitting in one of his log chairs drinking coffee at this time the previous morning. Damien studied the sky suspiciously. The haze was definitely smoke related. They had no cell coverage, but they had a radio. Things had been fine the night before and there shouldn't be any need to worry, but wildfires were fickle devils and could shift on the whim of the breeze — literally.

A cool, wet nose at his palm startled him. He looked down to see John's lab, Tug, at his side and reflexively pulled his hand away. Dogs and thoughts of fire didn't mix in his mind, but Tug's friendly, huge eyes and hopeful, wagging tail implored him for a pat. With a sigh, Damien stroked the soft, black fur. He needed to get over his mental feud with dogs. They weren't to blame for his issues. It had always been easier to ignore them and the memories, however partial, they evoked.

"Well, you're up," he said. "Where's your boss?"

Tug's tail-wag speed doubled, and he turned and trotted toward the barn. Damien followed, his skepticism high. Dogs did not understand human words they hadn't been trained to understand.

"Where you headed at six in the morning?"

He turned back and found Kelly in jeans, boots, and a sleep-wrinkled red T-shirt, rubbing her eyes and yawning. Asta was beside her and sprinted joyfully toward Tug.

"I don't know." He allowed a self-deprecating laugh. "Following a dog, I guess. I asked Tug where his boss was and he headed off. I had nothing better to do."

"Huh. Okay, well I woke up with nothing to do, too. Can I follow you?"

"I dunno; it could be dangerous."

"Don't you worry your pretty little head. I'll protect you."

He grinned at her. "You know? I believe you could."

The barn aisle was empty except for Tug and Honey, both standing in the middle of the row as if waiting for them.

"Hey, pups," Kelly said. "What's up?"

Tug gave a quiet woof and turned; Honey followed and they padded toward the back door.

"This is just silly," Damien said.

"We've been up to our armpits in mystery since Day One," she replied. "Might as well follow them. Maybe they're being controlled by aliens."

"I can't believe you actually said that."

There were no aliens. Instead, outside the rear barn door stood John holding the reins of an unfamiliar horse. It was a pretty little chestnut Arabian with a flaxen mane and tail, a crooked blaze, and two white socks. Fully tacked up, it stood quietly while John ran a big hand down its neck

"Good morning, Damien. Kelly."

"Hey, John," Kelly answered the greeting. "Who's this beauty?"

At that moment, a girl stepped from behind the horse. Damien's stomach gave a leap of recognition even though he'd never seen her from the front before. Short and athletically built, with a heart-shaped face and a long, black braid slung over her shoulder, she was probably sixteen or seventeen. And he guessed she could run like an antelope and disappear into the woods like a rabbit.

She looked first at Kelly and then Damien, her expression a mixture of nervousness and defiance.

"The beautiful horse is Real Love," John said. "But the beautiful girl..." he placed a hand gently on her shoulder, "is Kaiah Barns, my grand-niece. Kaiah, this is Kelly Crockett and Damien Finney. They've been looking forward to meeting you."

"Hello," she said, her voice so quiet it was nearly a whisper.

Kelly held out her hand. "Kaiah, hello. It's good to meet you in person."

For a moment the girl contemplated Kelly's offered hand, but when she took it, her gaze dropped to the ground.

"I'm sorry I broke into your house. I know I should have talked with you."

The speech was practiced, but the girl was clearly embarrassed and sincere. Kelly tilted her head in curiosity.

"Why didn't you?"

"I didn't want you to tell me I couldn't camp in the

canyon."

"I might not have, if you'd had a reason to be there."

"I did."

Damien wanted to know more, wanted far more detail. Kelly was more patient. She seemed to consider for a moment and then reached into her back pocket. Slowly, she drew out the now-familiar medicine bag. Kaiah's eyes went wide and then shiny with relief.

"I guess this is yours."

"Yes," she whispered. "Thank you." She took the pouch almost reverently and stroked the beading with a forefinger. "It carries the spirit of my first horse. Well, hairs from her tail. And a ring I used to keep on her bridle. She was a mustang. She was my best friend."

"Was she a smoke horse?" Damien asked.

Kaiah shook her head and looked up at John. "Onyx was not a grulla, but my uncle told me the stories of the Cloud Band when I was very little. I was away for a long time, but I always knew I would come back and look for them."

"Why didn't you come and tell us this when you were looking for the medicine bag?" Kelly asked. "Does it have to do with why you were camping in Ancestor Canyon?"

Again, Kaiah looked up at John.

"I sent word to my brother's daughter, Kaiah's mother, that we needed to speak with her. I wasn't certain anyone could reach her. Kaiah rode three hours already this morning to get here and I am proud of her for that. But now…" He nodded at her to continue.

"I was camping because they were there. The smoke horses."

"On Paradise land?" Damien's heart hammered behind his breastbone, almost painfully. "You saw them?"

"I drew them to prove I did."

"Those beautiful drawings!" Kelly said.

"And," Kaiah swallowed, "I know where they are now."

"Kaiah, are you serious?" Kelly touched the girl on her shoulder.

"Yes. And I will pay for breaking into your home by taking you there."

They gave Kaiah time to rest after her morning ride, while everyone stocked up on bacon, eggs, and pancakes again. They set out into the hills with Kaiah and Real Love as guides. Skylar had been ecstatic when Kaiah joined the group.

"You were in the drawing class with me at the Community Arts center. Do you remember?" she'd cried, giving the other girl a huge hug. "You drew the most beautiful horses. I couldn't understand why you were there. You could have taught us all."

That had opened up Kaiah for the first time, and she'd shown everyone her sketchbook—the one Damien and Kelly had seen the day they'd found her backpack.

"I don't have a smoke horse," she'd said, "but I saw four of them one day about a month ago, and I knew because Uncle told me, that seeing them was almost as lucky as having one. I decided then I had to find out if there was a whole herd, as the legend says. I've been following them for weeks. I have to leave and go back home every so often—that was the deal I made with my parents, so I had to search a few times. Ancestor Canyon was as far from here as they got."

"Did you find the herd?"

"I saw ten horses together once. I don't know if that's

a whole herd."

So now they rode to where she'd last seen several. Damien kept a watch on the hazy sky but it was his heart he followed. He couldn't explain to anyone, even Kelly, what it would mean to see the horses. They would answer his questions; of that, he felt absolutely certain.

"Look!" Rory's Largo had stopped with ears pricked toward movement off to the group's right. "There must be twenty deer. And they're kind of running."

Damien followed the boy's pointing finger and saw the tawny sea of mule deer loping across the grass. A large-ish herd wasn't unusual, but to have them moving at such a clip was. Asta caught sight and started for them, but Skylar managed to call her off.

"They are looking for new grounds quickly," John observed. "We should check the fire reports closely when we return home."

"There's no smoke close by," Damien said. "But, yes, something they know but we don't is driving them."

It took two hours and travel through thick scrub between a winding maze of hills to find the valley Kaiah sought. Kaiah and Skylar magpie-chattered their way into friendship during the ride. Marcus taught Lucky, Rory, and Aiden the late-summer wildflowers because he told them all ranch workers had to know everything that grew on their land. Joely and Raquel seemed to be discussing wedding plans for Grace, and Kelly rode silently beside him, her uncharacteristic quiet the only thing about the day that worried him. She claimed to be worried about what she'd sent to the chef in San Francisco, but he didn't believe her. She was the most optimistic person he knew. The application wouldn't throw her.

"There!"

Kaiah's sudden call stopped them all and Damien's heart pounded in his chest. He looked over a broad expanse of grassland, still tall and green in a wide, U-shaped valley that was well-protected from drying winds. Scattered stands of ash and pine gave plenty of shade and good places to shelter.

"Where?" Lucky asked. "Are they here?"

"This is where I left them this morning. What I've learned is that they like to find a sheltered place and then stay for at least a couple of days."

"Let's dismount right here. We can tie the horses in the shade and go sit on the hillock over there and watch for a while."

They loosened cinches and replaced bridles with halters. Apollo was still being ponied along, riderless, doing a stellar job. When they left him tied next to Jellyman, however, he was the only horse of the twelve who seemed on full alert.

"Keep an eye on him," Joely said. "He might be interested in Kaiah's little mare. Sooner or later Apollo is going to figure this whole boy-girl thing out."

They all sat silently. Damien pushed his pessimism down deep as minutes ticked past and no horses appeared, but Kaiah was confident enough that she took out her sketchbook and got Skylar to do the same, prepared to capture the horses when they arrived.

"Do you believe her?" Damien asked John. "They do exist?"

"I have no reason not to believe." The old man smiled. "But do not worry. It isn't the finding, Damien. It is the search."

At that moment, one of their horses let out a whinny that shattered the air and rang long and plaintively into the valley. Damien nearly twisted his neck looking to see which it was and just as Kaiah called softly, again, "Look!" Apollo raced past their viewing spot and into the clearing, his lead rope trailing, his silver coat flashing, and his black tail fanned.

"Apollo!" Skylar cried and then covered her mouth as she watched.

Everyone was stunned into silence again as seven grulla horses, ears pricked forward still as stone, watched the colt tear toward them. They neither shied away nor made a sound until Apollo reached them, and they tossed their heads, baring teeth and snorting in warning.

"They'll hurt him!" Skylar cried.

"No." John stood beside her and placed a hand on her arm. "They know he's a baby. He's no threat. These are outlier mares, probably older, no longer breeding. They're wise."

"How do you know all that?" Kaiah asked.

"Too many years of watching herd behavior," John replied. "But this group...oh my."

Damien barely heard the conversation. Lightness filled his head and numb disbelief at the mares' smokey, shimmering beauty tied his tongue. He stared at the legend come to life. Seven horses from a herd that was supposedly not even real. He took a moment to glance at Pan, who, along with Bird, was watching calmly. She was no longer wild and his heart rejoiced. Yet, without her, he never would have found this place. A sudden burn behind his eyes had him pressing the heels of his hands against the sockets, but the tears flowed anyway.

This. This was it—the epiphany. John had been wrong. These animals were part of him. They were guiding him. His out-of-control emotions proved he would have his answers.

"Hey." Kelly moved in beside him and encircled his upper arm in a hug. "Pretty powerful, huh?"

He nodded, his throat too clogged to speak. Her eyes rested on him; he could feel their assessment, but she said nothing. She laid her head on his shoulder and let him watch.

"We need to get Apollo," Sky said. "He'll follow them off if we don't."

"I agree," John said.

"Can I go down there?" she asked.

"Slowly. Talk to the colt. Don't pay attention to the mares."

"Right," Skylar joked. "That's like saying don't pay attention to the giant unicorn in the room."

But she pulled it off. It took twenty minutes, but with slow movements that proved what an able horsewoman she was, Skylar got Apollo's attention long enough to grab his rope. The mares skittered away from her but were too fascinated by the young horse to run off. As soon as they saw she wasn't after them, they followed halfway to where the group sat and set to grazing a mere thirty feet away.

In the end, they watched for over an hour, drinking in the sight of the perfect horses. Skylar and Kaiah drew picture after picture, Joely took countless photographs, and the littler kids named each mare. Queen, Stormy, Dove, Cloudy, and Mommy. The latter by Aiden who claimed his choice "looked like she was the mommy of the group." Kaiah added Whimsy and Dancer but didn't correct the rest, even though she'd given them all names in her sketchbook and knew each horse.

But eventually they had to leave. The kids grew

restless, the mares moved away, closer to the protective trees, and they wouldn't reach John's place until dinnertime. The first stab of depression hit Damien as they mounted up. Apollo gave one more long call, but it wasn't answered. The wonder of finding the horses remained, but Damien's euphoria drained away. He'd seen them and felt the magic, but he was no different inside. All the horses had done was show him that this was who he was, and it would have to be enough. His part of the ride was done. Cole would arrive in the morning to bring him, Pan, and Apollo back to the ranch. He'd promised to help with the calves and so he would. He couldn't decide whether he regretted missing the two-day ride back or was relieved he didn't have to figure out his feelings in the company of nine other people.

His dejection took second place, however, when they came in sight of John's ranch and everyone stopped as one to look out over the horizon. The memory of smoke horses turned into the harsh reality of real smoke. Still far to the north, and not the dangerous billowing clouds attached to a visible fire, the gray wisps were nonetheless clearly distinguishable as remnants of a closer fire and not just haze.

"Well, shit," Damien muttered, his brain working to calculate what it could mean.

"What's wrong?" Aiden asked, wide-eyed at the eerie patterns of gray-blue light in the distance.

"Nothing here, sweetie," Kelly said. "But maybe the wildfires are getting bigger up north."

She looked at Damien and he tamped down his worry to give her a reassuring smile.

"Yup, we're fine," he said. "But when we get back to John's we'll pull out all our maps and get on the radio to find out exactly where the smoke is coming from. Okay?"

He looked around, checking everyone's reactions, his instincts to assess and decide on the next moves kicking in. Everyone nodded back. Joely and Alec instinctively put the three younger kids together and rode beside them. John led the way across the pasture. Kelly sent him a grateful half-smile and fell in beside her sisters. He and Alec took the back.

"You worried?" Alec asked, his eyes darting to the north.

"I don't like that we're seeing actual smoke," he replied. "I think it's a good fifty or sixty miles away, and the wind is coming from the east-southeast and blowing away from us. I always worry when fire and nature get into a duel."

Alec huffed a laugh. "Right? In a duel, somebody always loses. Thank God we've got guys like you on the front lines."

Damien's stomach dropped. He wasn't on any front line; he was worried about his own problems—in his head when nothing mattered but the safety of the people with him. Even though they weren't in imminent danger, he kicked himself for his selfishness. He should be out doing his job, not whining internally that some crazy magical fantasy hadn't solved his problems for him.

If there really was magic in the world, it was the invisible force that suddenly slapped him upside the head and steeled his reserve. He couldn't get to the front lines, but he could use whatever expertise he had to make sure this group of people he cared about stayed calm and safe.

Even if deep beneath the newly steeled spine, he felt the warning signs of something much bigger than himself.

Chapter Twenty-five

KELLY KNEW THEY were in trouble when the wind picked up at one in the morning, rising from a shooshing lullaby through the trees to a roaring gale that shook the nylon tent sides like a wolf shaking its prey. They'd ridden another long, long day after leaving John's that morning and after studying topo maps and checking on fire updates with Damien.

When they'd left, the fire just north and west of Wolf Paw Pass, covered over a thousand acres and was only about eight percent contained. Its path was taking it north of the little town and south of Jackson, but hotshot crews were clearing and evacuating and claimed a fair amount of confidence that they could keep both centers safe. Rain was in the forecast, and Damien believed the fire was headed away from Paradise land.

Still, they'd ridden out at first light, leaving Damien and Alec, Pan, Apollo, and Alec's Barney to wait for Cole to pick them up. Fire threat or no, ranch work went on and fifty calves needed to be branded and become steers.

Nobody questioned that the five kids and three women would navigate the way home with no problem. They'd all planned the shortest route together and along with Joely, Raquel, and Kelly, Skylar and Marcus were superior map readers. Joely would have preferred sending Lucky home to Ty and Grace, but the girl had insisted she was going to finish the trip with everyone else. At seven she was a pretty amazing kid, riding like she'd been born on a horse, and smarter than half the adults Kelly had met in her life.

Now, however, with the wind howling, Lucky, who was sandwiched between two of her soon-to-be-aunts, snuggled into Kelly's side, shivering.

"Aunt Kelly?"

Even though Ty and Lucky weren't officially married, the title felt lovely.

"Hi, honey. Did the wind wake you?"

"Yes. I'm a little worried. Didn't Damien tell us we'd be okay if the wind didn't shift? I think it's coming from a new direction."

"Oh, Lucky, I don't know. I think it's just that rain moving in, faster than predicted. That would be a good thing."

"Maybe." Brilliant Lucky couldn't be placated like a normal child. "But when we went to sleep, it was the right side of the tent that was blowing in and out. Now it's the left."

Kelly pretended to assess the situation and finally nodded. It wasn't fair to lie to any kids, but smart ones would catch you out anyway.

"Maybe you're right. We could go check on the horses and the weather at the same time. Want to help me?"

"I can help, too." Raquel's disembodied voice came

from above their heads, where she lay squeezed along the back of the tent.

"Me three," said Joely, and patted Lucky's leg. "You okay, sweetpea?"

"Yes. I'm worried about Skylar and Marcus and Rory and Aiden. They don't have any grown-ups in their tent."

Kelly laughed and gave her niece a squeeze. "Marcus and Skylar are pretty smart. And they're right next door."

"No, we're right here." Marcus's voice outside the door startled them all into laughing, but his next words stopped them. "I think you need to come out here."

Kelly scrambled out of her bedroll and heard Raquel do the same. Joely found her flashlight first and illuminated the tent so everyone could find boots. When they finally stood outside the tent and looked to the north where Marcus pointed, they could see for the first time, actual licks of dancing flames visible above the tree line.

"I'm guessing it's about thirty miles away," Marcus said. "And this wind is wicked and coming our direction now."

Kelly's pulse throbbed in her temples and the first flush of fear made her momentarily light-headed. She had no time for panic, however. With a deep breath, she turned to Raquel and Joely.

I tried my phone last night and we aren't in range of the towers yet. We've got the radio. Raquel, can you try getting the fire update frequency on that? If this kind of wind is driving the fire into our path, it can travel six to ten miles an hour depending on terrain. What do you think about packing up and heading out in the dark? It's not the safest, but we don't want to get trapped here."

"I say absolutely we go. We've got flashlights and the two small lanterns." Raquel said and climbed back into the tent to find the radio.

"I agree," Joely said. "We've pushed our poor ponies, but they're all ranch tough. So are we, right guys?"

Raquel reappeared with the crackling radio and massaged the dial until the temporary emergency broadcast flared to faint life. Kelly ducked into the tent and found the topography map where they'd marked their route. With flashlights and heads together, they listened to the updates and followed the projected fire path.

"It's curved southwest," Joely said. "It could cut the northwest corner of John's land and head straight between Ancestor Canyon and our main ranch yard."

"So much in the potential path." Raquel's eyes were liquid in the dim light. "Wolf Paw Pass. Harper's studio. The canyon… Oh, Joely, your house is right there west of town."

"I know. I know." Joely hugged her.

Kelly put her arms around both of them. "Protecting the town will be the priority. Everyone at Paradise will have ears on this, and Damien is there—he knows what to do. The rest doesn't matter as long as we keep each other safe. Right? So, we can't head to Ancestor now. Even if we made it, the box canyon is a fire trap, so let's go straight east to the Kwinaa and follow the river. It adds half a day to the trip home, but if necessary we can ford and get to Wolf Paw Peak. Then we have our choice of going around to the cabin or cutting across to home if it's safe."

"It's a good plan," Raquel added quietly. "Thanks for being calm under pressure."

It was the kindest thing Raquel had said to her most of the trip. Tears welled in Kelly's eyes. They had to fix this issue between them. She missed her sister's unwavering support. And she hadn't thought about restaurants or cooking more than camp food for four days. It only proved to her that her family was still more important than anything else—and that, at least, was reassuring. She wasn't totally selfish.

"I'm not as calm as I'm pretending," she whispered. "Don't tell."

"I never would." Raquel hugged her.

"Okay, guys. How fast can you all pack in the dark?"

***

"Their planned route would take them straight across the projected path of this damn thing." Ty looked up from the dining room table that had become Paradise's own command central.

Damien clearly read the lines of worry carved into his forehead and understood completely. Ty's daughter was in the midst of this unexpected horror show, and nobody knew exactly where the group of eight campers was located. They'd left John Red Wolf and his grand-niece almost thirty-six hours earlier. They would have camped one night and been underway this entire day—or so everyone hoped. They were due home tonight, but if they were nearing the ranch, they'd be within cell phone coverage. All their phones went to voicemail. The two scouting forays Cole and Bjorn had made had found no trace of them on the trails they'd have taken.

"Joely is there," Grace said, rubbing Ty's back in an attempt to comfort him. "She might have been the beauty queen, but she was always one of the first to plan a camping trip. She knows the skills as well anyone. And Kelly was Harper's little shadow growing up – those two have serious outdoor chops. I have every faith that they know what's going on."

"They're due home but this thing is only a few miles

from the canyon now." Cole ran a hand through his hair. "Where's the crew, Damien?"

He'd been in contact with the commander in Wolf Paw Pass and spoken once to Anna before she'd boarded the plane for her jump. She was on the crew jumping into remote Paradise land. She understood fully his family was missing.

"The hotshot crew went down into the Angel Valley from Wolf Paw Pass. The West Yellowstone jump crew dropped in behind Ancestor to try and build a break that'll hold the fire at that point. The girls wouldn't have gone to the canyon, right? Kelly knows how I felt about the safety of that place. They'd be sitting ducks in there."

This question had been asked and answered fifty times. Nobody knew for certain, but the words of hope had to be repeated to stave off panic.

"They'd have figured that out, I'm sure." Cole's voice held far more confidence than his eyes. "If they knew the path the fire was taking, they went away from it and are circling around."

If. Everything hinged on if. Damien knew exactly what equipment the little group had with them. Flashlights. Maps. Cell phones and a battery-powered radio. If they were using the tools properly, they'd be as prepared as they could be. If. What he wished more than anything, however, was that he'd ignored their skills and preparedness and insisted they all come home instead of finishing the trip. There should have been no guesswork, no assumptions that weather reports and containment strategies would hold true, no trusting that all would be well. All was far from well.

He wandered away from the maps and the endless repetition of hopeful encouragement into the living room

to check on Grandma Sadie and the baby. He knew how
everyone felt. The Thorsons waited for news of Sky,
Marcus, and Aiden. Gabe and Mia were barely holding it
together worrying about Rory. Grace and Ty had nearly
been hog-tied to keep them from going after Lucky
themselves. And Grace's fear for her triplet sisters showed
in the panic permanently shining in her eyes.

He got the terror. He understood it because he knew
well what it was like to be behind the wall of fire with no
way out but to fight. And the thought that Kelly might
now be in that position ate away at his gut like acid. It
hadn't been long enough for him to fall so hard for her, but
that truth didn't matter. He'd fallen. And he knew,
without regard to logic, that wherever she went, whatever
state his broken brain was in, whatever he ended up
doing, he was going to talk her into going together. Fear
was a great equalizer. You found out very quickly what
things mattered and what didn't when you faced ultimate
loss.

If. If only there were anything tangible he could do.

He sat on the sofa next to Grandma Sadie and she
smiled, serene and resigned to the wait. This wasn't her
first crisis. She'd seen more in her ninety-six years than
any of them. She took his hand.

"You have no idea how much you've helped, do
you?" she asked.

"I've done nothing."

"You've explained everything. You've contacted the
fire crews on the ground. You speak optimism. Most of all,
you care about this family and show it."

"I feel like those could as well be my own kids out
there, and I can't save them, Grandma."

The kids. His own kids. With absolutely no warning,

for the first time in hours of this ordeal her suddenly and completely, he lost it. Tears flowed with no hope of stopping them, and he closed his eyes, letting the Crockett family matriarch pull his head to rest on her shoulder. She stroked and stroked his hair.

"I can't save them."

"They'll be all right, Damien."

"I couldn't save them. I couldn't. I didn't. I—" He sat bolt upright, his head pressurizing painfully with an exploding memory. "Oh, God. Oh, shit. No." He bent forward, hands over his face.

"Damien, honey, what is it?" Grandma touched his back.

"Damien?" Grace followed her grandmother's voice and knelt in front of him.

He barely heard them. His mind was back in the past. The house around him was burning to the point where there was no hope for him and his partner to save anything more. He stared into the hole where the second story floorboards had burned through.

"Don't look down, Damien." His partner, Billy Hendricks, yanked at his shoulder. "We've got to get out. There's nothing we can do, they're already gone."

"No, I'm going down." He stared at the two little figures in their beds, barely visible. A crashing ember fell on the foot of one mattress. "Hold that damn rope, Billy."

"This floor won't hold *us*. The kids are gone. If you go down there, there's no way out."

"Hold the goddamn rope."

He got halfway down and crashed. The next memory was of bright lights in a hospital room.

Damien floated back into the present.

"Damien, come on. It's just the exhaustion," Grace

said. "Come on, you're all right."

He looked into the hole again.

Not dogs.

Boys. Two.

"Shit, shit, God, shit," he moaned. "I didn't save them. I couldn't."

And now there were four kids. Four behind a wall of fire. And he had to do something. Anything. He sat up, looking crazy he knew, and the memory returned. He scrabbled away from it and forced it back purposefully this time. Stunned and numb, he knew he would somehow have to pull up the pain again and deal. But he couldn't take time to process the truth here, even though this was the entire, horrible answer to everything.

"I need to look at the map again," he said.

Grace let him up, skeptical but unable to stop him. He wiped his eyes, well past embarrassment just as he'd been with the horses, and gave her a quick kiss on the crown of her head.

"I'm...all right," he breathed. "I can explain." He swallowed against the pain. "But not now. Now, I have an idea."

Chapter Twenty-six

KELLY LET OUT a long, slow breath and leaned back against a tree while Joely led the kids to the creek to fill water bottles and wash the sweat from their faces. She couldn't believe how brave they'd all been or what leaders Sky and Marcus were for the younger three. They'd been mostly successful keeping ahead of the smoke, the dance of flames always visible now in the distance behind them. In truth, she'd never believed the fire was close enough to overtake them, but she also had to remind herself that it hadn't been supposed to come in their direction at all, so she couldn't assume anything.

They'd finally crossed the Kwinaa River late that afternoon and were now at the base of Wolf Paw Peak. In forty-five minutes, they'd reach the far side of the mountain and one of seven outback cabins on Paradise land. The thing she was betting on was that they'd be safer with the mountain between them and the fire path. Paradise had already lost land, and she wasn't sure Ancestor Canyon had been spared. But the terrain around the peak would provide some natural fire breaks. They'd rest at the cabin and in the morning, barring a true disaster where half of Paradise ended up in flames—a nightmare the possibility of which she didn't even whisper out loud—they could make it to one of the secondary roads leading through the ranch property and hopefully find cell service to let their families know they were safe. She felt terrible that they hadn't been able to get word out already; everyone had to be worried.

"Hi."

She looked up as Raquel sank down beside her. They hadn't been fully alone in six days and Kelly impulsively wrapped her hands around her sister's arm squeezing tightly.

"Hi."

"Are you doing okay?" Raquel asked.

"Yeah. I'm exhausted, but we all are. How about you?"

"Same. And scared. How are you keeping it all together?"

Kelly scoffed. "One step at a time. We're going to be fine, Rocky. I'm tired of going away from home, but I don't dare turn until we're well south of the fire path."

"You know, I can balance books, make a marketing plan, and organize events, but I couldn't have guided us out of this mess. You're amazing."

Kelly looked at the ground and bit her lip against the emotion that welled up at Raquel's words. She rested her head against her shoulder and sat quietly, gathering the right words.

"Are we okay? I don't want you to be angry with me anymore."

"I'm not angry."

"Come on, Rocky, you don't have to pretend. You were honest about what you want to do in Denver, and I'm messing that up. Let's promise to talk about it when we get home—we can work it out."

"There's nothing to work out. I'm okay with you going to San Francisco."

"It's not a done deal. I haven't been accepted and I'm not a shoo-in. But that's the future. I want to be honest now. This whole misadventure is showing me how stupid it is to let anything come between us. So I admit it. I want to stop being jealous of you and Joely. I miss you."

"Jealous? That's silly, Kel."

"Is it? You two have talked non-stop since this trip started. I'm totally paranoid."

"Okay." Raquel turned and looked her in the eye. "We haven't been talking about you, except to promise we wouldn't bug you during the trip about Damien."

"Damien?"

"Now you come on. I see the way you are with each other."

"We aren't any way." Kelly's face heated at the half-truth. "He's fun to cook with."

"Oh brother. Yeah, that's it. Cooking." She shook her head as if Kelly were a student who wasn't understanding the lesson. "He's a unique man—a special one. Fun, yes, but deep. And he'd be your exact opposite and all wrong if he wasn't so perfect for you."

"It's way too complicated for that." Kelly sighed. "He won't get close because he thinks he's somehow broken. I thought for a while I could make him forget his traumas, whatever they are, but that isn't what he needs. Or wants."

"Love is complicated, Kel. I might not have found it yet, but I sure have watched it play out in more-than-complicated ways around this family. Do you love him?"

"After three weeks? I'd be foolish to say I did." Kelly rubbed her eyes.

"No. You wouldn't."

"I've always had the reputation of being flighty and foolish. Why ruin that now? I love what I see in him. The important thing is, I like him." She shrugged. "And, yeah. I want him."

Raquel gave her an elbow to the side and a naughty wink. "Have you had him?"

"Shame on you! Good thing Grace isn't here."

"I'm taking that as a yes." She held up her hand. "Don't answer. I don't want details. As for what else Joely and I talked about, mostly ideas for getting Grace a permanent chef. I'm going to Jackson for a few days to pre-interview two candidates." She looked around at the smoke-dusky evening sky. "Because we are getting out of this alive."

"Of course we are. And that's wonderful. How did you find the candidates?"

"A lot of calls and LinkedIn searching." She hesitated. "Joely and I also talked about Grace's wedding and what to do about food."

Kelly's heart dropped. "Oh? You didn't think the cook would want to talk about food?"

"Of course we did, but we didn't want to put pressure on you. Grace would love you to help with food, but you'll be in San Francisco by then and nobody wants you to feel torn."

"I told you. San Fran—"

"Isn't a shoo-in. Except, it is. You are. You might know how to navigate past a wildfire, but I know stuff too. They'll want you at Opus."

Kelly waited for the thrill of hopeful anticipation at the vote of confidence, but it didn't come.

"I can take time off to plan my sister's wedding."

"Kelly. I remember when you worked for Landon right after school. We didn't see you for months on end. The man gave you one weekend off every six weeks. You work like a fiend at those jobs."

"Yeah." She covered a shiver at the memory of the hours, challenging and inspiring as they'd been. "But how about this? Let me help with the food planning anyhow."

Raquel grinned and hugged her as if an entire boulder had been lifted from her shoulders.

"Neither of us wanted to be the one to hurt your feelings. We were cowards and figured Grace could decide what to ask you."

"You're horrible." Kelly held her tightly, so grateful that the world felt suddenly a little less tilted.

"Kelly! Raquel! Asta? Is Asta here?"

They both shot to their feet as Skylar came tearing up the rise from the creek, her face twisted in fear.

"Sky, stop. What's going on?"

"Asta disappeared. She never leaves us and she always comes when she's called. But she's gone."

Kelly bit her lip and raised her eyes to the heavens, offering a desperate prayer for wisdom as much as for the dog's safety.

"We'll find her. I promise."

"What if she fell in the creek? What if it took her downstream?"

"She can swim," Kelly said. "And it's a little tributary; she wouldn't drown."

The others followed up the hill, Lucky and Aiden calling for the dog. Joely joined them with a worried frown she hid from Skylar.

"She's herding a rabbit somewhere. She's tired and bored, too," Joely said, shrugging at Kelly.

"That's right. Check around the horses. Then we'll mount up and head for the cabin. When we get ready to go, she'll show up."

They searched as long as they dared in the area, but Asta never responded. In near hysterics so unusual for her, Skylar threatened to stay behind and wait for her dog to return, but Kelly was firm.

"You cannot stay here. We don't know how much further the fire will spread and nobody is getting left behind. Asta is the smartest dog you've ever known. She will find you."

The fickle wind shifted again as they rode. It had played with them for the past two days, gusting and calming, coming from one direction and then another. The rain hadn't materialized yet and the fire remained miles behind them. Still, it followed. With this wind shift, smoke and a dusting of ash surrounded them, and visibility and breathability disintegrated by the minute. She was glad for the mountain's presence on their right as they navigated the rolling and rocky terrain around the peak. This time it was Rory on his trusty Largo who led the way. The little bay mare had spent more time in the hills of Paradise than any of the other horses, and she found the path, ever sure-footed and unflappable, even tired as she was and with the scent of fire that made the other horses dance and fret.

The going was so slow that Kelly felt a first rise of panic that they'd miss the cabin and lose their way in the smoke.

"Asta!"

"Asta, here, girl!"

The kids' constant calling was wearing, too, and only induced more worry. She didn't want their only casualty to be a beloved animal. It made her think of Damien and the story of his accident. He didn't like dogs because of the memories they raised. On this ranch, every dog was as important as a person.

"Wait!" Lucky held up a hand. "Did you hear that?"

"Asta?" Sky cried.

"No. Listen."

At first, there was nothing.

"Asta!" Skylar called.

"Kelly?" The deep voice was far away and muted, almost imagined.

"Hello?" Kelly shouted.

"Kelly? Raquel? Joely?"

And then she recognized the voice. Tears of relief spilled free, and ten steps later, he appeared. Damien ran toward them, his features an unabashed mask of relief and pure joy. Beside him, barking as if she were simply playing the best game in the world, raced Asta.

Kelly halted Jellyman and swung out of the saddle in one fluid motion. Five seconds later, she was caught up in Damien's arms and he kissed her, unabashed and uncontrolled, peppering her face, her eyes, her lips.

"Thank God," he said. "You brilliant girl. You came here, just like you told me you would."

"I did?" Her legs barely held her upright the relief was so great, and she let him take over being strong, sagging into him, letting him rescue her.

"If you were ever in trouble, this is where you'd come. Safest place—by the ranch's mountain."

"You remembered that?"

"Oh, sweet girl. I remember a lot of things."

Before she could ask for an explanation, he kissed her again and she barely heard the reunion around them as Cole, Ty, Gabe, Alec, and Bjorn all appeared and grabbed their loved ones. Skylar, after assuring her father she was fine, fell to the ground beside Asta and wept. When Damien noticed, he pulled away from his kiss, regret in his eyes, and led Kelly to where the girl and the border collie all but rolled on the ground in joyous reunion.

"She saved us," Damien said, and Skylar looked up, her eyes round and wet with tears. "I was leading us in the wrong direction after leaving the cabin. Then Asta appeared out of the smoke and led us back to you. John Red Wolf was right. It's always been the dogs."

"Always?" Kelly asked. Those were two enigmatic statements.

"I have a lot to tell you when we get back," he replied. "Right now, we have three horse trailers and three big trucks to pull them waiting at the cabin. Let's take you all home."

"Can I ride with you? I need to make sure I'm not hallucinating from the smoke."

"Kelly Crockett, you have no choice but to ride with me. Everywhere I go, I hope for a very long time."

She was so tired she didn't even blink at that third enigmatic thing he'd said. Maybe she was hallucinating, but she didn't care.

Chapter Twenty-seven

TWO WEEKS.

The world had changed completely and yet not at all in two weeks. Kelly closed her computer and stared numbly at the silver cover of her laptop. The temporary command center in their little town had been shut down, and the hotshots and smokejumpers had returned to their bases. September had brought rain and relief, and ranch life had gone on. Cattle were branded, kids were telling endless stories about smoke horses and harrowing camping. Cole estimated that approximately eight hundred acres of Paradise land had burned, including a swath across Angel Valley in front of Ancestor Canyon, but the canyon itself was unharmed. Some of the lost acreage bordered the old Double Diamond ranch where Harper's art studio stood. She'd lost no buildings, but the views were forever changed. Still, Skylar and her new best friend Kaiah had already gone back to two art classes and were making a project out of painting the new panoramas. Kaiah still followed the Cloud Band but would have to let them winter alone, according to her parents and her great-uncle John, once school started in a week.

Planning for Grace and Ty's wedding, set for mid-December, swung into high gear. Raquel had spent six days in Jackson and returned with a perfect candidate for Peas Porridge's head cook. A new graduate from a highly regarded culinary school in Boise looking for a place to grow her wings. Grace's friendly restaurant was ideal.

And Damien.

Kelly smiled. Her Damien, at least for now. His story still threatened to tear her up. He was, in fact, doing better than she was. He was seeing his counselor twice a week and had made arrangements to go back to Montana for a month-long boot camp refresher. Then he was going to jump again. Something he'd nearly given up on. She was thrilled for him.

Everything was like the wrap-up of a long-running television series—everything settled, everything way too perfect and tidy.

It only left her.

She gave the top of her computer a fatalistic tap. Her fate had been sealed as well, from the moment the email had arrived half an hour ago from Mark Lansbury at Opus. Raquel had been right. Kelly was, he'd said, exactly what he was looking for. She'd come up with an elegant but simple menu and executed it with creativity and success. He would be proud to mentor her as one of his sous chefs. And, she'd done exactly what she had to do even though, having made the decision, it set her adrift from everything she knew and loved.

She stood and checked her watch. Groaning, she grabbed her jacket and purse and headed downstairs. Everyone was gathering at Peas Porridge to celebrate the safe outcome after the fires, and to welcome Bethany, the new cook. People had hinted at other surprises, too, and that was the biggest change at Paradise – everyone suddenly seemed bent on keeping secrets.

"There she is!" Cole called out to the crowd when Kelly entered the restaurant half an hour later. "Fearless camp leader and fire dodger."

Her family all clapped, Bjorn and Melanie's family clapped, and Damien came to meet her with a bouquet of wildflowers.

"What on earth?" she asked.

"Part of this night is for you," he said. "We have seven eyewitnesses who said you kept your group together when it would have been easy to panic. We're thanking you for getting home safely."

"This is nuts, you guys," she said, fighting the flush climbing her cheeks. "We were a team. Sky and Marcus deserve just as much credit. The younger ones were so brave. And Rocky and Joely—you don't think they got us all through?"

"Whatever." Raquel stood up. "My sister here never backs down from a challenge. And it's a darn good thing for all of us. Get the girl a glass of wine and a Damien Finney Bacon Burger!"

"Oooh, low blow!" Kelly laughed.

"I have one more surprise for you," Raquel said and pointed to the kitchen doorway.

Marley Beckham stepped out and made her way to Kelly and Damien while everyone clapped again. Marley was becoming a fixture in Wolf Paw Pass.

"More interviews and filming, Marley?" Kelly asked. "Your viewers do not want to see all this crazy footage."

"Au contraire, Kelly dear. They will not be able to get

enough of you." She looked at Damien then. "And you. If you agree to my proposal."

Damien shrugged, but Raquel let out a squeal of excitement. Marley put a finger against smiling lips.

"What's going on?" Kelly asked.

"I showed footage of you two cooking together to my producers, and I'm here to tell you, it was love at first sight. They want to make you a part of my show, for a trial run. The gourmet and the firehouse cook. The plan is to have it lead to your own show, set right here in Wyoming. It would be once a week, and the format would be up to you as long as you stay as funny and fun as you were when I watched you."

The room spun in front of Kelly's eyes. Not in her wildest dreams had something like this crossed her mind. She looked to Damien, who was clearly as stunned as she was. And then, he began to laugh.

"Wow," he said. "This is a right turn I didn't see my life taking."

"I am so honored," Kelly said. "I— I have something to say first, that might change everything, though, before we go too far with this. I, ah, got the internship position at Opus. The email just came in before I came tonight."

The shocked silence only lasted ten seconds and then the room erupted in applause and shouts again. Damien whipped her into a bear hug and placed his lips against her ear.

"I am so proud of you."

"Thank you," she whispered back and then pushed him gently away. "Hold on." She motioned everyone to sit down. When it was quiet, she looked at the room full of faces she loved. Then she fixed her eyes on Raquel. "I turned it down."

This time the crescendo of disbelief took no time to swell.

"You did what?" Raquel cried.

Kelly shushed everyone once more.

"The camping trip, the search for a special herd of horses, the time spent with family in close quarters, and, yes, the fire scare—it all gave me time to think. To remember how much I hated being alone prepping for that dinner here and how horribly stressful it was to need everything to be perfect. I'd forgotten how long the hours are and how dreadful a three-star chef can be as a boss. And when I thought about how much fun it was simply to make new things in a restaurant or even to roast dough on a stick over a campfire, I knew I'd be miserable following my dream. So, Raquel, let's go back to Triple Bean and make it bigger and better. If you'll still hire me on."

Raquel had covered her face with her hands. Kelly turned to Marley.

"I'm so sorry. I don't see how it could work. I'll be in Denver. Damien will be in Montana. The logistics…"

"Wait." Raquel uncovered her face. Her smile blossomed. "I have something to say, too. A few weeks ago, Kelly said something I didn't want to hear. She said I was scared to move away from my comfort zone. She was so right. So, when I was in Jackson, meeting with Bethany, I found a property in an older part of town—one that would make an incredible space for a new restaurant. I was going to look into it for when you got done in San Francisco. But now…"

"Are you kidding me?" Kelly launched herself into a hug with her sister. "Thirty minutes away? We can build what we want?"

"I can follow it start to opening!" Marley rubbed her

palms together in glee.

"My turn," Damien said. "I talked to Stone Rayburn this week. Once I finish my training, he'll approve my transfer to the West Yellowstone crew if I want it. That would let me stay close to Paradise and Pan." He pulled her away from Raquel and bent close. "And now, to you."

"And to my wedding venue," Grace called.

"And to your newest niece or nephew." Harper made her announcement from the middle of the room, her arm securely around Cole's waist. "I mean, as long as everyone is sharing...stuff."

That was too much good news for anyone to keep order any longer. After squeals and hugs and a lot of disbelief, Kelly grabbed Damien's hand and returned to Marley.

"Give us one minute to talk about your offer," she said and dragged Damien away from the chaos and out onto the patio.

"I hope you're stealing me for really immoral reasons," he said.

She rocked into his embrace and pressed tightly to his long, hard body. There had already been more than a few long, wonderfully naughty nights together, and the still-unbelievable idea that she wasn't going to have to leave him or him her only heightened the desire that flared every time she touched him.

"This can't be happening," she said. "It's too good. It's..." She repeated her thoughts from earlier. "It's like a too-perfect script. When does the next shoe drop? When's the next bad thing?"

"No, Kelly, no. All the bad things have happened."

"But so many..."

"They all needed to happen. I made a list, starting

with my whole misbelief that dogs had died in that fire so long ago. Why dogs? I can only believe that they really are some kind of guide. They protected me until I could face reality. Without them, I never would have quit the department in Sheridan and gone to Afghanistan. I never would have needed Gabe or found Pan or Paradise. When I failed on that plane I searched out the horse because I'd learned to ask for help. Without the horses and John Red Wolf, we wouldn't have taken the camping trip and left you to get stuck. And without the fire, I wouldn't have remembered the boys, Asta wouldn't have appeared out of the smoke to bring me full circle. I'd be a broken truck driver in Sheridan."

"That's a crazy list, Damien."

"Simplified. It's not a perfect script. I'm not magically over everything that happened. But I can think about jumping without panic and that's a good enough start. And if you're always there to catch me…"

"And if you're always there to tell me the truth about myself…"

"I have another idea."

"Uh oh." She laughed.

"What if Marley's television show chronicles me asking you to marry me and you saying yes? Wouldn't that boost ratings?"

"I don't know…" She laughed. "It might be old news by the time the first episode airs."

"How's that?"

"Why would you ask me on television, if I've already said yes right here?"

His rich, happy laugh echoed against her ear from deep in his chest. His breath, warm and familiar, raised goosebumps along both arms and down her spine.

"That, Kelly Crockett, is a very good question."

Their lips met, and she flew off with him, certain that no matter what leap they took in the future, whether from a plane, a mountain, or of faith, they'd land safely. Always. Together.

THE END

ACKNOWLEDGEMENTS

This book dragged its heels for two years, not wanting to be "born." Both Damien and Kelly were reluctant (an understatement) to let their secrets out and kept me frustrated for a very long time. They may have kept those secrets forever had it not been for two amazing women who became my fellow (2020) pandemic Musketeers and coaxed, cajoled, brainstormed, and encouraged this book into being. Cat Schield and Nan Dixon—I thank you and I love you!

Thank you to my family who listened to me worry this story like a collie with a bone for nearly two years, and kept on patting me on the back without too many rolled eyes: Jan Selvig for your patience, Tami Richie for listening to the plot multiple times, Grace Feuk for telling me every single day to "be brilliant" and knowing I could be, and to my grandkids Evie, Riley, and Zoey who keep me young and never wanting to quit.

Thank you to Michel Prince of Royal Touch Photography, and to Lance Johnson and Jenni Marie, for the beautiful photo shoot that made Kelly and Damien of this book come to life; to Dana Lamothe for turning the photo shoot into a cover, and to Anna Grace and Robin Selvig for reading first!

Finally, a huge thank you to all the courageous men and women—smokejumper firefighters—who risk their lives leaping out of planes directly into the paths of raging wildfires to get where nobody else can reach in order to save property and lives.

ABOUT THE AUTHOR

Award-winning and No.1 Bestselling author Lizbeth Selvig writes heartwarming contemporary romance. Whether set in a small town in Minnesota, a huge ranch in Wyoming, the Scottish Highlands, or a Kentucky racetrack, her strong, fun and funny characters will poke at societal norms even while finding their ways home to family and love. Lizbeth turned to fiction writing after working as a newspaper journalist and magazine editor, and raising an equine veterinarian daughter (handy, since there are usually too many horses in her stories) and a talented musician son (also handy because she's been known to write about rock stars). She shares life in Minnesota, where her first book series is set, with her best friend (aka her husband, Jan), her two pretty horses, Jedi and Largo, three human grandchildren, and her four-legged grandbabies of which there are nearly thirty, including two alpacas, a couple of small goats, a mammoth-eared donkey, two miniature horses, a pig, and many many dogs, cats and regular-sized horses. In her spare time she loves to hike, quilt, read, and horseback ride. An incorrigible extrovert, she also loves connecting with readers—so contact her any time.

www.lizbethselvig.com